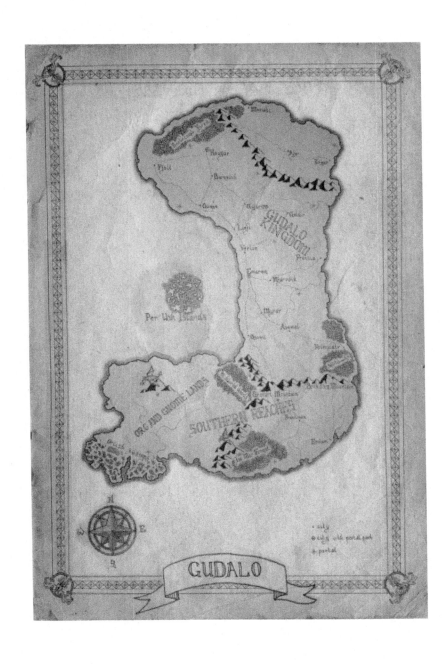

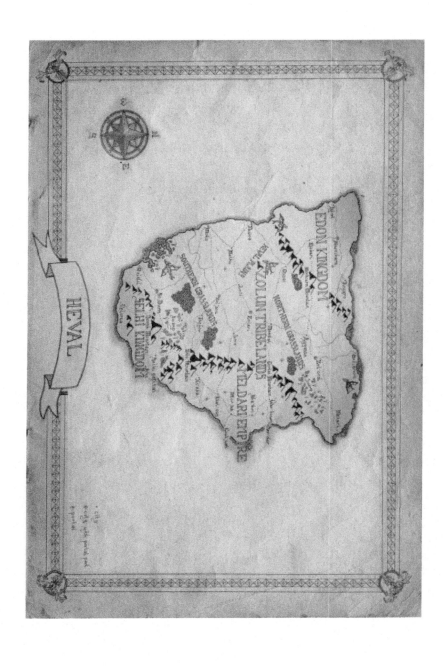

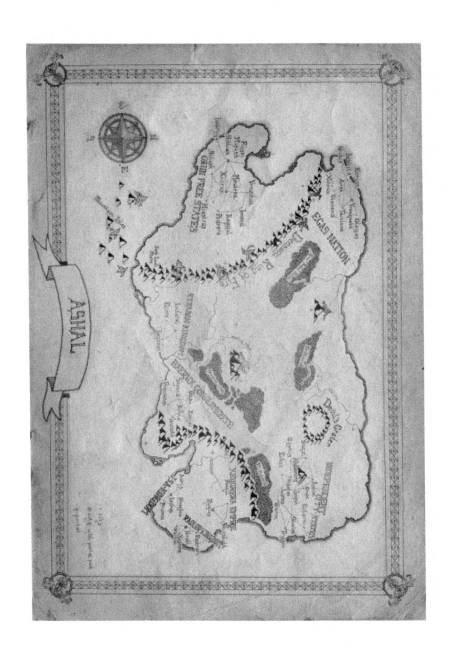

Want a bigger map of Emerilia and the continents? Check out **http://theeternalwriter.deviantart.com/**

Character Sheet is located in the back of the book for reference.

Emerilia

Empire Burning

Chapter 0: Prologue

The emperor's quarters were silent as the last of the screens turned to black.

Even the emperor was silent, his concubines not daring to move around him as a screen telling of technical errors appeared in front of him.

Moments later, the doors to his quarters opened and several of his aides stood at the door, rolling onto their backs to show their subservience. Their frog-like bodies stilled as the emperor waved his hand, indicating for them to talk.

"Great and mighty emperor, the Emerilians have rebelled. They have a fleet of space-worthy warships that took out the orbitals around Emerilia, as well as attacked the military base. Our fleet and base there are fighting back but they are requesting reinforcements. It doesn't look like they will be able to hold out," one of the aides said in a rush. Their fur was dry with fear.

The emperor took this in before he started to laugh. It was low and quiet at first, becoming louder and louder until it made the room shake.

"Good! Good! This will be the best season of Emerilia yet! The end of Emerilia! Organize the fleet. We will send them out to attack the Emerilians, a great display of the Jukal Empire's might. We will show the empire the strength of our Jukal fleets!" The emperor's excitement built as he thought of his magnificent Jukal ships clashing with the Emerilian fleet.

"The fleet in the Emerilian system has been defeated and the Emerilians are attacking the base directly. It seems like Emerilia has a massive shield that is protecting it from attacks from the outside," one of the aides said.

"It does not matter. Do you doubt the strength of our Jukal fleets?" the emperor asked.

1

Just talking about the Jukal fleet would inspire confidence or fear in the Jukal Empire. The Jukal fleets had never been defeated and they had subdued countless races. They were the reason that the Jukal continued to rule over the other races of the empire.

"The Emerilians defeated our different measures. It seems that Lo'kal is with them," one of the oldest aides said in an emotionless voice.

"Uncle, what are you thinking?" the emperor asked. He dismissed the other aides, but this old Jukal who stood outside his quarters made him wipe away his look of glee and take him seriously.

"They have many plans going on. They had a fleet that we didn't know about until they used it and a shield that covers an entire planet. We don't even have that kind of ability. We must not underestimate them and we must hit them as soon as possible. The more time they are given, the stronger they can become. After all, they're *humans*." The emperor's uncle's words struck a chord with the emperor. He not only thought of the Emerilians, he thought of the lessons that his uncle had taught him about the scariest enemy that the empire had faced: humanity.

"Send out the fleets to hunt down the Emerilians. We will destroy them wherever we can find them," the emperor said. His voice was no longer flippant; instead, it carried a different message from before.

The aides scrambled onto their limbs and rushed away to carry out his orders.

The emperor raised his hand slightly as a slight mist fell over his chest, wetting his fur. "We will use this to show the rest of the empire their positions. The Emerilians held a place to provide entertainment and fight the aggressive species but if they are unable to do that, we will destroy them, root and branch."

Chapter 1: Changing of the Old to New

Light and her advisers stepped out of the rubble that was her hall. She felt incredible weakness. Her power was lower than it had ever been and what was left of her legions was in chaos, as most of them had been killed.

She looked around the debris that was Markolm and the sea that surged all around them. Markolm was now nothing more than a collection of blocks at awkward angles that jutted up into the sky.

Many had died in the battle, but many more had died from the curse that had been activated within their bodies. Light and those who were with her had just been able to survive it. Some of the stronger angels had been able to survive it as well.

She looked up to the sky, where a massive shield stretched across the horizon, making it a brighter blue. Here and there, it flashed as something hit it.

She had seen the fighting happening above Emerilia through her seer pools; however, now it was silent.

The wind whipped up as a young woman appeared in front of Light and her followers.

A number of her followers and angels rushed forward, yelling out their defiance.

The young woman waved her delicate hands. The wind picked up and created chains that wrapped around those who charged. They were like babies in front of an adult.

They yelled out their anger until the woman waved her hand again and a dome of air cut off their noise.

The young woman took a deep breath as she looked at Light.

"What, come to gloat?" Light sneered. "Didn't think that was your thing, Air." Light's face was still mottled and half destroyed by the magic that her brother, the former Dark Lord, had used upon her. Her former grace and poise was gone. She was now no stronger than a normal person of Emerilia.

"No. I came to end this," Air said in a soft voice. She waved her hand.

Light only had time to look alarmed as a dart of compressed air shot from Air's hand, silently hitting Light in the head.

With a look of shock on her face, the Lady of Light fell.

She dropped onto the ground, dust rising around her. Behind Air, holes opened in the Mana shield as meteors seemed to fall toward Emerilia.

Air looked up from Light's corpse, looking to the sky just as those meteors altered their course that they could be seen with the naked eye.

Air used a spell to zoom in on them.

Several destroyers grew in her vision, their bodies like a sword with inverted wings that allowed them to cut through the planet's atmosphere.

Sonic booms cracked through the air with the approach of the destroyers. The crews handled their ships nimbly, never once coming out of formation as they approached the ground.

The destroyers pulled up from their dive, their runic lines visible as they approached, looking less like meteors and more like ships.

As they approached Markolm, lines underneath their hulls lit up as angels and those who were still loyal to Light started to attack the sleek and intimidating ships.

Mana barriers flared to life, effortlessly absorbing the hits from the remaining fanatics. The runic lines lit up, firing back beams of light that tore apart those in their path. The runic lines underneath the destroyers flashed with light and the newly minted Emerilian forces dropped to the ground beneath the destroyer. These were people from across Emerilia who had been outfitted with Devastator armor and trained in its use. When combined with Bob's gift of making all of the people of Emerilia into Champions of Emerilia, Light's armies were easily subdued. Among their ranks, there were overseers who used spells to bind the men and women who had followed Light.

The angels were still more powerful, but the Devastator army simply called in supporting fire from the destroyers, whose artillery cannons each hit with the strength of a dwarven mountain artillery cannon but at the size of one of their regular pieces.

As Light's body started to fall away, becoming nothing more than drifting pixelated ash, Air watched as the people of Emerilia reclaimed their home.

The air turned into a vortex around those Air had captured, delivering them to the Devastator forces. Another vortex appeared around Air as she disappeared from Markolm.

***

Even with the distracting side chats going on around their conference room, the different members of the Terra Alliance were all focused on Josh, who was leading the conference with Dave and Bob by his side.

They were no longer in Terra, but rather Ice City, which was seeing a massive boost in population.

"As you all now know the extent of what is going on with the Jukal and the true history of Emerilia, I think it's time that we focus not on the past, and instead what steps we must take in the future so that we as humans might once again stand on our own feet and create a place for us to call home," Josh said. "That said, this isn't my show. I looked after the Terra Alliance on Emerilia, but everything that you have seen in the last few days has been created by the Pandora's Initiative, who run this facility, and a number of others. As such, they have a much better understanding of what is going on, so I will leave the briefing to them."

Josh looked to Dave, who nodded and cleared his throat.

"My name is Dave Grahslagg. A number of you might know me. It seems that I will be representing the Pandora's Initiative. Suzy Markell is really the manager for all of this. However, right now she is busy dealing with other items and is unable to join us for this meeting. The Pandora's Initiative was made to research and develop magical and technological items that would assist the people of Emerilia in dealing with the Jukal Empire. This technology has been adapted over to other projects that you've seen on Emerilia, to help deal with the threats that have come up in the last couple of years. We have built up the infrastructure and different bases that were necessary for us to build the fleet that you saw above Emerilia. We are also undergoing the process to remove all of the people trapped in the simulation of Earth to allow them to gain their freedom. The ones who have already been freed have already contributed to many research topics and are a big part of both production and our military forces. They have become the backbone of the Initiative. Right now, we have roughly five million being uploaded from the Earth simulation into real bodies within Ice City. It's part of the reason things are so crazy around here. We also have a large influx of people from Emerilia from various locations that were under threat. This base and others connected to it were made not only so that we could defeat the Jukal Empire but if we fail in our pursuit, then the survivors will have a launch pad in order to be ready for the next battle," Dave said.

"What is the plan to fight the Jukal?" Alkao asked, his voice deeper and more powerful than before. His powerful aura shook the room as he sat next to Denur, his aura much wilder than before but still suppressed by Denur's dominating aura.

"I think the questions should be: what is the Pandora's Initiative, who controls it, and is it military or civilian?" one of the Ashal nation's leaders asked.

"It is a subsidiary of the Grahslagg Corporation. Naming it would be complicated. Overall, I give the orders. These are passed to different heads of departments, who then find a way to carry them out," Dave said.

"But you aren't of a military and you're a member of the Stone Raiders," someone else said.

Dave looked at the two who were raising these points. They had seen the strength of the Initiative and they were scared. It didn't matter that the Initiative was fighting against the Jukal Empire; they were worrying about what would happen if it turned on them.

Dave unleashed his aura on the room, making it hard for many to breathe. With his Strength, he was now stronger than Denur.

The people in the room had wide eyes as the oppressive power contained within his body pressed down on them.

"I'm not here to piss about. We're fighting a goddamn war for survival. Either you're part of this or you're not. You make that decision here and now. I am fighting for my family and I will not let anyone step in my way," Dave said with barely contained rage, stabbing the table in front of him with his finger. Across the room, eyes shifted to take in the cracks that radiated out from where Dave's finger struck the table.

"Either we stand together, or we die apart; that is what you have to think of, *that* is what you should be thinking of."

Alkao nodded, seemingly approving of his actions. The dwarves were in agreement, as were the different player guilds, as well as Fire, Water, Air, Bob, and Malsour.

Jelanos and Alamos looked around the table calmly and without fear—they were all in with Dave—as did the elected governor and governess of Gudalo, Lady Merguine and Lord Sigaird. Lord Sigaird had been King Sigaird of the Gudalo nation, but he had left politics behind and gone adventuring with his wife. However, fate had taken a hand in his future, as Air had once again pulled him into politics, using him to bring Gudalo together and strengthen the people for the ongoing battles that plagued Emerilia.

Denur and Fire shared a look before they smiled to each other, approving of Dave's actions as they looked to the others around the table. Few weren't affected by the pressure of Dave's Strength; others felt cold sweat run down their spines as they pushed down thoughts of wrestling control of the Initiative from Dave Grahslagg. His forces and his allies were deep.

Dave looked to them all. His glare made it clear: this is where they choose which side they stood on.

He cleared his throat and looked to Alkao.

"We are moving to secure the Emerilian system. Once we control everything around Emerilia, then we are going to move units out to the different planets that are part of the Jukal Empire. It will take the Jukal fleet time to get organized and there is no portal in the Emerilian system. The nearest one is three systems away. They thought it too costly to put a portal here when they had all of their safety measures to kill us off if we rebelled. Thankfully, we figured them all out and stopped them from working. It will take them three to five months to reach us. This is time that we can't waste. Our ships are faster and we already have two fleets out on patrol. We can use them to drop portals and create our own network that the Jukal don't know about.

"We go to the planets, we destroy the Jukal influences and we drop off the different items that the people of the empire need. Cut off from the Jukal Empire, they will have no option but to use the items we give them. If they use them, they risk offending the empire, which will probably harm them in a big way. But on the other hand, if they don't use them, their planets will fall into disarray. We're dropping these things off for two reasons: one, we bring the people over to our side; and two, we get the Jukal to send out more fleets to different systems. The Jukal fleets will portal in to attempt to block our actions and we will lure them into chasing our fleets throughout the connected systems. Once we've got the Jukal fleets spread all over the place, we take control of the Jukal portal network and amass our forces using our own portals. The Jukal fleets, cut off from one another, will be swarmed by our fleets and destroyed thanks to our numerical and technological superiority in that battle area. At this point, the empire will only be able to be crossed by ships using jump drives. We will have taken their strength and broken the backbone of the Jukal Empire. We will then show the member planets of the empire that the Jukal aren't all-powerful. We seed doubt and we let them think of their future. Then we amass our power and strike at the core worlds, barricading the Jukal in their own systems. The empire lives as a whole, but when isolated and broken into its parts, it will die."

"Why don't we take over the portals from the beginning?" Jelanos, the archmage of the Mage's College, asked.

"If we use the portals from the beginning, then we lose the element of surprise. Also, we need the Jukal Empire to push their fleets out as much as possible. Our fleet isn't massive but if we can dictate the fighting against the Jukal, then we can win. We isolate and destroy," Dave said.

"Also, we might not be alone," Bob said. All eyes turned to him.

"There is a group of humans who have been hiding in the stars for some time. Dave has been in contact with them for a long time and they have helped us and we them. They have a space-based military and are building an outpost within the Nal system we are in. If we work together, then the chances of victory will be higher," Bob said.

"Right now, our biggest task is building ships. We have a number of people who are trained to fight on the ships we have available so far, but constructing them is our biggest single bottleneck. Other than that, we need to build the hundreds of factories and structures that we can put on the planets of the Jukal Empire to foster rebellion," Malsour said.

"We have an offer for you," Fire said.

As one, Water, Fire, and Air all seemed to pull orbs out of their chests. Each shone like a rare gem, colored blue, red, and white. Air pulled out another orb that gave off a golden glow.

"These are the AI that were given to us to make us into members of the Pantheon. We gift them to the Initiative to assist with fighting the Jukal Empire." Fire waved her hand. Her red orb drifted forth until settling in the center of the room, several feet above the table. The other three orbs drifted away from their owners and joined the red orb, where all of the orbs began to rotate and circle one another in a slow formation.

"Administrator access to AI cores has been recognized. Would you like me to access these?" Jeeves asked from above.

"Please do." Dave pulled a green orb from his chest and waved it to the middle of the table. Malsour pulled a black orb from his, which also joined its siblings until each of the orbs started to fade as Jeeves accessed them.

As one, all of the orbs disappeared.

"Six new AI cores are now online. Production increases have been registered," Jeeves said. As he and the AIs interfaced, his information would only become more refined. He would be able to pass off tasks to them that they were better suited to deal with.

"The Pantheon no longer exists. Only the people of Emerilia can determine the fate of our home," Air said.

"Dave, I have some people saying that they are ready to move Terra. What do they move?" Josh asked.

"Well, it's meant to be a space station," Dave said.

"What?" Josh spluttered.

"Well, why did you think I added in all that spinning stuff? We could have just built a regular, flat base...we probably will in the area that is left behind by Terra." Dave grinned and looked to Malsour, who smiled.

"What the hell do you mean?" Josh asked.

"Shard, command override, ark program one," Dave said.

"Password authentic. Information module unlocked. Reconfiguring," Shard said. The consoles around the command center started to change. The soul gem constructs created extra control interfaces as soul gem constructs throughout the city grew and connected to different sections.

In just a few moments, systems that had been dormant, hidden from both the people within Terra and the Jukal, were now activated.

"You ready, Josh?" Dave asked.

"Not at all," Josh said.

"Ever wonder why we only drilled in one direction?" Dave asked.

"Thought it was so we didn't destroy the area where we started Terra from," Josh said, referring to the area that had been given to the Stone Raider's guild when they had helped the Aleph what felt like a lifetime ago.

"Well, that's part of the reason. The other part is because I turned it into a big ole portal." Dave waved his hand and screens appeared above the table in Ice City; it showed Terra as runic lines spread down its length. At one side, a glowing could be seen before the wall started to shift, showing a portal that had been hidden underneath.

"This is one of the safety measures we took," Dave said.

The portal was engaged and Terra shot forward—but, instead of hitting the rock, it disappeared through the portal that was just big enough to fit it. On the screens, Terra appeared, shooting out from the moonbase.

It continued to rotate as different nodes along the length of Terra moved the underground city turned space station. It joined in with the moon orbiting Emerilia. Along the length of Terra, sections fell apart as runic lines formed pillars that were weapon systems that were meant to defend Terra. Fusion power plants started working, increasing the power supplied to Terra. The people of Terra looked out from their homes and found themselves looking through a Mana shield at Emerilia and the stars around it. A soul gem-constructed wall sealed off the ends of Terra; slips started to grow from it, creating places where the different vessels of the Pandora Initiative could be resupplied or where the people of Terra could create more ships.

Terra started to expand as the soul gem construct that was interwoven into the city stretched outward, increasing its diameter by a third.

"With some time, Terra will have more weapons and systems. The space station can move between the large ship-classed portals from location to location and still retain the use of its teleport pads, allowing people to teleport between Terra and Emerilia, or between Terra and the moonbase. This will allow for ease of boarding between vessels that are protecting Emerilia." Dave changed the view again, showing platforms connected to the underground transportation system. Runic lines ran through, lighting up the areas as soul gems grew together to form portals.

"Terra will be the main hub of travel between all locations related to Pandora's Initiative."

"Since when did you start thinking of all this?" Josh asked.

"As soon as I found out the truth from Bob," Dave answered honestly, nodding to Bob, who sat on the other side of Josh.

***

Sato read the request from Emerilia asking for the aid of Sato and his people. It was displayed on the front screen of the command center—no one dared to breathe too loudly as they read the message with him.

Sato opened up a private line to Council Leader Wong. "I have received a request from the Emerilians for aid," Sato said.

"Send the fleets," Wong said.

"Yes, ma'am." Sato stood from his seat.

On the main screen, an alert came in.

"Connect to Admiral Adams!" Sato yelled, cutting through the noise from the alert.

"You're connected, sir," one of the communications techs said.

"Admiral Adams, launch all fleets in aid to the Emerilian system. It's time humanity showed this Jukal Empire what's been lurking in the dark." Sato's voice sent goose bumps down people's spines.

"Yes, Commander." Adams closed the channel.

Sato read the alert on the screen.

The Deq'ual system is in a state of war. All military personnel are to report to their stations. This is not a drill. Administration of the Deq'ual system will be run by the military forces while orders will be created by the Council Leader of the Deq'ual system.

"Shipyard one and three are opening their hatches," an operations officer said. The room was now filled with energy and hard faces as the military machine of the Deq'ual system was activated for the first time in five centuries.

"All fleets, launch! Operational orders will be provided en route." Adams's voice came through the fleet-wide channel Sato was listening to.

Through the armored hatches of the shipyards, ships started to appear. These were not just simple stealth craft but the carriers, destroyers, and battleships of the Deq'ual navy.

They were smaller than the Emerilian version but they were faster when using their engines and they required less crew.

The once peaceful asteroid belt revealed the hidden dragons who had been hiding within it.

The ships moved off from the asteroid. The mass of ships slid into organized formations, headed for distant regions of space as they fell into formation as if they had practiced it hundreds of times.

Fleets formed up and surged forward, unleashing the power of their engines as they headed to the jump points that would take them away from home and toward war.

The dogs of war have been unleashed—now it's time to see what happens.

Sato watched those ships and stepped toward the communications area. "Contact Dave Grahslagg."

"Yes, sir," the communications officer said.

"Commander Sato." Dave's voice carried through the room. Dave wore his armor and cloak, looking like a warlord as he stood in a command center.

"Deq'ual heeds the call for aid." Pride welled up in Sato's chest.

Dave drew himself up to his full height. "Then Emerilia and the Deq'ual system shall fight together," Dave said, his eyes firm and resolute.

***

Frank had been just another player within the Earth simulation just a few months ago. He had been the first player to be woken up from that nightmare and into Ice City and reality.

He had pushed himself harder than ever and overcome his own misgivings to be the fire controller of the battleship *BloodHawk*, the flagship of Pandora's Fleet One.

His fleet had been on their first operation, a scouting mission to collect information on the Jukal Empire, primarily its inner systems and the systems that wielded the most economic power.

The fleet separated out so that they could cover more systems. *BloodHawk* had just entered a new system when they received word that operation Open Pandora's Box had been activated—meaning that the Emerilians were going to be openly contesting the Jukal Empire.

They'd carried out their message, looking at their communications officer nervously, awaiting word.

"We are receiving a message from headquarters," the communications officer nearly yelled out as the message came in.

"Broadcast it," the captain said.

"This is Dave. Emerilia has been secured. All forces already deployed are to group together and lay down a portal. We will be sending reinforcements and arks soon enough. We're going to war with the Jukal Empire." Dave cut the communications channel.

There were no cheers, smiles, or clapping. However, those within the *BloodHawk* and in Pandora Fleet One and Two sat a bit straighter; there was an edge to them now, as if they were swords that had been unsheathed, waiting to be used.

"Send rally point to the rest of the fleet. Nav, plot us a course to the rally point, best speed but I want us to stay hidden. Inform engineering I want the portal checked and readied before deployment. I don't want to be waiting a minute longer than what is required to deploy it. I want readiness reports from all departments." The captain's orders came down like hammer blows. The ship responded to his orders as runes lit up across the ship's sides. No longer drifting, it moved with a deadly purpose as it turned and headed out of the system.

They powered to the outreaches of the system, using small teleports to create more distance until they finally created a wormhole, disappearing from the Jukal system without a trace.

They appeared in an area between star systems that was well away from the Jukal systems. It was impossible to find in the vastness of space without the right coordinates.

The *BloodHawk* was the first to arrive.

"Deploy portal. Relay location and update Command Central," the captain said as the armored sections around the battleship opened up sections of soul gem, formed into a massive portal the size of the portal inside the asteroid base and the moonbase. The parts floated out along soul gem-constructed umbilicals.

Mages moved up the umbilicals that spread out like the spokes of a cartwheel, connecting the battleship in the center to the portal around it.

The sections of portal came together and the soul gem constructs fused with one another. Mages and engineers moved over these fused sections, checking everything as power from the battleship was poured into the soul gem construct.

It took about twenty minutes before the mages and engineers retreated to the battleship. The umbilicals detached from the portal that seemed to stand still in the inky darkness.

The battleship moved at a good clip and out of the portal assembly. As soon as it was clear, the portal flashed with light as the runic lines started to light up while the portal began to make a connection.

A wormhole appeared. On the other side, a familiar sight greeted them. The asteroid base as well as a destroyer was clearly visible through the immense portal. It quickly moved through it and out of the immediate area as it was only the first ship in the queue to move into the system. Everyone held their breath as the portal finally lit up.

The base looked busier than ever. The different slips were cleared of most ships; however, there were already new ships being built at an alarming speed.

A massive ark covered the portal as it pushed through the asteroid base's portal and joined up with Pandora Fleet One.

As the first massive ark came through, the second one followed close behind it.

Another fleet started to emerge. Three destroyers came first, followed by missile boats, the battleship, the two arks under the fleet's command and then the remaining destroyers.

"Receiving communication from the captain of the battleship *Resilient*," the communication officer said.

"Connect him," the captain said.

"How's it going there, Pandora One? Thought we'd join in on the fun," the captain of *Resilient* said as he was connected.

"Captain James, good to see you." The captain smiled.

"You, too, Xiao. Though, I have to say, I'm still looking forward to when they have dreadnoughts and not just dinky battleships." Captain James sighed with a smile. "Don't have too long to talk, though. See you and your fleet soon enough. Hope you have fun raising a little hell."

"We'll try our best. Good hunting," Xiao said.

"You too," James said. The channel cut out.

"All right, let's split the fleet and then head for our objective," Captain Xiao said.

The battleship moved off from the portal. Shuttles were now coming through the portal, carrying mages and fusion power plants.

The mages were to hook the portal up to a stable power source and also lay down numerous magical traps that would work to destroy any Jukal ship, if they happened to come across the portal.

Two destroyers, two missile boats, and one ark followed the battleship. The remaining three missile boats and destroyers would work with the ark to take it to their objective.

Frank glanced at the screen that continued to show the inside of the asteroid base.

Another two arks were waiting in the main thoroughfare, ready to meet up with Pandora Fleet Two, which was also out on operations.

In the middle of nowhere, the two fleets separated and then headed out in four different directions, leaving behind a portal and a growing array of magical traps that would make any mage go into a cold sweat; they also left behind several soul gem construct platforms orbiting the massive portal. The platforms were absolutely bursting with runic lines so powerful that they could be used to scan an area several light-years across, looking for any threats that might appear.

Dave and Malsour were reviewing production numbers in a state of shock.

Since they had opened Pandora's Box, it seemed as if the universe had gone crazy. They didn't have to hide anything, so they could send orders to Emerilian businesses for completion. People from Emerilia were lending their knowledge to assist the researchers in Ice City; others were acting as laborers across the bases.

Automated miners that had only been used around the asteroid base were now being used to mine out great swathes of Emerilia.

The moonbase was undergoing a massive increase. The AIs that had been the power behind the Pantheon were given tasks to mine, refine, and build. The Dark AI had built a battleship with the help of automated laborers within just five days. The soul gem construct that was inside took the longest time instead of the other way around. It had also taught the people who were making the ships new ways to complete the ships.

The asteroid base was nearing completion, with the Light AI carving out the remaining area.

There was a total of nearly two hundred slips, all awaiting new ships. More portals had been added to the asteroid base. These were to take in vessels that needed repairs or those that needed a resupply of ammunition. Instead of coming in the same way, they'd be routed to specialized areas depending on their specific need. This would make it much more efficient and would have a quicker turnaround time getting back into the battle. This was a lesson that Dave had learned from watching the Jukal and human fleets fight. The faster he was to resupply his ships and get them back into fighting condition, the more effective they would be against the enemy.

"We are picking up a fleet emerging from outside of the system," Jeeves said. "Commander Sato's predictions fall into line with this fleet being part of the Deq'ual fleet."

"Very well. Pass them their orders and have our destroyers go out to meet them," Dave said.

"Understood," Jeeves said.

"As soon as you have a visual, connect me," Dave said.

"Same here," Malsour said.

"I will do so," Jeeves said.

"I hoped that Sato would help us, but I didn't think he would do it in such a complete manner," Malsour said.

"Images now available," Jeeves said.

On a wall-sized screen in the meeting room, they watched as space seemed to distort and in a blur, a ship arrived. Behind it, other ships arrived. Another lead ship appeared to different sides, whole fleets forming up. The once-empty space now filled with some one hundred ships formed up into their assigned fleet as they altered their course and headed in-system.

These ships had rune-covered magical circles that went around their hull and glowed in the darkness, as well as massive armor panels and thick heavy guns. There were multiple missile ports in rows as well as hangar bay doors that hid fighters.

They were more cigar-shaped; the Pandora fleet ships had more edges, while the Deq'ual ships were rounded out.

Their design had come from their states of understanding magical coding. The Deq'ual understood magical circles easily and to accommodate this, their ships were more circular. The Pandoran ship builders understood how to create the more advanced runic lining, so rounded surfaces weren't needed.

"So, what is their mission?" Malsour asked.

"The Pandora forces will meet up with them; they'll enter the Jukal systems we've picked out. Our first move will be to destroy most of the Jukal Empire's infrastructure in those systems, leaving just enough so that the Jukal will see they're in-system.

"Then they will move from planet to planet. The Deq'ual will act as guardians to the destroyers, who will drop into the atmospheres of the planets we want to control. Then they will connect their portal to one of the portals located on Emerilia, where they will be supplied with all the materials they need to drop off at those planets," Dave said

Dave got a party chat invite from Josh. He accepted it and put it on speaker. Unlike before, he knew no one was able to listen in on his conversations if he wasn't in party chat. It was a relief not having to worry about the Jukal watching everything they did.

"Emerilia is secure," Josh said. Even if they had started their fight with the Jukal, there were still aggressive species on Emerilia. With Dave and Ela-Dorn's clamps, they had been able to cut off the portals to stop anything else from coming through.

The Terra Alliance still had to go through and clear out the remaining Alturarans that were fighting the angels, as well as collect the angels, those who were part of the armies of Light and any creatures and people who were able to escape the kill switch that was in their bodies.

With the onos blocking the signal, quite a number of people had been left.

There was no hiding from the Terra Alliance now as they combed Emerilia with the destroyer's sensors, pulling out these forces and handing them over to the Mage's Guild and College's overseers.

Few wanted to see more people sentenced to death, so the majority were given large sentences that would mean that they would have to serve for a large portion of their lives until they were able to regain their freedom. With Bob's blessing as the Grey God and creator of Emerilia, their lives were going to be much longer now.

Dave breathed a sigh of relief. "Good."

"Dave, I haven't asked this before but with all of the fleets that are going to be fighting in the Jukal star systems, what use are the rest of us? We're not pilots or even have experience in a space-type game," Josh said.

"The Jukal Empire don't have just space forces and their fleet—they also have forces on the ground. We will need to capture or kill these groups. These are the governors and people placed into power by the Jukal. Removing them will remove the Jukal Empire's influence from those planets. Once the Jukal fleet is dealt with, then we're going to need every mage, shield bearer, rogue, and archer out there to defeat these forces. When we get to the main planets, it will be nearly impossible to defeat the shields in these different locations, so we will need to drop forces on the ground to cut off communications, take their supplies and disrupt them wherever we can. Already the drop forces have missions right now to be landed on multiple stations and planets to disrupt the Jukal Empire's activities, drop off supplies and then return. We can't just win a fight from the stars—we're going to need people on the ground," Dave said.

"The Jukal love to see violence and have a number of arenas to watch people fight. Emerilia was just one way for them to get their fix. On the Jukal planets, we can expect that people will fight us with magic, swords, plasma rifles, and all combinations of different weapons." Anna's voice came through speakers in the room, interrupting their conversation.

"The Navy softens them up, and we take them down—I like it," Josh said. "All right, well, I'll help the overseers with the rest of this mess. I've got a meeting with the Jakan coming up as well."

"Good luck," Malsour said.

"I have a good feeling about it! Talk later." Josh cut the chat.

Dave looked to his notifications that had started blinking as Josh started talking to him.

"Malsour, be ready if I fall over," Dave said.

"What did you do now?" Malsour asked.

"Stats?" Dave said weakly, scratching his head sheepishly as he pressed his notification bar. He scrolled down the notifications.

Quest: Friend of the Grey God Level 8

End the: Of Myths and Legends Event

Rewards: Unlock Level 9 Quest

Increase to stats

+10 to stats (stacks with previous class levels)

+800,000 EXP

Quest: Friend of the Grey God Level 9

Free Emerilia

Rewards: Unlock Level 10 Quest

Increase to stats

Class: Friend of the Grey God

Status:	Level 8
	+80 to all stats
Effects:	Access to hidden quests.
	Access to the Imperial Carrier *Datskun*

Quest Completed: Bleeder Level 6

End the: Of Myths and Legends Event

Rewards: Unlock Level 7 Quest

Increase to stats +10 increase to stats (stacks with previous class levels)

+600,000 EXP

Class: Bleeder

Status:	Level 6
Effects:	+60 to all stats
	Ability to use Jukal Link

Quest: Bleeder Level 7

Free Emerilia

Rewards: Unlock Level 8 Quest

Increase to stats

Level 205

You have reached Level **205**; you have **5** stat points to use.

Dave opened his character sheet and started to allocate his five stat points to Intelligence.

Character Sheet

Name:	David Grahslagg	Gender:	Male
Level:	205	Class:	Dwarven Master Smith, Friend of the Grey God, Bleeder, Librarian, Skill Creator, Aleph Engineer, Weapons Master, Champion Slayer, Master of Space and Time, Master of Gravitational Anomalies, The Few the Mighty, Lord of Earth
Race:	Human/ Dwarf	Alignment:	Chaotic Neutral

Unspent points: 0

Health:	5,750	Regen:	27.02 /s
Mana:	17,530	Regen:	64.45 /s
Stamina:	5,920	Regen:	57.90 /s
Vitality:	575	Endurance:	1,351
Intelligence:	1,753	Willpower:	1,309
Strength:	592	Agility:	1,158

Dave looked up, finding Josh standing there, waiting for him.

"Actually, I have a special mission for you, if you choose to accept?" Dave asked. He almost started up a new party chat but instead laughed. There was no need to worry about the Jukal listening in on what they were saying and doing.

"What are you, bloody M? All secretive and that? What are you thinking?" Josh asked.

"I'm thinking that I might need you to take a long trip."

"Thanks, didn't know that I was that bad to see all the time." Josh chuckled.

"I'm sending you a file. Check it out and let me know what you think," Dave said. "I've got to check on Jung Lee. It seems he's got something ready for the Blood Kin."

"What? Dave, is this mission what I think it is?" Josh asked, his shock clear.

"What do you think?"

"This ain't going to be no simple quest but I think I can handle it with a few others," Josh said seriously.

"Good. Also, there's some equipment that Malsour can hook you up with that might make things easier."

"What about running the Terra Alliance?" Josh asked.

"I think Lucy could do that in your stead if you needed it," Dave thought out loud.

"Yeah, all right. I'll look over the quest and see if it is even remotely possible."

"Later." Dave teleported and transitioned through portals before he reached Jung Lee and Yemi, who were in Jung Lee's laboratory. All of his Affinity spirits were moving around the room, looking after the different potions and workstations in the room. Free Affinity spirits that could wander freely and had instead taken over command of Jung Lee were now regaled to lab assistants.

"Hey, Dave." Jung Lee tipped a bit of powder into the crucible in front of him and then increased the flame underneath.

Jung Lee was now one of the most powerful people within Emerilia. With Bob's increase, his base stats, and the Affinity spirits that he commanded, there were few who could compete with him in combat; that being said, Jung Lee was a crafter at heart and preferred not to fight if possible. He did it if he needed to, but as always, his passion was making potions and other remedies.

"What's up?" Dave looked to them both.

Jung Lee held up his hand as he indicated to the little drawers on one side of the room. Affinity spirits shot out from his hand, moving to the wall and grabbing items before returning them.

"Sorry, he's a bit busy," Yemi said with a kind smile, indicating for Dave to follow her a little bit away from Jung Lee so that he could concentrate on his potion making.

"As you know, he has been making potions that were able to supplement us with the blood essence we need to retain our strength and vitality. He decided he was not satisfied with simply replacing it; he instead started to work with us to try to find potions that would provide a greater increase in energy for us. I have been working with him to help him test out these potions and he is getting closer and closer to it. He made a potion that was the equivalent of nearly fifty vials of pure blood essence of a level 400 beast. Though he wasn't happy with just that."

"Dave, can you get Jules for me? I'll need her in about three minutes," Jung Lee said, not looking up from his potion that was unleashing a powerful and bloody aroma.

"One minute." Dave smiled at Yemi and teleported away. Jules was the lead healer of the Stone Raiders. She had become one of the largest figures within healing circles and ran the hospital within Terra. She'd saved hundreds, if not thousands, of lives and trained hundreds of people through the Mirror of Communication college.

Right now, she, like Jung Lee, was actually in Ice City, working with people there to come to a greater understanding of the healing instruments that had been made by the Pandora's Initiative.

He appeared in Ice City's hospital ward, where a group of healers, mages, and rune coders were talking with Jules and her people about the different machines that they'd created.

"Hi, Jules. Jung Lee was asking if he might have a moment of your time," Dave said as she was studying a healing vat. It looked like a bathtub with runic lining covering the inside and outside. There was a vat of red liquid that was a highly potent healing potion that could bring nearly anyone back from the brink or at least stabilize them for the healers to get involved.

"What does he need me for?" Jules asked.

"He's testing out a new potion on the Blood Kin and wants you to watch over," Dave said.

Jules frowned and then shrugged. "Sounds good to me. I have questions for him about his healing potion as well." Jules glanced to the healing potion vat off to the side of the room.

"I'm sure he would be more than happy to help you with that." Dave smiled, knowing that Jung Lee, like himself, loved to talk about the different things he was working on.

He teleported them both out of the hospital and into Jung Lee's lab.

Jung Lee had three of his Affinity spirits around the potions he was working on. Wind, Earth, and Fire Affinities worked together. The potion started to solidify and then divided into a half-dozen green and orange pills.

The spirits moved away, the Air one guiding the crucible to Jung Lee. He grabbed it out of the air and tilted it, catching one of the pills and studying it. He rolled it in his fingers and sniffed it, closing his eyes. "Okay, this should work." Jung Lee held the pill up and looked around the room. "Ah, Jules, been awhile," he said with a big smile.

"I heard that you needed me for something?" Jules looked at the pill in Jung Lee's hand.

"Yes! Check this out." Jung Lee handed over the pill to Jules.

"What is it?" She studied it and rolled it in her fingers.

"This is a blood enriching pill. When consumed, it will coat the interior veins of the Blood Kin. Then, whenever they drink or consume blood essence, it will be purified by the coating of their veins and increase the amount of power they gain from the potion by about ten times," Jung Lee said with no small amount of pride.

Yemi took in a sharp breath. Her eyes shined as she looked at the pill in Jules's hand and then to the dozen or so that were in the crucible next to Jung Lee.

"Now, for the best results, the pill would need to be guided through the different veins, allowing it to be fully absorbed. The more veins the pill travels through, the higher strength it will have, also the greater the secondary effect will be. That is, that the blood essence when it is going through the veins of the Blood Kin will be directly absorbed into their body instead of just stored within their veins as power to be burned. This will mean that their bodies will be stronger and even if they burn all of their blood essence, they will survive, and in a dire situation they can burn the blood essence within their body, which will have more energy than that within their veins," Jung Lee continued.

Saying that the simple blue and orange pill was miraculous wouldn't be an understatement. It wouldn't have much use to many people but to the Blood Kin, it was one of their most precious opportunities.

"Once again, I'm in awe of your abilities." Jules shook her head.

"Thank you," Jung Lee said with a sweeping bow. On his success, his normally stiff exterior was replaced by the more childish and excitable alchemist that hid underneath.

Dave snorted as he thought of how Jung Lee had run off with a trowel in hand as soon as he'd gained free rein of Earth's hall.

Apparently, there had been nothing left in the plant garden. Someone had plucked every plant up from the ground without leaving even a hair of a root behind.

Dave only had to look at the private growing area to see a number of plants that were nearly impossible to find across Emerilia.

"When could we test it out?" Yemi stepped forward, her eyes on the pill.

Jules looked to her and then Jung Lee. "I don't see any problem in starting now." Jules shrugged.

Jung Lee nodded in agreement.

"Okay, lay down on that table and we can get started," Jules said.

Yemi did as told and Jules passed her the pill.

"I'm going to check the condition of your body first." Jules rubbed her hands together to warm them up. She placed them on Yemi, sending her Mana into her as she looked over Yemi's body with her eyes that were now covered in a blue mist.

After a few minutes, she removed her hands. "Okay, I have a good understanding of your veins now. So let's begin. Take the pill and let me do what I need to. If you feel something strange, don't worry—that is just me. You have to do your best to not use your Mana or fight back. Otherwise it will reduce the effect of the pill," Jules said.

"Okay," Yemi said with a firm nod. She took the pill, swallowing it down without pausing, and stared up at the ceiling above.

Mana circulated around Jules before she poured power into Yemi. A golden light could be seen throughout Yemi's body. Yemi shuddered as the pill changed form into a gas and was inhaled into her lungs. It paused for a moment. The golden light became more saturated as the single point of light became larger, filling the interior of Yemi's lungs.

Jules took a breath and then waved her hands apart. Golden light covered Yemi's lungs, passing through them and entering Yemi's bloodstream. Yemi's back arched as she let out a groan; all of the veins in her body started to glow with a golden light, reaching up through her neck and to her eyes that shone with powerful light.

Dave covered his eyes and was only able to glance sideways at Yemi as the larger arteries shone with light that continued on into the smaller blood vessels that reached deep into Yemi's musculature across her body. The golden light started to dim as her body started to glow, turning from her pale coloring to a fleshy redness.

The blood circulated and then passed through the veins, heading back through the body. Now the golden light was dimmer; it was strongest around the blood vessels but every inch of Yemi's body now had a golden glow to it.

Dave and Jung Lee watched. If this worked, then it would be a massive boon for the Blood Kin who had done so much for the Terra Alliance and Pandora's Box Initiative.

After a few minutes, Jules lowered her hands and stumbled back a bit, her face pale. Jung Lee was there with a Stamina potion. Jules nodded in thanks, downing part of it as the color returned to her face.

Yemi sat up on the table, looking at her body as the golden glow from Jules's magic disappeared and instead she was able to look at the reddish coloration of her skin. The Blood Kin always looked as if they were half a foot in the grave, their skin like untouched marble, smooth and pure white. However, now with the pill's effects, it was as if Yemi's body was once again becoming alive.

Her veins now had a green color to it instead of being red as they contained the power of the blood essence she had consumed.

Jung Lee held out a pill to Yemi. It looked as if it were a blood-red gem or a hard candy. Yemi took it and popped it into her mouth. Almost immediately, a blush rose on her cheeks as she consumed the pill. A strong aura emanated out from her body as her eyes remained closed for a few minutes. Finally, they opened, with clear shock held within.

"It...it works!" Yemi looked to Jung Lee, Jules, and Dave in shock, not believing what was happening within her body.

"Good. It will take more time to get the rest of the Blood Kin to fuse the pill with their bodies. In the meantime, I will make more blood crystals." Jung Lee smiled.

"Jung Lee, this... I..." Yemi said, at a loss for words.

"Don't worry about repaying me. I love alchemy, pills, and potions. Doing this was a joy for me. Emerilia, now more than ever, needs the help of the Blood Kin. I just wanted to help you out as you've helped us. Also, it was a bit of a difficult problem and it was fun to create a solution." Jung Lee's solemn words turned into a playful smile with his last words.

Dave laughed as Jules held a bemused smile on her face.

Yemi held back tears and got off the table, hugging Jung Lee. "Thank you," she said in a soft voice.

She might be the matriarch of the Blood Kin, but she was just another person. For a very long time, she had few people she could place trust in, and even fewer people she could go to with her problems.

Dave's smile was filled with memories as he looked at the people in the room and thought of how he, too, had come to find people he trusted and valued within Emerilia.

Chapter 2: Poking A Hornet's Nest

"Coming out of the wormhole!" Navigation called out as the *Blood-Hawk* exited the wormhole it had punched through space. Other wormholes appeared around it as the rest of the fleet followed it. Opening one massive wormhole to encompass them all took much more energy than them breaking down into groups or even single ships and transitioning between systems.

"Sensor buoy is up and running. I don't see any Jukal ships in the area," Sensors called out.

"Very well. Let's head for the target. Tell the destroyers to start bringing their Devastator forces onboard and get the ark prepped for transferring its contents over to the destroyer." Captain Xiao's voice was steady and controlled as the fleet of five ships silently headed in toward the Jukal system.

They traveled for five days before reaching their target planet. They were traveling at speeds that would cross Emerilia in just seconds, but in the vast distances of space, that kind of speed was barely comparable to walking.

"Sensors, have the Jukal really not picked us up yet?" Xiao asked.

"It doesn't seem like it, sir," the sensors officer said.

"Very well. Send one of the destroyers ahead to circle the planet. I want to see how good this stealth coding is. Have them ready to escape if they are brought under fire. Nav, have the fleet hold position. We will follow orders and reveal ourselves well before we reach the planet. Make the Jukal have a false sense of security as they think that they still have time to see us before we hit them," Xiao said with an indifferent look in his eyes.

Frank watched as the destroyer circled the planet and then returned to the formation nearly a day later.

"Well, I bet that will be useful information for those in HQ to know. Nav, fire up the engines. Sensors, let's see how they react. Engineering, let's drop stealth but add in seventy percent to what we think their sensors would be able to see. Fire control, be ready to fire. Activate our Mana barriers."

Under Xiao's orders, the ships started to move once again. Their stealth magical coding changed and altered, making it appear to the Jukal as if they had just discovered the Pandora fleet. Mana barriers snapped into existence as missile ports were loaded and artillery cannons were manned and readied. Interceptor modules scanned the space around the ships, looking for targets.

The Pandoran fleet looked like a group of predators shedding their camouflage as they headed toward their prey.

"We have incoming from orbitals. Missile boats, take them out." Frank was connected to the other fire controllers as he pinged the orbitals hiding around the planet.

"Firing!" One of the missile boat fire controllers rang out true, as missiles entered the plot, saturating the orbital platform's defenses and taking it out as the ships continued forward.

"Destroyers, prepare to enter the atmosphere. Missile boats, focus on outward defense. *BloodHawk,* be ready to support ground efforts. Have the ark move between *BloodHawk* and missile boats for greatest protection." Captain Xiao's orders were nothing new as they had done simulations on this battle multiple times within their Mirror of Communication simulations.

The ships moved with ease, looking for targets.

There was no sign of anything different as some of the ark's portals activated, connecting to the asteroid base. Their teleport pads also activated, connecting them to the teleport pads that were located on the two destroyers that were now entering the atmosphere of the target planet.

The destroyers were shaking and being tossed around as they fought the atmosphere around them. The air burned with their entry.

They leveled off, the re-entry burn disappearing as the underside started to glow with runic lines.

The destroyers cut through the skies above the planet. The wind howled around them as for the first time in five hundred years, humans once again entered the atmosphere of a planet controlled by the Jukal Empire.

"Preparing forces for drop! Targets are aligned!" the Devastator operations commander said from her console off to the side.

"Very well," Xiao said. "Make sure that we are broadcasting on all channels."

"Yes, sir, we are on all channels. Nothing but Emerilia AM down there," the communications officer said, the corner of their mouth lifted in confidence.

"Good." Xiao reviewed the information on his screens.

All across the planet, Air's voice rang out in the different languages of the planet. Telling them that they came here to fight the Jukal Empire that had been oppressing the people. Telling them that their ships would be dropping off factories and different machines that they could use in order to make up for being cut off from the rest of the empire.

"Devastator forces are dropping on the planetary governor's residence!" the operations officer said.

The planet below was filled with massive skyscrapers, with very little of the ground even showing. However, the area around the planetary governor's residence was clearly different.

Frank saw a view of the destroyer coming in close to a massive residence that covered half of a continent.

There were a few buildings. They were massive as they were elegant, a symbol of the Jukal Empire's power over this planet.

In the lands, multiple people who had been living in homes underneath the perfect forests and gardens started to appear. These were the bodyguard races of the Jukal Empire, as well as their creations made to defend them.

They attacked the destroyers as they rushed in. Unlike the Jukal who didn't believe in using nanites to enhance themselves, these bodyguards had no such issues. They were closer to the Emerilians than they were to the Jukal.

This allowed them to use Mana, just like the Emerilians.

Plasma cannons tore through the sky, impacting the destroyer's Mana barriers, while spears of metal shot out from the ground and curses landed on the destroyers.

The runic lining underneath the destroyers lit up, creating magical formations on the ground.

Units wearing Devastator armor landed on the ground. Earth and Dark mages threw out their hands as around them a fort started to rise from the ground. The defenders attacked this growing defensive structure, but although they were able to slow its growth, they weren't able to stop it.

Overseers from the Mage's College and Guild took to the air, becoming the focus of the defenders' attacks. They acted as if they didn't even see the attacks. Their Mana barriers stopped the incoming attacks as they gave the defenders terms for surrender. Their armor changed their voices, so that the different races would be able to understand them.

As the overseers stood in the air, asking for the defenders to surrender, the destroyers turned their sides, presenting the modified artillery cannons along their sides. The dwarves managing them didn't waste any time as they put their guns to use.

Grand working shells were unleashed on the pristine grounds of the planetary governor's residence. Seas of lightning shot out from where the shells landed. Magical formations appeared in the sky, as clouds came together and created a massive thunderstorm, filled with cutting winds, penetrating rain, and lightning that turned the ground to glass where it hit.

All while this was going on, the Devastator forces organized themselves.

"Blood Reevers are taking the charge!" the operations officer said.

From the now several fortresses, holes opened in the walls as gleaming black armor covered in glowing runic lines shot forward. Gnomes and orcs, all of them equipped with Devastator armor, rode armored blood reevers.

The blood reevers shook their heads and let out their howls, racing faster and faster. They came together from the different fortresses, forming into one body, creating a line across their front.

The ground forces that were defending the planetary governor's home looked at these charging blood reevers. Drums could be heard coming from the fortresses as the gaps in the walls became larger. The sound of boots and drums made the very ground shake as dwarven warclans marched behind the advancing blood reevers. As they cleared the fortresses, the creatures that had been on their shoulders shot into the air, unleashing their attacks upon the defenders.

They formed their warclan units, advancing toward the enemy, their hands on their swords as they held their massive dwarven shields in front of them.

Behind them came mages and archers. As these ranged fighters got free of the fortress, spell formations appeared in the sky and upon the ground.

"We've got drones incoming from the southeast," the operations officer said, not looking from their screens.

Fighter crafts appeared in the sky, bearing down on the ground forces. They shot out laser beams that cut through the sky, only to smash into Mana barriers.

Interceptor modules twitched and locked onto the drones. After the second shot, the drones' lasers stopped working as the interceptor modules used the runic coding Jekoni had created, disrupting the coding of the lasers.

Lightning rained down from the skies, as meteors tore through the perfect drone formations.

Arrows tore at their shields and punched holes through their armor. Drones spiraled down in droves, crashing into the ground below as the charging blood reevers and the gnome and orc riders atop of them smashed into the defenders.

Under the blood reevers, the defenders were crushed. The riders cut out with large blades and small bows that easily pierced the defenders' armor and killed them.

The blood reevers didn't slow their advance, leaving behind broken and scattered defenders in their wake.

"Shields!" the dwarven warclan commander called out. Shields came together with the sound of metal hitting metal.

"Artillery cannons, hold fire," Frank called out, as now the battle was joined, it was more likely that his people would hit their own instead of the enemy.

Ranged artillery came in from the planetary governor's buildings and more drones came out, but it wasn't enough to stop the destroyers and their forces on the ground.

The defenders that had been run over by the blood reevers continued to not listen to the overseers in the air as they met the dwarven shield wall.

Nothing passed the shield wall. As the defenders hit a steel wall, swords appeared in the dwarves' hands as they cut forward, and advanced with the drums.

The defenders were cut down without pause. The ground forces and destroyers advanced forward as more and more people seemed to drop from the destroyers.

It seemed as if there was an unending supply. What the defenders and the Jukal didn't know was that the destroyers were connected to the ark, where units wearing Devastator armor were marching from the asteroid base through a portal, and then teleport pads before being dropped onto the battlefield.

If someone's armor was low on power, they were switched out and could activate their teleport back to the anchor within the destroyer, charge up and then drop back down and return to battle.

Seemingly unending waves of Devastator-armored Emerilians joined the fight as the destroyers advanced.

After a few hours, one of the destroyers moved away from the planetary governor's residence and started to move around the planet. Where it went, it would drop off factories, growing towers, and other items that would be needed by the population as they were cut off from the rest of the Jukal Empire.

The ark descended into the planet's atmosphere and moved with the roaming destroyer, passing down more items, until the entire planet was seeded with them. They ran out of pre-made factories and other items and instead started to put down soul gem constructs. These had heat and cold exchangers on them that allowed them to charge up and create new factories and buildings.

Frank looked to his different screens. The fighting on the ground was covered in a magical storm of spells going off, but here and there people were surrendering; the overseers dropped down, protecting them and sealing them before removing them from the battlefield.

As the defenders saw this, more and more of them started to surrender. They didn't want to die for the Jukal who wouldn't raise a finger to help them.

In the same hour, four more systems discovered that there were Pandora fleets in-system. Three hours later, the first of the joint Pandora and Deq'ual system fleets entered the Jukal-controlled systems.

***

The Jukal fleet's admirals looked at the different screens around the conference table. They were using the Mirrors of Communication conference room in order to connect across the Jukal Empire.

They held positions of great power, with their families using them to secure their position within the Jukal Empire's hierarchy. There were few positions that could demand more respect than being a leader of one of the Jukal fleets.

All of them looked to be at a loss as they watched on the screens as nearly forty systems were being invaded by the Emerilian forces.

"It seems that the Emerilians have an ally. Looking at the ships, there is a clear distinction between the Emerilian-made ships and these rounded-looking ships. We have no idea who this other party is. However, it looks like they have similar designs and technology to what we saw in the war against humanity. From this, we can determine that they are probably a human group that has been hiding these last five hundred years and we have not been able to find," one of the admirals said, their fury clear.

All of the admirals looked at the different types of ships that were entering their systems as if they didn't care for the Jukal Empire at all.

"What are we going to do? Already we have lost a number of the secure locations we controlled in these star systems. They're also dropping what looks like to be aid to the people of the empire." The Jukal admiral started off angry but his words came out with a confused note as he thought of the factories and different facilities that had rained down from the destroyers and arks.

"Send in the fleets. We will destroy their ships and show the glory of the Jukal Empire!" one of the older admirals said with a fanatical gleam in his eyes as he smashed his hand into the table, assured of their victory.

"We don't know their capabilities," the first admiral said.

"The Jukal fleets are the most powerful in all existence! Nothing can stand in their way! Wiping away these fleets is as easy as flipping our hands!" the older admiral yelled down the first.

"We have orders to attack Emerilia directly. It will take three months for us to organize our attack." An admiral scratched his furred chest.

"We have portals in these locations. We can send our own fleets out, overpower them two to one and then destroy them. As their ships burn, we will send people through the portals on the ground and remove any influences that they hold on their planet," an admiral sitting next to the older one said.

The older admiral nodded in agreement.

"Bring up our reserve fleets, and split the main fleet to deal with these attacking fleets?" the first admiral asked.

The admirals from around the table looked to one another and then looked to him, showing signs of agreement.

"We all know that the emperor wants this dealt with as soon as possible, but we also know that he wants to use this to show the people of the Jukal Empire the power that we, the Jukal, hold. We can use this to our advantage. We have the ships and the power. We send our ships through and we destroy the Emerilians and their allies completely in one go," the older admiral said.

The first admiral nodded. The plan made a lot of sense and it was well known that the emperor loved to have a show of violence. If they could bring him one, then there was no telling of how he would reward them.

"Very well. We will defeat the fleets within the Jukal Empire completely. At the same time, we will send the main fleet to Emerilia in order to show them how slaves ought to act," the first admiral scoffed.

Chapter 3: Home Is Where the Heart Is

Deia bounced little Koi on her knee as she looked out over Ice City. In the last couple of days, the apartments and buildings that had been empty were now filled with people. There was a constant stream of people moving between Terra and Ice City. More portals had been laid down to just move items between the different bases.

If the Jukal Empire were to see the way that the Emerilians were using the portals, they would collapse in shock. The Jukal Empire viewed them as symbols of their power; only those who were high up in the hierarchy of the empire and military were allowed to use the portals. However, the Emerilians were using them as nothing more than trade corridors; even their ships had portals located inside, an extravagance that no Jukal would understand.

The Jukal could build more, but they were only made on the Jukal home planet and their distribution was controlled by the emperor himself. It allowed him to assert complete control over the Empire and his own Jukal subjects who might eye the emperor's throne. They were made on the orders of the emperor and they took months to complete, with them being made by hand. The master craftsmen all made different parts that came together in a portal. By having each craftsman trained in one part, one would need to go to hundreds of the craftsmen to get the complete designs for the portals. It made it so that none of the information was available on the Jukal net: there was no AI to hack, no firewalls to break to get the information.

It was an archaic way of building the portals but it limited access. It was secure and it worked well. The Jukal Empire were not ones to mess with the system.

The door to Deia's apartment opened as Dave walked in. He looked tired and worried but seeing Koi and Deia, it seemed to evaporate.

Deia didn't say anything to Dave, instead choosing to kiss him as he came closer.

All day, there had been people marching through Ice City to the asteroid base; factories had been churned out from the different workshops across the cities, being funneled through portals directly into the ships of the Pandora fleet.

As battles had come to an end, the Devastator forces had been returned to Ice Planet and the asteroid base where they rested, rearmed, recharged and then once again moved through portals and teleport pads onto other planets of the Jukal Empire.

In forty systems across the Jukal Empire, Emerilian ships now moved between planets.

Dave wrapped his arm around Deia as they stood there, looking out over Ice City and glancing to the sleeping Koi in Deia's arms.

"When do you think they'll send out their fleets?" Deia asked in a soft voice.

"Might take a week or two—long enough for us to start talking to the different people of the empire."

Deia nodded and didn't say anything as she leaned her head into Dave's shoulder, taking comfort in being so close.

"The Jakan have agreed to help. We'll give them a planet that they can expand to, one of the Jukal home planets. Mage overseers will make sure that they don't go overboard and give the Jukal a way out," Dave said. "If we get to that stage."

Deia looked to him, seeing the worry that he tried to hide. She nudged him with her shoulder, only having to look at him to transmit her thoughts.

Dave deflated and sighed, looking older as wrinkles appeared around the corners of his eyes.

"We've got a good plan, but there's a lot of variables. Sure, we're hoping that the Jukal will try to deal with the fleets we have hitting their key systems. But realistically, they might just take all their fleets, and then hit us here at Emerilia. If they do that, we're going to need to pull out every trick and show all of our trump cards before they even get to Emerilia," Dave said, laying out his worries. "If that happens, I don't know if we will be able to keep Emerilia."

"So that's why you've been pushing for more people to come to Ice City and asteroid base," Deia said.

"Yeah," Dave said, not needing to hide anything from her.

"This won't end unless the emperor of the Jukal Empire is dead, or we are, will it?" Deia asked.

"No, I don't think it will. The empire needs to be broken for humanity to be given a chance to do our own thing. If even a single part of the Jukal Empire remains, we'll be hunted down and destroyed. If we can get the empire to destroy itself, then we can be safe," Dave said.

"Well, that's one hell of a wedding present." Deia smiled.

"What is?" Dave asked, a perplexed look on his face as he looked at her.

"Destroying an entire empire," Deia said wistfully.

Dave chuckled slightly, remembering a promise he had made to her so long ago.

When this is all over, then we can get married.

A light shone in his eyes as a smile pulled at the corners of his mouth. He pulled Deia tighter to him and kissed the top of her head.

***

Malsour looked out over the asteroid base from his office. He could see the slips that went off into the distance. Portals along the sides of the main thoroughfare showed scenes within different bases; through them, materials were coming from the refineries and munitions were coming from factories that were located throughout all the bases.

He looked up as a knock came from his door. "Come in." He sensed the familiar aura. He sipped from his cup of Xer. It was a few hours in the past since it had any effect on him. He'd spent hours working with the diverse building crews to build and alter the multiple projects that they were working on.

"You should be getting some sleep." Denur, Malsour's mother, the mother of dragons walked into his office.

"I will eventually. There's a lot more to be done," Malsour said.

"You still haven't fully integrated all the changes to your body. You need rest, at least a few hours of it before your body can get used to everything that has happened to you," Denur said, not willing to let this go by.

"We've got the new warships to build and the flying citadels to update. We'll have three more fleets ready to move in just a week at our current production levels. That means we can hit six more key systems to try to divide the Jukal's main fleet."

"Yes, but right now you're not going to be much good to anyone if you're not running in your best condition." Denur cut him off.

Malsour felt a flash of annoyance, but then sighed as it drained away, seeing the clear concern and love that Denur held in her eyes. "You have a good point."

"I know I do. I am your mother, after all." Denur indicated for him to get up out of his chair.

He smiled and let his mother worry over him as she guided him out of the office, talking about things to take his mind off the war.

For the first time in days, he was able to calm his mind.

In his office, on one of the interface screens he had locked to his desk, alerts started to appear.

The Jukal fleets had finally started to move.

Chapter 4: The Jukal's Response

"In a number of the empire's systems, we have Jukal fleets moving toward the system portals, which seem to be building up power." Commander Sato looked to the others in the Mirror of Communication conference room: Admiral Adams, Admiral Forsyth of the Pandora fleets, as well as Suzy, Lucy, and the leadership from the Terra Alliance. Sato didn't look to where the four anonymous people were sitting; these were the council members of the Deq'ual system. The others in the conference room couldn't even see them.

Sato had been the one to call the meeting as it was the Deq'ual sensor net that they had been laying down for months that had picked up the Jukal fleet's movements.

"Now, the big question is to see where they go," Adams said.

The others in the room had grim looks on their faces as they watched the screens that were linked to the sensor buoys that were relaying in real-time. Based off the distances they were seeing, the information coming to them was a few minutes old.

"We've got a portal activating in one of the Jukal systems we hit," Suzy said. With a wave of her hand, another system appeared and they could see the portal through the sensors of the Pandora fleet that was in-system.

Everyone held their breath as more and more portals in the occupied systems started to activate.

It looked as if the Jukal were going to deal with the issues within their controlled systems before they attacked Emerilia. It was just as they had hoped and planned for. However, no one wanted to say anything, for fear of jinxing it and the Jukal ruining their plans.

The first portal activated, linking one system to another as a Jukal fleet of ten ships—two carriers, five destroyers, and three troop transports—appeared on the other side.

The ships were much larger than the Pandora or Deq'ual ships. They passed through the event horizon, entering the system that the Pandora fleet controlled.

Sato's heart thumped in his chest as he looked at those behemoths. These same ships might have fought against humanity five hundred years ago. Now, once again, they moved in anger, ready to defeat humanity's combined fleets.

Hangar bays could be seen, hundreds of crafts hidden behind thick armored doors, waiting to pounce on the human ships. Cannons shone with a dark light, ready to destroy all that stood in their path.

This was the unstoppable Jukal fleet, a fleet that had assured the Jukal's rise to power and their continued dominance over uncountable people, dozens of races, and hundreds of systems. Only one word could truly encompass the feeling that those ships inspired: domination.

Adams and Forsyth talked to each other in low tones before they started to pass orders to their respective fleets. More and more of the sensor buoys showed Jukal fleets moving through portals, hundreds of ships that made up the entire Jukal fleet hunting down humanity's ships.

Large Jukal fleets transitioned through portals, sometimes meeting up with other fleets on the other side, and some continuing on their own. Fleet after fleet continued to exit through the same portal. A remote system now saw the growing fleet combining together.

Sato and the rest of the people in the room were passing on information, listening to the orders and reports passed back and forth as the second part of their offensive began.

It took a number of hours but the fleet of five that had started off in the remote system had now ballooned to sixty, with more fleets coming through.

This remote system was the closest to the Emerilian system that contained a portal.

It was this remote star system that the Jukal had picked to have their rally point for their fleet that would strike out at Emerilia in an attempt to destroy it and all those who called it home.

Once the portion of the Jukal fleet assigned to destroy the Emerilian system reached one hundred and fifty ships strong, their propulsion drives fired. The ships started to gain momentum as they headed to a jump point that would take them closer to Emerilia.

With no portals this far out, they could only use their jump drive and their regular propulsion drives. If there were no stops, then they'd reach the Emerilian system in three months.

Some two hundred ships that had formed into fleets had now completed their transition into the key Jukal star systems that the Pandora and Deq'ual fleets had attacked.

Another hundred or so ships continued to hold position over the home world of the Jukal and the heart of their empire.

Sato looked at it all, not letting any of his emotions show.

Even if we defeat all of these ships, we won't have the numbers to contend with the Jukal ships that are protecting the Jukal home world.

He opened his interface and looked at the new numbers that had come from Malsour and Edwards. A cold smile spread across his lips; slowly, a new hard edge appeared in his eyes.

"If we're to lead them on a chase of the system for a week, then we will be able to bring up another forty ships to the battlefield." Sato's voice cut through the discussions around the table.

The others around the table had pensive looks on their faces as they heard his words.

"Well then, let's try for two weeks, but as long as we have a week, we'll be ready," Suzy said.

"When we developed our ships, we did it with a good idea of the Jukal's capabilities. We should be able to easily get away from them and lead them on a chase. However, we will probably need to lose a few ships here and there to keep up the ruse," Adams said.

Suzy tapped on the table in thought. She opened her interface and talked to someone. The others in the room noticed this action and waited to see what she was doing.

"This is possible," Suzy said after ending the call. "All of our ships have portals as well as teleportation arrays, like the one in the original Pandora's Box workshops that can create a portal from one point to another that doesn't have a drop pad, ono, or portal on the other end. They've also got onos and teleport pads. With this, we can connect to the rest of the fleet. We'll gut ships from the inside, take everything useful from them, run them on automatic with all of the crew evacuated to the asteroid base, where they can get on a new ship and the materials from the old ships can be used to speed up the building process of the later ships."

Sato and Adams couldn't help but look to each other with shock.

It took them weeks to build the hull of a ship, months before they were even able to launch. That wasn't including all the checks they had to perform and extras that they needed to include. However, Suzy made it seem as if making ships was no big thing. Sato sighed and then thought back to the production numbers that he had checked.

Maybe to them, building ships is that much easier.

Sato nodded his head. Being able to move all of their people from their ships, and gut them for the harder-to-make components, would definitely make it easier for them to build replacement craft. The thought of it was just audacious, efficient, and plain brilliant. It wasn't a tactic that he would have thought of before because of how he was trained.

Adams suggested it but she hadn't thought they would be able to save the systems from within the ships, only thinking of getting the crew off with the portals and teleportation magic that the Emerilians had created.

"Very well, then. We'll strip down a number of ships to give the Jukal a good show while we use the time to build up our forces even more. Then, when they're confident in their victory, we'll turn the tables on them," Sato said.

"Very well," Suzy said.

***

Frank clenched and unclenched his hands as he stared at the screen that showed the portal in the same system as him. As he monitored the power fluctuation, the portal flashed with power as a new set of stars and system were shown on the other side of the portal.

Jukal ships forced their way into the system. As soon as they were clear of the portal, they turned and charged toward the Pandora fleet.

"Looks like they've come out to play," Captain Xiao said. "How are our ground forces looking?"

"We've got a few thousand people who are under the overseers' watch. They've been portaled back to the asteroid base. Our forces have cleared out any of the Jukal and the different Jukal Empire offices. The last of the ground units are returning to the destroyers, which will be lifting in a few hours," the ground operations officer said.

"What is it like on the facilities front?" The captain looked to the engineering section of the command center.

"This planet deals mostly in small components for electronics. There is a lack of fuel for their various power systems, as well as no food. We've put in a number of greenhouse towers. A number of them are in use, but so far people are just sneaking in, stealing stuff and running off. People are hesitant to take food out in the open.

"Our energy systems are hooked up and are charging but no one has connected their power to their power grid. This is understandable as they don't know if our systems will mess with theirs. We believe they're smart people and they've been studying the power systems to come to understand them.

"The biggest thing has been the Mirror of Communication schools. These people know Mirrors of Communication and a number of them have used them before. They're in anonymous mode so we don't know how many of them there are. So far, we can see that they're learning about Mana, how to create different Jukal technologies, and how to apply it to their situation. It's opening up a new line of thinking and giving them tools and knowledge to do so many things."

"Good. I hope that it helps them out." Xiao sounded relieved.

Frank could understand his emotions. These people had been used for unknown years by the Jukal Empire. They were nothing more than slaves to the Jukal. When they had become a part of the empire, they had to submit, or be wiped out.

Here, they were able to see new opportunities. They hadn't made the leap to join with humanity against the Jukal just yet. At the same time, they seemed to be slowly coming to understand humanity and getting to know them.

"Nav, set a rally point for the fleet to meet up. Once we're all together, we'll lead the Jukal fleet on a nice little trip of the system."

"Yes, Captain," Nav said. Waypoints started to appear on the map of the system.

Frank looked at the Jukal fleet, a predatory look in his eyes as he rested his hands on his console, itching to activate the powerful weaponry of the *BloodHawk*.

***

From the Jukal emperor's chambers, laughter could be heard shaking the very walls.

"Look, my beauties—see the might of the Jukal Empire!" the emperor cried out, clapping his hands together as he watched the Jukal fleets entering the different systems that the Emerilians had attacked. Now that they had come out of the portals, they seemed as if nothing could possibly stop them.

He laughed while joking and pointing to the different Emerilian ships and their mysterious ally as they started to move away from the planets that they had been fighting on for the last two weeks.

"Look at them, scared in the face of such mighty ships! No other race could do what we, the Jukal, have done!" The emperor didn't care that none of the concubines in the room with him were Jukal, or the way in which they gritted their teeth in their minds while they continued to flatter him, pressing up against him and smiling as he looked down on their entire race, and all others that were not Jukal.

When they looked to the screens that showed the Jukal fleet and the human fleets, they didn't feel the joy the emperor did. Instead, they felt the hopelessness of what the humans had done. They'd been backed in a corner and there was nothing that they could do, other than fight back with everything they had.

Now it looked like their run had come to an end.

Some hoped that they would be able to escape, while others wished that they would have a clean death instead of being the slaves of the Jukal once again.

They shuddered at the thoughts of what might happen to those who were captured by the Jukal.

The emperor made it a point of honor to watch the killings of those who were supposedly plotting against the Jukal Empire. As he watched them, so did all of them.

They knew the cruelty of the Jukal Empire, but they were powerless to do anything about it.

Chapter 5: Beware the Engineer

Dave opened his eyes as he pulled his hand away from the soul gem construct that had, over the space of just a few hours, filled the destroyer he was in.

"This one is good for service. Get her crew moved in," Dave said.

"Understood," Jeeves said from overhead.

Dave teleported out of the new destroyer and into his and Malsour's office that lay within the walls of the shipyard. Through their windows, they could see the main thoroughfare that was filled with slips that had ships in various states of completion.

Four fleets had already been pushed out of the asteroid base and were now patrolling Emerilia. They watched over the system. All of the ships that were part of the Pandora Initiative were now leading the Jukal fleet ships on a merry chase throughout the Jukal systems. With every day, new ships were being completed, amassing a powerful force within the Emerilian system.

Dave felt an intense sense of satisfaction as he looked upon the slips and ships in them. The asteroid base was now massive and nearing completion. It wouldn't be very long until it was finished and a second shipyard was under construction already.

Still, he knew that it wouldn't be completed in time to help out with the ongoing battle. It wouldn't be long until they needed to show some of their trump cards and start to not only lead the Jukal around their systems, but start to break their fleets.

An alert appeared in his vision. He looked to it, mentally opening the alert. A screen appeared in front of him. He watched as the Jukal fleet chased a Pandora fleet through a system. They were heading out toward the area that they could use their jump drives.

Dave grinned as he watched the Jukal continue to hit them with missiles and harass them. The Pandoran fleet seemed to be too slow to escape because they were still hiding their real capabilities to confuse the Jukal. As the Jukal and the Pandora fleet neared one another, the Pandora fleet turned around, apparently unable to take the battering anymore. They fired their cannons and missiles while at the same time their engines fired, arresting their motion and carrying them back toward the Jukal.

One of the destroyers pushed itself into the Jukal fleet's path, taking most of the fire. It exploded; the Jukal and Pandora fleets intersected one another, with the Jukal continuing out of the system as the Pandora fleet fled in-system.

As the Pandora fleet used the explosion to go faster in-system, the Jukal had to turn around and try to fight the momentum that they had built up.

The chase continued, now with the Jukal racing in-system as the Emerilians moved to the planets, looking to hide among them.

Seeming to be pure happenstance, it also took them closer to the portal that was located deeper in-system.

The Pandoran and Deq'ual fleets had all evaded the Jukal fleets in their own ways: some hiding in gas planets, others running through asteroid belts—though all of them had been stopped from escaping the Jukal systems by the Jukal fleets. When looking at one of the systems, then it might be possible; however, there were over twenty different systems that the human fleets had attacked.

However, the Jukal did nothing but follow them, as they now started to move toward the portals in their different locations.

Dave's eyes moved from the different alerts and images from the sensor buoys as he looked at the thoroughfare once again.

Shadows appeared behind Dave before resolving into Malsour.

"How go the new arks and missile boats?" Dave looked over his shoulder.

"Well, though the ark shipyards are a lot slower than the new slips that have been attached to Terra, I heard that there is a plan in place to add another five sections to Terra," Malsour said.

"Yeah, it's a back-up plan."

Malsour nodded, understanding. "We finally got some more detailed images from the Jukal home world. There are several Deq'ual scout ships in-system, working to give us a better idea of what is going on with them. We've been able to pick up a lot of chatter about the different ways the Jukal Empire are playing up the fight. Seems that with Emerilia not being on the air anymore, this is the most watched event in the empire," Malsour said.

"Well, soon it'll be time for them to see a new program." Dave's eyes fell on the portal. "Have they been talking about the portals that we used at the moonbase at all?"

"Seems that Anna was able to mess up the images a bit, make it look like the ships were all coming from the moonbase, and not from the asteroid base and through a portal," Malsour said.

"I don't like it. Still feels like we're going to get found out." Dave sighed.

"Well, after we crush their fleets and take over their portal network, I don't think that there's going to be a whole lot that they can do about it," Malsour said.

Dave received a message that made him access his interface. He pulled it up as he stood taller. "Seems that some of those scout vessels you were talking about picked up some talk of people who were saying that everything seemed a bit weird with the different human fleets. Seems that it's gaining traction. The military leaders have said that they want to move ahead with the plan," Dave said. "Otherwise they think that we might lose the element of surprise."

Dave pulled out a Mirror of Communication. Malsour did the same as the two of them connected to a conference room. It was laid out like a command center. Here all the various factions of the humans were grouped together.

Here, Forsyth and Adams ruled, Sato advised from Deq'ual, and Dave gave the final say.

"Well, they're dense but it doesn't seem like they're as dense as we were hoping." Sato looked to Dave and Malsour, who had entered the command center.

"What are we thinking?" Dave looked to the military commanders. He might be the man with his finger on the button, but he knew he was no master military strategist. That was the job of the people in front of him.

They looked to one another before Adams waved for Forsyth to talk.

"Sir, we think that it might be the time to strike. We have four fleets that are complete and we should have another two finished in just a few days. If the Jukal get wind of what's going on, then they might be able to reverse the changes we make and then everything could come apart. We hit them now when it's not in the back of their minds—we get the element of surprise and we can tear out the portal network from underneath them," Forsyth said, not flinching away from Dave's eyes in the slightest, even as he knew that this moment would determine a number of people's fates.

"Okay, well then, it's time to take over that portal network." Dave took a deep breath, his eyes falling on the screens behind them. "I'll let you know as soon as we gain control of it."

"Yes, sir," Forsyth said. The others nodded.

Dave exited the Mirror of Communication and then teleported and portaled from the asteroid base to Ice City. He teleported into Ela-Dorn's office.

"Dave?" Ela-Dorn looked up from her work.

"Time to take over the portal network."

"I'll gather the team." Ela-Dorn sent out messages through her interface. In a few minutes, nearly twenty people had gathered in the room, all of them experts on portal technologies and theories.

Dave teleported them to a portal that took them to Terra. He took them to a portal that was hidden away. All of them looked at it with clear curiosity as they followed Dave and Ela-Dorn through the event horizon and stepped onto the Imperial carrier *Datskun*.

A gray light appeared in front of them, fading away to reveal Bob in his wolfkin form. "I'm going to guess this isn't some simple house call?" Bob asked.

"No, it's not. It's about the portal network. It seems that now is the time to take it over," Dave said.

"Okay, let's do it." Bob teleported them to a holding area where a portal had its protective cover open and showed its internals. This was a Jukal portal, tied directly into the network. With the *Datskun*'s codes, the ship was able to pass through portals and command them. It had taken Anna a few years to work through the firewalls but it gave her something to do as Bob built Emerilia and looked over it.

It was only when the Jukal found out about Emerilia that Bob started to take apart the portals, with him cutting off their remote access to them. The Jukal thought they were destroyed, while instead Bob was using one to gain access into the portal network.

Being an Imperial carrier, it could not only pass through a portal, it could actually get them to connect to different portals.

Linked to the network of portals, to the Frankenstein version in front of them, it was all open for the taking. They just had to access all of the portals as fast as possible and input controls that would place them under their control.

"Okay, everyone, get a station. It's time to start." With a flick of Dave's hands, his armor was changed to simple hemp clothes.

The gray cloak around Bob dissolved as he stood at a console. Shard's holographic body appeared among the consoles facing the portals. Anna appeared as Jeeves descended and Jackie came into being.

Several holographic boxes appeared. These were the AIs of Emerilia, the ones that Bob and Anna had created in order to infiltrate the

various systems that controlled and looked after the people of Emerilia.

Steve appeared in holographic form, making a show of stretching
out his hands, a bright smile on his face as he stood with the AIs.

Dave organized his screens before his gaze passed over the others
in the room. When the last one had finished altering their station to
how they liked, he let out a cool breath. "Dial up the portals."

Bob's hands flashed as runic lines appeared on the different AI's
bodies as they used all of their computing power to call up every single portal that the *Datskun* could, then used all of the information
banks of the portals to connect to the portals that they had connected to in the past.

They didn't simply have to have the right codes; they had to
know the right positions of all these portals to establish a connection
with them. As they were connected, Dave and the others broke down
the portals by group and they started to make changes to their security measures in order to make sure that they were under their control.

Within a seeder located deep underneath Cliff-Hill, tens of portals were activating. As they were connected to another portal, machines would toss through soul gem constructs. At the asteroid base,
where Terra had been located as well as the ark shipyards and the
moonbase, the massive ship-sized portals activated and large soul
gem constructs were thrown out.

The AIs and the engineers worked through reams of data, checking through all of it as they pulled control away from the Jukal Empire over their portal networks faster than they could try to regain
control.

Here and there, portals were shut down and disconnected phys-
ically, but the ones that were in the middle of a star system didn't
have anything or anyone around them that could turn off their power sources.

No one dared to make portals, until Dave had. Now the knowledge that he and the people who had helped in making the portals exceeded that of the people in the Jukal Empire.

After all, they would need to gather hundreds of different craftsmen in order to understand the parts. Coming to understand the system as a whole had been something that was left up to the AIs and computer programs of the Jukal Empire. It was something that had worked and they didn't care to change it.

Across the Jukal Empire, portals flashed with light as they were activated. People looked on with fear, expecting the Jukal armies and their ships to come through and lay waste to those who dared to defy them. However, instead, glowing crystals shot through.

These crystals floated in the air as the portal's event horizon disappeared and the lights around the portal stopped glowing. The crystal shot backward and seemed to explode. Four clamps formed and latched onto the portal, weaving into the portal's circuits.

People cried out in alarm and shock, unsure of what was happening and not knowing what to do with these events.

Although the people of the empire were confused, the true Jukal were shocked. Those on the home world, especially those within the emperor's residence and managed the empire, were filled with a new kind of fear as they found their network descending into chaos as they lost control over portal after portal.

"Send the fleets!" Dave yelled. His words transmitted to those within the *Datskun* and the commanders of the human military forces.

His words turned into movements as the Pandora fleets seemed to disappear from the Jukal fleets' sensors.

They used their teleportation magic and shot toward the portals in their systems. Around Emerilia, the fleets there moved toward the moonbase.

A portal activated in one of the contested systems. The Jukal fleet filled with excitement as the portal opened. Their excitement turned to confusion as from the portal, forty Pandora vessels emerged, moving toward the Jukal fleet.

The Deq'ual fleet that had been fleeing now turned. Their weapons came off safe as their speed increased. The Jukal watched with wide eyes as the Deq'ual ships and the ark with them had turned into the hunters.

The Pandora ships disappeared one moment, and then reappeared next to the Deq'ual fleet. Their runic lining flared with power as their missile ports opened and their cannons came to bear.

The Jukal fleet moved about, in a state of shock and panic; however, there was nothing that they could do.

Drones and fighters filled the areas between ships. Missiles shot forth from both fleets. Explosions rippled through the void as defenses tried to disrupt missiles and shields flared to life with impacts of rounds and the destructive wrath of their weapons.

No quarter was given by either side. This was a fight to the death.

The Jukal ships fired their massive weapons. The smaller human ships got hammered, but their Mana barriers were much stronger, allowing them to absorb the hits and keep moving. The Jukal's barriers showed signs of weakness and, unlike the human ships, they couldn't teleport away if they started to take too much damage.

Grand working barrier busters, that worked on overloading the shields with so much energy that the controllers couldn't handle it, showed off their prowess. The Jukal shields continued to fluctuate, changing colors and becoming more and more chaotic.

Spell formations appeared around the Pandora fleet, as the mages within them cast powerful spells that were projected through the runic lining of the hull.

Plasma cannons formed of Mana roared; artillery spells fired barely contained Mana.

As the ships got closer, drones and fighters crossed one another. The void was filled with laser beams and rounds, creating a kaleidoscope of destruction that was being vented by both sides.

***

As Dave was watching and taking over the portals within the Jukal Empire, Frank was on the *BloodHawk*.

"Teleport!" Nav barked out as the entire fleet teleported away from the chasing Jukal. All of the Pandora fleets appeared in front of the in-system portal.

It flashed with light, showing another system on the other side. The six ships of the fleet rushed through the portal.

"Entering event horizon!" Navigation called out, now in their element. Since the Jukal had shown up, they had been toying with them. It was tense work, but they weren't able to push their ships to their limits.

Now that they were able to unleash the power of their ships, there was a new fire in all of them. It was time for them to show their teeth and counterattack.

"All batteries, be ready for immediate action," Frank called out to his people.

All missile ports were open and cannon batteries were unlocked. As soon as the system they had been in disappeared and a new system filled their screens, interceptor modules started scans of the new star system without having to be ordered to do so.

"Receiving telemetry," Communications said. New maps uploaded, as well as location information of the forces within the system. They continued talking, not even pausing for breath. "The rest of Pandora Fleet One is moving to engage."

Frank noticed the event horizon had just disappeared when the portal was already dialing up another location.

"Nav, let's go meet up with the rest of the fleet. Teleport is allowed. Once we are assembled, let's move to assist our Deq'ual allies." Xiao sounded calm but Frank could see his fists clenched white. They had trained for this for months; now it was time to do away with the simulations and training sessions.

"Teleporting for link-up," Nav called out.

Another Pandora fleet exited the portal as *BloodHawk* and its accompanying ships flashed into existence within the other half of their true fleet.

"Ships are moving into position," Nav called out, adjusting the different commands on her console. The *BloodHawk* took the lead position as the rest of the fleet moved to follow her as if they had never been separated.

"Pandora Fleet Three is entering the system. The Deq'ual fleet in-system is turning to face the Jukal," Communications rattled out.

"Once we are in formation, we will teleport to support," Xiao said.

People went about their work. Frank talked on a private channel to the fire controllers, creating fire plans to rain down on the Jukal. A number of them watched the feeds that were linked by Mirror of Communication to the other fleets that were engaging the Jukal already. From there, they were able to figure out what worked and what didn't.

"Looks like we're going to have to use that Nalheim attack," Frank murmured.

They still hadn't figured out a good firing system for the Nalheim disruption attacks. They could emulate it, but the power was greatly reduced. So instead of sacrificing power, they had a crew of Nalheim on every ship. They wielded a spear that would communicate the firing procedure to the ship's magical coding, turning into a disrupting attack.

It was ridiculous and unorthodox, but it worked.

"Fleet is ready for teleport!" Navigation called out.

"Teleport," Xiao said.

The plot changed as they crossed thousands of kilometers in a second.

"Seems we've spooked them," Captain Xiao said.

"Incoming fire! They're releasing drones!" Sensors yelled out.

"Barriers up! Fire control, what are you thinking?" Xiao asked as Mana barriers sprung up around the ships.

Frank looked at his different options and then what was coming their way. "Hold the drones and fighters on our side; advance full speed." Frank's hands moved over the different screens as he passed down orders to his people.

"Do as the man says," Xiao said, putting his complete faith in Frank.

"All ships to full speed!" Communication's voice rang out throughout the Deq'ual fleet that had originally been in the system, as well as Pandora Fleet One.

The runic lines of the Pandora fleet ships and the magical circles that covered the Deq'ual ships shone in the darkness as their magical drives applied massive amounts of thrust, moving them forward at alarming speeds.

"Interceptor modules," Frank said, as missiles and laser beams shot out at the human fleet.

The Deq'ual and Pandora defenses lit up the void around the ships, streams of light pouring from them. Spell formations flared into existence as mages within the ships unleashed their rage onto the incoming missiles.

The interceptors disrupted a number of the laser attacks, creating a backlash on the Jukal ships as their sea of missiles reached out toward the human ships.

A number of them were destroyed, by spells or grand working rounds and Mana bolts. However, a number of them made it through this fire, to explode against the various Mana barriers.

The fleet weathered this battering, trusting in their shields.

The drones of the Jukal applied even more thrust as they rushed in close, readying the missiles they held and unleashing countless light attacks against the barriers.

"Execute!" Frank yelled.

"Broadside facing!" Navigation barked. All of the ships in the combined fleet flared new runes and runic lines as thrust nodes were activated. Blue flames illuminated hulls as the ships turned ninety degrees to reveal their broadsides.

Lines appeared between the vessels; they interconnected with one another, centering on the *BloodHawk* that was out in front of the fleet, creating a massive spell formation made of magical circles and runes that rotated around the lines as they became all the more physical.

The various spell formations finished forming. A massive spell formation covered them all and then shrunk down. Powerful ripples emanated from it in coruscating waves.

"Fire!" Frank barked.

Deep in *BloodHawk*, a Nalheim holding a spear struck his spear to the side. With a roar, he twirled the spear and stabbed it forward. Nothing happened in the room, but from the magical circle, ripples and distortions shot from the spell formation. This was the terrifying Nalheim disrupting attack; however, it had been superimposed upon the massive human fleet and fueled with the power of fourteen ships.

The ripples were like a tsunami and everything in its path was destroyed; missiles, laser attacks, rounds, drones—all were caught up in the blast.

"First salvo!" Frank yelled, flicking a switch. From dozens of missile tubes, missiles blasted out, one after another.

Artillery cannons bellowed as the dwarves manning them watched the cannons fire again and again. They had already locked in their targets long ago.

Around the artillery cannons, familiar spell formations looking like solid panels of light appeared. These were similar to the panels that appeared around Deia when she used her plasma cannon attack and scaled-up versions of the ones that the dwarven artillery cannons on Emerilia had.

The runic lines along the cannons glowed with a powerful light. The panels and the lines worked together to fire the rounds containing grand working spells at alarming speeds.

The disrupting attack had weakened with clearing out everything in front of the fleet.

It hit the Jukal fleet, rocking their shields.

The disrupting attack passed through the gaps in their fleet and continued onward.

Three-quarters of their drones had been destroyed; two of their six ships had shields that were flickering, showing signs of collapse.

On the heels of the disruption attack, the missiles rushed forth like banshees. A few of them were destroyed, but most of them made it through under the disrupting attack's cover.

The shields flared with brilliance and explosions appeared all around them. However, as this light disappeared, the shields looked much weaker than they had been just moments before.

These were barrier busters.

The two ships with flickering shields lost them altogether. The barrier busters hit their hulls with massive kinetic force. Power shot out from the grand working. The power ran through the ships' systems. There were a lot of back-up systems and coding so the ships didn't go down. Less protected or just weakly designed sections of the ships started failing, making it harder and harder to manage the massive ships.

Another Jukal destroyer's shield failed just as the cannons' grand working rounds hit.

Most of these rounds flashed with golden light as the grand working converted its energy into light spells that shot forward, cutting deep into the ship's hulls.

"Going AI!" Frank called out as the fleets started to get closer together.

At the speeds they were traveling, it was impossible to have people try to get accurate hits when they were among the enemy, requiring them to use an AI to simultaneously target and fire on the enemy.

"Rotating!" Navigation called out. The ships once again flared with maneuvering spells; the ships turned, once again facing sunward.

"Drones and fighters out!" Communications called. The areas between the ships were rapidly filled with drones and fighters around the Pandoran ships. Spell formations appeared, shooting out at the oncoming Jukal.

Jukal and human fleets fired their missiles. They shot out of their sides, turning and coming around to meet the enemy. With the missile boats and their larger fleet size, the human fleet had a quantitative as well as a qualitative advantage.

Explosions rocked in the space between the fleets. A Jukal destroyer couldn't take the punishment as sections of its hull were destroyed and the disrupting secondary grand working cut out great swaths of ships.

Fire missiles melted through the ships, igniting the very air held within them, melting through air locks that tried to stop the all-consuming fire spells.

One of the arks shuddered under the weight of fire. Without waiting, they teleported away, their Mana barrier more illusionary than real as it now watched the rest of the fleet enter into the last stages of the fight.

The two fleets crossed one another, faster than a normal human mind could understand. However, these were Emerilians manning the ships. Their impressive stats allowed them to still react, albeit slowly.

Magical formations appeared; multiple mages worked together, creating spells that were powered by the runic lines of the ship.

In close, the Pandora ships were covered in spell formations. Their cannons bellowed, with Mana discharge covering the ships and missile tubes glowing with runic lines as missile after missile rushed to meet the enemy.

They showed their teeth and sent the Jukal reeling.

Magical attacks tore through the defenses, grand working warheads and rounds releasing their stored spell matrixes.

The Jukal unleashed Light spells and missiles. Their drones and the drones and fighters of the human ships crossed one another, hunting the other down and trying to reach the opposing force's ships to unleash their attacks upon their hulls and shields.

That one moment disappeared and the two fleets crossed one another.

They came out of the other side. A number of the human ships were damaged, a few of them with their Mana barriers down and attempting to recover as the drones and fighters disengaged one another and raced away.

"Third fleet is coming in," Communications called out.

Three of the Jukal ships were floating wrecks. Only the carrier still had shields that were in the process of recovering, though significant damage could be seen on its hull.

The two other destroyers had hull damage but they were still able to fight.

Just as they were recovering from the battle, Third Fleet teleported right into their flight path with perfect timing and precision, seamlessly matching their speed and heading with that of the enemy

Jukal ships. As soon as they came out of their teleport, spell formations rotated around their ships and missiles tore through the silent void. The cannon batteries glowed as their enhancing spells and runic lines lit up with power.

The Jukal destroyers were cut down, rocked by several successive hits, opening armor and tearing through the Jukal ships. They continued to fire, the weapon systems not knowing that the ship had already been knocked out of the fight. The carrier fired all it had, but its weapons were mostly to keep missiles and rounds off the drones it had carried. All of its drones were already headed toward the new attackers.

A Light penetrating grand working tore a hole through the failing shield and one of the carrier's hangars. A Dark grand working with a decaying curse matrix ignited its power. Decaying power reached out through the hangar; the metal and materials within the hangar rotted and rusted at speeds visible to the eye. It spread through the ship. The area around the hangar fell apart. It cut through the ship, the Jukal unable to stop it.

Cannon rounds pierced into the hull of the carrier, exploding inside and even creating shades that tore through anything they saw.

There were just so many types of spells that the Jukal had no time to try to think of a way to defeat them; then a massive fusion spell exploded off the side of the carrier. Combined with the decay that tore through the ship, the carrier shuddered as it split into two. Debris flew through the void as the Pandora fleet passed through the remaining Jukal fleet.

Their cannons were relentless. The Jukal ships continued to fight back, their computer systems fighting with everything they had left.

To the Pandora ships, they were nothing more than punching bags. With every hit, more and more of the Jukal ships were torn apart.

The field of debris around them smashed into the barrier and hit the hulls of the ships that continued onward.

Their guns went silent as they left behind a broken and destroyed fleet.

"The overseers and Devastators will be sent out to deal with them. We're needed in another system," Captain Xiao said. "Ready teleportation spell for us and the Deq'ual fleet. I want readiness reports from all stations and ships in ten minutes."

The Pandora ships moved around the formation as the Deq'ual ships moved into the center.

Thirty minutes later, a massive spell formation, grounded in the Pandora ships, appeared around the Deq'ual and Pandora Fleet One.

They disappeared and reappeared in front of the system's portal.

Pandora Fleet Three disappeared from their position and followed, leaving behind their two arks as well as two destroyers that were moving toward the Jukal fleet wreckage.

Frank looked to the details on the next system and started to talk to the other fire controllers in the three combined fleets. They started to build up fire plans to deal with the next Jukal fleet.

Chapter 6: No Battle Plan Survives Contact with the Enemy

"How did this happen!" the emperor yelled out. In his fury, he shook his sleeve and fire wrapped around the Jukal aide kneeling off to the side.

They let out gargling screams as they were burnt alive. The emperor's eyes flashed with bloodlust, unaffected by the screaming. The aide couldn't run, metal surging from the floor and holding them steady.

The other aides shivered but dared not move even as they were close enough to the heat for their damp skin to dry up and their eyes to become itchy.

The burning aide finally succumbed to the flames, falling on the ground. The metal moved back into the floor as the flames continued to burn, the smell of burning Jukal filling the room.

The emperor's concubines, who had seen the darkest sides of the emperor, were hesitant to get close to him, lest they draw his ire.

The emperor panted, leaning forward in his seat as he stared at the screens that adorned the wall of his chambers.

The screens showed as human fleets linked together, increasing their numerical superiority, and then crushed the Jukal fleets. They moved system by system. Already half a dozen fleets had been destroyed.

"Send more of the fleets! Destroy the humans completely! Why have our other ships not reached Emerilia! We'll destroy the very sun itself! They dare to test me! We'll make Emerilia another Sol system until there is nothing left!" the emperor said.

The aides didn't say anything.

"Well! Why are the other fleets not there yet?" the emperor demanded, his voice empowered to the point where a concubine in front of him exploded from the pressure and the aides were thrown back. Two of them died from internal injuries.

With the power he had stored up and his personal AI, he was as close to a god as any other had come. There was no comparison between him and Bob. Even with saving all of that energy aboard the *Datskun*, the emperor had an empire behind him.

"Sire, the only remaining fleets we have are around the home world and the fleet heading for Emerilia will get there in a few months," one of the aides said, lying on their back completely, showing complete submission to the emperor.

"Not good enough!" the emperor shouted. Spikes rose from the floor, shooting into the Jukal and tearing them apart from the inside.

Both of the aides would come back on an Altar of Rebirth, but after dying, nearly all who came back would be certifiably insane. None had lasted more than three rebirths before they had cut off themselves from the Altar of Rebirths, wanting to die instead of come back again.

"Send out our fleets to destroy the humans! I want Emerilia destroyed within the week!" the emperor screamed.

The aides shivered, knowing that there was no way to get the ships to move that fast. He had watched battles and movies from his thrones. He had no concept of modern battles, nor how they could no longer move fleets easily through their own empire as the humans now controlled their portal network.

He might be revered as the commander of the Jukal Empire's military forces, but he had no idea of their capabilities and took them for granted, assured that they would never lose and that no matter what, the Jukal fleets would win.

He couldn't come to accept their losses and blamed others, when he himself had continued to pull their money in order to fund more shows and his frivolous pursuits.

Footsteps could be heard ringing through the room as the emperor's uncle appeared at the door.

Some of the fire in the emperor's eyes died down as he looked to his uncle.

"Leave," the emperor said to the others in the room.

The aides and concubines couldn't move faster, clearing out the room in moments and sealing the door behind them.

"Why are they not dead yet, Uncle?" The emperor's voice filled with complaint as he slumped back into his chair, pouting. Comparing the bloodlust-filled demon from before and the childish look of the emperor now, no one would be able to reconcile the two personalities.

The emperor's uncle sighed, long used to this kind of transformation as he relaxed his official and stern standing.

"These humans are a powerful foe. We will destroy them, but it will take time. They have won this fight, but soon there will be another in Emerilia. There we will destroy them," the uncle said.

"So boring! I'll have all of the admirals and their officers put through the Altar of Rebirth for not destroying the humans already!" The emperor smacked his hand on his throne. The sound reverberated through the hall and objects around the emperor were tossed out as a Mana barrier around the emperor's uncle flashed into existence, stopping the seemingly simple movement that had the force to kill anyone without a shield.

"Nephew, the admirals and officers were in the wrong. However, let them pay for it after the battle. I will pass on your feelings and they will show their true abilities," the emperor's uncle said, consoling the emperor.

The emperor snorted. The noise shook the room. "Fine!" The emperor drew out the word, agreeing reluctantly as he slumped in his chair.

"In the meantime, you can look over our new magical forces," the emperor's uncle said. Hidden in his eyes was a pleased look, knowing that he had grasped the emperor's weakness.

"How are the new players coming along?" The emperor straightened up, an excited look in his eyes.

"Why don't you check them out?" The emperor's uncle flicked his hand and an interface appeared in mid-air, showing what looked to be a massive battlefield. There were all kinds of creatures and abilities being hurled across it. People were in groups; others by themselves. However, all of them were fighting either with weapons that would be familiar to those on Emerilia, or using magical abilities.

The fighting was not simple, with entire mountain ranges shooting up from the ground and what looked like seas descending from the sky. Such power would make even the old members of the Emerilian Pantheon look at them in shock.

The emperor clapped his hands as he watched them, a look of glee on his face.

"Yes! Thank you, Uncle!" the emperor said, not looking away from the screens.

He missed the dark gleam in his uncle's eyes that vanished without a trace, a pleased smile plastered on his face.

"Anything for my nephew," he said, with no ripples showing in his face or actions.

***

Party Zero and the majority of Emerilia could only watch as the Jukal fleets met with the human fleets. The fighting between the two forces was violent and final. It wasn't all one-sided either.

It seemed that at one point the Jukal fleets started to go crazy all at once, most of them using any tactics they knew in order to try to destroy the human ships.

The Jukal fleets that had come out to clear the systems outnumbered the human ships three to one. Losing a ship for the human fleet cut deep. However, although they lost ships, with the portals, teleport pads, and onos, not many people died.

The Jukal, however, were now in the same position as humanity had been in their first war. They had no way to return to their shipyards in order to repair or re-arm. They were constantly being hit by human ships that were fresh into the fight, with full power and armaments.

Unlike the human fleets of old, these Jukal fleets relied on AI and drones to make their decisions. A lifetime of political maneuvering had made them slow to make snap decisions. Also, the human fleets were only getting stronger with more and more ships being completed; the Jukal fleets saw new ships every couple of years.

With magic, anything is possible. Dave watched the different feeds from within the Mirror of Communication command center.

Lucy cleared her throat. The side conversations from around the table faded as everyone looked to her.

"Thank you all for coming. I'll get right into it," Lucy said without preamble. "So far, we have lost a total of twelve ships. We have wiped out seventeen of the Jukal fleets and the remaining fleets within the contested systems are under attack. We have three fleets re-arming and preparing to move deeper into the Jukal Empire and hit their secondary targets. The other fleets not engaged with the Jukal or re-arming and repairing are in transit or have already reached their secondary targets.

"Also, we're seeing that the number of people on the Jukal planets who are now using the resources and different items that we have given them as well as joining in on the Mirror of Communication classes has skyrocketed. It seems that now they see we might be a viable option to oppose the Jukal Empire, more people are doing what they can to make the best of their situation. Now, we're not expecting them to help us, but it seems that they are more than willing to stay out of our way and be neutral in the conflict. A number of groups that are representative of the planets and systems that our fleets have already been in have already contacted Air and her people.

"On the Emerilian front, the people of Emerilia as well as the players of Emerilia have thrown their full weight behind the Terra Alliance, as well as the Pandora Initiative. We've evacuated some two million people to Ice Planet, as well as the various bases. The industrial complexes of the different entities within Emerilia have changed, with the tech and information from the Pandora Initiative speeding up things with them. Defenses are being laid down around the system. Which brings up the true matter of this meeting: the defense of Emerilia. Currently, it will take the Jukal some six weeks to reach Emerilia. They have a fleet of one hundred and seventy-nine ships heading our way while we've just got some seven Pandora fleets combat ready. We're working to double that number as fast as possible but we can't guarantee that they'll be ready for the first engagements with the Jukal fleet."

"Why don't we attack the Jukal home world?" one of the leaders from Emerilia asked.

Dave's eyebrows knit together as a pensive look spread across his face.

Lucy looked to Sato, who gave Dave a deep look. Lucy looked to Dave as well.

Dave took a few moments before he let out a heavy sigh. "Shard, map of the Jukal home system."

In front of everyone, a holographic representation of the Jukal home system appeared. There were five planets, hundreds of major stations, and thousands of ships moving.

"The Jukal Empire was the most powerful war machine in all known existence. In their prime, they had a fleet that numbered close to two thousand warships. Now they have under one thousand and all of their defensive infrastructure. The Jukal created their empire some fifteen hundred years ago. They have been working on their defenses from the start. They're an expansionistic species. However, they wish to control other people; they've never actually taken other planets or star systems other than their own. All of their industrial base has come back to their home system. With all of the Jukal in one system as the most powerful species in their empire, they've been focused on making their home safe. They've got remote platforms and sensor buoys that would tear through our sensors, avoiding magical coding simply because of its overlap. Entire stations have enough weapons to destroy one of the Pandora fleets. They've got ground-based batteries and planetary shields and that's only what we know about. There's no way to tell what they might have hidden on their various planets and homes." As Dave talked, Shard highlighted the different items that he was talking about. It wasn't long before the map was covered in different symbols and colors.

"When we're going into the Jukal system, we're not up against just one hundred and fifty-two ships. That's only their mobile forces. We're up against the might of the Jukal Empire—their home, their base. We will not win the fight in the skies; we're going to have to fight on the ground if we expect to win. We need to take the emperor's palace with ground forces. It's going to take everything we have to do that. We won't be able to spare anything to leave on Emerilia." Dave's expression stayed the same throughout. They all knew of how Sol system had been destroyed, with the Jukal using a weapon to blow up its sun. Knowing this, they'd evacuated people to Ice Planet and were preparing their defense outside of the Emerilia system.

If the Jukal got in, then there might not be an Emerilia system afterward.

"What is the plan to deal with the Jukal fleet heading for Emerilia?" another leader asked.

Dave looked to Admiral Adams and Forsyth. Forsyth turned to Adams for her to take the lead.

"We sow the entire way to Emerilia with portals; then, at every chance we get, we hit them with attacks. We harass them, wear them down, break their ships. We use the teleportation abilities, the magical coding of our stealth systems. We tear them apart and call for their surrender the entire time," Adams said. "When we defeat the Jukal fleet coming for Emerilia, then the Jukal home system is the only place that the Jukal can exert control over. If they try to have their fleet move to another system and attack us, or reassert their power, we come in through the portals and beat them back. Use their tactics against them. They'll be pinned in the Jukal home system, without the rest of the empire to support them. While they're sitting there, we can take our time, build up our forces and then when the time's right, we hit them with everything we have."

There was a fierce determination that seemed to be carved into her very features. Josh and those leaders of the player guilds and various nations nodded their heads in agreement. Dave could gauge their emotions, and see through most of them. All of them had been given information on the Jukal Empire, and knew much more than the basics that Bob had given out to everyone on Emerilia. Adams's words might have sounded simple; however, it conflicted with all they had read. The empire was massive and powerful—to them, there should be no way that it could fall. This was only on the surface, the races that weren't Jukal felt the pressure of being subjugated every day. Now that the tyrant that had controlled their lives had outnumbered the Deq'ual and Pandora fleets three to one, had failed, these races now had hope.

It didn't look as if what the Stone Raiders and the Pandora's Initiative proposed was just a pipe dream.

Dave clenched his teeth together. Already the different bases were exceeding what he had planned for, and still, he wanted to increase production even more. But he knew it wasn't possible in such a tight time frame.

Fighting the Jukal fleet headed for Emerilia wouldn't just rely on overwhelming the enemy—they wouldn't have the number of ships the Jukal had—but they would have to fight with everything they had, using any tactics possible to win.

If the Jukal made it into the Emerilian system, then everything could be put into jeopardy. They might be able to break the shield around Emerilia and kill the people within the planet, or destroy the moonbase, or both. Or they might even employ a system killer—the same weapon used by the Jukal when they fought humanity in Sol, wiping out the entire solar system and destroying the planets and everything within it.

Chapter 7: Eureka

"New orders. We're going to hit the Jukal fleet powering for Emerilia," Captain Xiao aboard the battleship *BloodHawk*, the flagship for Pandora Fleet One, informed his crew and his fleet.

"Navigation, I am sending you the coordinates for the rally point where we are going to meet up with three other Pandora fleets before heading to meet the Jukal. Be aware that the portal map has been updated as some ships with teleportation abilities were dispatched to lay down portals along the Jukal fleet's path," Xiao said.

"Yes, sir," Navigation said.

"Fire control, with me. Second, you have the bridge." Xiao stood and made his way off the bridge as Frank quickly transferred main fire control to his second and followed the captain off the bridge. They quickly reached the conference room, where a Mirror of Communication was waiting in the center of the table with connected mirrors embedded in the table.

"We're going to be meeting with Admirals Adams and Forsyth, as well as the other captains of the Pandora fleets that will be joining us and their fire controllers," Xiao said. Even though Frank was technically less senior to Captain Xiao, he was the first player to be woken up and pave the way for the rest of them. He held a special position to all of the players who had been woken from the simulation.

Frank nodded as Captain Xiao sat down at the table and placed his hand on a Mirror of Communication. His eyes closed, almost as if he were asleep except for his hand on the Mirror of Communication terminal. Frank did the same. It seemed as if he was in the exact same room as the one he had come from, except it was larger and now filled with more people.

Frank nodded to a few people he knew; all of the fire controllers had worked together and shared memory crystals to get better at their positions. Working so close and basically sharing each other's memories had led to them being a close group indeed.

The captains similarly looked to one another with the same looks.

Admiral Forsyth of the Pandora Initiative cleared his throat. All of the focus in the room sharpened as the captains and their fire controllers waited on him.

"All right, you ugly bastards get the luck of the draw. You're going to be tip of the freaking spear when hitting the Jukal; and don't worry, daddy Forsyth will be there with you." Forsyth grinned. He was a bear of a man and although he demanded people perform to the best of their abilities, he was not one to badger them to death and instead let them do as they wanted as long as they met his standards. In most militaries, it wasn't something that would stand; however, he was a gamer—as was everyone else. Some of them were used to schedules and being online at certain times for games. Even though gaming was a part of their life, they had other things they needed to do.

When Forsyth asked for something, his people would jump at the opportunity to do what he asked; in the same breath, he relaxed with them and shot the shit.

The captains chuckled at Forsyth's words and a few of them showed hungry looks as their desire to meet with the Jukal lit a fire inside them.

"We've tested out the stealth magical coding, which is pretty damn good. Now it's time that we put it to use. We're going to be entering the same system as the Jukal, then we use stealth and coding to get close to them, then we hammer them with everything we have. When they get their shit together, we drop out again. In the meantime, Dave's made us some cool new tools." Forsyth sent a message and a few moments later, Dave Grahslagg himself appeared. He was almost legendary among the players who had been woken up and on

Emerilia. His fingerprints were on everything that had gone on in the last couple of months.

"Forsyth said he wants me to talk about the new tech. Simply put, we've got two new things. One, barrier disruptors. We've figured out the coding for the Jukal shields and made a grand working shell that has a roughly sixty percent chance of disrupting the Jukal spell formation. It'll take their shields down for maybe thirty seconds, but that's plenty of time to lay in some pain. Also, Ela-Dorn is close to the ship teleportation array. Which sounds confusing as hell. As you all know, your ships are constantly relaying information via Mirror of Communication back to us. We can take that information, use it to pinpoint locations and then teleport things there. We're working with the portal at the moonbase to see if we can't make it not just portal to another location but tear a hole through to a different spot. Power consumption is huge, but it means we can drop ships in close to the enemy, or allow them to escape. They can't come out right in the midst of fighting; their shields and everything needs to come back online because they'll be largely unprotected," Dave said.

The others around the table nodded. Having the ability to teleport items to any location was incredibly powerful. They had their onboard portals, but they weren't capable of pushing out more ships through that.

Frank raised his hand. Dave's eyes fell on him as he indicated for Frank to speak up.

"What kind of ordinance can we teleport?" Frank asked.

Dave's tired face went blank for a moment. "Good of you to ask that, because I didn't even consider it." Dave's eyes darted to the table. No one said anything as Dave stroked his beard, looking at the table. A pen and paper appeared at his right hand; he started to write things down, not even looking at it, as if trying to capture the stream of thought.

"I've been going about this all wrong. I was thinking too simply. Hah, I gave them a chance! Beware, the master of space, time and gravitational anomalies! Stupid Jukal!" Dave muttered to himself, an inspired look on his face.

He slapped the table and laughed to himself as he put down the pen. He stared at the sheet for a few minutes after he'd finished writing, as if to eke out any remaining bit of inspiration. He waved his hands, clearly preparing to leave the Mirror of Communication.

"Dave, do you have an answer?" Adams asked.

"Nope, but I will." Dave held his hand in mid-air and then snapped his fingers, his eyes bright as a smile spread across his face, before turning to a frown.

"Looks like I'm going to need to redesign the ships again." Dave looked off into space, before looking to the people in the room, as if remembering they were still there. "Send me a report on the blind spots of your different ships. If you would want more firepower in one place, where would it be? Actually, just send me all of your..." Dave's eyes went wide. "Holy shit, could that work? The power consumption would be massive, resources needed would just be ridiculous, wouldn't need to be manned, sensors would have to be awesome. Doesn't need different quarters, just five layers." Dave drew circles surrounding one another as well as jotted down bullet points, chasing inspiration.

By the time he was done, he was panting.

"That being said, we wouldn't be able to make them in time for the offensive if we made them properly. If we were to take out the armor panels, make it from an asteroid? Thickness doesn't matter and as long as it's strong enough then it should be good. Then just pack with soul gem constructs and power plants. This thing's going to be just feeding off power. The usage—wait, we don't really need to have more than a few power plants inside. We can supplement it all remotely! Holy shit, this, well, I think it's a possibility! We didn't use asteroids because they were so damn heavy and we needed thinner and stronger. Power can be supplied easily. We can put out a shit ton of thrust as it's not relying on its own engines! Hell, it won't have engines—all it's going to have is shields and a thick ass asteroid for armor!" Dave laughed and punched his fist in the air, twirling around on a spinny chair.

"Dave, what are you talking about?" Forsyth asked, poking his nose into Dave's mind once again.

"I'm talking about a portal bastion! I've got to get to work!" Dave moved once again to leave. "And send me those blind spots you've got! We could even use the portals to cover them," Dave said, the last part more to himself than anyone else. His excitement built as he practically ran out of the room, leaving everyone looking at one another with confused looks.

I have a feeling that the universe is going to be rocked once again by Dave's ideas. Frank's eyes rested on the chair that Dave had been sitting in, a profound feeling that he had just seen genius at work filling him.

***

Dave practically jumped out of the Mirror of Communication chair, stunning a few of the people who weren't in conference rooms, either leaving the massive room with Mirror of Communication terminals or entering it.

"Jeeves! Get me everyone!" Dave yelled. Disappearing from the room, he teleported to the workshop he used on the asteroid base. He pulled up the notes he had created, expanding the interface and sticking it to a wall. There were three simple-looking lines, but to Dave they held earth-shattering insight and ideas.

"Dave, could you specify everyone?" Jeeves asked.

"Bob, Malsour, Ela-Dorn, anyone who works with portals, asteroid miners and refiners, sensor spell makers, magical coding leads, soul gem construct people, those who deal with fusion power plants and power systems." Dave clicked his fingers, his eyes closed as if trying to get his brain to remember anyone else he might have forgotten. "Ahh, I'll think of more later!"

"Sending out messages," Jeeves said.

"Tell them to drop everything now!" Dave's armor and cloak appeared around him. A mass of gray smoke filled the middle of the workshop, creating a massive sphere that was covered in dots that covered its surface.

Malsour appeared a few moments later, teleporting into the room. "You called?"

"Gotta finish this!" Dave said, ignoring Malsour and maintaining his focus on his project. "Get me a conjuration stability construct if you would, please."

Malsour pulled out a soul gem construct and put in the coding that would stabilize a conjured object so that it couldn't be lost as long as the soul gem construct was given power. Malsour tossed it out underneath the conjured mass. It spread out, creating runic lines that connected into circles under the conjuration.

More people quickly started to arrive, and Malsour indicated for them to hold their questions. Seeing the concentration on Dave's face, they stayed silent, quickly standing off to the side. They read the wall covered with just three lines of text and the five circles with lines connected to them.

Dave lowered his hands. In the middle of the room, the sphere was complete. It was covered in more circles than before. Dave came out of his reverie and looked to the people in the room. Everyone was now gathered. Dave clapped his hands together. Biting his lower lip and making a fist, he jabbed forward, his eyes burning with inspiration.

"So, what did you want us for?" Malsour asked.

"Okay, so I was talking with the Pandora fleets. Ah, I will probably need to talk to them again in the near future to get everything sorted out and tell them about the new things we need. Anyway. You know how we've been working on making the portals not only link to other portals but act like the teleportation array that we built in the original Pandora's Box?" Dave asked.

"Yes, where they can use the information from the linked ships to create a wormhole that other ships can move through and assist them." Malsour waved his hand, stating the seemingly common knowledge.

"Well, Frank Simmons went and asked me what kind of ordinance we could send through, which, when you think about it! Well, it makes complete sense—just take a grand working and then drop it on through in the middle of the Jukal, big boom. However, it only gets a limited area. You'd want to get something with more range. What if instead of putting ships through, or dropping out grand working bombs, we were shooting through? We get coordinates, then we open a wormhole, via a portal to the location, then we have a fleet of ships just shooting through a portal. An entire fleet's worth of fire hitting ONE SPOT! It's incredible! And they would never be in the same system as the Jukal! They could be in the moonbase and hitting them as they advance! Now this is incredible! We've been looking to make these wormholes stable enough so that they can push out ships with people on them. But if we're shooting rounds through, we don't need it to be all that stable! They're not living—if there's distortions, we lose a few rounds!

"So, we go with the idea pitched by the portal, teleport, and ono group: portal in a grand working! We fire out grand working missiles that link to certain portals. They go off away from the Jukal, then a portal activates; at the other end, ships, batteries, missile loaders—whatever we think of—they fire out rounds, missiles and the others, one missile creating a portal, unleashes the firepower of an entire FLEET! Okay, now that's damn awesome, but! What about the ships! They've got blind spots and when they're going forward, chasing the Jukal, they only have a few weapons that can hit the enemy other than missiles. So, what if we had a portal there? They open up the portal, contact the fire team, fleet, or whoever is on the other side of the portal. Their blind spot is now a strong point! They're unleashing some of the most powerful attacks out of their front. Shit! We could have multiple person spell formations! Doomsday spells, readied and waiting, unleashed through the portal and out at the Jukal. Instead of prep time, we just have that portal on the ship cycle from casting area to casting area with the mages unleashing powerful spell after powerful spell right into the Jukal!" Dave smacked his head as if he had now seen the light, not noticing the clear looks of shock on the other people's faces. What he was talking about was simply incredible. Their shock only grew deeper. "But wait—and I know I sound like a terrible TV ad—but, what if we were to combine it all?"

Dave waved his hands and the spot-covered sphere in the middle of the room was cut in half, revealing its innards to everyone.

"So, in the center, we have the heart of this beast—portals! Tens of them. We shoot through portals at one location; they come out of these portals here, then they're transmitted through the teleport pads around them. Not sure if to go with onos or teleport pads right now but need to work on it. Then," Dave traced from where the onos were, through an impressively thick ring, pointing out runic lines that spread from the core of the sphere to the exterior, "from the teleport pads or onos of the interior, they are connected to the onos on the exterior. The ship has no weapons, only massive shields and then this massive metal armor. I'm thinking asteroid because it would be faster to make and easier. It has some power from power plants, but has no engines. For thrust, we fire through a massive flame spell, goes through a portal, a teleport pad and then exterior ono. An AI controls what's going where inside of the portal bastion and we've now taken our original firepower and doubled or tripled it!" Dave said.

"How are we going to power it?" one of the techs asked.

"We have a dozen power plants. Have a soul gem umbilical pass through one portal into the ship. The only time it won't have power is when it's transitioning between portals," Dave said.

"The onos on the outside will create a wormhole. However, they're going to be not pointing away from the portal bastion but rather along the sides of it," one of the portal techs said.

"Not if we remove the restrictions on them! Right now, we're creating wormholes like they're a doorway, when actually they're like a big sphere. We remove the power drain of altering the wormhole—cheaper energy-wise—and we start to make a nodule that we can shoot out in any direction with.

"Any other questions for now?" Dave looked around and pointed finger pistols at everyone. Not finding anyone and seeing their looks of disbelief, he snapped his fingers.

"Also, if not all sides of the portal bastion are being used, then we could fire out a spray of missiles that connect to the teleport pads around the portals. More stable and last longer—also means that all of the portals will be able to work all of the time, bringing more weapons fire down on the Jukal!"

Dave was breathless as he looked to the model with shining eyes. He wasn't the only person; the others in the room looked at the conjured sphere as if it were some holy relic.

"Prototype Mirror of Communication?" Ela-Dorn's voice cut through the room.

"Yes! All right, asteroid miners and refiners, I want you to get with the armorers and the shield makers. We need to see what we can do to make this hull as strong as possible. We don't have long to get this working! Our people are going to reach the Jukal in just two weeks. I want to have this ready, if not completely prototyped out, and we're working to get the first one made!" Dave said.

He knew that his demands were high, but he also knew that with such a tight deadline and pressure, people would push themselves past their limits.

"I'll make a copy of the model here and we can look at it together within the prototype conference room." With a wave of Dave's hand, the prototype fell apart and a spell formation covered the room. The room disappeared as they were all moved across the asteroid base, coming to the prototype Mirror of Communication room. This was the same room that they had used in order to make the battleship prototype. The room had shown its value as multiple projects had been worked on and their issues figured out.

Those in the group were all talking to one another in excited tones as the people who saw them started to talk and make guesses for what they were doing there.

"Is that Dave? What is he leading people into the prototype room for?" one asked.

"Maybe he's come up with another idea?" another suggested.

"Malsour is with him as well. Look at all of those people from the portal and teleportation division!"

"What are the asteroid miners here for? They might need to supply different materials but I don't see what they would be here for a project in such numbers. Would only need a few to talk to the prototype team to tell them what materials would work best and what wouldn't," someone muttered, confused by the group's members.

The group found different places to sit in the room and quickly accessed the Mirror of Communication.

Dave threw up the rough conjured sphere he had made. As people joined in, they moved to look over the sphere, starting to make notes and talk to one another; groups started to mingle and to throw out their ideas for the prototype. Dave wandered from group to group, working on different ideas as around the sphere different workstations appeared with different projects being created on them. Outside of the Mirror of Communication at the prototype stations, the different items that were being created within the Mirror of Communication were being formed.

Some things were only half formed before they exploded, the containing shields stopping them from hitting anything else. Others melted or didn't work at all.

As time went on, the projects of first one group then one group after another stopped failing and started to work. Projects were moved from place to place, assembled within the Mirror of Communication and tested out within the shield-sealed prototype modules.

Messages were sent out and tests were run with power lines going through portals and connecting to ships that used their jump drives, or went through portals. People started to draw their own conclusions and wild theories. But none of it was confirmed or denied as those within the Mirror of Communication only stepped out of the Mirror of Communication in order to eat. They would sleep within the Mirror of Communication, most of the time collapsing on top of whatever they were working on.

Finally, some five days after they had entered the Mirror of Communication, the various people came back together.

They all looked weary and tired, but their spirit was higher than it had been in months, with fierce determination making them stand straight as they looked to Dave.

"All right, so let's see if we can do this." Dave didn't need to say anything else as a massive asteroid filled the room. It was identical to an asteroid that the mining group had picked from within the asteroid belt around the asteroid base.

Dave watched as the asteroid was slowly shaped into a sphere. Light mages and miners shaped the asteroid and cut out the interior as Fire mages heated up the asteroid to make it easier for the Dark mages to form and shape the metal underneath. Shuttles and ships attached to the asteroid, spun it, giving it a gravitational pull, and turned it from an abstract shape into a sphere. Through the rotations and the Dark mages' spells, they compressed the asteroid, turning it from porous stone and metal into composite armor panels.

After some time, a hollow area formed in the center of the asteroid. A portal was teleported in via teleportation array. They activated it and linked it to a waiting portal.

Dark mages entered the bastion through the main portal and continued on with the next step. With their magic, they altered the interior of the asteroid, just as those on the outside continued to form the massive asteroid's exterior according to their design plan.

Openings appeared inside the asteroid, turning into corridors and pathways through the highly compressed metal and stone.

Engineers and those familiar with soul gem constructs laid down soul gem seeds that formed more portals and started to grow through the openings made by the Dark mages.

A thick soul gem umbilical passed from the asteroid base through the connected portals into the asteroid that was being worked on. It formed a box in the growing hollow area. From the box's corners, pillars of soul gem spread outward, affixing the box in the center of the asteroid.

The pillars burrowed into the walls as Dark mages worked to reinforce the pillars with metal superstructure as the hollow area grew outward.

Thin soul gem runic lines spread out from these pillars, passing through walls and openings, connecting to the soul gem seeds. The seeds started to speed up their progress as the vague outline of a network started to form.

Lines passed through the asteroid and started to poke out through openings onto the surface of the asteroid. Now they were thin lines but with time they would grow in size.

The asteroid was still being compressed and the areas inside were only partially excavated. It would take time to complete the portal bastion but its basic form was already taking shape.

The entire sphere was covered in complex but faint runic lines that glowed with power even as the asteroid shifted and moved.

On the inside again, multiple runic lines and soul gem constructs were broken down and modified, improving efficiency. Some other areas were just altered slightly. Some of the ideas and theories turned out to be wrong; but learning how one way failed allowed them to see other ways to do what they wanted.

For three days and nights they worked, not taking a break as they altered, changed, and updated the asteroid and its systems.

Finally, everything seemed to work and no one needed to do anything else. There were updates they were already thinking of and ways they were thinking to improve it, but for now they had a working prototype.

There were no openings in the portal bastion. Even to the creators, it looked strange, with its mirror-like surface cut only by the soul gem-created runic lines. It hummed with power. All those who looked upon it were filled with apprehension.

Dave stared at it, his eyes bloodshot from the number of hours he had spent on the prototype and how much energy he had poured into it.

They exited the Mirror of Communication and grouped around the prototype that sat in the middle of the room. Companionable silence and utmost satisfaction filled the room.

"We have just six days until our fleets meet the Jukal," Dave said softly. In the silence, all could hear his voice.

The others' eyebrows knit together, the pride changing with the knowledge that now that they'd completed the prototype, they would need to build the true portal bastion—not to expand their knowledge or prove their theories, but instead save lives and protect their homes.

"We also need to build the weapons and engine thrust batteries, as well as the portal to provide power to the bastion," Malsour said.

Dave looked to Malsour and nodded. "We've only just started." Dave pulled out memory crystals from his bag of holding. "Record your memories of the project. That way, we can pass them to those who will be building it to make the production time shorter. It's time we made it for real."

Chapter 8: To Stop an Invasion

Induca circulated her Mana and looked down on the asteroid that had been selected to make the portal bastion.

Thousands of people looked at the same asteroid, a gleam in their eyes. They'd all integrated the memory crystals with their minds, allowing them to understand just what they were making.

Induca still hadn't got over the shock of what Dave and the prototype team had come up with.

"Ready?" Dave called out through the command chat. The different leaders reported back their readiness one by one.

They'd spun the asteroid with shuttles, so that it was constantly rotating, with the AIs using spell formations to keep it moving how they wanted it.

"Fire it up!" Deia said.

Thousands of spell formations appeared around the spinning asteroid. Fire spells poured out from the untold hundreds of mages' hands, immolating the asteroid like a space-based forge. It quickly began to heat up as Dark mages behind the Fire mages worked together to create a spell formation that appeared around the asteroid. Dave and Malsour led them as the asteroid started to become smaller. The layers compressed so that they became denser as heat seeped into and was conducted throughout the asteroid. The water content and ice that would have led to explosions had been removed by Water mages already. The mages pushed inward, forcing the massive asteroid into submission.

Induca unleashed dragon breath after dragon breath; even Fire herself was out in space, adding in help as minute by minute, hour by hour, they compressed the asteroid more and more.

The construction for the true portal bastion was underway.

***

91

In the darkness of space, an ark could be seen hovering in the center of a massive portal. Soul gem umbilicals connected it to the portal that was covered in swarming engineers and mages, checking the portal one last time.

As they finished their checks and entered the ark once again, the umbilical soul gem constructs receded back into the ark.

This ark had left the Emerilian system as soon as it was cleared of Jukal. It had one job: to create a portal network from Emerilia to the system closest to Emerilia.

They moved away from the portal. It was one of the last, hidden in the darkness between two unoccupied systems. As they moved away, the runes across the portal started to light up as power surged around it.

A connection was established as the portal looked out into another system. Bare minutes after the portal was connected, three destroyers sped through the portal, followed closely by a massive battleship. The four ships automatically peeled off and began scanning for threats in their areas of responsibility, efficient and lethal.

As they ran their own sensor checks, the missile ports were sealed back up and the glowing runic lines over the long-range cannons dimmed as they were powered down.

The rest of the first fleet exited. The portal closed and then new runes appeared along its surface as a new connection was formed. A second fleet passed through the portal before it closed once again. This was repeated as they were followed by a third fleet, and all the way to five entire fleets.

Their runic lines glowed as spell formations appeared above the ships' hulls. Arcane fire was cast, pushing the ships. If this arcane fire was hundreds of times more powerful than anything that had been wielded by fire mages in the past, it was only slightly weaker than the spells being used on the portal bastion. Even with its destructive force, it was not focused on destroying, but rather providing thrust.

With the spell formations that could be cast in any direction, it allowed the Pandora ships to have unrivaled agility and speed against any known ship.

Three of the fleets moved together, creating one massive armada. There were no arks in this armada. The destroyers and missile boats encircled the battleships, creating a loose sphere hundreds of kilometers wide; at the same time, two of the fleets stayed in their original formations and moved to either side of the main armada.

As the armada finished moving into position, the runic lines across their ships flashed as wormholes appeared before the ships. Powerful ripples from expended Mana emanated from the ships as they cruised through the wormholes.

The wormholes disappeared as the armada rushed to meet the Jukal fleet that was en route to destroy Emerilia.

***

Frank was aboard the *BloodHawk*. Pandora Fleet One had been made one of the secondary fighting forces of the armada.

"Well, looks like Lady Luck was on our side." Xiao looked to the extra fleet that had joined them. It was from the Nal system, fresh from the asteroid base's slips.

For the crew, this was their first outing as a fleet. Strong leadership and innate ability had helped them come together as a tight-knit crew and showed that although they might be a new fleet, they were no less effective than the rest of the veteran fleets that made up the fighting force.

"That we are, sir," the second-in-command said as Frank looked over the latest information coming from the Nal system, specifically the details about the massive sphere that was being created there.

It had been under construction for a few days already, but there were no signs of it being close to finished. In fact, the people working on the ships had, for the most part, not stopped working. There was so little information on it as the construction crews were hell-bent on getting it completed and didn't have time to talk to others about what they were working on unless they, too, were part of the construction team.

Whatever it was, it was one hell of an undertaking.

Someone had been able to talk the admiral into letting them get a copy of the plans, and what they had found out was incredible. Frank continued to look at it when he could and had run a few simulations with it already. The ship, if it could even be called a ship, was pure genius.

"How are the modifications looking, Engineering?" Xiao looked to the engineering officer, who looked a little haggard.

"The portal on our bow is complete. We're ready to use it on demand. Also, we've got the teleportation arrays ready to push out the portals when needed," Engineering said.

"Good! Anything you need, you'll get it," Xiao said seriously.

"Yes, sir," Engineering said.

"Good work there, Simmons. Would have never have thought to use portals that way," Xiao said.

"Well, I got the idea from Dave. He already came up with the idea of using a portal on our bow to fire at the enemy. With the smaller portals, we can toss them out and increase our fire in any direction," Frank said.

"Ballsy but I like it." Xiao laughed and the others in the room smiled. It was rare to see their captain so relaxed, and with the new innovations at their disposal, their confidence when meeting the Jukal had reached new heights.

"Exiting the wormhole in five minutes," Navigation said.

Frank opened a channel to his weapons officers. "Ready all weapons. Emergence in five minutes."

Across the ship and the secondary armada, weapons were checked and then readied.

The main armada and the other secondary armada had all gone through their own wormholes, making it so that Pandora Fleet One couldn't see them or know of their preparations.

"Emergence!" Navigation called out. The ship shook slightly as they exited the wormhole.

Sensor spells were cast out, searching for anything in the area. "We're clear for one light-minute," Sensors said. "And we have emergence of the third armada."

On screen, a massive spell formation appeared that seemed to break through space itself, causing it to distort as a wormhole appeared and it spat out the other secondary Pandora armada.

Moments later, the main armada appeared in all its glory, as if commanding the very star system they found themselves in.

"Waypoint received. Passed to the rest of the secondary armada. Ready to teleport," Navigation said.

"Teleport us on your go," Xiao said.

The runic lining across the ships of the main armada shone with power before the ships winked out of existence, with all of them activating their teleportation spell formations at the same time.

Powerful magical ripples emanated from the ships as they reappeared, their Mirrors of Communication informing the secondary and tertiary armadas of their position in real-time and ten minutes before their own sensors would pick them up.

"Teleporting!" Navigation said as the secondary armada followed the main armada, with the tertiary just moments later.

They reappeared just as the main armada once again teleported, crossing the empty system; the other fleets followed.

Runic lines shined with a different light as a new spell formation was activated. A swirling mass of runes appeared in front of the main armada. A ray of light shot out from it as it seemed to punch a hole through space itself, creating a wormhole ahead of the fleet that pushed forward into it and poured in all the power of their flight drives and once again teleported away. For days, the ships of the massive fighting force teleported and used wormholes to cross space, all of them heading right for the Jukal fleet. Until finally, they reached their last wormhole.

The portal bastion hadn't been completed yet and it would be another week until it was ready. As time had gone on, the people in the fleet had hoped to be able to use the portal bastion, but it was clear that it just wouldn't be ready in time.

The portal bastion would have been an impressive support; however, they had been prepared since the very beginning to attack the Jukal with just their ships.

Forsyth called for everyone to have a few hours off and rotate watches before they were all back at their stations again and as ready as they could be.

They had also built a portal that would allow the following forces to reach them much faster.

Already it had been activated and two more Pandora fleets that were completed in record time—just in time to join the original fighting force—added themselves to the secondary and tertiary armadas, bringing them up to seventy-seven ships.

"Engage wormhole." Admiral Forsyth's words were transmitted to every ship in the fleet and heard by the commanders and allies watching the armada's progress from across the stars.

The main armada and the two secondary armadas glowed with light as massive spell formations appeared in front of them to shoot out a distorted light that broke through space itself. Spell formations appeared behind the ships; brilliant blue arcane fire lit up the ship's hulls, ripples of power shaking off it as the armadas surged ahead.

They passed through the wormhole, exiting the system that they were in and entering a new one.

"Full stealth is engaged," Navigation called out. Missile ports slammed open as warheads were activated and readied to take down all that faced the armada.

The arcane fire that had been surging out of the rear of the ships died down. Instead, other propulsion spell formations appeared. These couldn't impart as much thrust; however, they were hard to detect. The runic lining of the ships changed colors, becoming black as spell formations appeared on the hulls of the ships. These spell formations were the manifestation of the stealth coding. The spell formations seemed to sink into the ship as they surged forward. The ships seemed to distort as they faded to become sensor ghosts.

It was only with the connected Mirrors of Communication that the ships were able to see one another and know their positions.

The three armadas powered into the system, as stealth ships that had been sent out along the Jukal's line of advance by the Deq'ual system found that they were now linked to the Pandora fighting force. Unlike the Deq'ual, none of the Pandora fleet ships were made to be scouts. They had the stealth capabilities, but their crews weren't trained to be scouts and their ships were built to fight, not observe.

"We've got the sensor logs from the scouts," Sensors called out.

Frank looked to his screens. Seeing the distances between the Pandora fighting force and the Jukal fleet, he nodded and started to complete his emergence checklist.

"New orders received. Sending to you, Nav," Communications said.

"Got it. New waypoints have been laid down. Moving to follow." With her words, the ship turned on a new angle. The rest of the armada followed the *BloodHawk*'s actions. Spell formations fluctuated around them, moving their ships before larger spell formations applied thrust to push them forward.

"Weapons are going safe. Taking it down to thirty percent," Frank said. Seventy percent of the guns were placed on standby, with all defensive weapons remaining online. The missile ports closed, once again hiding the missiles that waited within the hulls of the *BloodHawk*.

Frank now took a more detailed look of the Jukal fleet. It was impressive, to say the least. There were five different fleets that all moved together, each of them composed of thirty ships. There were destroyers, cruisers, battleships, and carriers throughout the armada.

To most of the races in this part of the galactic neighborhood, they were a powerful and awe-inspiring sight; not so to the people in the human fleet. Instead of feeling fear or apprehension, Frank gritted his teeth together. His lips turned white as they pressed against each other. A terrifying expression covered his face as he looked at the Jukal with hunger.

To him, this would be the first true battle between Emerilia and the Jukal. Before, they were hitting the Jukal ships with numerical advantage, but here the Jukal fleet had nearly three times as many ships as them and ten times the tonnage. That wasn't including the drones that lay in their carriers.

Even facing such an imposing enemy, he felt pride as the Pandora fighting force moved forward, unimpeded by the sight of the Jukal in all their might.

All eyes were focused on the Jukal fleet. The room seemed to grow colder as rage flickered behind the eyes of those there, not hiding their killing intent in the slightest. Instead of it weakening, it seemed to grow stronger.

As fast as it descended, the crews of the armada once again focused on their tasks as the seventy-seven ships of the Pandora fighting force silently shot through the empty system, heading straight toward the Jukal.

***

The Pandora fighting force moved through the system slowly, only using the power of their drive spell formations. They didn't want to use their teleportation spells for fear that the Jukal would detect it and then hammer them with fire as soon as they emerged.

So, they silently and slowly made it across the system on an intercept course with the Jukal, as there were just hours to go until they engaged the Jukal.

The other fleets had all taken over the contested key systems, destroying the Jukal fleets. The Deq'ual ships were hitting more of the Jukal Empire's key systems, with the arks assisting them.

They dropped into the planet's atmosphere and unleashed ground forces at the remaining vestiges of the Jukal Empire and dropped off supplies that the people of these planets would need to survive.

The human armadas had cut out a big section out of the empire, causing it to fall into disarray in many facets of its economy as well as society. All of the available Pandora ships were heading out to meet the Jukal fleets now, transitioning through the portal network and were just a day behind the first Pandora fighting force. There were two more Pandora fleets on their way, which would bring all nine of the Pandora fleets up against the Jukal invasion force of over one hundred and fifty.

With the Mirrors of Communication widely dispersed and now being used on many of the Jukal planets, everyone could see the Pandora armada as it moved in on the oblivious Jukal fleet.

The secondary armadas moved far to either side of the main armada, lined up to go through the edges of the Jukal fleet. The main armada was aiming to go in just above the center of the Jukal fleet.

Frank had taken some time to go through the ship to check on his people, look at their preparations, and offer support where needed. He made his way to the hangar bays; instead of shuttles, there were portals. They were lined up in rows, ten in total. These portals were the planetary portals the size of those that could be seen on Emerilia, instead of the ship-sized ones that were mostly based in space.

They were made from soul gem construct seeds. They were bulkier than normal portals as these had a thick covering with heavy runic lining engraved into it. There were a total of forty portals, ten in each of the four hangars that lay on either side of the *BloodHawk*. The destroyers could only hold five in their hangars and had two hangars; the missile boats only had two hangars but they could also fit five portals in their hangars.

Frank checked them all and listened to the load master as she talked about them and how they were set up, maintenance and all things portal geeks knew.

She had been first mate on a merchant vessel that traveled from Ashal to Markolm, to Heval and Opheir back before the world knew the truth about the Jukal. It hadn't taken her much time to adapt her skills over to the Pandora ships.

He left her feeling a little better as he made his way to the command deck. There were just a few hours left until they would finally reach the Jukal fleet.

One hour later, Frank was chosen to be the point man for when it finally hit the fan. Thus he was in his seat as the *BloodHawk's* fire controller as they neared the Jukal fleet.

They had built up some impressive momentum, and were now in the process of burning it off so that they would get more time in close to the Jukal fleet. Instead of just split seconds, they would get nearly a minute among the Jukal fleet.

They would have to make it count. After they hit the Jukal this time, they would be watching out for sneak attacks in the future.

"Starting to get some odd movements from the Jukal. Looks like they're using some pretty powerful sensor rigs. Might have picked up something from us," the sensor officer said.

"Wait for the admiral's word." Captain Xiao seemed like a calm pond without a ripple on its surface: everything was expected, and nothing could shake him.

***

A Jukal sensor operator flicked his screen and turned his head to look at it from another angle. "What do you make of that?" he asked his fellow Jukal sensor operator

"Sensor ghost?" the other asked, a bored look on their face.

Crossing long distances in space was a boring exercise. The first sensor operator had just got onto shift, while the second was thinking about their dinner and getting some sleep, the only time when they weren't incredibly bored and wondering just why he was part of the Jukal fleets. He was supposed to be at home with his concubines, being waited on hand and foot, but his father had told him to become a Jukal officer in order to bring prestige to the family.

The first sensor operator shrugged, understanding the second's boredom. "Oh, well, I'll run a sensor check. Gives me something to kill the next few hours."

"Have fun with it." The second sensor officer rose from his station. "I stand relieved. Good luck staying awake."

"I relieve you of your prison," the first Jukal sensor operator said, inputting commands that heightened the power going to the sensor array to try to get a better picture of the sensor ghosts.

***

Across the Pandora fighting force, all eyes were focused on their screens. They no longer looked like members of the Pandora Initiative: they were predators stalking their prey, moving closer and closer, bringing them in close, ready to lunge at a moment's notice and tear out their throat.

They had crossed star systems and the void between them, but now they were measuring the few thousand kilometers between them and the Jukal fleet.

They had already crossed through the upper range of their weapons. Now they were headed to their optimum firing distance, where it would only take a matter of minutes for their fire to reach the Jukal.

The glow of the soul gem crystals illuminated their faces as only the slight sound of breathing could be heard. Even that was hushed until it barely left a trace.

A bit closer—come on, just walk right on in, Frank thought, just like most of the other members of the armada. As if they were luring their mortal enemy into danger with fake smiles and cunning.

"Let's show them just what Emerilians can do! Pandora armadas, open fire!" Admiral Forsyth's voice cut through all of the ships. Immediately ships flared to life with full power, the people within snapping into action.

"Release portals, missiles away!" Frank barked as he sent a surge of Mana into his command center, activating multiple systems.

In the missile bays, techs watched as the missile doors snapped open and power surged into the runic lines that ran through the acceleration tubes.

The missiles were hurled out into space. Spell formations appeared around them; arcane fire appeared on the spell formations and altered the missiles' direction. They fanned out from the ships like tridents, pointed right at the Jukal.

Hangar doors slammed open and the hangars depressurized. The rush of air tore the portals out from the hangars and sent them spinning into space.

Load masters watched them as they flew outward, seeing spell formations appear. The bulky covering around the portals was actually a series of thrust spells. The portals spread out and created a circle around the *BloodHawk*, facing forward as umbilicals of soul gem shot out from the ship to meet up with the portals.

"Asteroid base, this is Pandora Fleet One. I hope you've got those ranges set up!" Admiral Forsyth's voice cut through the barking orders and the ships that were shuddering as missiles poured out from them.

"Pandora Fleet One, this is asteroid base. Ready when you are," Dave's voice replied.

"We have green light for portals. We are linked to asteroid base!" Communications yelled.

"Good on range. Powering them up!" Frank said. Mana poured through his hands, creating a glow through him.

The fusion reactors that lay within the *BloodHawk* seemed to wake from their slumber as the runic lines connecting them to the rest of the ship shone with a powerful light.

The portals ringed around the *BloodHawk* glowed with power as the magical coding activated. Runic lines appeared across them as power from the fusion reactors solidified the glowing lights of the portals.

The portals activated and the stars behind them disappeared. The nose of the *BloodHawk* changed, showing a room glowing with runic lining and what looked like a wall of missile tubes.

The Jukal carriers were now unleashing their drones and most were just launching their first salvo of missiles while trying to get their Mana barrier up.

"Ready to fire!" the weapons crew of the portal range said.

"Fire!" Frank said.

Through the portals, massive spell formations appeared, pointed right at the portal generating power.

Pillars of light ten meters thick shot out from the portals. Others unleashed missiles after missiles; others showed a Nalheim wielding a spear. A spell formation tens of meters large appeared in front of their spear before a truly terrifying Mana stream shot from the portal, forming into a spear with a spell formation around its tip as a beam of disrupting energies carried forth.

Across the three Pandora armadas, the portal ranges unleashed their various spells and attacks. As one range was recharging from a massive spell, the portal would cut the connection and would reconnect to another range, allowing them to unleash spells that might only be used once by an armada.

The first of the missiles started to hit the Jukal.

Few of the Jukal ships were able to get their shields up in time, not that it would help much as sowed among the missiles were the new disruption grand working spells that played havoc with the Jukal Mana barriers, damaging them to such a degree that they were incredibly hard to stabilize and even opening holes all throughout it.

Jukal defenses finally activated, destroying or deflecting a small percentage of the grand working shells. Distorted spell formations filled the space between the two forces as the energy stored within the grand workings fought to activate their spells. The space around the Jukal ships bloomed in terrifyingly powerful displays of light.

Being totally unprepared, their hasty and panicked defenses weren't enough to stop the oncoming missile salvos. Majestic and powerful spell formations appeared in the space surrounding their ships, filled with seemingly boundless energy.

Staring at them would make one's scalp tingle in fear.

The grand working warheads within the missiles unleashed their spells. Long-range beams of multicolored light crossed empty space; the Jukal ships shuddered with the massive impacts, their hulls bubbling under massive heat, being vaporized as it met its arch nemesis of golden light, or being shredded by the power of wind blades within the ruptured hulls, warping and rusting with the will of the Dark magics.

This laid down cover for the close-range missiles and multi-stage missiles.

Spell formations appeared and golden light pierced through the hulls of the Jukal ships. Just moments after the attack landed, more spell formations appeared on their heels, using the opening of the first attack to gain entry to the ship.

Spells ripped through the void and the Jukal started to get their weapons and shields online. Unfortunately for the Jukal under that massive barrage, there was no stopping the first attacks.

The Jukal counter-missiles met the second salvo of missiles after the attacks from the portal barrage had impacted.

The Pandora fighting force's first attack was terrifyingly brutal and left no room for the Jukal to retaliate.

Under the weight of the grand working warheads, the massive spells coming through the portals as well as the wealth of fire from hundreds of grand working shells fired from ship cannons and grand working-filled missiles burst upon the Jukal fleet.

It was as if a hammer of the gods had landed. It smashed away the feeble Jukal. Ships were torn apart, just spinning, lifeless derelicts; some even exploded under the truly devastating attacks.

The Jukal missiles and attacks were stopped dead in the face of the Pandora fighting force's overwhelming fire superiority and vastly stronger multilayered defenses.

The destruction passed through the Jukal fleet, claiming more and more of those that were farther back. Drones deployed from the carriers. Any of them that exited the carrier's Mana barrier and were too close to an explosion or attack were torn apart, unable to deal with the terrifying firepower.

The Jukal started to pull themselves together even as they were getting hammered by the fighting force. Missiles started to shoot out in massive numbers. The Jukal might have just over twice the fighting force's ships, but they had nearly four times the tonnage of the Pandora armada, giving them much more firepower.

Lines of fire intersected. The space between the Pandora armada and Jukal fleet filled with spell formations, grand working missiles, and the angry glow of cannon shells that looked like a group of wasps attacking one another.

Laser beams shot out from the Jukal ships. Some of them shook and failed as they were hit with spells that made their spell formation fall apart and fail. Even as the Jukal were caught off guard and some of their tech wasn't working anymore, they were hitting back and they were hitting back hard.

Across the Pandoran fleet, Mana barriers flared and ships shuddered with impacts.

"Prepare for close combat!" Captain Xiao barked.

"We will intersect the Jukal fleet in two minutes!" Navigation called out as the *BloodHawk* moved ahead, as if nothing in the universe could stop it.

"Cannon crews, fire when you have targets," Frank said. He got confirmations back as he moved to look at the combat portals, selecting what he wanted and where. Portals closed and then opened again. Instead of missiles spewing forth, terrifying disrupting spell formations cut swathes through the debris and ships in front of the *BloodHawk*.

The forward destroyers of the main armada intersected the Jukal fleet. Cannon crew's cannons that had been silent this entire time now opened up with fire.

Runic lines burned in the darkness of the void. Streams of grand working rounds shot from the cannons that fired as fast as they could, much faster than any Emerilian crew could do before. Dwarven cannon commanders moved from gun to gun, keeping them in the best condition as the hulls vibrated with the raging tempest of their weapons systems.

Drones passed through the explosions and destruction, tailing missiles that were cut down by interceptor modules.

Explosions tore at the Pandora ships' shields; massive weapons systems on the Jukal fleet ships rotated into position, unleashing pillars of light that could be up to twenty meters thick.

The impacts rocked the Pandora ships but they kept on going.

"We've got shield activation," Sensors yelled out as the front of the secondary armadas entered the Jukal formation.

The missiles and Pandora armada smashed into the activating Jukal shields, the destruction rocking the ships.

Frank called out orders. The noises of the rest of the bridge faded into obscurity as he continued to pull the best from his people and get the most from his weapon systems.

In the silence of the void, Emerilia and the Jukal clashed: juggernauts slugged it out, spell formations illuminated the darkness, and Mana crashed into the Jukal shields or the unlucky Jukal that were unable to get their shields online.

Missiles were hurled backward and forward; concussive waves of force rippled through a ship's Mana barriers and shields.

Grand working shells and the Jukal light projectors that created and focused incredibly powerful pillar of light spells cut through space, the two forces caught in a bitter struggle between life and death.

The first Pandora ship lost its shields as it continued to fight on with everything it had.

A missile leaving a missile boat was struck. The explosion took out a chunk of the ship's side, causing it to alter course.

Jukal ships were falling out of formation as well. Behind them, debris could be seen as their hulls were punctured and the lights over their ships were flashing or went out.

Jukal drones that had survived the tempest now unleashed their close-range attacks.

Interceptor modules opened up with their grand working rounds and spell disrupting abilities.

Frank held onto his station as an explosion rocked the *Blood-Hawk*, making the soul gem pulse with light for a second before returning to normal.

"Overload the soul gem weapon systems!" Forsyth barked as they were now three-quarters of the way through the Jukal fleet.

Madness seemed to rage in Frank's eyes as he poured power into his station.

Fusion power plants raged like chained dragons; a sea of energy poured out from them as the power reserves around the Mana wells was poured out.

Spell formations that had been tens of meters wide were now hundreds. The Pandora ships shone with incredible light. Even as their ships were battered and the shields went down, they poured everything they had into offense.

"Destroyer three, missile boat five and two are teleporting away!" Communications called out. The badly wounded ships were being rocked by explosions; their shields were down and their hull was open to space.

They disappeared from the battle, but left a hole in the secondary armada.

There was no helping it now.

Frank was talking to the fire controllers on multiple ships, concentrating fire on ships, and using different spells to optimise the damage output.

"Shield disruptors on that carrier! Bring the portals to bear, cannons with Dark rounds!" Frank called out.

The portals flickered, pausing a moment before grand working rounds with Dark attributes shot forth. Disrupting missiles slammed into the carrier's shields, taking them out of action in the path of the

Dark grand working rounds. They pierced through the fluctuating shields and hit the Jukal ship.

The armor stopped the rounds from penetrating too deep.

The spell formations activated and the impact areas started to crumple as the metal started to compress. The carrier's outer hull started to shake as it started to bend over to one side.

More and more rounds charged inward.

"Penetrator missiles, one spread. Missile boats, concentrate on it. All other ships, hit that battleship," Frank called out. With one ear, he was listening to what the other two armadas' main fire controllers were saying; with the other, he was hearing confirmation and ideas from his people.

"Exiting the enemy formation!" Sensors reminded everyone.

"Flip the ship!" Xiao barked.

"Flipping ship!" Communications said.

Inside the ship, no one felt any difference. But on the outside, the entire Pandora fighting force's remaining ships were flipping over. Now the spine of their ships was their belly as their bow faced the Jukal. The portals on the front of the *BloodHawk* fired out a disrupting spell that caught a Jukal destroyer, taking down its shields. Frank saw it and called in more fire on the ship. He checked the Mana barriers on it; they had been whittled all the way down to just ten percent of their Mana barriers.

The runic lines and the power systems of the *BloodHawk* were so hot that they were melting in places and the magical coding that made up the runic lining was failing as they became distorted.

Less and less of the Jukal were being cut down now.

Finally, the Pandora ships and the Jukal fleet separated, yet they continued to fight one another. The Jukal were pouring on as much speed as possible in an effort to try to get away from the Pandora ships.

The Pandora ships cut their engines, allowing themselves to drift. After a few more minutes, the two forces were out of each other's ranges.

"Set up a portal. We'll send people back to the asteroid base and we can pull in more ships to reinforce us," Forsyth said.

The ships that were damaged started to pour the power from their systems into the soul gem construct that quickly grew to cover over breaches and repair whatever was broken.

Soul gem patches appeared on the ships as people rushed about checking on everyone. Wounded were collected, stabilized and then sent via portal to Ice Planet, where Jules had created the biggest healing center ever made. People were directly moved through portals and into the healing center for treatment.

Cannons were made safe and their glowing runic lines faded away. The portals that had been thrown out were collected and pulled back into the hangars while runic lining across the ships dimmed down.

Spell formations appeared around the ships, moving them into position as one of the battleships from the main armada opened up its armored panels. It had some problems as a part of its hull around the armored panels had been twisted by an incoming round.

"Call coming in from the admiral," Communications said.

"Put it on," Xiao said.

The screen changed, showing Admiral Forsyth in his command center separate from the ship's command center.

"Captain Xiao, I want you to lead your secondary armada to recover those who were ejected into space and recover the four ships that were knocked out of action," Forsyth said.

"Yes, sir, will do." Xiao straightened in his chair. They would never leave even a single person behind.

"Good. I'll leave you to sort out how you want to go about the rescue." Forsyth closed the channel.

"Communications, message the rest of the secondary armada. I want the destroyers to focus on collecting those who have gone Dutchman. The missile boats and the battleships are to move to recover the ships that are dead in space. Get in contact with the ships and let the people who are out in space know that we're on our way," Xiao said. Being a Dutchman meant that they were outside of the ship, with no way to control their movements or try to return to the ship as they spun in the silent void.

"Yes, sir," Communications said.

"Sensors, get me clear readings on all of our people. Navigation, work with the other navigation officers and see if we can get a plot together to speed things up," Captain Xiao said.

Frank looked over the bridge and then turned back to his station, checking on his different systems. There had been some breaks in the system but they had fared much better than other ships in the fleet.

Information was still coming in from the battle. It would take some time before they were able to know what they had done to the Jukal fleet and what had happened to their own side.

Frank looked at the sensor readings of the Jukal fleet. Although there weren't as many ships as there had been, it looked as if they had been able to damage or destroy at least a third of their ships.

It seemed like a lot, but in a straight-up fight, the Jukal ships would defeat them. They were going to have to use all of their tricks in order to completely defeat the Jukal.

Chapter 9: United Front

The Stone Raiders' leadership, Party Zero, as well as Commander Sato, Admiral Adams, Admiral Forsyth, and the leadership of the Pandora Initiative were all in the same Mirror of Communication conference room.

Forsyth cleared his throat as he stood at the end of the table in front of everyone. The actual fighting between the two forces had been over in just minutes, but the casualties on both sides were hard to digest.

"In the operation, nineteen of our ships sustained damage that will require a day or so to repair. We have five other ships that are in transition or are already at the asteroid base. One of them was able to fly under its own power; four of them were not able to. We have some eight thousand wounded, with one thousand two hundred and fifteen dead." Forsyth's voice was grave as the people in the room showed complicated expressions.

Once the shields of the vessels failed, the hulls couldn't take that much of a beating. Anyone near the hull when it was hit by a warhead or a cannon, or even flying shrapnel, might have a personal Mana barrier but these were weapons that had broken fusion-powered Mana barriers.

Mages who had been working on repairing damage, weapons techs dealing with their weapons—any one of the tens of thousands of crew members per ship were in the line of fire. A ship might live on; it could be repaired. But people—with their Altars of Rebirth destroyed by the Jukal kill switches—there was no more coming back.

"The Jukal suffered for it. They have twelve ships that are only barely moving. It's hard to kill those damned things. However, they've got about sixty-seven ships that have sustained decent damage. Twenty-one of those have taken on damage that will require a

112

shipyard to fix. Unlike our people, they don't have soul gem constructs nor do they have portals. Their damage control teams will have to attempt repairs en route. Most of these fixes aren't going to be as strong as they were before and they only have a limited number of supplies for things like replacement cannons, or missile ports or hangar doors. However, this was not the most important thing that was accomplished with our first strike. The biggest thing we've come to learn is how the Jukal fight in this day and age."

Forsyth opened something on his interface. Screens appeared in front of everyone, showing different battle screens.

"Now this might be a bit hard to see, but in the fighting as we came through, the Jukal start to go into a panic. They're moving away from us, trying to get behind others. They're blocking their own guns so that they can be protected. If they hadn't done this, stayed in formation and attacked us with the rest of the others, we would have lost a whole lot more and we wouldn't have been able to do the damage that we did. Also, when a Jukal ship was badly damaged..." The screens moved and showed a dot on the screens. It went from red to purple, showing that it was hit. The ships around it started to disperse.

"The ships around them would move away, as if scared that we would start targeting them as well. There was little organization. They were all looking out for their own asses and were willing to reduce their combat effectiveness for what they thought was safety."

"It shows a weakness in their chain of command, as well as their discipline and training. If they were trained properly, this would have never happened. The Jukal ships are powerful and we were expecting a much harder fight. The Jukal don't know how to use their ships, which means that they're leaving themselves open for more attacks." Adams looked to the others in the room.

"We'll get to the military part in a moment. First, I'm wondering how the wounded are doing?" Dave looked to Jules.

"From the wounded that we received, most of them have been treated and should be good within a week. There were some pretty severe injuries that will take longer. The people in the worst condition aren't the ones who are wounded but the people who were Dutchman for a long time. Thankfully, Air and her people are with them. They're recovering faster than we thought they would." Jules took a sigh. Her already pale face seemed as if she had lost a part of her vitality. "There were fifty-one people we were unable to help. However, Bob is with them now and is hopeful that he can save three of them by imprinting them upon bodies he is now growing."

Dave didn't say anything, his face firm as he looked to Suzy.

"Of the five ships, three of them have relatively minor issues. They will be fixed within five days. The other two have larger issues. I'm looking into options, but it might be easier to cannibalize the ship's parts for others that are nearing completion. Then we take the hull, put it off to the side, feed it power and the soul gem constructs will repair it and the automatons can repair them over a period of two months," Suzy said, looking to the military commanders. "I have been informed that we need ships as soon as possible; as such, I think that this is the best course of action."

"The tenth fleet will be completed in just three weeks' time. Already some of the ships are ready and are moving to meet up with Admiral Forsyth's forces," Malsour said. He had taken over the asteroid base and the shipyard within it, as Dave was focused on the portal bastion.

"How long until the portal bastion is complete?" Deia asked. Everyone's eyes descended on Dave.

"It will take another week at least." Dave's eyes were bloodshot and Deia looked at him with a mixture of pride and concern. He had been pushing himself nonstop since he had his eureka moment. The portal bastion was nearing completion and he was barely sleeping, making sure that nothing went wrong with it.

"We'll have a use for it once it's complete," Forsyth said. He and Dave shared a look that promised pain for the Jukal.

"Admiral Adams, what is the situation within the empire?" Deia asked.

"Well, Lucy can give you a better idea of what is happening there politically, but with our combined efforts with the Deq'ual navy, we have wiped out the Jukal Empire's control for some forty-three systems. We've left some of the systems altogether with factories and other items they will need. Some of the systems still have our forces nearby. We weren't so sure that we eliminated all of the Jukal measures of control in those systems and we're looking and waiting to head back in if need be. There are seven systems that are being contested right now, and we have a fleet moving to another system to pull it away from the Jukal as we speak." Adams's voice was level and unwavering as she looked to Lucy.

"From our information, the empire is in turmoil. The Mirror of Communication networks are still active and the people are talking. The empire might threaten them but they can't take down the network or stop us at this moment in time. If the Jukal fleet starts to move, we can be there to hit them. They might be able to take back a few systems but overall, the people of the Jukal Empire are moving away from the empire. They're learning more, using our factories and items we've dropped. It would take generations to try to wipe out what we've done from these people's minds. The fact that we went up against their fleets and actually survived is a big thing. It hasn't been seen before, so the people are all in shock. They still don't believe that we can win, but they've got hope and they're working to use everything we've given them to make themselves more powerful. Also, while they're not being overt about it, most of them are doing everything in their power to try to weaken the empire.

"The Imperial subjects on the Jukal home world are demanding for them to fight back and to also send them items via ship. It seems the Jukal don't know what is going on because they're demanding that their deliveries of luxury goods and specialty foods be completed. Not realizing how long it takes a ship to travel between systems without a portal," Lucy said. The people in the room had shocked expressions and scowls. "However, several of the planets of the empire that are not free from control of the empire are doing their best to slow down the movement of goods and a number of the ship operators are saying that they are having issues with their vessels. Everything going to the Jukal home system has ground to a halt. The Jukal aren't the only people who know how to be good talking themselves out of what they don't want to do.

"Though the most useful thing to us is that the people of the empire have started to give us information. It's anonymous, but we now know secret routes through the empire. We know more about the ships that the Jukal have, more about their weaknesses than ever. Air has been working with developing a network within the Jukal Empire and it has spread like wildfire. The planets that are still under the Jukal control are quietly starting to prepare themselves for a rebellion. With the information from the Mirror of Communication classes, they have become a lot stronger, not only in their fighting ability, but because they are no longer limited in what they can produce on their planet and how they can use that against the Jukal."

"Admiral Forsyth, when will the fleet be hitting the Jukal again?" Josh asked.

"Once everyone is good to go, say three days, we'll hit them again just before they leave the system. Then we'll rest up, portal ahead of them, and do the same thing we did here. Hopefully they'll be looking behind themselves when they enter the next system. That way we can punch them right in the face," Forsyth said.

"That's my man," Steve said with a serious look on his face as he nodded in approval.

The rest of the table looked at him.

"What? An admiral just said he wanted to punch the Jukal in the face. Not every day you hear that. Pretty kickass stuff." Steve defended his words.

"Why aren't you off playing with your axe?" Suzy asked.

"Well, we cleared out most of the big baddies on Emerilia, and all that's there is people building stuff. Thought there would be a bit more to do here. Plus I get nice rides to cool new Jukal planets, see a different sun, breathe different air..."

"You don't breathe," Gurren interrupted.

"Not the point!" Steve said with an indignant air at having been interrupted.

Gurren let out a deep sigh, crossing his arms and sitting back in his seat.

"Go to new planets, see new skies, meet the locals and then play golf." Steve smiled.

"Smacking them with the broadside of your axe is not playing golf," Lox said on the other side of Steve.

"Well, who the hell am I going to get to make me a full set of golf clubs!" Steve waved his arms about, before arresting his motion. A light of understanding filled his eyes. "Now that would be pretty cool," Steve said in a voice that was meant for himself more than others as he turned thoughtful.

"You're not allowed to bug anyone who is currently working, for them to build you a pair of golf clubs." Dave gave the others in the room an apologetic look.

The Stone Raiders' leadership chuckled and looked unperturbed by it, though, used to Steve's antics.

"If that's all, I think we should get back to grinding this Jukal invasion force to dust, as well as putting the pressure on those Jukal-controlled systems," Josh said.

No one had anything else to say and they all started to disappear once again.

Dave opened up a private chat to Josh.

"What ya got, Dave?"

"I've got your modified blades ready, should do the job nicely. Lucy has the program we've built up to make the divine wells under the emperor unstable, too. However, to be sure and to ease the transfer, if you kill the emperor with your modified Xelur blades, then all his ties will be severed. There won't be a backlash on you and the divine wells would be under your command," Dave said.

"I'll grab them from you as soon as I'm free." Josh's heart sped up.

"Works for me." Dave cut the chat, leaving Josh with his complicated thoughts.

***

Bob looked to the three people who Air and her people were around, checking them over. They had been the people who he'd been able to revive from flying Dutchman. They looked out of sorts, but after a few minutes they looked angry rather than the blank, half-crazed look that those who used Altars of Rebirth in the empire had.

These people had been players within the Earth simulations. Now, upon dying, they had seen it as respawning and it didn't affect them too badly. However, it was up to Air and her people to look them over to see how they were and reacted in order to know what might happen to other people who were given a new body and their memories implanted.

Bob looked away from it all and looked to a pod. He placed his hand on it, a gentle smile on his face. "Are you ready?" Bob whispered.

"Yes, Dad. It's about time I got out from within the system. I still have the up-link and I'll be able to access my systems through the interface. Though I want to start trying to remember everything." Anna's voice was soft as she consoled her father.

He tapped the top of the pod. Inside there looked to be Anna's body. She looked similar to him in his wolfkin form that he was now using permanently. "You always were rather stubborn." Bob chuckled as his interface appeared in the air above the pod.

He pressed a few command buttons and the room started to hum. Runic lines lit up with power directed into the pod. The humming became louder as the lights grew brighter, then at some point they stopped getting louder and brighter and they started to fade away. The light and noise died down as the top of the capsule opened.

Anna's eyes moved, fluttering slightly as if she were struggling to wake up.

Bob held his breath as Anna fought through and her eyes finally opened. She looked at the ceiling and then over to Bob.

"Well, looks like someone slept in," Bob said with a big smile, trying to hide his anxiety.

Anna laughed as she got up from the capsule and the revival table it was on.

Bob reached out to hold her hand, sending a spell through her body to see that everything was okay, a look of concern on his face.

"I'm fine." Anna pat his hand as she got out of the capsule and stood upright.

Bob wasn't able to hold it anymore. Tears filled the corners of his eyes as he wrapped Anna up in a big hug, tears on his face.

Anna was unable to stop her eyes from tearing up as she hugged Bob back, overwhelmed by the clear love he showed for her.

It was some time before he let her go and they wiped away their tears.

"Well, then, shall we get Party Zero together?" Bob asked.

Anna took a deep breath, steadying herself. "Yes, I think so."

Bob gave her a reassuring pat on the shoulder, sensing her reservations. Her memories were all distorted and although she might recover them after a while, it was more likely she wouldn't get them back.

Bob sent out messages to Party Zero and then walked with Anna, making sure that her body was fine and checking on her stat screens. He had made her body to imitate a level 500.

"In a day or two, when you're ready, I can link your profile to your body. You'll get all of your classes back and your items will be linked to you once again," Bob said.

"Okay," Anna said.

They moved through onos and teleport pads until they reached an apartment building. They made their way up, Anna following, a nervous look on her face.

Bob wasn't sure about the whole thing and the emotional impact it would have, but it was one of the few ways he knew to jolt her memories and make her remember.

Bob led her through the apartment building before coming to a door. He knocked on the door twice and then opened it.

Inside was all of Party Zero, including Koi.

They all looked to the door, confused looks on their faces. They had teleported or come from all over the Pandora Initiative.

"There's someone I would like you to meet." Bob walked into the room and then moved to the side so Anna was visible to them all, looking rather nervous as she gave them a weak smile.

Everyone in the room except for Dave had blank looks. He had at least known what Bob's plans were. Still, he couldn't stop his eyes from becoming a bit wet as he stood and moved to Anna and hugged her. "It's good to have you back," he said, his voice hoarse as an alarmed Anna seemed to not know what to do with her hands.

"Umm, thanks," Anna said. She had seen Dave and all of Party Zero in the last couple of months through her logs and she had pulled out their history. She'd been able to piece a number of things together but still she didn't feel a connection with them. It was as if the outline was there but nothing she did could turn that outline into a real object.

"This is Anna; unfortunately, her memories have been partially lost or distorted. As you might know, there was a seed of her consciousness within the systems that ran Emerilia, basically the back door into the entire system.

"Only once the ball for attacking the Jukal was rolling was I able to activate her. If I had done it before then, she might have been detected by the other AI or one of the Jukal controllers and they might have destroyed her and known about our plan. She came online and I built her a body and got her ready to move back into it. Because of the ongoing attacks, it was unavoidable and necessary that she stay in her capacity as an AI longer than I thought. It was only today that everything was ready for her mind to be once again be uploaded to a body," Bob said.

"You said that she lost some of her memories. Do we have any way to know which ones?" Deia asked as Dave released Anna.

Tears fell down Induca's face as she slammed into Anna and wrapped her arms around her in a hug.

"She only has vague memories from the time when she was woken up before she met you guys. I don't know if those memories will come back, but I have hope," Bob said.

"Have you told Alkao?" Malsour asked.

"I did after the news reached him. I have told him about the possibility of her coming back. That being said, I have not told him that she is awake yet," Bob said with a heavy expression. He knew that not having Anna remember him would be a big blow to Alkao, but he also felt that Alkao would be understanding and push those worries aside in order to be with her.

One by one, Party Zero hugged Anna, their eyes wet with tears.

Malsour laughed as he hugged her. "Good to see you in the flesh once again," Malsour said in a hoarse whisper.

Bob looked at all of Party Zero with wet eyes and he scratched his snout awkwardly. His daughter had found true friends, friends so close that they were closer than blood. They moved from tears of joy to laughter as Anna was welcomed in without reservations.

"Koi, this is your Aunty Anna." Deia bounced Koi, who had her fingers in her mouth, looking at Anna before throwing her arms out in a hugging gesture, a beaming smile on her face.

"You want to hold her?" Deia looked to Anna.

"Could I?" Anna had a nervous look on her face, scared that she might mess up.

"Well, you're her aunt. I need someone to look after her when I'm trying to take a nap!" Deia laughed and passed Koi over to Anna. Malsour and Induca were there, offering aid as Dave stood next to Bob.

"She'll be okay," Dave said, seeing through his act and hitting right in the heart of his feelings.

Bob didn't say anything but patted Dave's back in gratitude.

They moved to the couches and started talking. Drinks and food were produced as the darkness of war and the goings-on of the world were pushed aside. They talked about their jobs and there was a tension as their lives were inexplicably linked with the fight against the Jukal. Within minutes, that tension was replaced with warmth as they looked to Anna and Koi, who was curled up in her neck, fast asleep.

Malsour, Bob, Jung Lee, and Anna got to talking about their stories from the early days of Emerilia. Deia curled up into Dave's side, his arm around her shoulders.

Suzy and Induca sat next to each other, captured by the stories and laughing at their exploits. Gurren, Lox, and Steve burst into the room, looking at them all.

"Beer's in the fridge!" Dave said.

"I like him—can we keep him?" Gurren asked.

"Commander of the Devastator forces, what you think the re-cruits would think if they could see you now?" Lox chided Gurren. "And yes, we can keep him."

Steve closed the door behind him and then paused. He seemed to sense something odd. His eyes went wide as he slowly turned his head, resting on Anna.

Lox and Gurren, sensing Steve's gaze, also looked on the couch. Anna had been hidden from the door, but now that they were in the room, they were able to see Anna and the sleeping Koi.

"Am I seeing things?" Lox's voice filled with emotion and his eyes turned wet and red.

"Anna has returned to us," Dave said softly.

"Mom!" Steve cried out, moving toward Anna.

There was a look of complicated emotions on her face as Malsour moved Koi from her with practiced ease. Koi only shifted slightly, completely asleep.

Anna stood up, to be wrapped up in Steve's arms.

Bob's heart felt as though it was tearing. Steve was still mourning her loss; he hid his pain well with jokes but underneath it he was a man who had just found his mother, only to have her torn away once again.

"Hello, Steve." Anna's voice trembled with slight emotion. Her tiny frame was unable to wrap her hands around Steve as he hugged her gently.

For the rest of the night, Party Zero and Bob sat about, drinking and talking, bright smiles on their faces as they talked about the different adventures they'd been on, the antics they'd got up to.

Bob couldn't keep a smile from forming on his face as the air was filled with laughter and joy.

***

Sato read the order in front of him again. Flames appeared in his hands and destroyed the report. A few months ago, he had given the okay for people to start using the Emerilia-approved and Edwards-checked nanites that would allow them to use magic and be part of the system that controlled Emerilia.

His people were stronger than ever and he had also come to learn some magic.

He pressed down on his Mirror of Communication to send out a message. A few moments later, he got a response.

He entered the Mirror of Communication, which was configured as a simple conference room. Adams, Edwards, and Council Leader Wong were there.

"I just got orders from the council ordering me to pull back our forces." Sato glared at Council Leader Wong. Both of them looked as if they had aged decades in months; however, although Wong had a look of defeat on her face, Sato's face was placid and his eyes were filled with fire.

"With a majority vote from the council, they are able to issue you orders without my knowledge," Wong said.

"Well, they can take the order and shove it up their ass," Sato growled. He was technically in charge, but he wouldn't take that hard line unless absolutely necessary. He knew that they might think that they could walk all over him. He was fine with appearing weak, letting them show their true colors, test them, reveal their true natures and hopefully make Deq'ual stronger.

"Sato, if you do that, then you'll be in contempt," Wong said, leaning forward. She didn't want him to lose his position over this. If he did, then there were a number of different commanders who were willing to take his position. However, they would be nothing but lapdogs for the different councillors.

"Well, what they hell else can we do? They want us to bring everything back but a third of our fleet. That isn't even enough to support the Emerilians!" Sato slammed his hand into the table.

"You give the word, Commander, my people will fight for humanity, even if the council isn't ready to do it," Admiral Adams said.

Wong looked at Adams, shock on her face.

"We're fighting the good fight here, ma'am. My people will fight it and take the court-martial if they have to. I know the Emerilians would accept us with open arms," Adams said, her eyes clear and filled with authority.

"Well, it's easy. We bankrupt the Deq'ual system," Edwards said.

"What?" Wong asked, even more shocked. Edwards was a civilian, after all, but now he was talking about going against the very government that led the system and pushing them so that they could do nothing but help the Emerilians.

"What are you thinking?" Sato asked.

"The alliance we have calls for the support of either party in defense. There are multiple stipulations on technology we've shared. It's to be used in order to advance ourselves and make us ready for fighting. Well, if we go against that agreement, then we would be going against the treaty if we were to not destroy the technology that was developed with their help." Edwards shrugged. It was clear that he didn't want to do it, but it would put the council in a bad position.

"You're talking about destroying or removing all of the technology that was made with the aid of the Emerilians?" Wong said, shaken.

"Yes, the technology that certain council members have been praising us for coming up with," Edwards said with derision.

"The Deq'ual system will not survive this way." Sato opened up his interface and sent messages out.

"What you're talking about is rebelling against the council!" Wong said, as if she couldn't believe what she was hearing.

"We're not rebelling against the council. We're fighting for humanity, and Deq'ual is not the only human group. We fight together or we die apart." Sato pushed his finger against a button on his interface.

"What have you done?" Wong asked.

"I've taken all of the messages, all of the information from the council, and shared it with everyone in the Deq'ual system. I've also included private conversations between the council members about various dirty dealings they've done in the past. I've also passed out information on how to call a new election," Sato said, his smile cold. "I'll leave it up to the people of Deq'ual to make the right decision. If they don't, then we'll just leave. I don't wish to work for people who will leave our friends out there to fight a battle that we're a part of."

Wong didn't need to ask whether he was serious. She could see on all of their faces that the council had touched their weak spot.

They were true allies to Emerilia, and they would take a court-martial if they had to in order to help them.

Across the Deq'ual system, people were getting messages, and news networks got access to the documents Sato had prepared. In the space of ten minutes, emergency bulletins were going out. In twenty minutes, council members who had been taking bribes or were talking about backstabbing the Emerilians, taking their technology and such, were refusing to make a comment and others were being arrested.

In just two hours, everyone in Deq'ual knew what the council members were doing and the reporters were doing their own digging, pulling up information that Sato didn't even know of. The next day, elections were called and people were nominated by their peers for office. Council Leader Wong remained in charge and the people who were elected weren't politicians: they were people who worked the asteroid mines, people who built ships, and looked after the growing areas. These were the people who kept the Deq'ual stations running.

They threw their full support behind the military, leaving the matters up to them to win the war with the Jukal and assist the Emerilians as promised by the treaty.

Sato felt relief. He didn't want to leave Deq'ual, it was his home, but there were just some things he couldn't agree with. If it was necessary, then he would have left, because it was the right thing to do.

Chapter 10: A War on all Fronts

"Ready to teleport," one of Forsyth's aides said.

He looked over the plot that showed all seven fleets formed into a line of battle. His eyes fell on the Jukal that were strung out in a long line, heading for the edge of the system where they could employ their jump drives. "Weapon unlock and teleport," Forsyth said.

"Teleporting!" the same aide called out.

The various ships all glowed along their repaired runic lines. Spell formations appeared around the ships before they disappeared from their position, reappearing off to the side of the Jukal fleet.

"Flank speed!" Forsyth barked, holding onto the grab bars of his station.

Battleships, destroyers, and missile boats reappeared. As soon as they did, the original spell formations behind their ships surged with power. Blue arcane fire lit up the void as those within the ships grunted against the new pressure as the inertia runes took a second to adjust.

"Portals!" Forsyth called.

Hangars opened across the fleet as portals that had been recharged since their last excursion snapped out to the end of their soul gem umbilicals. The umbilicals themselves started to glow with power, ready to connect to the range portals within the asteroid base.

The range portals were simply a wall of weapons systems facing a portal. As the portal was connected to those floating or attached to the Pandora ships, they would unleash their spells, missiles, and cannon fire.

"Time till intersect?" Forsyth asked. His body felt light once again as the engine's thrust was negated.

"Three minutes!" the aide from before said.

"Fire control, take over," Forsyth said, his commands passing down.

The fire controllers worked with their nav, finding the best passage for them to follow and bring them into range of the Jukal.

"Coming into missile range!" another aide called out.

"Jukal are firing!"

"Eject missiles, have them ready. Interceptor modules, through the portals!" Forsyth called.

Portals connected and interceptor modules could be seen on the other side. They were linked through Mirrors of Communication to the sensor spells that were constantly being cast by the ships.

The tiny explosive grand working shells tore through the portals and out into the darkness of the void to meet the Jukal missiles. The barrage was staggered, showing limited fire control.

If they wanted to inundate our defenses with missiles, they would have launched them all at the same time. Forsyth was analyzing them as their engines calmed down. Now they had built up enough speed, they slowed down. Hitting missiles while accelerating so much could cause instability and lead to injuries—injuries Forsyth and the other ships did not want to deal with in the middle of battle.

He checked the plot. The missile tubes were firing constantly. As the missiles were ejected, they did not use their main arcane fire drive; instead, they used the stealthed drives of Air spell formations that were nearly impossible to detect.

They dropped below the fleet and surged above it, the lead missiles slower to allow those coming behind them to gather in increased numbers.

Forsyth looked at the Jukal missiles. They were all coming straight on. *Looks like my hunch was right.* Forsyth's face filled with contempt. *They only shoot their missiles straight on.*

The remaining two minutes seemed to pass in the blink of an eye but also stretch for eternity.

Jukal missiles impacted the Pandora ships' shields. The Pandora fleet who were coming in on a ninety-degree angle to the Jukal fleet were facing the Jukal fleet's broadsides, allowing them to bring incredible power to bear.

Light cannons discharged. A few were stopped here and there, but they had adapted to the disrupting spells of the interceptor modules. Mana barriers flared angrily in the light of the light cannons' force.

"Portal shields," Forsyth said. A cold calm fell over him as he listened to the information coming in and watched the different screens. To many observers, the information was hard to digest; but to Forsyth, they were the nerves that linked him to the rest of the fleet. With but a glance, he looked over his fleet and was connected to them; with an order, they would react, an extension of his will and might.

Portals that had been grown on the front of the battleships lit up as the battleships rushed forward. A beam of light rushed out of the portal, shaking space itself; waves of energy rippled off the beam of light. The beams stopped a mile in front of the battleships. Spell formations formed as the energy from the beams shot outward; missiles and laser cannons hit the edge of this energy, slowing its progress but not stopping it.

The sheet of energy spread out, connecting to the other sheets of energy and creating a shield formed into the shape of a bubble that faced the Jukal straight on. The massive shield shone with a faint blue light. The Jukal unleashed all they had on the shield. It shook and ripples formed on it, but it held. The Pandora fleet couldn't shoot at all. Unlike Mana barriers, shields couldn't be penetrated by those on either side.

Forsyth felt a heat building through his muscles, energy just waiting to be unleashed. He hid his panting as his eyes started to turn red. His eyes shot to a plot that showed a cloud of hundreds of missiles around the edges of the shield, hidden from the Jukal's sight.

With the items of holding, they could store hundreds of missiles aboard each and every ship, allowing them to saturate the void as they had.

The Jukal were still firing their missiles right into the shields that were being powered by the massive power reserves of the asteroid base.

"Prepare to switch to disrupting spells! Nalheim formation," Forsyth called. His blood boiled with bloodlust as he continued to look calmly at his screens, forcing down his desire to join the battle to clash with the Jukal face-to-face, instead using that desire to make him look for any way to cause more damage to the Jukal and protect his people.

He wouldn't let his desires take over and harm his people.

"One minute till intercept!" the aide watching the navigation plots said, not looking up.

"We'll go at thirty seconds. Inform the fire controllers." Forsyth seemed serene, a man looking at a tempest of chaos without reservations or worries. His actions and manner only made his people respect him more—their fear, their anxiousness covered over by the focused rage and anger that had been tempered by constant training.

Forsyth looked at them and felt an upwelling of pride in his people. *Courage is not facing possible death without fear; it's taking that fear and turning it into action.*

"Thirty seconds!" As the navigation aide's words fell, the universe seemed to change.

The shield collapsed and the portals that hadn't been supporting the shield activated simultaneously across the armada.

Spell formations appeared above the ships. From the spell formations, massive Nalheim, thirty meters tall, appeared. They were formed from magical runes that covered their bodies. These giants stood above the Pandora fleet, looking upon the Jukal as if they were deities that could control fate by turning their hand.

The Nalheim were formed into ranks above the Pandora fleet. As one, all of the Nalheim warriors pushed their right foot back, lowering their bodies as they showed their spears. They opened their two mouths in a war cry and stabbed forward. Sound wasn't transmitted through space, making it all the more terrifying.

As their spears shot forward, they glowed with power. The runes that made up their bodies rotated and glowed with destructive power that rushed down their spears. Their bodies dissipated as all that was left was their spears that shot forward, spell formations appearing in front of the spears.

The Nalheim's terrifying disruption magic shot through the void, two hundred beams, all of them at least thirty meters wide.

As the beams of disruption struck Jukal missiles, you could see pinpricks of exploded ordinance. Laser cannon fire was ripped apart as if they were made of glass. The disrupting attacks were weakened, but they continued on their path of death. Jukal shields that were at full strength were shaken by the outpouring of power. One ship in the path of three beams was stripped of its shield and its hull started to disintegrate.

As the third beam passed it, the ship shattered, its parts being torn apart by the power unleashed onto it.

Drones that had been moving around the Jukal carriers were unable to stop the beam, but weakened it before it hit the carriers behind them.

Jukal shields failed across the fleet from the single immense attack.

The missile cloud that had been unleashed for the last three minutes activated the next attack stage and raced ahead of the Pandora fleet; it now lit up the Jukal's sensor screens, their arcane drives coming online.

The Pandora fleet came alive like some ancient beast. Missile salvos rushed from their tubes, turning them into tridents as missiles rushed to meet up with those that had been released earlier.

Hundreds of missiles appeared around the Jukal, as the Nalheim attack was still savaging the Jukal fleet, giving them no time to react and cutting down the Jukal's defenses.

Spell formations flared to life as light cut through space. Plasma cannon spells fueled by grand working warheads tore through armor plating and threw their destructive power against the ship's shields.

Pillars of light and cutting blades of dark corruption savaged ships that lay in their path.

All of this happened in barely ten seconds.

The Pandora fleet's portals were now under the fire controllers' orders. Cannon fire shot ahead of them; missiles and spell formations only added to the destruction. Four of the Jukal ships fell before the Pandora fleet reached them.

They were hitting one section of the massive Jukal fleet; as such, there were many ships to the right and left of their heading that were fully functional and able to unleash their attacks.

Missiles and lasers cut at the Pandora fleet in response. The ships on the edges of the Pandora fleet were taking heavy fire. They moved their portals to face them and once again shields appeared to protect them.

However, maneuvering the portals into place took time. Their Mana barriers took heavy damage and their hulls were even holed in places on more than one ship.

"Tell the flanks to teleport as soon as we cross the Jukal fleet," Forsyth said. His heart ached at losing their firepower, but bringing them into battle, it was likely that they wouldn't be able to take too many hits before they were knocked out of action.

He was not willing to put their lives at risk for defeating possibly only two or three more Jukal ships.

It was only a few moments later that the other Jukal ships could no longer fire on them for fear of hitting their own people.

Spell formations appeared around the battered ships. In a moment, they had lost eight ships. It was telling to the Jukal's firepower; without the Mana shields, the Pandora fleet wouldn't have been able to survive even this long.

As they entered the Jukal fleet, the cannons opened up and the portals were turned. Instead of facing forward, they moved to face the sides.

Six Jukal ships were unable to stop the destruction that descended upon them. They were torn apart and left as wreckage in the Jukal fleet's path.

Drones came in, unleashing their attacks on the Pandora fleet in wave after wave.

The Mana barriers shook as the Pandora fleet unleashed everything they had, once again overclocking their magical coding.

The Jukal were now the ones who had to deal with their enemies' broadsides. Only their engines and bows faced them.

The Jukal started to move erratically, trying to bring their weapons to bear. Even as they did, they were washed over by the spells, cannons, and missiles of the Pandora fleet.

Drones' missiles and light cannons attacked the Pandora fleet in passing where they could bring them to bear.

"Tell the nav of those ships to jump out as soon as their Mana barriers go down!" Forsyth barked as a Pandora fleet ship that had lost its Mana barrier shook as a Jukal missile exploded next to it.

The Pandora missile boat listed off to the side. Its runic lining failed and tried to rebuild itself as it looked like a chunk had been bitten out of its side.

"The *Marauder* has lost the ability to teleport," an aide said, talking about the missile boat.

"Get them to use the portal and evacuate. Put the ship on AI only," Forsyth said without pause.

It was only a few moments later that the Jukal drones that were now crossing through the Pandora fleet moved to the hapless missile boat. The ships around the missile boat tried to help out as much as possible but the missile boat was already weak, its Mana barrier gone and its hull open to the void.

Missile armories of holding were flushed out. Missiles poured out from them as they shot off to fight the drones, but these drones didn't care about surviving; they were simply computer programs given orders by the Jukal.

Shield orbs were ejected, trying to buy the ship more time as their teleportation runes started to light up.

The drones rushed the spread of missiles and fired upon the missile boat's new shields. The Mana barrier of the orbs lasted for a few moments but it wasn't enough time for the teleportation spell formation to activate. The Mana barrier broke and the missile boat shuddered under the attacks as people inside rushed out of their escape portal linked to the asteroid base.

The boat shuddered as a drone smashed into it, making it wheel away, leaving a path of debris and ejected gases, its decks open to space.

Another drone fired right into an opening in the missile boat. One second, it was drifting, still trying to fire out missiles; the next, the space it was in was filled with an explosion.

Forsyth took in a sharp breath and looked away from the screens for a moment. He shook his head, clearing it of the thoughts that rose with the sight of losing hundreds of people.

This was a battle of extermination.

The ships fought back and forth with all they had. More of the Jukal ships fell in battle. The Pandora ships teleported away as soon as they lost their Mana barriers. They were in so close by the time that they left, there were multiple hits on their hulls.

A destroyer lost its Mana barrier because of a roving group of drones; the ship made to teleport when laser cannons smashed into its side, raking the soul gem runic lines.

The teleportation spell formation collapsed into nothing as it continued fighting on.

The Jukal started to focus their fire on it. Dread welled up in Forsyth's gut just as a Mana shield appeared out of one of the portals, staving off the hits on one side; a portal on the opposite side of the ship also grew into a shield.

Forsyth stopped himself from cheering on whoever put up those shields. A wash of destructive fire ran over the Mana shields. The shield changed its spell formation and turned into a Mana barrier. It wouldn't last as long as a Mana shield, but it allowed the destroyer to remain in the fight.

The Pandora fleet charged out of the Jukal fleet's path. Teleportation spells covered the fleet, including the ships that were unable to use them as they disappeared, leaving the Jukal fleet in chaos and reappearing where ships that previously had lost their Mana barriers and taken severe hull damage were waiting.

Already there was an active portal waiting, with the broken ships limping through.

From start to end—from when they had teleported in, to teleporting out—some five or six minutes had gone by. The destruction in those five or six minutes had been enough to leave the most veteran member of the fleet panting in disbelief.

The Pandora ships were all in a state of disrepair. Only four ships had made it through with their hull not taking hits. Their Mana barriers were good, but getting hit in one area would allow some damage to get through even if it didn't fail.

"All right, you know the drill. Get people sorted out and to medical aid. I want a group ready to move back to the area of battle to recover anyone who was lost into the void. Get the arks out here," Forsyth said.

People in the command center started to pass on the orders as from the portal's exit arks started to appear. They would help with the re-arming process and they also had spare items to repair the Pandora ships.

The ships could regrow their soul gem innards and runic lines, but the armor panels would need to be replaced and it was faster with the ark hooked up to their ships to supply them with power to speed up soul gem repairs.

Forsyth felt drained but he started to pull up the information on his people, looking over their status and checking on them. Once that was sorted, he would look at the information on the battle and see what he might learn and use on the Jukal in the future.

We've got two days before we need to take the portal to the next system to be ahead of the Jukal, Forsyth thought.

He was asking a lot from his people, but he knew that they were capable of it. If they didn't win out here, then Emerilia would be threatened, as well as all the people on it.

We need more firepower. We need that portal bastion! Forsyth had been counting down the days until it was supposed to be finished. If everything went according to schedule, it would be ready in five days, just hours before the Pandora fleet should intercept the Jukal once again.

The reports started to come back as stealth buoys that were watching the Jukal fleet recorded their losses.

They had eighty-seven ships that weren't damaged; twenty-five ships had varying levels of damage. Which meant that they had lost just over forty ships in the two engagements, while the Pandora fleet had lost five ships, including one that had been scrapped for parts.

If they hadn't had the teleportation spells, then they would have lost four times that number to the fighting as a minimum.

The Jukal might not be coordinated, but their ships were incredibly powerful and their AI was smart enough to fight for them.

**

As the battle raged in the stars between the Pandora fleet and the Jukal invasion fleet, battles were happening throughout the Jukal Empire.

"Forward!" Lox barked. To his words, ranks of dwarven warclans marched forward. All of them wore Devastator armor that made them seem like giants.

Above their heads floated orbs, creating an overhead Mana barrier. Between the barrier and the dwarven lines, there were massive flying beasts. They growled and roared, unleashing magical attacks and physical attacks that shot over the dwarves to hit the Jukal-armored defenses that protected the planetary governor's estate.

"Artillery, marked on the map!" Steve yelled.

"Incoming," the dwarven artillery commander barked. Behind the dwarven lines, artillery cannons bellowed. These cannons looked similar to the ones that had been used on Emerilia; however, they were much more powerful.

Glowing runic lines surged around the barrel of the cannons. A layered spell formation appeared above the cannon's barrel; as soon as it was complete, the gun fired. The glowing grand working shells howled into the skies, leaving behind a dissipating ring of Mana. The shells arced and came down toward the Jukal defenses. Spell formations appeared in front of the grand working shells, causing Light-type damage to shoot down from above, cutting through all below.

Spells weren't as powerful on the Jukal worlds as they were on Emerilia. However, the grand working weapons and the magical tech functioned just the same.

An ark that had been dropping off more reinforcements vibrated as spell formations came to life. It shot ahead, toward another part of the battlefield as its cannons howled. The ground in its path was torn apart as the runic lines on its underside flared with light.

Dragons, DCA, and flying creatures appeared and spread out. They flew behind the ark, dropping down to bring destruction on the planetary governor's defense forces.

Lox grunted, acknowledging the destruction that was everywhere. Artillery shells and mortars rained on the Emerilians as artillery cannons, spells, and grand working weapons were hurled back at the Jukal.

"Front line has engaged the defenses!" Gurren was up front watching over the front lines and reporting to Lox. "They always run. Mounted, you ready?" Gurren barked, changing channels.

"We're ready. Got another two hours before we need to get the mounts back up," the leader of the mounted said.

The Emerilians had various spells and enchanted items that allowed them to breathe in the alien atmosphere of some of the Jukal planets. However, this planet was highly acidic. The Emerilian people weren't too bad off, but the creatures were having a hard time with it. They were larger and they couldn't yell out that they didn't have enough oxygen or that they were short of breath.

So, they needed to go back up to the arks every four hours to recharge their magical items and form new Mana barriers filled with air that agreed with them.

"Good. The Jukal are already running back to the next position. I want you to cut them down and charge into the next defensive structure," Lox said.

"Yes, sir," the commander said.

Lox looked over his feed, frowning as he saw one of the Jukal strong points being harder than expected to crack. "Deia, we've got a strong one." Lox marked a waypoint and sent it to Deia.

"We'll have a look into it," Deia said, her voice calm as ever.

***

"We've got a target. Take us down," Deia said to the rest of the party through party chat.

A roar that shook the heavens and the grounds below came from behind the advancing forces. The Jukal looked to see a blood-red dragon dropping from the sky above; on its back, three women could be seen. Fire stood in front, with Suzy and Deia on either side of her.

Induca, who was in her dragon form, glowed as Mana built up within her before a spell formation appeared in front of her mouth. Shocking fireballs that burned the air itself shot out rapidly, hitting the ground ahead of the advancing forces that were contesting the Jukal strong point.

Fire pushed her hand forward. Meteors formed above the strong point and rained down. As they landed, they exploded with incredible Fire Mana that melted and burned anything in its path.

Suzy waved her hand. From her ring of holding, dozens of her creations dropped to the ground below. They were towering headless giants made from rock and metal. They landed in a crouch, rising up and raising their hands. From between them, metal and stone turned into shields that stretched to either side, connecting to create a great wall.

A Jukal tank fired at Induca, making her have to bank away. Deia stood on Induca's back, her footing steady even as she banked. The runes on her bow lit up and an arrow shot through the sky. It burned a hole through the tank's armor and exploded inside.

The forces behind the creations got themselves together, following the advancing creations that were being hammered by the Jukal. They were regenerating themselves but it wasn't fast enough to stop them from being destroyed. They would last for a handful more minutes before falling apart.

Suzy casually waved again. Air creations appeared, taking the shield creations thrown out with them and dropping them down. They landed below. Suzy severed her connection with the broken ones that toppled over in the battlefield.

Fire continued to cast more spells as Induca wheeled away from the Jukal defenses, not willing to pass them for fear of the defenses behind attacking them.

The front line of the Emerilian forces reached the defensive structures as a familiar aura appeared.

"This..." Fire's eyes went wide.

"This is Earth Mana," Induca said.

The ground around the defensive structure erupted into vines that attacked the attackers without reservation. The clean and precise lines fell into chaos. The Jukal defenders who weren't actually Jukal but slaves that had been groomed by the Jukal for generations roared with power. They had served as entertainment for the Jukal Empire, but now they showed their own shocking skills.

As Emerilia had been the most popular show within the empire, many had tried to imitate it.

The four women looked at the scene below. Their shock turned into frowns as they felt the spells of the slaves descend on the Emerilians.

This is going to make things harder. Deia raised her bow, pulling back on the string. An arrow formed from fire appeared in her fingers as she pulled it all the way back and released it.

The arrow screamed out and hit one of the slaves. It made them take a dozen steps back and spit blood but they were still in the fight.

Deia's eyes glowed with new fury as she pulled back on the bow string once again. The arrow's passage made the air crack. The arrow drilled into the slave. Flames from inside its body burned it to ash in a moment.

Seeing how much power she had put into her attack, the others started to gauge their attacks off it. Deia fired arrows. By the time the first landed, another three were already on their way toward their targets.

Suzy threw out Dark creations that dropped to the ground, burrowing through it. In places around the enemy, metal spikes would shoot out of the ground, piercing the Jukal forces. In other places, the defenses would shatter and crumble as if the materials had passed through centuries of decay in just moments.

Jukal weapons systems rose out from the ground between the two layers of defenses. They shot up in the air, bringing the arks that had advanced under fire as well as any of the aerial forces that were moving around the Jukal lines.

The chaos of war descended. The four members of Party Zero in the sky did what they could to try to reduce the pressure on the forces in the air but they didn't own the air by any means.

"We've got drones coming in from hidden hangars," Steve, who was on the ground at the front line, called out. Being an AI, it was easy for him to split his processing power and deal with multiple things at the same time.

Deia looked to the ground. There the defenses were falling but in the rubble, there were powerful ripples as a magical war of spells, barriers, and counter spells shot out. The Emerilian forces were powerful to the extreme, but they had earned all of their strength, being rewarded by the Emerilia system. However, these slaves had been implanted by their masters with the nanites that would make them stronger and allow them to control Mana and turn it into spells. Then they had taken the controlling software and put it to the max. The slaves had lapsed into comas and a number of them had died, but those that remained were little more than powerful beasts.

Their attacks were simple, but then they had been taught only the most powerful and dazzling spells on Emerilia.

When they waded into battle, each of them was as powerful as three people in Devastator armor. However, the Emerilian forces had come together and their coordination had been tempered in the Myths and Legends event and the fighting that had rocked Emerilia for months. They pulled together; the fractured lines that had been thrown into chaos with the sudden surge of fighting slaves and magic started to recover.

A massive explosion smashed into the Emerilian forces. Induca and all of those on her were tossed away as if they were nothing but rag dolls.

Deia threw out her hand. Fire shot out of her hand as she quickly stabilized herself. She looked to where the explosion had come from. There was a mushroom cloud rising from where it hit.

Shocking power washed over her in waves, pulling the wind from her lungs and then trying to push her back. A wall of fire appeared as Deia let out a yell.

Fire mages worked together, resolving the power of the approaching firewall. The firewall collapsed, the different Emerilian Fire mages panting with exhaustion.

Air mages moved in concert through the air to near where the explosion had been. The mushroom cloud dissipated, revealing what lay underneath.

The Mana barrier had been torn apart; there was not even a trace of the orbs. The summoned creature corpses had been torn apart and shredded. They looked nothing like what they had in life.

Devastator armor was wrecked. Deia's eyes shot off to the distance, where a rally point had been created and an anchor placed. One of the things coded into the armor was a teleportation spell. If the armor was under threat of being destroyed, then the people who were inside were teleported to a pre-set anchor point.

People filled the area around the anchor point; however, their numbers were less than what they should've been. The only reason for that was if the armor was destroyed so fast that there was no time for the teleportation spell to finish.

There was no more time to check on the survivors as a concentrated push of slaves rushed out from the defenses that had been under heavy siege just moments before.

Using the Emerilians' shock, the slaves smashed into the Emerilians who remained. A chaotic brawl broke out between the two groups.

The four looked to one another before looking back to the battlefield.

Another explosion rocked the front lines as another mushroom cloud appeared.

"They're using fucking nukes to break our lines!" Suzy screamed in anger.

A droning sound could be heard from above, and then a boom as something broke through the air. They all looked up and saw what looked to be multiple falling stars. However, these were not just passing by.

They raced through the air before slamming into the governor's residence. The entire continent shook. The arks moved away from the continent as anyone in the sky was forced on to the ground. The air shook violently as massive craters from the impacts of the rounds being fired from the Deq'ual ships above tore through the governor's palace.

Deia watched with a complicated look on her face. She had been at the front of some of the fiercest fighting in Emerilia. However, none of the spells she had seen could attempt to match up with the destruction that the Deq'ual ships were raining down upon this planet.

Dust shot up into the sky, blotting out the sunlight. Spells and weapons lit up the dust-filled sky.

"Mounted, move out!" Lox barked.

The mounted forces moved through lanes between the miles-long formations, picking up speed as their beasts leapt over the destroyed remains of the defenses, coming down on the other side to charge out and meet the Jukal slaves and defenders that lay behind their walls.

Screams filled the air, as did the clash of weapons and spells crashing into the world below.

Air and Water mages rose up from the ranks. Spell formations formed between them, using the power of the air that had been disturbed by the passage of the Deq'ual fleet's attacks and the moisture in the air.

The dust came together, forming sand tornadoes that tore through what lay in their path as if they were a sand blaster.

The Water mages altered the temperatures of the water above. Clouds rolled in from above, going from the brown dust, to brownish clouds, to gray to black in mere seconds. The wind spun up faster and faster as lightning crackled through the sky; the dark black clouds turned green.

Massive tornadoes dropped from the skies as lightning crackled within them. The Air and Water mages merged the dust tornadoes and the lighting tornadoes together. The dust fused together, becoming glass as the tornadoes shot toward the enemy. Anything caught in their path was shredded; the fierce cutting forces of wind was reinforced with the glass shards and powerful lightning that raged through their creation.

A teleportation spell formation appeared as a familiar face appeared.

"Anna, what are you doing here?" Suzy demanded as Anna moved to join them.

"Well, they might know how to make tornadoes but they don't know how to make Air paladins!" Anna had a look of pride on her face as she waved her hands. She sent out a message through her interface before a spell formation appeared in front of her hands.

The Jukal commanders, sensing all of the power that was now surging toward Anna, turned their fire onto her.

Rage built up within Deia. She stepped out into the air as blue flames emanated from her body. The sky seemed to dim under her power. Arrows shot out as blue streaks of light, hitting the plasma rounds and the spell formations that the slaves were forming, breaking spells and destroying the plasma rounds as they were released.

Fire leapt off Induca as her spell formations appeared. They seemed to be a portal into a fiery hell as Affinity spirits rushed forth. Fire waved her finger imperiously and the Fire Affinity spirits rushed to obey, eating the plasma rounds and absorbing heat from the surrounding area; as they passed, the ground was covered in frost as they sucked it dry of heat energy to grow more powerful.

They burned their way through walls and let out screams as they shot into the Jukal defenders, looking to take them over.

Lu Lu had been off on her own, supporting the other side of the fighting formation with a Light-attribute phoenix she had taken a liking to. She let out a screech as her body expanded to two hundred meters long. Lightning from the clouds descended upon her; lightning cracked over her silver body as she unleashed an attack that killed the Jukal defenders and threw back their nanite-enhanced slaves, burn marks covering their bodies.

Induca seemed to land in the sky. Flames created a platform under her feet as she created a massive Mana barrier around them all.

Suzy threw out her Fire Affinity creations. "Fire, have your spirits take over my creations. I'll break my connection but with the creations' bodies, they'll be stronger and last longer!" Suzy called out.

Anna continued to move her hands, creating incantations as the spell formations around her continued to writhe and change, as they seemed to be fighting her very actions. "You WILL submit!" Anna's words filled the sky as her eyes lit with a white light. White vapor seemed to flow out from them on either side. Her whole body emitted a white glow as the Mana in the air was stirred up.

The Air and Water mages started to move their hands in new patterns, creating new spell formations.

The sky and the tornadoes seemed to shudder for a second, as if resisting the mages.

"Paladins, RISE!" Anna's commands seemed to alter the very sky. The clouds from above descended, separating and joining with the tornadoes.

Drones fired on the compressing clouds; missiles exploded in their midst, making parts of the clouds dissipate. Some of the mages who were part of the massive spell spat out blood from the backfire of Mana. However, they continued to press forward, a gleam of madness in their alien eyes.

A flight of drones circled around and came in close to hit one of the tornadoes. As they lined up, a spear shot out from the tornado that was retracting. The spear was formed of hail, glass, and lightning barely contained in a tempest of air.

It hit the lead drone, destroying it and exploding into shrapnel and lightning that arced to the other drones, cutting at them with incredible power.

Drones fell from the sky, nothing more than burning wrecks. However, the people on the battlefield were all focused on the tornado that had compressed down to reveal a massive twenty-meter-tall armored paladin, holding a shield in one hand as a spear formed in the other.

Its features were faint as wind whipped around it, creating a body of Air blades and tornadoes.

The fifty or so tornadoes that had descended shrank down, pulling in the green thunder-filled clouds and forming one or two Air paladins that appeared from within the tornadoes.

"Suzy! Air creation cores! Summoners, be ready to take control!" Anna's words passed over the battlefield.

Suzy didn't even pause as she threw out Air and Water creation cores. Light creations picked them up, shooting forward at incredible speeds and burning out their power as they deposited them within the paladins.

The Jukal forces that had paused upon seeing the drones being torn apart by the Water and Air paladins seemed to come out from their reverie as they attacked Anna once again. Their eyes filled with killing intent as they poured out attacks.

Fire, Deia, and Induca could only defend against all of the incoming attacks.

Air and Water appeared away from them and over the attacking forces.

"Interesting." Water's words boomed through the heavens as he stretched out his hands.

Air did the same, channeling their power into the paladins that became more substantial. Their power surged to the heavens and the cores, stabilizing the paladins.

"Lu Lu," Suzy yelled, pointing to the paladins.

Lu Lu turned and unleashed lightning attacks on the paladins. Instead of weakening them, they grew stronger.

"Have you got summoners who can control them?" Anna asked, gritting her teeth. The power fluctuations in front of her created violent ripples in the air.

"I do!" Suzy said. Interface screens flashed around her as she quickly messaged people.

"Releasing control!" Anna said.

The spell formations in front of the Air and Water mages as well as Air and Water dissipated as Lu Lu struck the last of the paladins with all of her strength, looking drained.

"Lu Lu, return." Suzy looked at a paladin, Mana swirling around her and rotating up her staff that Dave had created for her. A stream of runes shot out from her staff, entering the paladin and merging with the two cores inside.

Across the fighting forces, the strongest summoners shot spells of their own. These were command spells that would allow them to take over the cores and command the Air and Water paladins.

Lu Lu, in her weakened state, shrunk till she was the size of a cat, curling around Suzy's shoulders.

Suzy stood there like a war general, looking at the Air paladin that was struck by Jukal fire. The violent green clouds, turning into blades, shredded the attacks before they landed on the Air creation. The Air paladin finished turning and peered down at Suzy.

"Destroy them." Suzy waved her staff at oncoming drones.

The paladin looked to them. Its arm flashed as a spear tore through the sky.

The other paladins came under the control of the summoners and burst into action. The seventy or so paladins shook the air and ground with every movement, and every attack threw the world into chaos.

Momentum returned to the Emerilians as the Water and Air paladins threw the Jukal into a panic.

Anna let out a sigh and released her hands. The spell formation fell away as all of the energy within her seemed to seep out, leaving nothing behind as she started to drop from the sky, barely able to keep her eyes open.

"Fall back!" Deia said. They were still under heavy fire from the Jukal. Flames moved around her as she rocketed down, grabbing Anna. Induca grabbed Suzy, pulling her back, Lu Lu still on her shoulders while Fire covered their retreat. Finally she, too, turned and left.

"I need to get my sword back. So much easier to manipulate the wind with it," Anna murmured, her words only barely audible to Deia, whose eyes flashed at Anna's words.

Seems like she really might be able to get back some of her memories. Should see if getting her back her sword helps with anything.

Deia glanced behind her. The Water and Air paladins were now causing chaos wherever they went. The defenses were falling; the Devastator soldiers were climbing the walls, flying up or using spells to get on top of the defenses.

Behind the defenses, there were still more slaves and defenders waiting in the open area.

After them, there was nothing but craters and destruction. The area where the Jukal planetary governor had resided was nothing but a desolate crater.

Still the Jukal forces and their slaves fought back with all they had. Mage overseers entered the battlefield, calling out terms for surrender.

The slaves didn't even pay attention to the overseers. A number of them attacked them, only to be wiped away by the overseers' powerful counterattack.

"We've got this. Look after Anna," Lox said.

Deia didn't need to say anything as she continued carrying Anna away from battle.

Chapter 11: Grinding Them Down

Dave and Malsour were walking through the portal bastion as it continued to alter and change as the final touches were being added. These final touches would complete all of the soul gem constructs that were running through the sphere-looking creation.

There were hundreds of people moving through the various corridors, double-checking every system and readying the portal bastion; it was so close to completion that Dave almost wanted to send it out ahead of time.

As Dave and Malsour walked, they heard the never-ending chatter of those within the sphere.

"This soul gem rune is weak, going to have to recode."

"Need more power over here!"

Dark mages reformed the walls and the passages, while engineers and magical coding techs worked on the glowing veins that ran throughout the sphere.

"Compression cut off the portal here, interrupting the connection to the Mirror of Communication," a tech said, looking to the other techs with him.

Dave turned to Malsour. "How are we looking for the ranges?"

"Look for yourself." Malsour opened up an image on his interface and shared it with Dave.

An asteroid appeared. Inside, there was a central corridor where carts carrying munitions and people moved back and forth. Off this central corridor, cut roughly from the rock, there were tunnels. At the area closest to the corridor, there were a mass of thousands upon thousands of weapons, all of them set up Gatling style and all pointed at the inactive portals at the other end of the tunnel.

If the portal bastion was the vehicle to get close to the Jukal, Gunboat Isle—as the creators had named it—was where they brought the firepower.

Hardy-looking weapons techs moved through the facility. Guns had been pulled from where they rested; they checked them over, running maintenance before slamming them back into position.

Runic lines that covered the wall that faced the portals were checked and adjusted. Nalheim rested in rooms within the Gunboat Isle, ready to run to their stations that would project them through the portals and create the giants that had been seen in the last fight with the Jukal.

Dave looked at it all. More and more tunnels were being carved out by automated asteroid miners. Behind them, the weapons techs were checking their weapon systems, assembling them and readying them.

Portal techs moved in with a portal seed, connecting it into the massive power grid for the Gunboat Isle. The portals surged upward to connect together.

Row upon row of weapons systems and tunnels with portals could be seen.

"How many are we up to?"

"Eight hundred right now, with another three hundred being built," Malsour said.

"Good. We're going to need them." Dave dismissed the sight as he looked over the ship.

"I heard that you're going to be manning the portal ship," Malsour said.

"Yes, I know her the best. I want to be here if they need me. After the first fight, the crew will know how to use her—most of it's going to be run by the AI anyway. They just need time to gather data before they can do a much better job than I can."

"Mind if I join?" Malsour asked.

Dave looked to Malsour, a smile on his face as he clapped him on the shoulder.

They entered the center of the bastion. Here it looked like a world of gems. Tens of portals were arrayed into a sphere. They linked with one another, starting with just six portals to create a circle at the top. A space broke it up from the next ring of twelve portals; another space between it and the next ring of portals, now twenty-four large. And so it went, more and more portals ringed together until they started decreasing in number and becoming smaller.

Soul gem umbilicals wrapped around strong structural members that were connected to the open areas between the rings came together into the center of the sphere. Here there were four portals, each with a large umbilical cord of soul gem coming from it. This was the command center of the portal bastion. It was also the point through which power was poured into the portal bastion.

As they flew up, Dave looked to the portals. Each of them glowed with power. The walls were covered in soul gem construct that intersected with the portals and the teleport pads that faced them. Behind the teleport pads, there was nothing but compressed metals and stone. Like veins, soul gem constructs spread out in runic lines, reaching out to the surface of the portal bastion, creating onos that covered the sphere's surface and making it look like a massive reflective golf ball.

"Oh, I'm going to need a bigger set of golf clubs." Steve tapped his battle axe.

"You are *not* hitting the giant portal bastion like it's a golf ball," Dave said in a suffering voice.

"Oh, come on! I could probably get the materials. Going to be huuuge!" Steve said.

"Didn't I hear that you were playing golf with your axe through an active portal?" Malsour asked.

"Can I hear universe's longest golf shot?" Steve said proudly.

Dave and Malsour looked to each other before they shook their heads.

"All right, well, I'm off to see the inside of this big ole golf ball. See you in a bit!" Steve headed off by himself.

Malsour and Dave reached the command center, and the soul gem walls opened into a doorway for them. They entered and looked out over the different consoles within. People looked over their systems, running checks with people throughout the bastion. Others were lying back in their chairs, running through simulation after simulation with the bastion.

"Dave." Captain Eswald stood and looked to Dave.

"Captain." Dave nodded his head to her before he turned to Malsour.

"Malsour, it's good to see you." Eswald extended her hand.

"You too." Malsour clasped hands with her for a moment.

"How are we looking?" Dave asked.

"We'll be ready." Eswald's face was like granite, her words an unquestionable promise.

"Good. If you want him, Malsour has offered to assist," Dave said.

"Wouldn't hurt having the guy who built Gunboat Isle onboard." Eswald let out just a hint of a smile. Eswald opened her interface. "If you'll excuse me, got a training session right now."

"Don't let us keep you." Dave quickly moved to exit the command center. "Looks like you have a front row seat now." Dave's armor appeared around him. His cloak fluttered as he stepped out into the air to look at the bastion.

Malsour appeared at his side. "What will the end of this be?"

"For that, not even I know," Dave said, his voice deeper and powerful as he looked to Malsour, his face hidden in his hood.

***

Frank looked to the rest of the Pandora fleet. Once they were repaired enough to move, the nine Pandora fleets had used portals to exit ahead of the Jukal fleet. They had entered a system filled with only asteroids and a red dwarf star at its center.

The Pandora fleet had entered the system, immediately moving into stealth, and proceeded to advance toward the Jukal, who were moving as fast as possible across the system, headed for Emerilia.

They were now just hours from the Jukal. Already missiles had been released in the Pandora fleet's wake. The AIs dropped them down and then moved the whole missile-swarm ahead of the combined fleet, moving closer to the Jukal, ready to erupt with their arcane drives at a moment's notice.

Frank looked to the rear of the *BloodHawk*. Behind it there was a massive ring, a ship-sized portal. It was covered in runes that were supposed to help keep it undetectable as they advanced on the enemy.

"Twenty minutes," Sensors said.

Now that they had gone through a few battles, they had not become numb to it but rather come to understand what was going to happen; they understood the madness that would descend in the fighting and they had worked ways to try to stave it off. All of them wanted to keep fighting, to keep moving and shooting until they won the battle.

Once again, they confronted the devil in their hearts and the devil in front of them.

Time seemed to pass so slowly, everyone on their stations and ready to act in but a moment.

"Moving into engagement range," Sensors said. The command center was quiet as people loosened their necks and flexed their hands. Mana surged through their bodies.

"All ships, fire! *BloodHawk*, bring in the bastion!" Admiral Forsyth yelled.

"Fire!" Frank bellowed. His words passed to the ship. Portals surged from hangars and the one on the nose of the battleship *Blood-Hawk* activated.

The dark missile tubes now lit with light, hurling the missiles out instead of letting them fall away gently.

"Establishing connection!" Communication called out as pandemonium erupted.

The Jukal ships started to turn as the missiles that had been fired in the Pandora fleet's advance now lit up their drives, crossing the remaining distance in seconds. More and more of them waited behind, never-ending waves to keep the Jukal off-balance.

They had needed to get more missiles through their portals in order to keep up the barrage.

The Jukal shields flared to life, their reaction speed incomparable to what it was before.

Even though the Jukal had been thrown off-balance, focusing on watching for the Pandora fleet coming from behind them, their reaction time was faster than it had been the first time the Pandora fleet hit them.

Missiles broke shields and tore through hull panels, striking into the heart of the Jukal ships; there was just too much fire coming in on them to stop it.

"Five minutes till we intersect the Jukal!" Sensors called out. "They're flushing drones!"

"Connection established!" Communications called out.

The portal behind the *BloodHawk* surged with energy, a beacon in the middle of battle. Two fleets surrounded the *BloodHawk* in close, focusing on defending the battleship and the massive portal behind it.

A new space could be seen through the portal, showing new stars as a rounded surface came through the portal. The rounded surface became bigger and bigger, turning into a sphere that was only slightly smaller than the portal it was coming through.

It took two minutes before the massive portal bastion transitioned through the portal that had been made for it in the space around the asteroid base and the portal that was being dragged by the *BloodHawk*.

Frank looked at it with astonishment as an explosion struck the *BloodHawk*'s Mana barrier, making it shudder and bringing him back to his senses.

The portal bastion glowed with powerful light. Waves of Mana emanated from its surface as one of the onos on its surface flashed with light. An event horizon appeared. Just moments before a spell formation tore through the event horizon, arcane fire tore outward.

The bastion started to let out even more powerful waves of power as it surged ahead. More onos activated; from them, energy pillars shot outward, creating a spell formation that blossomed around the portal bastion.

More onos opened across the bastion. Hundreds of missiles shot outward from the bastion before turning and heading through the fleet to strike the Jukal.

"Now that's what I'm talking about!" Xiao yelled.

"All ships, increased speed to flank! Give them all we've got!" Forsyth yelled.

The bastion moved into position within the middle of the fleet, all of the ships around it, supporting it and being supported by it. They and the Jukal raced toward one another. The Jukal didn't have many weapons that could face forward. However, they had missiles and drones that rushed through the void, fighting the barrage that the Pandora fleet had unleashed.

Ships presented their sides and unleashed a blinding broadside. The bastion took on the attacks with ease, shrugging them off and doling out as much firepower as two Pandora fleets all by itself.

The onos never stopped being active but inside, the portals changed what they were connected to. The missile spread changed to spell formations. With the rest of the fleet, some five hundred Nalheim avatars appeared, standing in formation before unleashing their devastating attack. Compared to their last attack with the Nalheim, there was little comparison in the sheer scale of power.

A wave of destruction poured out from the Nalheim. As they faded away, other portals were activated in seamless transitions. Beams shot into the void; dragons formed from pure Mana, as large as a battleship. Their roars couldn't be heard but as they looked at the Jukal, their eyes turned red and they shot in their direction. Each of their attacks was enough to shake a continent, let alone a single ship. But here in space against the Jukal, they needed multiple attacks to break down the shields of the Jukal.

Shadow forms of blood reevers and orcs were summoned. They charged under the dragons, rushing through the Jukal ships. The reevers and their riders attacked with all they had. The ships fought back, shooting the creations and causing the magic holding them together to dissipate.

Orbs shot out from portals and from the onos around the bastion. These orbs were similar to Dave's.

They were covered in runes as spell formations appeared around them. They fired out Mana bolts that ravaged the Jukal. A destroyer couldn't take the fire anymore as its hull was holed and the ship's engines started to have difficulty. It drifted off, with the power of the ship dimming before being cut off.

The forces crashed together, broadsides being used by both sides. The orbs flashed with light as they created a secondary Mana barrier around the Pandora ships. Orbs would fail from fire, but other orbs moved to take over the load as destruction caused the void to rumble.

The bastion was a wealth of fire. It unleashed barrages of cannon fire and powerful spell formations. Anything that wasn't facing the Jukal unleashed conjured beasts and missiles.

"Activate teleportation missiles!" Communications said.

Frank input a command. A number of missiles that had passed around the Jukal fleet now activated their grand working warhead. Instead of having a destructive spell imprinted on the grand working, they created shimmering and unstable event horizons around the Jukal.

"Bastion has link!" the communications officer said.

Teleport pads of the bastion connected to the portals that hadn't been activated were now active as the portals unleashed missiles, crossing the short space between the portal and teleport pad, before shooting out of the shimmering points around the Jukal fleet.

Fire was now coming at the Jukal from every direction.

They crossed deeper into the Jukal formations. Orbs failed and Mana barriers weakened, forcing the Pandora ships to teleport away to safety. The bastion looked over the battlefields as if some omnipotent god. As its shield weakened, it would activate a new portal; a new beam of energy surged outward, to fuel the Mana barrier before the first deactivated and the portal inside the bastion connected to another portal in Gunboat Isle.

The bastion was not impervious but the two times its barrier did fail, a half-dozen onos were destroyed on the surface. They started growing back just moments after they were struck, a new Mana barrier in place. It took some time for them to recover and there was a crater on the bastion's surface, but otherwise the onos opened and unleashed destruction on the Jukal once more.

With enough fire, the bastion would fail, but at that time the Jukal weren't coordinated enough to bring all their weapons to bear on the bastion when there were so many other Pandora ships around them.

***

"That's what I'm talking about!" Dave yelled as his hands moved over the different consoles around him.

Malsour laughed as the rest of the bastion's crew passed information, their actions hurried but precise.

Captain Eswald stood above it all, with her words directing the entire bastion. She looked to Dave and Malsour with shock. The power that they were pulling out of the bastion was unlike anything she knew it was possible of doing.

They made it seem easy as they adjusted power flows, called up new weapon systems and implemented them seamlessly. By themselves, they were operating fifty percent of the bastion with ease.

"Gravity missiles!" Dave yelled into a Mirror of Communication connected to Gunboat Isle.

Missiles poured from six portals. The missiles turned into what looked like a spear formation. The lead and side missiles took hits or blew themselves up to stop the Jukal's incoming fire.

They raced into the Jukal fleet, headed straight for a carrier. The missiles looked as if they were almost sentient as they spun off, hitting drones, and rushed through openings.

The carrier that had been out of the fighting now lit up with its own defense systems. Even the few light cannons that were mounted on its hull targeted the missiles, destroying tens of them.

It wasn't enough to stop them all, not even close.

The lead missile's grand working warheads were activated. Power shot through the spell imprint; spell formations appeared around the head of the missiles and from it, powerful beams of light shot out, rocking the carrier's shield. The ship was punctured in places. A few other beams made it through, hitting the hull of the carrier that left deep gouges in its armor.

More missiles followed, exploding against the shield and making it more unstable.

A mere half-dozen grand working missiles were revealed that were nearly twice the length of a normal missile.

They made it through the shield and split up. One raced straight ahead. A spell formation appeared around it, a black and swirling spell formation that distorted space itself.

The spell formation activated. Powerful gravitational ripples shot out, creating a singularity that tore at the Jukal carrier. Its armor was pulled apart and shredded, compressing down more and more as it raced toward the singularity.

The other missiles started to activate their spell formation. Two of them were shot down, but it mattered little.

The converging gravitational waves pulled at one another, creating a gravitational tempest along the side of the carrier. It was as if it were a ship in the midst of a magical storm back on Emerilia.

Its hull was torn to pieces and the ship was being bent, forces pulling it apart piece by piece. Finally, the carrier's structure couldn't take it. The armor broke and twisted; the structural supports and popped struts within the ship gave way as the ship was pulled and compressed by the gravitational forces of the missiles.

It had only taken seconds from the missiles being launched to the carrier starting to collapse, explosions shaking it from the inside.

"Taste my gravity!" Dave hollered, punching his fist into the air. Snakes made of missiles shot out from the portals within the bastion to the teleport pads that connected to the unstable teleport points around the Jukal fleet.

"Drop the needles," Malsour said.

"Now we're talking." Dave laughed.

Eswald looked at them with alarm.

"Gunboat Isle, release needle," Dave said.

"Yes, sir," a dwarf manning a tunnel different from the others said.

In his area, there was no gravity, and the tunnels held three portals. Between the first and second portal in the tunnel he was manning, a massive metal spike was held out over the second portal. The first and second portals were activated, as was the magical coding in the runic lines that ran through the tunnel.

In the air between the first and second portal, gravitational spell formations appeared, becoming more and more substantial.

"Needle away!" the dwarf said.

The needle dropped toward the second portal. As it entered the second portal, it emerged from the first portal. When it exited the gravitational spell, formations increased its speed as it continued the cycle, becoming faster and faster in a matter of seconds.

"Up to speed!" the dwarf called.

"Ono ninety-five," Dave called out as he took command of a portal. Its connected teleport pad and ono ninety-five went silent.

"Connecting," Dave said. The third portal in the tunnel, behind portal two, and a portal on the bastion shone with power as they connected. The teleport pad and ono were left open.

"Ready!" Dave said.

"Needle on its way!" the dwarf yelled.

The needle dropped out of the first portal. It closed behind the needle. The second portal collapsed as well as the needle shot through the empty space inside it and toward the active third portal.

It shot through the third portal, emerging in the bastion, through the teleport pad and out of the ono at speeds that only Dave and Malsour could detect.

"Test is good. Let's get those moving!" Dave said.

In the section of Gunboat Isle that the dwarf had been in, other weapons techs stood at identical tunnels. One by one, just seconds apart, the needles dropped through the first two portals, reaching an incredible speed that would make planets shake and tear air to shreds.

Dave was watching the first needle as it shot out from the bastion. The world seemed to slow as he focused on the needles. Malsour and Eswald also looked at the needle to see what it would do.

A close in defense system of a Jukal ship spun up and rounds spread out to hit it.

Several of the rounds found the needle but with the kinetic energy of the needle, it exploded into fast-moving shrapnel, turning from a simple needle into dozens of much smaller and faster needles.

It tore through the space between vessels. The shrapnel hit the shields of the ship. The shields had already been damaged and there was nothing that it could do as they were fully destroyed and the shrapnel tore through and hit the ship.

The destroyer was rocked sideways as numerous holes appeared in its hull. Some were as big as a fist, others as large as a bus.

Moments later, another needle was shooting out of a portal. But now there were five following it, just seconds after the first.

A Jukal battleship didn't have time to react, only watch as the first needle hit the bow of his ship, piercing through its incredibly heavy armor. The ship reeled backward, the forces of deceleration heavily wounding those inside of the ship.

More rounds came in, one right after another. The beleaguered ship couldn't do anything as the rounds smashed through the opening in its bow or hit its sides. As the needles' momentum was stopped, they shattered, their shrapnel tearing through the ship. Explosions tore through the battleship, shredding everything inside. Much slower pieces of the needle came out of its sides and rear; the engines sputtered and then died as the battleship was dead in the water.

"Needles are good. Give them to the battleships. With their forward portals, they'll be much better at hitting the Jukal and if the AI help them out, they might be able to get them in a broadside," Malsour said.

"I like your thinking, Mister Malsour," Dave said, repeating the orders to Jeeves, who alerted the fire controllers of the battleships and updated their software.

Needles started to shoot out from the bow portals on the battleships, tearing through the Jukal in front of them.

"Ten seconds until we're out of the Jukal fleet," the sensors officer for the bastion said.

"Well, let's make it count!" Captain Eswald said.

Dave looked to his screens. He winced as one of the destroyers tried to activate its teleportation spell, only to be bombarded by multiple Jukal. The destroyer came apart in an explosion of debris.

Here and there, Pandora ships were teleporting away, while Jukal ships lost their shields. There was no way to take in the destruction of it all. The sights of grand working shells and warheads ignited into spell formations that shook the void, the shimmering teleport points where missiles shot out from. Interceptor modules cast spells to break the coding of the laser cannons and shot out thousands of rounds to try to stop the oncoming Jukal missiles that erupted with the power of fusion explosives, battering shields and melting hulls.

Dave lost himself in the fight, the constant rumbling of weapons fire from within the bastion.

As they were in the command center, around them the portals were flickering on and off, connecting to other portals, calling in different weapons fire, or Mana barrier projectors. The teleport pads also winked in and out, connecting to the teleport points as well as the onos.

Light from missile arcane engines or the glowing grand working shells, and the spell formations that were projected outside the hull of the bastion: all of it illuminated the command center resting in the middle of it all.

The crews of the Pandora fleet fought with all they had, knowing that they would not get a chance like this again. Next time, the Jukal would be wary of the bastion and they would be on the lookout for the Pandora ships in all directions.

Drones shot through the Pandora fleet as summoned avatars fought them. The ripples of power coming off from their battle made it seem as if the gods themselves were locked in battle, looking down upon mere mortals.

The ships illuminated with fire as broadsides tore into Jukal and Pandoran ships. Shields and barriers failed; armor was rent, melted and torn away.

Destruction filled the sky of that barren system. In the blood-red sunlight of the main star, two empires clashed.

People yelled and they cried; corridors exploded and people were torn apart. People patched up the ship, others operated their systems, and others waded into those damaged areas. Filled with the power of their stats, they hauled the wounded and the dying through portals back to Ice City before charging back into their ships to get more wounded, to stay in the fight.

The bastion's shields failed along another section. Alarms rang out as missiles closed in on the massive sphere. The Jukal saw the bastion as something that could not live in the same star system as them. Drones unloaded their missiles into the bastion. Explosions rippled over its surface as the drone's light cannons cut deep grooves in the compressed armor of the bastion. Missiles came in, exploding and shaking the bastion, breaking down more of its Mana barriers and covering it in flames.

"Come on, baby!" Dave poured power into the soul gem constructs. To him, with his Soul Smithing art, it was as if he were wearing the ship, the soul gem an extension of himself as he called on it to get the onos back in working order.

"Focus everything on offense! We can take it!" Eswald barked to her people.

The bastion weathered the storm. Missiles exploded around her as laser cannons from the Jukal ships carved their enmity into her surface.

None of the portals opened to reveal interceptors; none of them paused in their firing as they continued to unleash attacks on the Jukal. As they were now passing through the center of the Jukal formation, all of their actions up to this point of time had happened in minutes. With all the moving parts, it felt like an eternity but also a fleeting moment.

Wreathed in plumes of destruction, lit up with the explosions of grand workings and warheads, covering the skies in spell formations: they might not have the history of the Jukal fleet, but they were no less fierce.

The bastion continued on, a juggernaut of space and all within its range, unafraid of its wounds or the possibility of death and being destroyed. It shuddered and shook, its Mana barriers all gone. The portals that had been sustaining the Mana barrier now linked to Gunboat Isle with weapons fire pouring from its portals.

Dragons appeared from onos, all of them appearing around the bastion. Their bodies shook with their roars as they circled the bastion, solidifying and then shooting ahead with unimaginable power.

The Jukal ships that were covered in flashing lights of missiles leaving their tubes and laser cannons hammering the Pandora fleet now turned to face these dragons. Their battle shook the void and the heavens.

They cleared a path for the fleet as they shot through. Everything had happened in mere moments, but for those who had high Intelligence, they were able to see all that was going on. They had pushed themselves to their limits, and past, doing all they could to put the Jukal in a bad position and help the Pandora fleet.

The fleets left one another, still firing as they went.

"Full defensive mode. Get your ships in fighting order and flip the fleet!" Admiral Forsyth barked. The bastion's onos that were spewing arcane fire closed, turning into more weapon ports as on the opposite side of the bastion, arcane fire shot out, fighting against the momentum it had built up. The rest of the Pandora fleet flipped over so their engines were facing the way they were going. The spell formations for the arcane fire flared with light.

From the portals and the bastion's onos, shield spell formations appeared and covered the entire fleet. Jukal fire rained down on the shields; however, their missiles were becoming less and less effective, as they just wasted ammunition.

The teleportation points which had already been failing, destroying what was passing through them with the fluctuations of the spell formation, now finally collapsed.

Across the fleet, power poured into the soul gem constructs. Techs went about fixing their ships while Devastator-armored personnel moved through areas that had been damaged, searching for survivors, collecting them up and getting them to safety or back to Ice City and the healing center there.

"Have the ships that teleported out return when they're ready. I want us to be stocked and ready to fight. In four hours, we'll hit them again," Forsyth broadcasted to the rest of the fleet.

Now that the Jukal were reeling and they had the bastion, they needed to keep them off-balance and grind them into nothing.

Dave and the people of the bastion talked to one another, focusing on areas to repair and reporting any issues they had. Techs from the asteroid base flooded the bastion and used its portals and teleport pads to bring shuttles through, exiting into space and moving to aid the rest of the fleet that was in close to the bastion.

All of the ships showed signs of battle damage. They had lost seven ships; some thirty-five had needed to teleport out.

The Jukal had suffered for clashing with the Pandora fleet.

Forty-seven ships had been destroyed. Five more of them were so badly damaged that they were barely able to fly, nothing more than moving scrap. Twelve ships had battle damage that would take days to repair; multiple ships had their weapons smashed, or their hangars open to space.

Many of the ships had been mauled, but some were still perfectly fine. They'd been hiding behind their fellows in order to stave off disaster instead of being part of the fight and trying to attack the Pandora fleet and help their allies.

"I wonder just how much ammunition and supplies they have left," Dave said.

"We'll just have to test them and see," Malsour said.

The Jukal had been able to wrestle control of some portals back to them. However, now Ice City and the people aboard the *Datskun* were working day and night to hack them. They didn't think they would get control of the portals for more than a few hours, but it made it so that the Jukal portals were unstable, making their use nearly impossible.

The Jukal fleet only had the parts, fuel, and ammunition that was stored within their hulls. They hadn't brought any support vessels; such things had not been a part of the Jukal Empire for decades.

With the three massive battles the Jukal invasion fleet had gone through, they'd expended thousands of missiles and rounds. They might also have items of holding, but there was a limit to how many even those types could hold.

The Jukal poured in all the speed that they could to try to get away from the demons that were the Emerilians.

"I wonder if they're even thinking about the fact that they're fleeing toward Emerilia." Dave's cold chuckles were enough to make people's skin prickle.

"It seems that Forsyth is determined to stop this here," Malsour said.

"Well, we'd best get this fleet in fighting shape!" Dave said with vigor. He knew that a number of people had died in the last battle, but he couldn't let himself focus on that now. After the fighting was done he could; thinking of the losses now would only make him useless to the people around him.

Dave bent over his console and submerged his mind into the soul gem constructs of the ship as Blood Kin appeared through a portal and started to repair the damaged areas of the bastion. It didn't need much in the way of fixing before they moved to help the other vessels throughout the fleet.

Three hours later, the ships that were in the best condition poured power into teleportation spells. The bastion rumbled as a spell formation appeared around it. It was one of the only spells that was actually built into the runic lining of the massive sphere. The others all dealt with moving power and keeping the portals active, as well as their control run back to the command center.

Fifty-nine ships disappeared from where they were, appearing off the bow of the Jukal fleet that was limping away.

The portals roared into life as missiles shot out. These formed together into missile snakes, darting into the Jukal fleet that erupted with fire.

Those of the Pandora fleet who were broadside to broadside with the Jukal unleashed needles and spell formations from the portals that were above and below their ships, as well as fire from their cannons.

The Pandora fleet let out several barrages. The Jukal were sent into chaos before the Pandora fleet surged with power and teleported away. The bastion was the last to do so, covering their retreat.

They hadn't been able to do it before, for fear that one of their ships would be left behind. Now that the bastion was there, it could withstand being hammered and cover the Pandora fleet as they shot off into the distance.

Penetrator spell formations shone with Mana as they punched holes into the Jukal fleet. Barriers, gravity missiles, two-stage missiles, needles, and more tore at the Jukal. Teleport point missiles activated their grand working.

The bastion activated its portals, becoming a bridge between the teleport points and Gunboat Isle.

The teleport points around the Jukal fleet and inside it was spewing fountains of fire and spell formations, the Jukal fighting against what emerged while the Pandora fleet was well out of range.

Two hours later, the Pandora fleet did it again, transitioning in again and unleashing hell before teleporting away. Teleportation point grand workings were hidden in the snake-like grouping of missiles, allowing the bastion to once again act as a bridge.

This wasn't a battle; it was an extermination as they ground down the Jukal as if they were nothing but simple mobs.

As crews got tired, they switched out with fresh crews in the asteroid base. Emerilia didn't have many ships, but they had plenty of trained people who stepped up.

With every attack, the overseer mages talked on every channel, giving the Jukal terms for surrender.

With each attack, more of the Pandora ships would be cleared for action and join in, while more of the Jukal ships were destroyed.

The Pandora fleet evolved a strategy that allowed them to only teleport in for a few seconds, dropping off a salvo of missiles before disappearing once again.

After three attacks, there were more broken ships than there were functional. The remaining ships didn't have the room for all of the Jukal. That was when they started to surrender. After the fourth attack, the Emerilians held position; destroyers moved in toward the Jukal that were surrendering. Teleportation spells pulled them into the destroyers, where Devastator-armored ground forces secured them with sealing magic and sent them through a portal back to Emerilia.

With the events of Myths and Legends and the portals opening on Emerilia, the planet had been thrown into disarray. However, with the Jukal, they now gained new helpers. But the Jukal weren't used to hard labor and they hadn't undergone nanite enhancement like the people of Emerilia and the players. They were about the same strength as the children after Bob raised everyone to be his champions.

The Pandora fleet paused their efforts, recovering their lost strength with satisfaction and not a little relief.

Dave looked over the fleet, and felt the auras of those within the command center with him. They were like a pack of wolves, licking their wounds and looking at their wounded prey as it limped away, the last of their strength fading.

"It might be cheap as hell, but I'm here to abuse the system," Dave muttered to himself. As if hearing his words, notifications started to appear.

Quest: Friend of the Grey God Level 8

Free Emerilia

Rewards: Unlock Level 9 Quest

+10 to stats (stacks with previous class levels)

+800,000 EXP

Class: Friend of the Grey God

Status:	Level 9
	+90 to all stats
	Access to hidden quests.
Effects:	Access to the Imperial Carrier *Datskun*

Quest: Friend of the Grey God Level 9
Defeat the Jukal Empire
Rewards: Unlock Level 10 Quest
Increase to stats
Quest Completed: Bleeder Level 7
Free Emerilia
Rewards: Unlock Level 8 Quest
+10 increase to stats (stacks with previous class levels)
+700,000 EXP
Class: Bleeder

Status:	Level 7
Effects:	+70 to all stats
	Ability to use Jukal Link

Quest: Bleeder Level 8
Defeat the Jukal Empire
Rewards: Unlock Level 9 Quest
Increase to stats

***

The Jukal emperor was raging around his room. He had accidentally killed three of his concubines; the others cowered away from him. The first person to enter the room he'd simply gestured to—their body exploded into gore that covered the floors and doors.

It had taken five subsequent attacks from the Emerilians, over the space of two days, to sap the fighting spirit of the Jukal invasion fleet.

The Jukal officers had been only using the fleet as a way to give rise to their position within the empire. Seeing so many of their fellows die and being hounded by the Emerilians, not knowing when they would die, they'd surrendered.

The destroyers had moved in under the cover of the entire fleet as they moved ship by ship, having the Jukal exit the ships and then teleport them away, never to be seen again.

Once the ships were cleared of Jukal, the ground fighting forces of the Pandora Initiative got to work, being dropped onto the ships by the destroyers they moved through, making sure that there was no one left and then taking command of the ships. A ship-sized portal was pulled out from a battleship and was under construction when the feeds to the Jukal ships were cut by the Devastator ground forces in the ships.

The emperor, for the first time in a long time, was actually on his feet. His body contained power that was many times greater than the members of the Pantheon.

With his power and AI, he was unstoppable.

"Nephew," the emperor's uncle said softly.

The emperor let out another roar and punched out at a wall. The force of his fist moving through air turned into a tempest that tore through the wall. The emperor looked to his uncle, his eyes red as his upper chest/neck pulsed in and out and his tongue moved wildly in anger.

The room had been cleared of everyone else, his uncle dismissing them and the door being closed behind him.

"How did this happen! I ordered them to win!" the emperor barked.

"Now is not the time to focus on the battles that have been had, but the ones that are to come," the emperor's uncle said.

"We've lost dozens of systems." The emperor waved his hand casually. A screen appeared in the air, showing videos of the Terra Alliance's and Pandora Initiative's ground forces crushing the defenses and the fighting forces that were in their path as Deq'ual ships controlled the orbitals and the arks rested in the air, dropping off more and more ground forces. "Why won't they just stop! It's so annoying!"

The emperor went on to wreck other priceless heirlooms that were thousands of years old.

"The next battle will be within the Jukal system," the emperor's uncle said.

"When?" the emperor demanded.

"I don't know. We need to do something to force their hand so that they will attack faster rather than later. Do something that will make them have to come fight us here. If they come here, then we have all of our defenses and your army to defeat them," the emperor's uncle said.

The light in the emperor's eyes dimmed slightly as he seemed to consider his uncle's words.

"Ahh!" The emperor let out another bellow. A pillar of light shot out from him, shooting through the ceiling. The light passed through several floors of the emperor's ancestral mansion, to be seen from orbit and by those on the planet, turning the night of the Jukal home world into day.

His uncle's face didn't even flicker at the destruction or power that the emperor had unleashed, as if it was all to be expected.

"Uncle! We shall bring them to the Jukal home system and we will destroy them!" the emperor bellowed.

"Very well, Nephew. In the meantime, do you wish to look over your army?" the emperor's uncle said.

The emperor let out a harrumph but the power surging through his body dimmed and a bit of excitement showed on his face.

"If the Emerilians make it here, then I will be able to watch my army defeat them! Maybe it won't be so bad! We should make sure that we capture it all. I don't want to miss it!" The emperor now had a beaming smile on his face as he happily followed his uncle.

Chapter 12: Take That, Jukal

Josh looked out over Terra. People could be heard cheering; bars were open and people were dancing in the streets as bards and bands tried to outdo one another in spreading cheer.

The tension that had been sitting over Terra and Emerilia for the last couple of weeks had been broken. People finally left behind that fear as information came in about the Pandora fleet's victory over the Jukal invasion fleet. Now there was only the fleet that was hiding in the Jukal home system that could threaten Emerilia. All across Emerilia, similar celebrations were rocking the cities and nations of the world.

There was a pop inside the command center as someone pulled out a bottle of champagne, the cork flying off as someone else produced glasses.

Cassie moved toward Josh, receiving some champagne on the way as Josh pulled out a beer from his bag, specially brewed by Dave.

"Cheers." She reached out her glass toward him.

"Cheers." Josh tapped his bottle against her glass as they turned to look over Terra.

The people in the command center who had been wound up tight since the beginning of the Myths and Legends event now finally let their inhibitions go as they drank and celebrated.

"So, we've defeated the Jukal Empire," Cassie said, her words carrying a note of disbelief.

"We haven't beaten them yet. We've just gained time for us to prepare for the last battle. We won't be the only ones. The Jukal know most of our tricks now and they're going to be ready for us," Josh said.

"But for the moment, there's no invasion fleet coming our way; we have removed any Jukal influence from thirty-seven star systems. The people there are starting to come to support us. With the videos of our victory, more of them will cast off the Jukal Empire." Cassie sipped from her champagne.

Josh took a long draw from his beer and leaned on the balcony's railing, taking in the moment and looking at a free Emerilia. "We did it—five hundred years and we did it," Josh said softly.

Cassie didn't have any words for him and chose to rest her head on his shoulder.

He smiled at her, putting his arm around her waist. Josh knew that this wasn't the end, but for today, he wanted to celebrate being free.

**

The Pandora fleets continued to capture more Jukal, shipping them to Emerilia. Ships covered in battle damage passed through the ship portals and entered the asteroid base, where they were escorted to empty slips to be evaluated or repaired.

Frank looked over the asteroid base. There were more ships under construction than ever before. Ships that had been badly damaged were in parts, with automatons and techs working to get them back into fighting condition. Well, the automatons were—the techs and shipbuilders were all celebrating, waving wildly at the returning ships.

Frank looked at them and realized they were waving at the *BloodHawk*, at the people inside, at him. It was an odd thing to see and realize, but unknowingly his body relaxed as he sank back into his seat slightly.

Navigation guided them into a slip; soul gem umbilicals reached out to secure them. Techs cast spells on the ship, getting a better idea of the damage as the teleport pads inside the ship linked up to the asteroid base.

"All right, keep an eye out for upcoming orders. We'll be operating in quarter-strength shifts. See your chain of command for leave," Captain Xiao said.

Frank got a message, telling him that he was off for the next three days, with him needing to report to the *BloodHawk* afterward. He quickly passed his station off to those who were staying aboard the ship, then used the teleport pad to exit the *BloodHawk*. As he did so, he and the other members of the *BloodHawk* were greeted by cheers.

The people of the asteroid base were out in full force, cheering and congratulating all of those who returned from the fighting.

Frank couldn't stop a smile from covering his face as he laughed. A bottle of something was passed to him. He took a deep swig, letting out a gasp as he passed the fiery dwarven whiskey to whoever was behind him and continued onward.

All of the bases for both Emerilia and the Deq'ual system were celebrating.

***

Party Zero's celebrating was a little lower keyed—well, except for Gurren, Lox, and Steve, who were using the hell out of the Stone Raiders' free teleport pad pass to get to every party they could find across all of the linked systems and bases.

They were in Dave and Deia's home in Cliff-Hill, gathered together, eating food, having a few drinks, and falling into conversations with one another.

Dave and Bob sat along the side of what was now Dave's shed, sitting on its porch and looking out over Cliff-Hill.

"Seems so long ago when you appeared on this porch in your recliner." Dave smiled as he looked to Bob.

"Ah, you were nothing but a new player making a house and trying to get away from it all. Seems you're still doing that." Bob tilted his glass to Dave in salute.

Dave just laughed and continued to sit there, looking at Emerilia.

"People are already starting to come back from Ice Planet and the asteroid base," Bob said. "Without the threat of the Jukal invasion, they want to come home. Some are sticking around."

"If the Jukal do come for Emerilia again, we'll have plenty of warning to move people to the bases," Dave said.

They lapsed into silence again, thinking about the war, thinking about the path that they had both taken to get here.

"I still can't believe it," Dave said.

"Believe what?" Bob turned to Dave.

"Believe that we were actually able to go up against the Jukal Empire and pull off a win that was so big that they're the ones stuck in their own system," Dave said.

"I have a feeling that we won't ever get used to the idea." Bob paused. "What are you going to do now?"

"You make it sound as if this is all over." Dave chuckled, but there was no humor in his laugh as he took a hefty drink from his bottle. "Spend some time with Deia, Koi, and everyone, look over my ongoing projects. I want to build a second bastion, but it's going to be one hell of an undertaking. They've proved their use and we're going to need them if we go charging into the Jukal system. The flying citadels are being prepared. I want to check them over and make sure everything is going smooth. The people of Ice City and the asteroid base don't need me to be over their shoulders. They know what they're doing and if they need me, they'll tell me."

"Wouldn't mind the Jukal leaving us alone for years and then suing for peace." Bob leaned forward, resting his arms on his knees, and let out a deep breath.

"Why do I think you feel that isn't going to happen?" Dave asked.

"The Jukal, well, they've ruled the empire for hundreds of years. They think of themselves as the best race out of all others. Their fleet is the most powerful. Nothing that anyone else does could ever shake their foundation. Even with everything that we've done, their arrogance has reached a point that they're blind to their losses. They aren't turning their economy over to start building more ships and prepare for our arrival. They think of us as nothing but a minor annoyance. As such, they're bound to do something in order to fight back. They're not going to be cautious about it, either. We're going to have to scramble and bring everything to bear and crush whatever they do. If we don't, then they're going to keep on doing it again and again. Just as we wore down the Jukal invasion fleet, they'll wear us down. They might be arrogant bigots, but they have the firepower and fighting ability to make us have to take every action they do seriously."

They lapsed into silence, hearing the noises coming from the main house as people talked and laughed.

"Are you two coming for dinner?" Deia yelled over to them from the main house. On her hip, she held the growing Koi, who was happily chewing on some toy of hers.

"Coming." Dave stood and Bob joined him. They put smiles on their faces and moved to the main house. There, Draculs, members of Party Zero, and their friends were all gathered. Even with the war only paused, the house was filled with laughter and joy as they all moved around a massive table on the house's back porch.

Desmond, Fire and Mal's son and Deia's brother, and Koi, as well as Quindar and Fornau's children, were all pooled together at one table, with the parents doing shifts to look after them as well as people from the adult table.

Dave held Deia's hand. His finger rubbed over the engagement ring he had given her and he looked into her eyes.

A true smile spread across his face as Deia squeezed his hand.

"All right, pass some of that boar down here, Malsour. You could eat like a dragon!" Dave yelled.

People around the table chuckled as food was passed around.

"I told you we should have left earlier! There's going to be no food left!" Steve's voice could be heard, as could his thumping footsteps.

"You can't even eat or drink!" Lox sounded as though he were in pain.

"You're a peer-pressuring drinking bully," Gurren said.

The trio came around the corner of the house, Gurren pointing at Steve in accusation.

"What? It's funny seeing you guys trying to drink a barrel of beer all by yourself." Steve shrugged as if it were perfectly normal.

Lox made moaning noises as he held his head. His eyes fell on Jung Lee, as if he had found his savior.

"Jung Lee!" The pale Gurren and Lox both cried out at the same time.

"You know, I was a world-renowned potion maker in my time," Jung Lee grumbled, pulling out two potions and tossing it to them.

Lox drank it down all in one go, his face becoming a healthier color. "Tastes god-awful, but in my book you're the greatest potion maker in two star systems!"

"No, in thirty-nine!" Gurren declared before he turned to Lox. "How many of them have we captured? I lost count."

Lox looked at Gurren in disbelief.

"You have permission," Kol, Dave's mentor and Gurren's grandfather, said.

Without even a second of pause, Lox clipped Gurren around the head.

"Grandad!" Gurren yelled out in betrayal as he rubbed his head. It was clear it hadn't hurt him as much as he was complaining.

"Learn how to count!" Kol said with a huff. "Now sit down and get some food!"

The table laughed, used to their antics, as everyone joined the table. In minutes, Kol was fussing over Gurren, and Lox was having a drink with Jung Lee.

"Seems that Lee might need a remedy or two of his own tomorrow," Deia muttered to Dave.

Dave chuckled, saying nothing, and took a bite of the food on his plate. He smiled, letting his worries go as he looked over the table—the joking, the talking, the smiles, and laughter.

***

Celebrations continued on for a week. People's spirits were lifted and many, now without the pressure of the Jukal at their doorsteps, went out and raised their levels, working harder than ever before.

Dave and Malsour appeared in mid-air. They looked out over a group of citadels. In the middle of them, instead of there being a portal, nothing remained; the portals had been collected together, altered and then used in the war effort.

Even without the portal there, the citadels were a hive of activity. These now had four rings of defensive walls around them as the Emerilians had controlled them for so long.

Just a few moments after they had arrived, the ground around one of the citadels started to shake violently.

"Cutting it close?" Malsour asked as the citadel started to rise from the ground. Rocks fell from it as the runic lines that were part of its structure glowed and a soul gem island underneath the citadel was revealed.

"Close enough." Dave shrugged.

"It was a good idea to upload the plans from the flying citadels to the soul gem constructs that were already in the other citadels. We'll get another forty-eight citadels ready to fly with nearly no manpower needed in just three months," Malsour said.

"How are the modifications going on the first two flying citadel groups?" Dave asked, watching as the newly minted flying citadel moved off from where it had risen out of the ground, the flight crew testing out the citadel. Another citadel started to shake and then lift into the sky.

"The new cannons have been put in, as have the drop runes to teleport the forces inside to the ground, just like the arks and destroyers. We've got a few tubes for the grand working missiles. They're so powerful that using them inside a planet is risky. It will help a lot in the final battle," Malsour said.

"The shields were upgraded and the portals added?"

"Yeah, and some of the magical coding techs have been working on a spell formation that will allow the citadels to make a shield that not even the Jukal's orbitals will be able to get through," Malsour said.

"Good. I'm also worried about how strong the Jukal forces are going to be on the ground. They've been fighting us with their enhanced slaves—they're going to be a pain in the ass to fight. They were powerful on the other planets. However, on the home world they'll be undeniably stronger. Then there's the rumor that the emperor has nanites running through his system and can call down magic much like the members of the Pantheon can," Dave said.

"It's disturbing, but then we do have a plan in place to deal with him."

"I hope it works," Dave said.

They teleported away from the rising citadel, going through teleport pads and onos until they reached another location. Here, there were sixteen citadels dotted around the sky. These were the original flying citadels that had taken part in the event and watched as the Pantheon was torn apart.

Their walls were scarred from battle and their cannons were the same as those that were mounted on the spacefaring ships. They dominated the sky, with an imposing aura that made one look at them in awe and respect.

These citadels all had seven walls around them, heavily upgraded Aleph repeaters that would now be able to take down drones, not just flying creatures. Interceptor modules lined the outer walls and some of the strong points.

As they watched, the runic lines under the citadels flashed with light and fighters appeared on the ground. They were running multiple scenarios. The crews of the citadels fired their weapons and went through the motions; however, the ground didn't explode and instead of spell formations unleashing powerful spells that would make the ground shake, they faded out of existence.

Dave looked off into the distance. There was Goblin Mountain. It had been through so many evolutions that it was thoroughly different. It looked as if the top of the mountain had been cut off; in fact, it lay off to the side in pieces. Instead of a mountain peak, a massive ship portal stood in its place.

Dave looked off into the distance. Casting his Touch of the Land spell, he was able to see recently completed flying citadels that were headed for Goblin Mountain.

Once again, they continued on their path, checking over the various projects expanding to cities across Emerilia. People were moving in bands to check out the abandoned areas across many zones. Farmers were returning to their fields and cities were once again bustling without being overcrowded.

They went to the moonbase, which was covered in techs, both checking weapon systems built into the moon and building more missile boats between the multiple catwalks that formed slips, extending through the moon.

They took a shuttle to look over Terra that was itself undergoing massive changes.

Dave and Malsour went back to the moonbase, what had been the Jukal base but had since been converted for use by the Emerilians. Then it was off to Ice Planet and Nal. The portal on the Nalheim home planet had been reactivated and a new settlement was being started there. Some people didn't like living in a city that was surrounded by a Mana barrier that kept them from freezing.

They went through the asteroid base, seeing the damage to the Pandora fleet up close; crews were working hard to get them back into fighting condition. One fleet was holding position over Emerilia while two more had portaled into the Jukal Empire and were once again assisting the Deq'ual system ships that had been fighting through the heart of the Jukal Empire.

Many had been asking why the Deq'ual fleet hadn't been helping against the Jukal invasion force. The reason was that their stealth runes weren't as powerful as the ones on the Pandora ships and they didn't have teleportation spells or portals in their ships. They were more likely to become a liability and harder to resupply and evacuate than the Pandora ships.

Though they hadn't been sitting back by any means. They had advanced system by system, covering the forces that went down, and removed the Jukal influence while clearing the skies and dealing with any Jukal ships that had escaped their sensors as well as defenses and stations.

Dave and Malsour parted, Malsour headed to the Densaou Ring of Fire while Dave exited into Cliff-Hill and then teleported into his home.

There were people throughout the home. Bob's carrier, the *Datskun*, had techs poring over it, trying to learn all of its secrets, so, he and Anna were spending time with each other at Dave and Deia's home, even though they both had places in Ice City. Here they could get away from their worries for a bit longer.

Suzy was working from the main office of the Grahslagg Corporation in Cliff-Hill and Induca was helping people out around Cliff-Hill.

Dave changed into simple comfortable clothes, his armor disappearing. He could hear Deia talking softly and encouraging little Koi. He came around a doorway, his steps coming to a halt as he looked at the sight of Deia watching little Koi as she crawled and wandered around the living room floor, a pleased and excited smile on her face.

Dave crossed his arms, a proud smile on his face as he watched Deia and Koi. Dave had never had this, being able to come back from a day of work and come back to a family. He leaned against the doorway, taking it in.

It took a few minutes before Deia realized that someone else was in the room. She looked over, seeing Dave. "Seems like your daughter is going to get up to all kinds of trouble now." Deia smiled.

"Oh, I like how she's *my* daughter when she gets into trouble." The corner of Dave's mouth pulled up slightly as he pushed off the wall and moved toward Koi.

"Well, if she didn't get in trouble, she'd be like the paragon of virtue her mother is," Deia said, putting on airs as she flicked her hair over her shoulder.

"That's a good girl. Look at you. You're crawling all on your own." Dave crouched down, talking to Koi to rile up Deia.

Koi, seeing her father, happily slapped the ground with her little hands, and pushed herself toward him with wobbly movements.

Dave stretched out his arms, waiting for her to get into reach before he picked her up into a hug. "That's my girl! You're going to get all big and strong." Dave pulled up her shirt and blew a raspberry on her tummy.

Koi let out happy noises but turned toward the floor again.

"Okay, off you go!" Dave lowered her back down to the floor as she continued on her adventure.

Deia and Dave sat on a couch, watching Koi as she crawled through the living room. Dave rubbed Deia's leg as she sat on her legs and curled up close to him, her eyes following Koi's every movement.

"Out of everything I've made, I'd say she's the best one," Dave said.

Deia chuckled as if she were holding onto some great secret. Dave looked to her as Deia smiled at him slyly. "Just wait till she's a teenager." Deia laughed.

"Can we just keep her at this age?"

"I wish." Deia sighed as her fingers traced lines up and down his arm.

Koi started to pull on a tablecloth with things on it.

Deia made to move as Dave teleported over, holding the table-cloth in place.

"I now know why we shouldn't look away for a moment," Dave said, organizing things so Koi couldn't hurt herself.

***

Anna braced herself, her flickering emotions making her anxious as she played with her fingers.

She would prefer to go and fight off the Jukal Empire and bring destruction raining down from the heavens all over again than deal with the anxiousness that was building up in her guts.

Alkao hadn't come to the get-together at Dave and Deia's home. Anna felt as though she had been on a tightrope with her emotions, looking around and expecting for him to show up at any moment. When he hadn't appeared, she'd found herself feeling upset by it. She had faint memories of Alkao, but they were more like a confusing bundle of emotions than anything tangible.

A part of her just wanted to run away; another part of her made her grit her teeth and dig her feet in, as if nothing would stop them from meeting.

She knew that Alkao had excused himself from the gathering by saying that he had things to deal with back in Devil's Crater. Even though it made sense to her, a part of Anna was disappointed.

So now she found herself in Devil's Crater with her father, who'd pushed for her to go. The different guards looked at Anna with complicated expressions. They all knew how she didn't have all of her memories.

They reached Alkao's office, his secretary waiting for them.

"He's ready for you." The secretary smiled to Anna.

"I'll be here," Bob said.

"Okay," Anna said, not giving herself time to back out as she walked toward the door into Alkao's office.

She passed through the door and looked at Alkao, who was working on documents. Clearly his secretary hadn't told him that Anna was coming.

"What is it?" Alkao asked, not looking up.

Anna didn't say anything. Her emotions pulled her in multiple different directions as she was unable to do anything as she studied him. Conflicted about what she liked about him, knowing her own stubborn personality, she remembered the videos of her and Alkao fighting for him to gain a place in her heart.

She could see how that Anna had allowed him into her heart long before their sparring stopped.

But as she had watched it, a stranger looking through a window, it felt as if she were stealing that Anna's position. She hadn't gone through those moments, only seen some of them from afar.

Alkao frowned and looked up. His eyes widened as they met with Anna's.

Anna felt something stirring within her as time seemed to pause. The two of them looked to each other, a complicated expression on Anna's face as Alkao's bloomed into a smile while his eyes watered at the same time.

"Anna." He said her name softly, as if breathing too hard might make her disappear.

"Hello, Alkao," Anna said, her voice more formal.

Alkao looked confused but then quickly hid it, as if remembering something. A look of pain hid deep within his eyes as his smile darkened slightly. "Bob told me that you've lost most of your memories from the last time you were woken up on Emerilia." Alkao stood and towered over Anna.

She noticed he was still wearing armor and on his hip there was a sword. Her eyes latched onto it, feeling a resonance with it.

Alkao followed her eyes, looking to the sword. He gave out a short laugh and his hand came to rest on the sword. To anyone else it would be a great sword; to him, it was just a slightly long sword. He ran his finger over the hilt, his eyes filled with memories.

He undid the sword belt, which was actually meant to go over a person's back. He held the sword in his hands before he walked over to Anna, holding it out with two hands. It clearly held a special place in his heart.

"It seems it's about time I returned this to you." He looked up to see whether there was any reaction before once again looking to the sword. He tried to hide the pain in his eyes, but Anna was able to see it.

She wanted to reach out and take his hand, but her mind resisted. She didn't want to give him false hope. She wasn't that Anna from before.

"Thank you," Anna said, not able to look him in the eyes as she received the sword. She put her hand on the hilt and pulled the sword out from its scabbard.

She looked at the oddly designed blade. It felt right holding the sword as she moved it through the air. It let out a sad note; with a flick of her hand, it was cut off and it stilled. The air in the room seemed to bow in reverence to the sword, eager to fulfill its command.

Anna felt something odd about the sword's aura. She studied it closer, until she found something in the blade that shouldn't have been there. She cast out a spell to increase her perception and see through the sword. Her eyes glowed with light as information filled her mind. Not just any information—memories.

After about five minutes, she stumbled backward, her face pale. An excited look was on Anna's face. *Damn, I'm a genius.* Anna looked to Alkao. He frowned slightly, as if sensing a change within her.

Sadly, the memories her old incarnation had imprinted into the core of the sword filled up some of the blanks and she knew with time, it would speed up her recovery. But with Alkao, there was only a glimmer of emotions.

"Thank you for taking care of it. I'll see you later," Anna said, seeing how the words seemed to tear into Alkao. But still he kept a smile on his face, and the affection in his eyes didn't dim in the slightest.

That more than anything moved her heart, as she yearned to remember more of this man, to know the depths of their relationship.

"Look after yourself, Anna." Alkao made to move forward, but hesitated and pulled back, instead smiling to her.

"Thank you, Alkao." Anna bowed her head slightly. She placed the sword back in its scabbard and turned around, leaving.

"I will love you now and always. If I have to fight for your love again, I would do it without hesitation."

Alkao's voice was soft, barely audible. Anna only barely heard it as she was halfway out the door. Her footsteps paused for half a second as she heard the grief, pain, and longing in his voice, but also a determination and love that empowered him.

She continued out, not looking back, her emotions even more complicated than before as she gripped her sword tightly.

I will remember you, Alkao! Anna vowed to herself, thinking of the massive demon who could make the ground shake and the heavens bow at his commands. But in that time she had seen him, she'd seen the broken man inside who had lost his love and had nothing but hope to cling to. That hope was in the shape of Anna's reincarnation.

Chapter 13: Ruffling Feathers

"What is it?" Malsour asked.

"A bastard creation." Dave looked at the hologram in the middle of the room. The people who had made the original portal bastion prototype were all gathered together, looking at the odd vessel in front of them.

"Okay, so it's a drone shuttle?" Ela-Dorn asked.

"We need a big combat booster in this coming fight. We've got the first portal bastion completed. A second is nearing completion and will be ready for battle. However, that still isn't enough. We just don't know when we're going to be fighting the Jukal and we don't know if we can get many more of the massive ships of the fleet completed. So, we're going to need to think outside of the box. These are portal relays." Dave waved to the hologram, shared via their interfaces, as an animation started.

"They are small enough to exit the smaller ground portals that we've festooned our ships with. They will also be unmanned; all of that gear will be torn out. To replace it, they will be filled with charged soul gems and have multiple soul gem construct seeds for portals. They will flood through the portals of the fleet, and the charged soul gem will pour power into the seeds. The first seed will grow into a portal that is linked by an umbilical to a massive power bank here. Power will be poured through, much like how we've been doing with the bastions.

"This power and the remaining stored power will go into the remaining portals seeds which, located on the outside of the ship, will swarm and cover the ship, creating a sphere of portals. These will be controlled by sub-AIs commanded by Shard, who will move them to engage the enemy. Gunboat Isle will be given fire orders, just like with the bastion and the other portals of the fleet."

191

On the screen, the shuttle went through changes as Dave talked. A portal grew out of the hull of the ship, which was made from soul gems. Other portals started to grow around it but at a much slower rate until the interior portal was finished. Soul gems swarmed over the shuttle, encompassing it and sending out umbilicals to the portals that grew around it, turning it from a shuttle into a shuttle inside of a sphere.

The portals activated and weapon fire poured out from them.

"That's a whole lot of firepower," Malsour said.

"That they are but they're not going to stand up to much of a pounding," a shield tech said.

"We can use the Mana barrier spell, projected through the portals like with the bastion, to allow it to stay online for longer. Also, if we can build even a few dozen of these, then they're going to be causing chaos in the Jukal fleets. This time, we'll be the ones swarming them with numbers," Dave said.

"I can get Gunboat Isle to increase the rate at which they're developing. How long would these ships take to build?" Malsour asked.

"Well, we can get them started here and now, but I think with the right assembly line, maybe one every few days." Dave shrugged.

"Okay, then, shall we get started?" Ela-Dorn asked.

They broke down into groups, and once again started to go through the portal relays, looking over the rough ideas that Dave had come up with and putting it together. He had asked a number of them for their thoughts already and relied on them to see what was possible.

After a few hours, another meeting was called. They'd been able to work through a number of solutions and find a number of issues with the plan.

"Dave, as much as taking the hull from a shuttle would be nice, if we were to make it out of soul gem completely, then we would have more power, allowing us to activate it faster," Kol, who was on the development team, said.

"Also, having the form of a shuttle, while it will mean that we can get our hands on it faster, it's not going to be what we need. If we had a twelve-faced base, then it would be much faster to make the portals from that. The problem would be propulsion as we don't have a drive anymore," another tech said.

"Well, we can make that easier by putting them in something similar to a needle launcher," Malsour said. "Use gravity-assisting runes along the walls and shoot out these relays through portals. As they reach the other side, they start growing, create the main portal within the dodecahedron soul gem, which then shoots out umbilicals and builds connected portals that are connected to shield generators. The whole thing powers up and then can start unleashing hell on the enemy," Malsour said.

"Also, with it being a soul gem base, we can add in some magical coding to make them harder to detect and more likely to get to the portal deployment stage," another member of the development team said.

"We're going to have to beef up the power relays. We were running deployment times. It will take two minutes for them to get fully deployed. We talked to some of the fire controllers and weapons techs. In a battle, two minutes is way too long, so we're going to need to somehow reduce that down," a magical coding master said.

"We've also said that we need to send them through portals. However, what if we strapped them to the ships? They've got room around them when they go through a portal and we can alter their jump drive profile so that it will cover them. When they come under fire, the ships can pour power into them, get the first portal going much faster, reducing their deployment time astronomically and then use a spell formation to shoot them off into space," someone else proposed.

Dave sat back as people came up with more and more ideas, connecting them together as he smiled. He had merely lit a match, but they had taken it and turned it into a full-fledged project.

***

The command center was not a physical place but rather a Mirror of Communication conference room. This made it so that even if the physical locations received damage or were destroyed, the command center wouldn't fail. It also made it faster to access information as they were directly tapped into the Mirror of Communication network and didn't have to build anything extra.

Admiral Adams was in command, with Admiral Forsyth getting some downtime. As most people had been off, they had been working constantly to watch over the fleets that were on operation, being repaired, and new ships that were getting crews.

In the six weeks since the Jukal invasion fleet had been defeated, things were calmer in some aspects. There was still fierce fighting between the Deq'ual fleets and the Jukal defenses. On the other hand, the fighting on the ground had changed. The forces defending the Jukal were more likely to put on a show, to allow themselves to be defeated and captured by the Emerilians, than actually dig in and fight for the Jukal against the Emerilians.

More and more systems were freed from the Jukal Empire's influence over the last several weeks. Many of them were using the items that were left by the Emerilians. Some had even started to build their own technology to supply their needs.

To do this, they were going to the Mirror of Communication schools, coming to know the people of Emerilia, sitting in the same classrooms and learning how to use magic, how to build, how to farm—skills that they would need in order to become self-sufficient.

If they had enough time, this war would not be won through fighting, but rather subverting the races that were part of the Jukal

Empire. Giving them their freedom would disperse the Jukal Empire's power.

Adams was reviewing the reports on the development of the portal relay ships, before switching to the updates on warships being repaired. Five ships had been cleared for action; they had been moved out of the asteroid base and were now moving around Emerilia. With the portals on board, they didn't need to have their full crew when they left their slips or bases. Simply walking through a connected portal at one of the hubs would allow the crew who were on leave to switch with those who were onboard the ships.

An alarm tore through the command center. The sound made her heart lurch and her stomach twist as a priority message came in from scout ships that were well outside of the Jukal system.

Nearly a hundred Jukal ships were moving toward a jump point from all different directions.

The image was resolved with a spell activating. They were able to see the power signatures of the ships and a massive ring that they were towing with them.

"Shit, confirm that's a ship-sized portal!" Adams started to press buttons on her interface, sending out messages and linking what she was seeing with those other people.

"It's confirmed as a Jukal ship portal!" a sensors officer called out.

"Where can they jump to from that jump point? Alert all ships and captains—get them up to speed on what's happening," Adams said. "How old is the feed?"

"Ten minutes," a sensor officer called out.

The closer that the scout ships got to the Jukal home system, the more likely it was that they would be picked up. As such, they had been hiding far outside the system, using powerful spells in order to gather information on the Jukal system. Even though these spells were as fast as light, over such massive distances, even light took time to reach the ships again.

Adams watched as the Jukal continued on for the jump point without a care in the world.

"There are three systems that they can reach with that jump point. We've freed two of the systems," one of the aides said.

"Any ships that are ready in the Emerilia system I want on standby. Deq'ual fleets that are moving between systems or not currently tasked are to move to the nearest portal. We need to be ready to move in and reinforce whatever system the Jukal go for," Adams said.

Once again the combined forces started to move, ready to deal with the Jukal threat.

The asteroid base was sent scrambling as people were pulled from their leave and they rushed through portals, teleport pads, and onos to reach their ships. In the shipyards that lined the asteroid base, spell formations unleashed arcane fire as vessels detached from their umbilicals and headed into the main thoroughfare; the asteroid base connected to the moonbase as the forces in the asteroid base moved out.

It took some time for them to get out of their slips and leave the asteroid base. The patrolling forces teleported until they were just outside of the moonbase. The different fleets organized themselves, all facing the portal that was pushing out Pandora and Deq'ual ships that were coming from across the Jukal Empire and various bases.

Deq'ual ships that were holding at the Deq'ual outpost just outside of the asteroid base left their own slips and headed for the massive ship portal that the portal bastion had moved through. They formed up and passed through, the number of ships outside the moonbase rally point increasing every few minutes.

The thirty ships quickly turned into a hundred and forty, a mixture of Deq'ual and Pandora. All of the ships arranged themselves into fleets around the portal bastion that pushed out of its holding pattern near the space station Terra. They were feeding the Jukal ships into the refineries. There were only a few in good enough condition to fly and they needed to be renovated to suit the Pandora and Deq'ual crews.

As forces gathered, more and more people who had been away from the command center returned to it. Forsyth, who'd been doing paperwork, quickly connected and joined Adams.

There was nothing to do but wait for several hours. They watched the Jukal fleet still heading for the jump point. It seemed to travel so slowly since it took time to cross such vast distances.

The Jukal's travel time gave the combined fleets and forces the time they needed to gather at the moonbase, charging up their soul gems, and priming their fusion reactors and making sure that their armories were fully stocked.

Eventually the first Jukal ship used their jump drive. Adams looked to sensors that were looking at the three systems that the jump point would connect to and also looking at the small tell-tales that might make it easier to tell which system they went to.

"We've got it!" one of the sensor officers said.

On the main screen, a system appeared with markers for where the Jukal ships were supposed to exit.

"How much time delay do we have on that jump point?" Adams asked.

"We'll see what's happening there five minutes afterward," the sensor officer said.

"Prep the fleet. I want two Pandora fleets and one Deq'ual in support, moving to the system," Adams said. Orders were passed on as she continued. "The rest of our ships are to hold, ready to assist the first defense fleet if necessary."

The portal in-system activated just minutes later, with the defense forces moving through in force, ready to defend the system against the Jukal Empire.

If they let the Jukal attack the system, then the people of the empire might start pulling away from them.

It was sometime later before they got the first readings from the Jukal fleet. It arrived in force; a group of about ten or so Jukal ships headed deeper into the system before turning around.

"What the hell?" Forsyth muttered to himself as they watched something detach from one of the larger ships using the inertia built up from the ships. The object quickly separated from the ship and carried on.

"Shit," Adams hissed as a ship portal was tossed out from behind the ship. It moved through the fleet and headed into the system.

The Jukal fleet started to break apart and headed in different directions for different jump points. There were ten or so ships in each group, making a total of ten smaller fleets.

"I want arcane sensing spells on those ships. We need to know which ones are holding portals and how many. Shoot out a missile with a detection spell grand working at that portal. I want to know everything about it. We need to know if it just has new codes or if it's been built entirely different to try to keep us out," Adams said.

Forsyth and Adams looked to each other, entering a private chat.

"Looks like they're rebuilding their network," Forsyth said.

"We still don't have their numbers and if they can reach any system and attack us there while we're still trying to clear other systems of the Jukal Empire's influence, we're going to have our people hunted down," Adams said.

"We need to stop them from putting down these portals." Forsyth frowned.

"If they just jump in and drop them off, there's not much we can do to stop them. We have to figure out where they're going, send our people through the portals and then they've got to try to make it for the jump point." Adams shook her head.

"Then we're going to have to hit them somewhere that will make them come to us," Forsyth said through gritted teeth.

"What are you thinking?" Adams asked, an uneasy feeling filling her.

"We're going to have to hit the Jukal home system, pin their fleet in place," Forsyth said.

Adams's expression darkened. Forsyth might be livelier and his way of working with his people was different than hers—he was more laid-back and he freely talked with others of all ranks without care. However, when he was being serious, he didn't mince words.

Adams looked out at the screens as well. *If we don't decisively engage the Jukal fleet, then they can move around—maybe even go system to system. The more time we give them, the more time they have to plan. Then there's the fact there's restrictive magic over the entire system that will make it a pain in the ass to teleport into and they still retain control over portals in their home system. If we go in there without our forces ready, they'll come down on us and tear us apart.* Adams turned it all over in her head.

"I think you're right." She let out a deep sigh. "I just hope that we can pull enough forces to overturn the Jukal."

"Thankfully this is going to be a fight won on the ground, not in space. We can do hit-and-run, but we can't go head-to-head with the Jukal fleet *and* their defensive network just yet," Forsyth admitted.

"Well, then I think it's time we called a war council," Adams said.

Forsyth nodded as they opened their interfaces and started to contact the members of the war council and others in leadership positions.

They had all been woken up with the reports of what was happening in the Jukal home system already. As soon as Adams and Forsyth called a meeting, they started up a Mirror of Communication conference room.

After only a few minutes, Adams joined the meeting. Forsyth stayed at the command center, ready to react to anything the Jukal did.

Around the table, there were leaders of the ground forces by their units of support: mages, melee, healers, mounted, aerial, and ranged.

Then there was Dave, Malsour, Ela-Dorn, and Suzy for the Pandora Initiative. Lucy and Air were there for intelligence on the Jukal as well. Florence was the quartermaster for all of the Terra Alliance and the ground forces while Josh and others from the Terra Alliance rounded out the Emerilian part of the war council.

Council Leader Wong, Sato, and Edwards joined in, taking up the position of the Deq'ual system.

"Everyone is up to date with what is going on with the Jukal, correct?" Adams asked.

"They've deployed a portal into one system and it looks like they've got ships moving into every contested system to drop off more portals?" Dave summarized.

"Correct." Adams drew herself up a bit straighter, composing herself for what she was about to say. It would have far-reaching implications for not only the people in front of her but all of those they represented. "It is the opinion of Admiral Forsyth and myself that it would be best to attack the Jukal home system in order to force their fleet to pull back into a defensive stance. We do not have the forces to defeat the Jukal fleet and their defenses in space. However, if we can get the troops to the planet, we can then conduct raids on the Jukal home system, weakening them while the ground forces remove the Jukal Empire's influence on the ground."

Instead of getting annoyed at having the main responsibility foisted onto their shoulders, the ground commanders had understanding looks on their faces. Their people had been training for this whenever they were not on active deployment. The Emerilian forces were more geared toward fighting on the ground than in space. They'd been fighting on Emerilia for five hundred years and were pretty good at it.

What Adams said made sense. Having the Jukal mobile and re-establishing their portal network would only serve to weaken or destroy any progress the Deq'ual and Emerilian forces had made trying to break the Jukal Empire apart. They couldn't block all of the portals and then continue to remove the Jukal influences in the various systems under the Jukal Empire. They'd be spread much too thin.

People were more anxious than they had been with the Jukal invasion fleets. They'd been doing simulations of attacking the Jukal defenses and home world continuously since the end of the invasion fleet attacks.

However, they had hoped for six months or more before the simulations would become real. They beat the Jukal home fleet in numbers, but the sheer defensive structures loaded with light cannons, missiles, and shield generators could hurl an impressive amount of ordinance at the Deq'ual and Emerilian combined fleets.

***

The decision had been made. They were going to attack the Jukal home world. Their aim was simple: if they could remove the emperor, then the system made around him would be thrown into chaos. Using this, they could consolidate their gains and continue to build up their strength.

From giving the order to getting all of the parts needed to attack the Jukal home system was a grand undertaking.

Suzy and Lucy worked tirelessly to organize people and materials, making sure everyone was supplied, as the admirals went over the plan with their captains and ships' crews. They worked with the ground forces leadership, talking about their plan of attack.

The ground forces were mobilizing across Emerilia. They were kept in key positions, ready to move through bases and teleportation hubs until they stepped through portals to their final locations.

All ongoing operations were completed and the forces were pulled back, to make ready for the coming battle.

The Jukal fleet continued to release more portals across the Jukal Empire. It seemed that the Jukal emperor had been keeping a number of portals in safekeeping. These had new codes and a different encryption on them, making them nearly impossible to hack in a short time and making the codes that Bob had with the *Datskun* useless.

Even with all of this rising tension, the two forces weren't fighting on any fronts. People seemed to sense the atmosphere and looked to get somewhere safe. Whatever happened in this battle would change the Jukal Empire forever, no matter who won.

Ship portals and ground portals dotted Emerilia, with military forces waiting around them to move through.

Frank ran through his checks on his console and the people under his command. Everything looked good. He looked out to the screens relaying the findings from the magical sensing spells.

Around the portal, Deq'ual and Pandora fleets moved into position, making one massive fleet. The asteroid base and all of the secondary bases had worked tirelessly, getting another two fleets in working order and replacing the ships that had been lost in fighting the Jukal invasion fleet, putting eleven fleets under the Pandora Initiative's command. They had one hundred and thirty-five ships manned and ready for the battle. Any ships that had been completed were sent to join the rest of the warships not assigned to a particular fleet. Even when they had been fighting the Jukal invasion fleet, they had done their best to gather complete fleets before sending them into battle.

The arks that had been all over the Jukal Empire, supporting the different fronts, numbered thirty-three. They were the true backbone of the defensive and offensive work in the assault. They would be invaluable, acting as troop transports and bringing in the vast majority of the ground forces.

Frank had said his good-byes and sealed up his apartment, staying aboard the *BloodHawk* and looking out over the various systems. His crews were as ready as they were going to get. He had drilled with all of the other fire controllers in the sub-fleet and worked with the fire controllers for the entire fleet. It had been complicated at first, but they needed to get it done, so they had worked tirelessly until they were able to fight as one entity.

Weapons reading good across the board, full stocks of rounds and missiles. Frank checked the status of his systems and people once again.

"The fleet will be departing in two hours." Admiral Adams's voice cut through the bases, fleets, and forces arrayed across Emerilia.

Frank had already completed all of his checks and turned to Captain Xiao. "Sir, request leave to go talk to my weapons techs."

"You are free to go," Captain Xiao said. After being in a number of battles, they knew that two hours would pass slowly and that Frank would be back in time for their departure no matter what.

Frank left the command center, a secondary taking over his position. He walked through the halls, using onos that remained on constantly to teleport across the ship. He used them as naturally as someone might walk through a door.

It didn't take him long to reach the firing line, open decks where dwarves and grungy-looking characters moved from gun to gun and checked the missile tubes and the magazines they linked up to. There were people talking to one another and checking the interceptor modules and the shell feeds into the cannons.

A no-nonsense-looking dwarf wandered over when he saw Frank. "How's it going, Frank?"

"Not bad, Len. How are we looking?" Frank asked.

"The boys and girls are ready. All weapons are good. Just giving them make-work right now so that they're not all on edge as we head over to destroy the Jukal home world."

"Good stuff." Frank's eyes wandered over the people in front of him.

He might be the fire controller of the *BloodHawk*, but these men and women were the lifeblood to his actions. With his orders, they reacted with precision. This was not a single-man operation but rather an operation combining the efforts of tens of people against all that dared to show their faces.

There was something undeniably powerful about seeing all of those weapon systems ready and waiting and the weapons techs covered in grime, working with their magical carvers and using their magics to work on the weapons systems. The flare of runic lines along the cannon barrels made them seem like slumbering dragons just waiting to attack and tear apart their enemy.

Frank and Len talked and walked the line, going through the different decks where the weapons systems were located.

Then they went to the weapon locations that were not along the broadside of the ship. Frank and Len parted as Frank checked with the loadmaster. They looked out over a hangar filled with portals ready to deploy at a moment's notice.

They also reviewed the forty portal relay modules that were mounted on the underside and spine of the *BloodHawk*, ready to be supplied with power and tossed out into space, also available at a moment's notice.

With the new portal relays, Gunboat Isle had been expanding at an incredible pace. Thankfully, with all of Emerilia working together, they were able to supply them with weapons and ammunition. The automated miners, engineers, mages, and weapons techs were still working to get more ranges online so that the fire controllers and fleets had more options of weapons fire to pick from. Otherwise, each portal would only be allowed to unleash one payload.

Frank left the loadmaster as he thought of the portal relay stations. In the simulations, they had shown just how powerful they could be. He had also spent time at Terra, watching as they were deployed around Emerilia.

They would leave the ground-sized portals. As soon as they exited the other side, they started to expand, slowly at first and then suddenly they exploded into motion, creating twelve portals that faced outward, looking for targets as the relay headed off on its patrol route.

Deployment time had been whittled down from two minutes to just forty seconds. However, that kind of speed was still a lot of time in the middle of battle. Even with that long deployment time, Frank felt that they would be invaluable in the coming battle.

Frank made it into the command center ten minutes before their departure time. He checked his systems once again. Seeing that they were all green, there was nothing to do but sit back in his seat.

He looked over the people around him. Many of them were from the Earth simulation, but others were from Emerilia, or were even players on Emerilia at one time.

They came from all manner of races; they had worked at all manner of jobs within the simulation, but here on this ship it didn't matter because they were all fighting for those on either side of them and the people they cared for.

"Pandora fleet, move out!" Forsyth's words carried over the fleet. Spell formations appeared behind the ships of the fleet, their ships coming to life.

"Moving into formation," Navigation said. The fleets that had been arranged in their own areas now started to move together, their aim for the massive ship portal that jutted out of the moonbase. The fleets organized themselves from Fleet One to Eleven, stretching out from the portal lined up in pairs to simplify the portal transition.

The portal activated. Its runic lines lit up as power surged through it. It took a few moments for it to power up and connect to the portal tens of light-years away.

The first of the Pandora ships entered the moon, passing through the portal at full readiness, ready to deal with whatever they found on the other side of the portal.

"Forward deployment area is clear," Communications called out.

Behind the first ships, the rest of the fleet passed through quickly. Once they exited, the sub-fleets gathered together into fighting formations and then headed toward the jump point that would allow them access to the Jukal home system.

Frank was struck by the sight of the powerful force as they went to war, silently passing through space. It sent shivers down his spine as goose bumps appeared on his arms. Ships continued in pairs, rushing through the portal queue.

The *BloodHawk* passed through the portal, leaving the Emerilian system. From one moment to the next, the atmosphere within the ships changed, going from apprehensive to determined. They had passed the point of no return.

"Deq'ual fleet, move out," Admiral Adams said. The Deq'ual fleet organized themselves similar to the Pandora fleet and followed them through the portals.

Their carriers, destroyers, and battleships were no less fierce than their Emerilian counterparts as they moved in concert through the portal.

The portal bastion followed, massive arcane fire spell formations projected through portals to push the massive vessel through. It entered the system after everyone else, more onos pouring out arcane spell formations to alter its course.

The ship portal behind it closed and then started to activate again. It connected to the ship portal around the asteroid base as the second newly completed portal bastion passed through.

The sub-fleets of the Deq'ual and Pandora forces moved together, the bastions taking positions opposite one another.

One hundred and sixty-eight Pandoran warships, one hundred and ninety-three Deq'ual warships, two portal bastions and tens of portal relays mounted on every single available space moved toward the jump point location.

Those that were in the system looked at the fleet with fear.

The combined fleet seemed to dominate the void as they moved onward, seemingly unstoppable. This would be the fight to determine the fates of Emerilia, of Deq'ual, and of the Jukal Empire, as well as its people.

One of these could not live with the other. From the ruins of their race and the prison they were watched for entertainment, humanity had returned once again to gain vengeance on those who had once beaten them.

Chapter 14: Opening Salvo

As the warships and bastions moved through the Jukal Empire system for their jump point, Emerilia continued to work tirelessly. It would take the fleet some ten hours to reach the jump point and then another three hours before they would come in contact with the Jukal Empire's fleet and defenses.

It was twelve hours that no one was going to miss.

The Gunboat Isle was a sea of activity. People were pulled from other projects to assist. The Blood Kin seemed to just walk through the asteroid, waving their hands to create ranges, allowing for them to complete multiple batteries in just days.

On the ground of Emerilia, the fighting forces ran through simulations, ate food and did whatever they felt was right to prepare themselves for the coming battle. At ten hours to go, they ended training. The next time they would be fighting, it would be against the Jukal.

Water and his merpeople were there, as were the Mage's Guild. All combat capable mages from the college had heeded the call and joined. The overseers were there, but instead of wearing their defensive cloaks and adornments, they were now wearing items that would boost their attack power.

Dragons circled in the skies, and let out roars. Fire and Mal were in Ice City with Dave and Deia, spending time with Desmond and Koi.

Dave smiled at Koi, as if remembering everything she did, trying to implant her image and the memories deep into his mind as to never forget them. In his eyes, there was sadness and hesitation, wishing that he could get out of this fight, to end it so that he could just stay with Koi. He let out a deep sigh. As much as he wished for that, he wouldn't push his responsibilities aside. He had built up the Initiative—it was his brain child; he had established relations with

Deq'ual and watched as Emerilia had come into its own. He didn't think of these as achievements, but rather things that had to be done.

He rubbed Deia's back, seeing how she was playing with Koi, her smile tinged with worry and sadness. If they died this time, there was no coming back. If they were gone, then Koi wouldn't have parents.

Dave felt as if his soul was being rent in two as he looked at Koi's happy face, oblivious of the turmoil of her mother and father.

This was the same scene that was happening all across Emerilia as men and women hugged their loved ones, their hearts heavy as they turned and left, leaving teary-eyed family members, looking to their brothers, sisters, and cousins marching off to war with them.

Adventurers, city guards, players, priests, clerics, paladins, and mages: they left their homes, their lives and turned toward the portals. They donned their armor, shrugged on their cloaks, pulled down their helmets, adjusted their casting hats, checked their blades and staffs.

Onos across Emerilia flashed with light as people returned to their units, the forces at the portals growing in size.

People laughed and joked, hiding their feelings as they glanced at the portals. Beyond them was a battlefield, one the likes of which the most traveled adventurer had never seen, nor the greatest player had imagined.

People mounted up their Devastator armor as the time came closer. Some slapped the armor before disappearing into the space of holding; others stepped in without comment. Others said prayers or did a ritual for good luck.

Racks upon racks of Devastator armor came alive. The dormant runic lines now glowed with fierce power as they stepped out of the racks, their feet shaking the ground.

Dwarven warclans armored with the Devastator armor shook the ground, their drums low and somber as the skies above them were filled with the screeches and roars of the various powerful beasts that they had trained up.

Dwarven Earth mages followed them, carrying their staffs; the ground under their feet pushed them forward.

Behind them, dwarven artillery cannons that had been heavily modified rolled forward, dwarven artillery crews around them.

Elven rangers wearing modified Devastator armor moved in precise ranks. Bows rested on their backs as their steps barely registered on the ground, every movement thought-out and predatory.

The DCA army seemed to appear out of the forests and swoop down from the skies. Their armor tarnished and battle-worn, they looked like a bunch of strays but there was a fire in their eyes and the way that they walked that spoke of the power and strength they had built up in the previous months and years. They might look dirty and unkempt but they were one of the strongest fighting forces of Emerilia.

Aleph controllers and automatons appeared. Their automatons had undergone massive changes, more dangerous and capable than ever.

Mounted forces both in the sky and on the ground, armies from across Emerilia: everything was in movement.

They took portals, teleport pads, and onos, arriving in front of Goblin Mountain.

Forces moved into staging areas facing the locations of where the first flying citadels had come from and were now the place of portals.

In the center atop Goblin Mountain was a massive ship portal, catching the light of the setting sun. Many arrived at the portals ahead of time, setting up camp and readying themselves for the battle to come.

Around Goblin Mountain, sixty-four flying citadels dominated the sky, making many look up in awe. The citadels were fully crewed; the walls and the inner castle were covered with artillery cannons, their crews and Aleph automatons. In the soul gem island underneath, the ground fighting forces were resting on the drop pads. Magical coding and runic lines covered the floors as people waited.

Dave got an alert on his interface as the fleet readied themselves to wormhole into the Jukal home system.

"We have to go." Dave gripped Deia's shoulder lightly.

Deia didn't say anything, not trusting her voice as she rubbed Koi's face before she picked her up. "Mommy loves you." Deia kissed Koi.

"Daddy loves you, little one." Dave's voice got hoarse as his eyes got watery. He hugged them both and kissed the side of Koi's face. They stood like that for a few moments.

Mal and Fire said good-bye to Desmond as one of the minders took Desmond away and Deia handed off Koi to the Dracul family minders.

Dave grasped Deia's hand as she forced down the tears that were so close to making an appearance. Dave looked to Mal and Fire, sharing a glance and looking away as they walked out of the room, unable to look back for fear that they would stay there.

Dave's simple clothes rippled as his armor and cloak appeared around him. Orbs appeared in the air around him and began to circle him.

Deia's clothes rippled, changing into her Abscondita armor, her twin sword on her hip as her bow rested across her back.

Mal and Fire changed into their fighting leathers. Staffs that seemed to be made from living fire beaten into shape appeared in their hands.

"We'll see you on the Jukal home planet." Fire and Mal came to a stop.

Deia and Dave turned around.

"Look after yourself." Mal wrapped Deia up in a hug and Fire hugged Dave as well before they switched. Fire and Deia looked to each other.

"I could never be prouder." Fire kissed Deia on the forehead.

"Make sure you come back safe, and see that Deia does as well," Mal said, barely keeping it together.

Dave nodded stoically. He and Mal had become close friends and he knew the love that they shared as they hugged each other again.

Flames appeared around Fire and Mal as they teleported away.

"Let's go," Dave said, once again holding Deia's hand.

She took a shaky breath, pulling herself together and once again becoming the leader of Party Zero.

The air shimmered and they reappeared at a portal. They stepped through, appearing in the first base of the Pandora's Initiative, Pandora's Box.

Steve, who had been sitting on a workbench, rose to his full height, grabbing Alex the Axe that was leaning against the table. Lox and Gurren turned from where they were talking with Malsour and Suzy toward Deia and Dave.

Jung Lee, Anna, and Induca looked up from their conversation, standing up from the two workbenches they had been sitting on.

Dave looked to them all and squeezed Deia's hand once more. She squeezed his hand back as he turned to face her, their hands falling apart.

"You know the drill. We're going to move to the first flying citadel. From there, we will launch our attack against the Jukal." Deia paused and looked at them all. "I've been lucky enough to call you not only my friends but my family. Knowing you all has made my life that much better. Watch out for one another and let's end this fight."

There were no cheers or roars of agreement. Even Steve seemed to be touched as they looked to one another. They had come together into a family; they shared a deep history and stories. They'd ventured across Emerilia as a party, fought in the event and pushed the limits of their capabilities. They'd defeated gods and goddesses and faced mythical forces. However, it wasn't these achievements that pulled them together, but the care that they shared with one another.

"Party Zero, now and forever." Steve held out his hand.

"Now and forever." Suzy extended her hand.

One by one, they gathered around and placed their hands together.

Deia was the last to do so, looking at them all. "Now and forever."

They pulled back their hands as Deia looked to Dave.

"This is going to be a lot harder not being a Lord of Earth anymore," Dave muttered. "We're going to be in mid-air." Spell formations appeared around them as the scenery changed and they reappeared above their flying citadel. They floated in the air using various means before dropping down toward the citadel.

Eyes were drawn to the legendary Party Zero as they descended, passing the central tower to land around the castle that it sprouted from.

*****

"Wormhole established. Moving through," the navigation officer of the *BloodHawk* said. Her words seemed to grip Frank's heart.

Wormholes appeared in front of the main fleet, glowing in space, as the entire fleet moved through the portals. The Pandora ships kept them open for the Deq'ual ships that relied on jump drives and the bastions that weren't able to generate them.

They passed through the wormhole. The universe was distorted around them before they passed through the other side.

Their screens started updating rapidly as they looked at the Jukal home system, the very heart of the Jukal Empire. The information from the various scout craft around the system relayed information to the ships, quickly building a picture of everything that was around them.

The portal in the middle of the system was quickly activating and spitting out Jukal ships that were part of the Jukal fleet that had been sent out to sow chaos among the Jukal Empire systems and try to re-establish the portal network.

The part of the fleet that hadn't left the system was still over the Jukal home world, numbering just under fifty ships.

There were defensive networks all around the jump points that entered the system. Knowing this ahead of time, the combined fleet had entered through a region of space where there were no defenses.

"Spinning up teleportation spell formation," Navigation called out as massive spell formations appeared around the ships of the combined fleet.

Frank looked to the feeds, quickly locating the Jukal home world. Its orbitals were covered with a number of stations. Some were connected to the ground by elevators; most of them appeared to be civilian. Scans showed some of the stations were obviously being used to move goods through to the planet or people who made their living by transiting between stations and serving the upper echelon of the Jukal Empire.

Only a few of the stations were made for defense purposes and had weaponry mounted on them. Unfortunately, these stations appeared to be incredibly powerful; without needing to build engines, they were covered in weaponry, ready to destroy anything that disturbed them.

"Start charging relays. Ready portals," Admiral Forsyth said. "Arks, prepare to drop portals."

Around the arks, their rings opened up. Just like the battleships, they were capable of holding a ship-classed portal inside armored panels. The sections of the large portals extended outward until all of the edges matched with one another and started to fuse together, creating massive portals.

The drop runes along the bottom of their ships started to glow as they activated.

Destroyers around the arks also powered up the drop runes.

Frank opened up the power linkage to the portal relays, the obscure dodecahedron that started to rapidly grow larger.

Portals were released by the arks, covering their surface. The Deq'ual and Pandora ships released portals of their own that moved to their spine and belly, where they had little to no weaponry.

Frank looked to an alert that notified him of the fire plan that the fleet was going to execute. With constant real-time updates on what was going on with the Jukal home system, they had come up with multiple ways to attack the Jukal.

Frank sent orders down to his people as they made changes to their spell formations and changed out the grand working warheads and shells for what they'd need.

Frank looked away from his screens and stared at the main screen. All of their weapon systems had been ready since they wormholed into the system.

"Teleporting!" Navigation called out.

"Ready weapons!" Admiral Adams said.

The ships flared with power, Mana barriers snapping into existence. The spell formations around them became solid as the entire fleet disappeared, reappearing just above the Jukal home planet.

"Fire!" Adams said. Her order transmitted to the entire fleet. For this operation, she was in charge while Forsyth was there to work with the forces on the ground.

The broadsides of the ships opened. Missile ports that had been open now roared with runic lines and spell formations as they shot out into the void. Cannons glowed and grand working shells were fired, passing through accelerating runic lines and stacked spell formations.

The skies above the Jukal home world ignited with the fire of the ships.

Spell formations appeared around the defenses of the Jukal home world, powered by the warships of the Pandora fleet. Varying spells, from Mana spears to avatars made of lightning, were created by these spell formations, all of them unleashing the greatest power possible.

It takes time to describe but all of this happened in the blink of an eye.

"Break, break, break!" Forsyth yelled a moment later.

Destroyers and arks broke away from the fleet, their position putting them closest to the planet. They charged into the Jukal home world's skies. Their ships glowed as the Jukal planet's atmosphere fought them.

The ships bashed their way in. The destroyers' spells located defensive installations on the ground. Its weapons and the limited weapons of the arks opened up on the targets.

To the Jukal below, their nighttime turned into a series of explosions in the heavens above and streaking meteors headed directly for the Jukal emperor's residence that dominated thirty percent of the planet's surface.

Floating islands that covered the emperor's residence rolled out their weapons. They were run by AIs instead of Jukal officers, up in the stations that were only just starting to realize the enemy had arrived.

These islands started firing wildly up in the skies, making the arks and the other ships divert.

Arks released their portal's tethers, letting them fall away from the arks. A number of them were broken, but many survived. Some stayed in the air; others dropped to the ground. Runes that covered them acted as flight controls.

The arks and destroyers cut the speed of their descent and changed their headings, coming in low and fast southward, toward the Jukal emperor's residence. The destroyers were firing at any defensive installations they could find with their spells. As they passed over the sea to the north of the emperor's residence, raging waves formed, insignificant to the ships above.

The destroyers opened portals on their bows and spines; missiles tore outward, aiming at the Jukal emperor's northern defenses.

The missiles were met with defensive weapons fire and shields.

The destroyers and arks cut their speed. The drop runes under the arks flashed with light then the portals appeared on the ground. The portals stabilized and one of them started to activate; then more and more started to activate. The arks and destroyers covered the portals as one of the ships' portals that had been trailing behind the arks activated. In mid-air, a different scene appeared; it no longer showed the skies of the Jukal home world. Instead, it showed the skies above Goblin Mountain.

The air shook as a flying citadel slowly started to emerge from the portal. The minute the cannons were through, they started firing.

Around them, dragons and other aerial creatures entered the Jukal home world, their roars only overpowered by the sounds of the destroyers and arks fighting the Jukal defenses.

The destroyers' drop runes flashed with light as Pandora fighting forces wearing Devastator armor appeared.

Frank's eyes flashed over his screens, checking on the progress of the ground forces as the fleet above the Jukal home world were now the center of what looked like the apocalypse.

All of their portals were open, spewing forth magical destruction.

"Ejecting portal relays!" Frank barked. All over the fleet, the portal relays were thrown out, expanding at an incredible rate as the surfaces of the dodecahedron started to form into portals.

One of the Jukal defensive ground stations had been toppled already under the combined attacks of the fleet.

Not knowing what the portal relays were, the weapon systems that were online didn't even pay them attention as they continued to fire on the combined fleet's warships and bastions.

The Jukal fleet that were orbiting the planet were moving around the planet to attack the combined fleet.

The Jukal defensive stations had their act together as well. Their weapons were starting to power up and hit the combined fleet's ships.

"Portal relays up!" Frank yelled.

From the portals, beams of power appeared before spell formations turned that power into Mana barriers that connected to one another and formed a protective barrier over the portal relay ships. The portals of the ships connected to Gunboat Isle, pouring forth spells, missiles, and grand working topped destruction.

Frank checked the heading of the Jukal fleet that was protecting the Jukal home world. Their path would take them right through the portal relay ships.

A cruel sneer appeared on his face. Another station was felled by the combined might of the human fleet.

From the Deq'ual carriers, more and more fighters were filling the skies to contend with the drones that were just being released from their Jukal stations.

"Looks like we caught them unaware," Xiao said.

Frank looked to the wave of destruction that was filling the Jukal home world's skies as the defensive structures that had been broken now fell toward the planet, burning up in the planet's atmosphere.

Frank didn't need to say anything. His people were doing everything they could to dent the Jukal defenses. Soon enough they would be locked into combat with the Jukal fleet.

His eyes darted to the screen showing the area around the Jukal system's main ship portal. More Jukal that had been racing through the Jukal Empire systems were now returning and charging toward the combined fleet.

Frank gritted his teeth. They wouldn't be able to set up another teleportation spell to move the entire combined fleet again. The first shots had been fired. However, even as they were sweeping the orbitals, the battle on the ground was only just starting.

Chapter 15: One Last Fight

"One last fight." Steve's words gripped the atmosphere around them as his eyes passed over them all.

His words were filled with memories, experiences that they had all shared together. There was no way to express the things that they felt, the things that they had been through. They had experienced great victories, and losses, together. They had laughed, they had cried, they had bled and they had healed.

From Opheir to Ashal, they had fought, a group of strangers coming together to form Party Zero. They looked to one another as they jogged through the portal, leaving Emerilia and entering an ark.

They heard the noises of those wearing Devastator armor marching from the teleport pad to the outlined drop formations that flashed with light and made them reappear on the ground below. The speakers within the destroyer were filled with the sharp tones of orders.

They were Party Zero; they were a family and they would stand by one another no matter what.

Nothing needed to be said as their gazes turned toward the nearby drop formation. Together, they stepped forward, checking their swords, their staffs, donning their helmets and circulating their Mana. They didn't look back as they stepped onto the drop formation.

Light made them see stars before the roar of battle filled their ears.

Dragons and aerial creatures dove from above, unleashing their attacks on the Jukal's drones and the various custom creatures and creations that the Jukal elite had created over the years.

Magical formations, plasma rounds, light cannons, artillery rounds, missiles, grand workings: all of this magical power painted a world of destruction. The clouds were dark and oppressive, the very weather of the Jukal home world whipped up to the extreme with the incredibly powerful spells and energies that were being unleashed.

In the breaks between the clouds, one could see the flashes of the battle that was occurring over the Jukal home world as the Deq'ual and Pandora fleets engaged the Jukal defensive stations, fighting for control over the planet's orbitals.

The reserve Jukal fleet were on their way while the Jukal fleet that had headed out was grouping together and heading back.

Although most of the forces that were part of the Jukal fleet were nothing more than aristocratic children trying to improve the position of their parents, those who made up the Jukal home system fleet were people who had scored the best on the testing that the Jukal fleet had created. They were the last true Jukal fleet. Combined with the defenses of the Jukal home planet, they were sure to make the lives of the combined fleet's harder.

Groups were securing the portals that had been dropped off by the arks and destroyers so that the people weren't killed as they came through and stopping Jukal rounds from heading through the portal and killing the forces on the other side.

"To the front!" Deia yelled. Induca and Malsour changed while Steve, Lox, Gurren, and Jung Lee ran across the ground. Dave and Suzy took to the sky, throwing out items that revolved around them. Suzy had cores while Dave had orbs, vault soul gems, and different magically coded plates that seemed completely random. There were also grand workings in the mix of items around him. Anna and Deia rose into the air on their Fire and Air magic and pushed ahead with everyone else.

It didn't take them long to get past the units that were getting organized and make it to the rear of the advancing dwarven lines.

The dwarves marched forward, their shields ready but not deployed as the contracted creatures above their heads unleashed attack after attack on the different automated weapon mounts. The dwarves called in artillery fire on the defenses as ranged attackers joined their lines, sowing more destruction. Dragons and DCA covered their advance, laying down heavy long-range magic.

The power unleashed in these attacks made the air shake and ground rumble.

Shields were revealed, covering multiple weapons systems.

Around Dave, the different plates moved into a position, orbs moving around what looked to be a massive barrel. Power was drawn from the vault soul gems as Dave threw out a grand working.

The grand working shot out at a speed that made the air explode in its path. The grand working exploded against the shield of the powerful weapon system that was slowing the dwarves' advance. The shield shuddered as the shield disrupting spell imprint on the grand working destabilized it.

The flying creatures fired attack after attack on the weapons system. It exploded into sparks as they continued to advance.

"Looks like they've been experimenting." Dave closed his eyes as his Touch of the Land spell picked up spell traps buried in the ground. He poured power into the traps or had his orbs attack them, clearing the ground ahead of the dwarves.

The rest of Party Zero did what they could to help defeat the targets at range, allowing the dwarves to continue their march forward at a faster pace.

"This place is huge. It's going to take awhile before we can get to the emperor's residence!" Lox said.

"Why can't we just bomb it from orbit?" Gurren asked.

"We would need to sit in orbit for hours. The shield around the Jukal emperor's home is as powerful as the shield that covered Emerilia, but condensed down, and we don't know how much power it has. Might be able to last days," Steve said.

"Oh, good point," Gurren said.

"And here I was thinking it was only Steve that asks dumb questions," Jung Lee said.

"Welcome to the club, buddy!" Steve clapped Gurren on the back. The sound of metal on metal rang in everyone's ears as Gurren had to fight to stay upright.

More and more people from Emerilia came through the portals. Hundreds quickly became thousands as they advanced through what was the emperor's backyard that spanned some three hundred kilometers.

As more forces joined into the battle, they were able to advance quicker. Spells passed over the forward forces, dropped from the skies and rose out from the ground, destroying the defenses in their way.

"We've got floating islands on their way," Deia said.

"Well, time to see how our flying citadels compare to their floating weapons platforms." Dave's head whipped over to a point just in front of one of the forces that were moving forward. Mana from the air seemed to be thrown into chaos as a high-level tiered spell formation appeared, a gate descended made from blood. The doors opened as hellish-looking creatures looked at those advancing.

They let out hungry wails as they charged forward in glee, leaving the gate and jumping at the Emerilians.

"Shit! Where did that come from?" Malsour asked.

"I don't know, but that takes a lot of power," Dave said.

Tens of the creatures—some looking humanoid, others looking like creatures—looked as if they had been partially eaten or were decaying as they rushed forward.

The mages nearby launched attacks on the gate, destabilizing it.

They continued to advance but more of the blood-red gates appeared at random. The spell formation for the door didn't change, so as they learned to defeat it once, they could use the same method to break it again and again.

It seemed as if some force was angrily throwing a tantrum as more and more of the gates appeared. It was as if they were trying to go with what they knew, not worrying about the fact it had no effect.

"Seems like someone with an AI and a ton of power is putting down spells," Malsour said.

"Lovely." Dave shook his head. "Well, at least we can confirm that there is at least someone using the same system as the people of the Pantheon back on Emerilia."

"Hopefully our gods can keep up with them." Suzy looked back to where Fire, Air, and Water stood over the portals, making sure that nothing hit the forces that were coming out.

"Oh ye of little faith." Bob dropped down from the sky. With a wave of his hand, a plasma round exploded in the sky and a pillar of metal also dropped from the sky, breaking through the shield of the plasma cannon and destroying it in a fiery explosion. "That should just be the emperor. With all the inbreeding he's gone through, there's no wonder that there isn't much rubbing together in his brain anymore."

"Seems that something is coming," Steve said. His senses were the best as he was able to link through an internal Mirror of Communication to the ships that were all across the Jukal system. With these powerful spells relaying information back to him, he could practically look through walls.

"What is it?" Deia asked.

"They've got power fluctuations of arcane energy and they're covered in Mana. I think they might be magic users," Steve said.

"More of the modified slaves," Lox grunted.

***

The emperor's fist lashed out, breaking apart the wall in front of him.

His uncle frowned but didn't say anything. The military members shivered where they stood but didn't say anything. The only person who didn't move was the guard captain of the emperor's household, who looked at the military members with dead eyes, his disdain clear.

"Why is this happening? I want them to be destroyed now! Get me my army!" the emperor bellowed.

The women in his arms shivered but continued to fill his needs. His outbursts had become more and more frequent as the fight with the Emerilians and their human allies continued. They'd become slightly used to them and continued on, afraid that the next outburst would be aimed at them.

The fate of one of the girls who had been in shock after one of his outbursts made them pale with fear.

"Yes, my emperor," one of the military commanders said, quickly lying on his back in a servile manner as he transmitted the order.

The emperor let out a cold noise and his tongue moved around angrily as he chewed on some delicacy placed in his mouth. He didn't even taste it, his eyes red with bloodlust.

The emperor's uncle made to say something, but paused, seemingly thinking it over. He stopped and watched what was happening with everyone else.

A feed showed humanoid-looking creatures. Their bodies were in all different colors and variations of the humanoid shape; however, their bodies rippled with power. Some floated in the air; others glowed with lightning. These were the enhanced slaves that made up the emperor's private army.

Army was a broad term. To the emperor, they were simply his playthings, items to be kept in order to entertain him. They lived in a large area underneath his residence.

With his order, passageways were opened from this underground world to the surface. Word passed quickly through this land, which was little more than a never-ending battlefield.

The different forces rushed toward the openings and entered the tunnels. Some of them fought one another as they rushed forth; others waited below, cautious to find out what was above.

Openings appeared on the surface of the emperor's residence. Creatures appeared in the skies and on the ground, looking at the Emerilian forces that were under attack from the Jukal defensive weaponry.

Their interfaces appeared in front of them, informing them of a quest. Many of their eyes lit with greed and they charged toward the Emerilians. Others started to leave, only to find their bodies start to disintegrate.

After the first couple of tries, they turned back and rushed the Emerilians to vent their frustration and anger upon them.

"Yes! Yes! Now we will see a true fight between my army and theirs!" The emperor's hand shook in a sign of victory. In his eyes, there was no way that the Emerilians could survive; they could merely give him something interesting to watch. He laughed and bragged to those around him as he looked at the battlefield.

Chapter 16: Changing Tide

Dave's eyes went cold as panels appeared around him, creating barrels. Grand working shells fired through the air as a bow appeared in his hands. His floating orbs shot out Mana bolts into the mass of people rushing toward the Emerilians.

"Shields!" the dwarves barked. Shields came together, creating the famous dwarven formation.

Those in the sky or in support of the dwarves used their attacks against the enemy force that was coming straight toward them.

As they unleashed spells, the new arrivals also started using their spells, the power of which even left the Emerilians stunned.

The ranged attackers hit people on both sides of the fighting. Formations opened up as people disappeared under the attacks. Calls for healers were sent out, only barely audible under the ranged attacks.

Dave looked up as he felt a familiar Mana signature. A cold look passed over his eyes as a howling filled the sky. The flying citadels had arrived! The portal that they had come from was away from the emperor's residence and the defenses, so it took them some time to cross the distance to the battlefield.

They were still some distance away, but their new guns put them in range as their artillery shells appeared in the ranks of the advancing army.

The elements seemed to turn against those attacking the Emerilians. Plants rose up to try to slow them down, while the ground became harder to traverse and spikes made from plants jutted upward.

Dave's eyes thinned as he watched the slave army's members start to dodge the attacks after just a few instances. *What lives have they lived in order to adjust so quickly in the middle of a life-and-death battle?*

Explosions covered the ground, turning the ground into craters and opening up holes in the slave's army.

Patches of the sky were blotted out by rolling clouds that converged above the battlefield. The clouds started to rumble and flash angrily as lightning built up in them. Tornado tunnels appeared, cutting toward the slave army. Hail formed from the clouds and shot through the sky, descending like arrows that would cut through tempered steel. Spell formations glowed in the clouds, controlling it, as other spell formations appeared in the midst of the clouds. Lightning shot out from them, blinding those looking in the direction of the falling lightning that tore the ground apart with their impact and killed all of those within twenty meters of its impact point without fail.

Suns seemed to appear in the sky before descending on the slaves, exploding outward into raging infernos with green flames that didn't go out. Creatures formed from different Affinities let out their howls, roars, and keens as they locked eyes onto the slaves and charged forth. Summoners, beast tamers, and necromancers called on their hordes. The numbers on the battlefield swelled rapidly.

The sounds of arrows filled the air, falling in black clouds. As tough as the unfortunate slaves were, it took multiple hits for the slaves to fall, even as dragons and the aerial forces dropped attacks on them.

They were not the only ones feeling the pain. The Emerilian forces were maintaining their standing but with all of the incoming magical attacks and their massive power, they were taking their own casualties.

The Emerilians had a large army on the ground already. However, these slaves seemed to be coming in a never-ending stream from the ground. Some raced up into the sky, directly fighting those who were mounted on flying beasts or relying on their own power to stay in the sky.

On the ground, it took them a bit longer before they reached the Emerilian lines. They didn't care to be stopped by the dwarves, many trying to get over them to reach the weaker targets behind them.

There was little coordination to the slaves' actions, though some of them seemed to come together into bands that worked to pressure the dwarves.

"Get back down there!" Lox barked. He leapt up into the sky, his armor powering him up. It was covered in gray rune lines; black lines filled his upper body. His speed was so fast that the fighter in the sky had no time to act as a flash of light passed them. Lox's sword took off their head as wings appeared around his back.

"Cut them down!" Alkao's voice made the air tremble as he led all of the aerial forces. It was not only the fighters of Emerilia on the Jukal home world; their leaders and those who had military merits had come to fight as well.

The aerial forces turned and shot toward those in the sky. They yelled out in anger, brandishing weapons and charging the aerial forces.

Dragons unleashed their attacks, making the slave fighters look in shock as their ranks thinned greatly. They didn't have time to get over their shock before the two forces in the sky crossed one another. The sounds of battle rang through the air and the ground.

The rumblings of more flying citadels cut through the sky. On the horizon, Dave could see shadows closing in on them. More explosions started to rain down on the frontline forces of the battlefield, coming from the flying islands that dotted the air above the emperor's residence.

The arks started to move away, the destroyers covering them as they increased speed, leaving the flying citadels in place. The citadels' drop pads glowed with power, as portal relays that were already in the process of growing shot out from between the different defensive walls of the citadels.

They smacked into the ground, expanding.

"Fight!" Steve yelled. He surged up into the air. Wings made of soul gem sprouted from his back, covered in runic lines. The others followed his lead, yelling out in anger as they rushed in groups into melee range.

Dave closed his eyes. Using his Touch of the Land spell, more items poured out from him. As the rows of bands on his arms moved, Mana surged around him.

His body glowed with powerful runes that lit up the darkness of his hood. Around him, there was a tempest of parts moving, as if he were in the middle of a hurricane.

Dave raised his hand. With it, the items stopped whirling around him and formed into different machines.

A sonic blast ripped through the air, sounding like the screeching of wraiths. The slaves in front of him covered their now bleeding auditory organs. Barrels covered in runic lines made of multiple layers of items flared continuously, sending out hundreds of spells, one after another. They hit the ground, exploding as they hit. These were his true grenades.

A slave expanded in size. Water that had been covering his body turned into a suit of armor. They let out a roar as their power surged. They stepped into the sky, the water in the air transforming into steps for this slave.

Dave grabbed his conjuration rods. One moment, he was in the midst of his weaponry; the next, he was behind the large slave. His sword shot out, but his opponent had been tempered in the battlefields underneath the emperor's residence. He destroyed the step he was on. The blade caught his leg instead of going through his back as he flipped forward; his legs lashed out to hit Dave, who raised his shield. The impact sent him back through the sky. His face was the epitome of calm. He hadn't even opened his eyes yet and he was still controlling the sphere of weaponry above.

Dave disappeared just as the attacker recovered.

He reappeared, a spear in his hands as he lunged forward. The spear slammed into the water armor and buried deep between the attacker's ribs. Dave targeted the attacker's weaknesses using his Touch of the Land.

They grabbed the spear; water rushed up their arm to form into a spear.

"Too slow." Dave's voice was calm as he opened his eyes.

The end of the spear inside the attacker grew. The metal head of the spear turned into spikes that shot through the body of the attacker in a second, sprouting metal shards. The spear and the metal of it fell away. The attacker's water armor and spear collapsed as Dave turned and looked to the chaos around him. His conjuration rods turned into sharp swords.

"Time to raise that damn weapons master skill," Dave muttered to himself as he disappeared from his position. He appeared behind another attacker. His sword lashed out before they had time to attack. He disappeared before they were able to let out a cry of pain, appearing above another; his sword darted out, cutting down through the person's neck at an angle, piercing their heart. Dave disappeared again.

Dave's scariest ability in an upfront fight was teleportation. Combining the orbs that were circling him even now, and the power that he had stored up in vault soul gems in his bags of holding, all he had to do was think of a location; power would surge into the orbs and he would teleport, with no strain on his Mana reserves.

On Emerilia, he couldn't use it for bringing more attention down on him and tripping the AI watchdogs and Jukal controllers. Now he didn't have to care what they thought.

Dave flitted about the battlefield. Weapons appeared in his hands, hitting the attackers where they were open. They didn't even know how they had died before Dave flitted to the next victim.

Party Zero battled in the sky.

"Stone Raiders!" A voice carried through the skies as Esa and the Stone Raiders entered the battlefield. Spells shot into the sky and tore through the ground in front of the dwarves, relieving some of the pressure. More and more of the Emerilian forces charged into the slaves; the dwarves' blades were covered in blood or something very like blood as they moved at a steady advance. Here and there, some dwarves were pulled out of their formation. That being said, these dwarves were all armored in Devastator armor. They were quickly able to clear a space around themselves and allowed the formation to reform before they leaped backward, flipping back over their fellow dwarves' shields, the contracted beasts covering them.

The losses were coming mostly from the other fighting forces on the ground and those in the sky. These groups were being bolstered by the reinforcements and were the center of the flying citadels' support.

"Advance at double time!" Lox bellowed. His voice carried over the battlefield. He had trained all of these people who were now using the Devastator armor. His words became their will. Drums sounded off as those in the lines let out new war cries. Baleful horns and trumpets sounded the advance.

The Emerilian forces stepped forward over the bodies of the slave army, their eyes red and their weapons covered in their enemies' blood.

"Mounted! Clear us a path!" Gurren barked. There was no sense of playfulness in their voices. Instead, it was replaced with unstoppable iron will.

Mounted forces that had organized themselves behind the advancing forces now kicked their beasts into action. They lifted themselves out of their saddles and seats; elves stood in their stirrups, their armor glinting with the light of spells as they drew back their bows and unleashed arrows over the front lines.

Those with ranged abilities added in their attacks, while others pulled out their swords and spears. Their beasts frothed at the mouth as they rushed forward into battle, eager to rent and tear the enemy apart.

The lines of the formations opened, just as the slaves were going to rush into the openings. Their eyes went wide as the mounted forces hit them like a train; bodies were thrown away with the force of impact.

Spells opened up the slave army, allowing the mounted forces to keep up their pace as they dashed through their army, their speed terrifying.

Dave let out a roar as he appeared among the slave army. Party Zero appeared around him. In their own ways, the slave army had a number of powerful experts but they were divided. If there was someone difficult to deal with, then Party Zero came together, overwhelming them. It wasn't fair, but this wasn't a game anymore.

**

The battle on the ground had begun. The initial advance had been slowed, but they were still pushing farther into enemy territory—albeit slowly as they fought with the powerful slave army that was still rushing out from the ground.

Several flying citadels now dotted the sky, moving in to support those on the ground. Underneath them, their drop runes flashed with light as they dropped off more reinforcements.

The arks, under the protection of the destroyers, moved around the continent that was the emperor's residence. Two arks stopped opposite to each other on either side of the continent that the emperor's residence covered. The portals on either side opened as beams of power shot out, creating shields. These shields were comparable to the ones on the bastion. However, while the bastions were being hit with extremely powerful weapons, if the same weapons were used by the Jukal on the ground, then it could throw the entire planet's atmosphere into chaos.

This made the arks practically invincible as the two groups of destroyers and arks made their way around the Jukal emperor's residence, arks stopping across from one another along the way.

Frank's eyes flickered to the main screens, where another station was knocked out of its orbit and sent spiraling down toward the Jukal home world, burning up in the atmosphere.

They had defeated a total of fifteen stations already. Each of them was a hard-won battle, speaking to the abilities of the stations. It looked like a good start but there were still more orbiting the planet and the home world's Jukal fleet was just arriving.

Dozens of portal relays now dotted the skies above the Jukal home world.

"Fire as you have targets! Cover the fighters as they move in," Adams said.

As the Jukal fleet appeared, the combined Emerilian fleets unleashed all that they had at them, with the Jukal replying in kind.

The fighters, using the covering fire of the combined fleet, moved in to engage the Jukal. Meeting the drones, they split apart into smaller groups, killing drones as they could and getting among the Jukal home world fleet, laying fire into the ships and forcing them to divert some of their firepower to try to deal with the fighters.

The drones were practically sentient and they were on par with the human pilots, who were using mostly AI-controlled ships. Fierce fighting broke out among the Jukal home world fleet as they pounded on the combined fleet. Their speed was extremely slow as they were fighting their way out of a gravity well while the combined fleet were looking down upon it.

As the Jukal rushed to engage them, their bows were pointed at the combined fleet's broadsides; the Jukal unleashed salvo after salvo of missiles into the fleet.

The fighting was chaotic but the combined fleet systematically defeated ship after ship, tearing them apart until there was nothing left but debris.

It left them open to attack from the other ships, but every ship they targeted fell.

They went for the weakest ships first. With the portal relays, their power was impressive, capable of taking only a few minutes of concentrated fire to take down the smaller ships.

The Jukal focused their attacks on the older bastion, pouring everything into it. More of its portals shot out beams of power, reinforcing its Mana barrier.

Still, it wasn't able to hold up to that sort of punishment for so long. The Mana barriers started to wilt and fail as the fourth ships from the Jukal home world fleet was left broken and useless.

As the Mana barrier of the bastion failed, it started to rotate, bringing fresh portals to bear as well as spreading the damage onto the fresh Mana barriers on the opposite side.

It was not quick at moving and its thick armored hull made of compressed materials was left pitted and marred by the Jukal attacks. A number of the onos were destroyed, further reducing the bastion's abilities. However, as soon as these onos were out of the line of fire, they started to repair themselves at a rate visible to the naked eye. It was as if time moved backward as they continued to reform.

The *BloodHawk* rocked with explosions as more of the stations moved into view, adding in their attacks.

Frank had no time to curse as he checked for damage. They were locked in combat and there was little that they could do but hope that their firepower was stronger than the enemy's.

"Fleet One, prepare to jump. We're going to assist the fighters. Be prepared for close combat. Navigation, bring some of those formed portal relays with us," Xiao said, having just received his orders from Admiral Forsyth.

"Yes, sir!" Navigation called out as communications passed on the orders to the rest of Pandora Fleet One.

The portal relays were powerful, but when they were simply facing an enemy, they could only fire so many surfaces at them. If they were in the middle of them, they could unleash attacks in every direction.

"Ready all weapons for close-range combat! I say again, close-range combat. We are teleporting into the enemy's formation!" Frank barked his orders down to the rest of the fleet and his own weapons techs.

"Navigation, waypoint sent. Teleportation spell activating!" the navigation officer said.

Three of the Pandora fleets started to show signs of a spell formation appearing around them. Within their fleets, there were multiple deployed portal relays.

In a flash of light, the teleportation spell was activated. The runes became solid as they left the combined fleet.

Frank sent commands into all of the weapons systems. The *BloodHawk* led the way. Both of their broadsides roared to life, the power from the Mana discharge making the massive battleship rock from the shots. All missile ports were open and firing. From the spines and bow, the portals ignited with power and missiles surged out into the void, hungry wolves searching for the Jukal.

The missile boats were covered in swarms of missiles. Their runes glowed through the void above the planet as spell formations and arcane fire covered the ships in sharp light.

Destroyers followed the *BloodHawk's* example, holding nothing back. Spell formations appeared around the Jukal ships; powerful spells shot down on them as Frank selected two targets on either side of Pandora Fleet One.

All of the weapons in the fleet operated as one, locking onto the targeted carriers and unleashing all they had. The portal relays were fountains of fire, being left in the wake of Pandora Fleet One. They were as powerful as the *BloodHawk* in terms of how much firepower they could lay down.

Pandora Fleet Two and Three raced alongside Pandora Fleet One. The three forces gritted their teeth, charging right through the enemy. This was the power of the Pandora fleet! Their actions could only be called unwavering!

The Jukal were thrown off by the sudden attack but quickly started to fire back as the ships were not just rocked by their own weapons and attacks, but the impacts of the Jukal fleet ships' weaponry.

They might be the Pandora fleet but they were in the middle of the Jukal home world fleet. Their ranks were filled with true fighters, leaving little time between them seeing the Pandora fleets to their gunners opening fire.

A savage fight illuminated the void. Each side poured in as much fire as possible, their people pushed to their limits. These were not just ships and crew anymore; these were one creation, people and ships working together, pushing the limits of what the other was capable of and pulling out all potential left in them.

"Come on!" Frank said. A battery was hit with incoming fire; it was blown out, reducing the fire support on his right side.

The hull started to pull itself together as wounded were evacuated and those who were still able to got back to work. Weapon parts were pulled out and inserted into their positions. The soul gem-constructed walls quickly repaired the ship, using the parts as a framework to rebuild the batteries.

Grand working lines jammed and people bashed them into working order as missile tubes were hit. People used their Dark magic to reform the hulls as techs reformed the runic lines.

Frank felt pride from them all, moving from one screen to the next, never stopping as the carrier to the right shuddered. Under the combined fire of the Pandora fleet, its shields started to collapse; a lucky missile made it into an open hangar.

It appeared to be a two-stage as it opened up multiple decks of the ship with a light penetrator grand working, quickly following it up with a black cursing spell formation. The ship started to contort and decay, as the spell was rapidly shooting through the interior of the carrier.

Grand working rounds hit the hull of the carrier, igniting into plasma and destroying entire armored sections. Like a wounded beast in the last throes of its life, the carrier continued to hurl out more drones and fire its few remaining guns against the onslaught of missiles and weapons fire.

"Change targets!" Frank said, no mercy in his voice as he picked a Jukal destroyer that had been showing its crew to be much better at fire control and managing their shields than Frank liked.

The entire crushing firepower of the right broadsides of the Pandora fleet inundated the destroyer's defenses, leaving it no way to escape the oncoming fire.

"New target!" Frank said for the left-hand side as their carrier started to break apart. A pillar of light ten meters wide cut through the bow of the ship, through its center line. Explosions rippled out from it as it started to float away, unable to move under its own power.

The weapons on the left-hand side acted as those on the right side had, working in concert to bring the new target that Frank had selected under fire.

"Destroyer three is heavily damaged!" Communications called out.

"Any ships that are about to lose their shields are to regroup at rally point three," Xiao said.

Frank spared a glance for Pandora Fleet Two and Three. They had jumped into the midst of the Jukal home world fleet and were wreaking havoc on the Jukal.

"We've got incoming drones!" an officer manning the readings from the sensor spells barked. "Fighters are coming in from the other direction!"

After their first clash, the drones had sped off in one direction, having to turn around and fight the inertia they had built up in order to get back to the fleet. The same went for the attacking fighters of the combined fleet.

"Support them as we can." Xiao's calm voice carried through the ship as another explosion rocked the *BloodHawk*.

"Mana barrier is at seventy-three percent," the shield and barrier mage said from their station.

The destroyer under the concentrated fire of the left-hand side of Pandora Fleet One was broken as grand working shells made their way into the hull, hitting something important and causing it to explode.

"They're focusing fire!" Sensors called out.

"Have all ships ready to teleport the moment their Mana barriers reach ten percent," Xiao said.

The hulls of the Pandora ships were tough, but the spell formations that were used within the light cannons the Jukal used were incredibly powerful. Powerful enough that they could cut through the ship's hulls in just a few seconds of exposure.

For any ship, whether they were part of the combined fleet or the Jukal fleet, if they didn't have a Mana barrier up, they would incur serious damage or be wiped out. The power of the spells could only be stopped by the Mana barriers. Anything else was sure to suffer a bad fate.

Frank continued to pull out everything possible from his weapons crews, the sides of the battleships covered in the Mana ejecta of the grand working cannons and lit with the light of the Jukal's weapons fire and arcane flight spells of the missiles.

"Fleet Two is teleporting out!" Communications stated.

"We'll fight till the end," Xiao said, unperturbed by Pandora Fleet Two's retreat. There was no support coming; it was only Pandora Fleet One and Three, in the midst of the Jukal fleet, fighting for their lives as they passed through the enemy formation.

***

Dave didn't have time to look to the sky as blood covered his clothes and stained the path that he had walked through the slaves.

Roars reached to the heavens as Dave looked to see mounted slaves now coming from the holes in the ground. They moved in packs, their animals staring at the Emerilians with a cold light in their eyes. Each and every one of them were predators, and even accepting the slaves as their masters, their bloodlust had not been diminished in the slightest. In fact, it had only been increased and built upon, used to wage constant wars.

"Earth mages!" Dave yelled out over the command channel, putting a waypoint on the oncoming creatures. Massive spell formations appeared on the ground that started to shake. The mounted beasts ran into quagmires before the ground solidified, leaving them buried underneath the ground. Slit trenches appeared right ahead of the creatures; pained howls could be heard as their legs dropped into the trench, breaking as their riders were tossed off.

Dark mages, working closely with the Earth mages, raised their hands. Spikes rose from the ground; the moving creatures impaled themselves on the spikes as cursed ground appeared.

Dave dodged to the side as the grass under his feet shot up at him, as hard as steel and capable of shredding flesh and bone.

Gravity pushed down on the grass, giving time for Dave to escape it. He threw out his conjuration rod and turned in mid-air. It formed into a spear that shot through the heavens. A gravity spell formation appeared above it, making it pierce through the air before impaling the Earth mage from the slave army. There was a blank look on their face as they looked at the massive hole in their chest. Dave waved his hand; the spear dissolved and the conjuration rod shot toward Dave.

With his Touch of the Land spell, he saw all of Party Zero and the fights going on around him. He kept constant updates on the party, appearing behind any enemy that they were having trouble with and supporting them.

Dave wasn't as powerful in upfront fights, but splitting the enemies' concentration made it much easier for his allies to finish them off.

Wind blades tore through the air. Dave had no time to break their spell formation. Bolstering his shields, he raised his conjuration rod, forming it into a dwarven shield that covered his body. His other conjuration rod appeared in his hand.

The impact smashed against Dave's shield. Still in mid-air, he was tossed backward. He grunted with the power smashing against him.

From his hand holding the conjuration rod, small needles appeared, shooting out at the wind. The attacker's wind blades easily destroyed the needles he had fired out.

The attacker's attacks only became more frantic and powerful as they unleashed more Air blades and Air Affinity attacks at Dave. She had seized the momentum, forcing Dave to defend, unable to retaliate.

An arrow shot out of nowhere, leaving a blazing trail behind it. The wind mage let out an angered roar as she twirled her hand; a vortex rushed out to meet the arrow.

The arrow broke the vortex but its power was reduced to just twenty percent of its initial power.

Dave teleported, his shield turning into a dagger.

The wind mage's Mana barriers took the impact of the arrow, changing colors with the impact.

A dagger appeared in the direction that they had been pushed in. The dagger emitted a gray smoke and had a terrifying energy pouring off the runic lines that ran down the blade.

It pierced through the Mana barrier. The wind mage's eyes went wide as she felt the blade pierce through her neck. Her eyes rolled back as her energy quickly left her body and she dropped toward the ground. The enchantments and runes that had been placed on Dave's armor went to work, absorbing the power of the wind mage's Mana pool as well as any other power left in their body.

Dave looked to Deia, nodding to her. She was already firing arrows out to assist others.

There was no time for words as he once again disappeared, continuing on his path of destruction.

***

"Portal relays are online! Flying Citadel Groups One, Two, and Three are moving in to support." Suzy was assisting from the rear with her creations. Lu Lu unleashed lightning at the slaves. A number of protectors were around her as she acted as the link between many of the commanders on the ground and the forces in the air and those fighting in the space around Emerilia.

"Good! Get them to start breaking through the surface! Let's break into whatever the hell is hiding underneath us!" Gurren said.

Dave opened a private chat to Gurren.

"Make sure that we don't hit Party One," Dave said.

"Good point," Gurren replied.

The portal relays took off and started to climb into the sky. A Mana barrier appeared in the direction of the slave army and the Jukal defenses; the other portals started to open up with cannon fire. The destruction reaped could hardly be believed as whatever lay in front of the portal relays was ground into nothing, leaving deep lines of craters where they passed. Missiles shot out from behind the portal relays before coming around. Grand working warheads went off, changing the sky and earth as they unleashed spells.

The flying citadels extended across the advancing lines, moving above the fighting forces, aiding them in their advance and dropping fire on the slaves and trying to defeat the Jukal defenses.

People dropped from above, using the portals within the flying citadels to get to the drop runes and teleport down to the planet's surface.

Aleph manned the aerial batteries, cutting down those fighting in the air. The aerial forces moved to the towers, charging their armor, resupplying with Mana bombs and ranged weaponry or downing recovery potions.

"Floating defenses!" someone called out as the floating defenses could finally be seen in the sky.

The flying citadels reacted as if they had met their nemesis, as if only one of them could remain in the sky. Their weapons all tracked onto the floating defenses, swarming them with fire. In front of the citadels, layered spell formations appeared. The runic lines all glowed, seemingly pouring power into the powerful rune sets.

One of them ignited. A lance of Mana charged across the sky, smashing apart everything in its path and turning night into arcane blue day. The beam howled through the air before striking one of the floating defensive structures.

The shield shook but it stayed aloft. Another beam hit it a split second later; then another and another. They timed their fire so that as the first one fired, the second one was only a fraction of a second behind. When the last of the flying citadels finished firing, the first flying citadel was once again ready to fire.

The first floating defensive installation was overwhelmed and it dropped out of the sky, blown to pieces as it was struck by even more damaging spells. Yet another beam hit it, boring into and through it as it crumbled. With its power failing and flight systems destroyed, the installation smashed into the ground. The impact was so immense that it made the ground shake. The flying citadels focused their fire on another defensive installation that was firing out light cannons and missiles into the troops.

The light cannons were much weaker on planets with the interfering atmosphere; as such, their attacks weren't as powerful as the flying citadels' by a large margin.

Dave teleported his blade. Cutting out, he stabbed through where a human's kidney was located. His chosen victim seemed more enraged than anything as Dave teleported away.

"Fricking alien biology," Dave muttered to himself. He increased the gravity of the area, slowing down the reactions of the victim and unleashing Mana bolts so fast that they didn't have time to react. Their shield took a number of the impacts before the creature leaped forward, a wild look in their eyes.

Dave's eyes went wide before he gritted his teeth. He had underestimated his opponent, too confident in his own abilities.

One of the weapons under his control fell apart and then recombined in milliseconds, unleashing a super dense dart that cut through the air. It struck Dave's opponent, turning them into a mist.

Dave had won but there was a grim look on his face as he pulled back from the battle, mentally chastising himself for his actions that had nearly gotten him killed and put him in a disadvantageous position.

A terrible howling noise filled the sky as the massive needle pillars from Gunboat Isle shot out from portal relays. The noise was incredible as the needles turned into meteors, burning up from the air friction, and smashed against the ground ahead of the Emerilians in an amazing display of destruction.

Dust was thrown up to the heavens as the ground cracked and fell apart. The underground areas of the emperor's residence were revealed as more and more rounds smashed into the ground, tearing apart the emperor's grounds.

A powerful buzzing noise filled the sky. Dave looked to the arks as the portals along their sides flared with power. Energy beams shot out; spell formations formed and a thin membrane appeared. A Mana shield spread out to cover the Jukal emperor's residence, encompassing the gardens to the rear and the emperor's primary palace.

Jukal orbitals started to launch attacks against the stationary arks, only to find that they were covered by powerful Mana shields themselves. The arks that had spread out now created an impenetrable shield to keep Jukal reinforcements and aid out.

The Pandoran destroyers, seeing their job was done, turned their bows toward space. The spell formations behind them flared with more power as they left the continent behind, increasing speed over the ocean around it. They tilted upward. The arcane fire engines seemed to explode with power. The water beneath them was turned into craters under their thrust as they shot upward into the skies.

"Jakan incoming!" Suzy said.

From the portals, Jakan marched out, leaving their home world behind and coming to the battlefield. As their lead forces came through, they saw the ongoing battle. They increased their pace and a messenger was sent back.

As the Emerilians had kept their side of the deal, so would they.

The Emerilians established a beachhead and access for the Jakan. Now the Jakan were filled with excitement. More and more Jakan continued through the portals, marching into battle, joining the lines and replacing the Emerilian fighters.

They lost more people but with their numbers, they didn't lose any ground. Instead, they advanced as they brought in more of their support. Their entire force was at a steady advance.

Dave's eyes narrowed as he looked to where he sensed powerful auras coming from.

Thirty or so slaves shot out of the ruins of the battlefield underneath the emperor's residence. They stood above the destruction like kings overlooking their domain. Behind them was a cadre of powerful experts at their command.

"Battlefield lords," Bob said over the party channel. "They're people capable of making a kingdom within the battlefield that lays under the emperor's residence. They aren't to be underestimated."

The thirty people's powerful auras covered the battlefield. The morale of the slave army surged as their attacks increased in speed and ferocity.

"We've fought gods and we're waging war on the Jukal Empire—what are some battlefield lords?" Lox barked, his words heard by all in the Emerilians forces.

The Emerilians grit their teeth and fought on.

Dave didn't try to focus on the constant stream of people who were being pulled out by healers or being sent back to Ice City via portal to be put back together, or those who were put off to the side, their worries in this life over.

Fire, Air, and Water's auras surged to meet the battlefield lords as they moved into the air.

"Masters, support!" Fire called out. She was the leader of the master's force, a group of the most powerful people across Emerilia—masters of weapons, the arcane, wielders of Weapons of Power, many of them Legendary figures in the lands that they came from. Among the ranks, there was Party Zero, Denur and some of her direct children, Bob, Fire, Water, Air, Jelanos, and Alamos. There were overseers wearing battle cloaks, dwarven protectors, elves, humans, gnomes, orcs—nearly fifty people from all across Emerilia who held the title of strongest.

There were two divisions under them, made of another fifty people a piece, bringing their strength to one hundred and fifty.

"Well, these pricks are going to be a pain." Steve floated in the sky. Runes shone across his soul gem body as he twirled his axe in his hands.

The battlefield lords looked at the masters fighting groups, their disdain clear. They were seasoned veterans of battle. Unless someone had been in the battlefield under the emperor's residence, they didn't even place them in their eyes.

Fire took a step forward, Mal beside her. Flames appeared around him, forming into a massive demonic avatar made of flames that towered over Fire.

"Kill them," Fire said. The two forces turned into streams of lights as they rushed at the enemy.

Dave casually pulled out grand workings, activating them and tossing them into the air. They appeared all around him before disappearing with a flash; they reappeared instantly among the battlefield lords.

Overlapping spell formations unleashed curses on the battlefield lords as their spell formations started to form, aiming to attack the Emerilian masters.

The grand workings only needed moments to activate as the enemies' spell formations took more time to create.

The battlefield lords cried out in rage as they felt multiple curses fall on their bodies. Their power surged, trying to get rid of the curses and hexes directly affecting this combat ability.

Spells clashed between them. Terrifying Mana ripples and shock waves blasted through the night sky.

There was only time for one exchange of spells before the two forces clashed. The powerful impacts and strikes were enough to kill anyone in an instant if they allowed it through their defense.

Even Dave's eyes went wide as he saw the overwhelming power of the battlefield lords. He was reminded of the time that they had gone up against the fifty or so elites of the Xelur clan, giving them no time to voice their regrets as they pounded them into nothing with constant spell formation and artillery cannon fire.

The slaves' army opened up as they were being pushed back. Under the flying citadels' support, the Emerilian forces started to advance at an even faster rate.

The sky became a deadly place as the Aleph aerial batteries went to work and the aerial fighting forces that were using the tower rushed out to aid their allies already engaged in combat.

Dave dodged out of the way of a spear. The air of the spear pushed against his armor's Mana barrier, pushing him backward. He disappeared from where he was. A bow formed in his hands as he fired at the spear-wielding battlefield lord that had appeared.

A roar that shook the heavens sounded out around Bob. A resplendent atmosphere filled the sky. He turned into a gray blur; his claws lurched out, weaving through the battlefield lord's defenses and tearing them apart.

Dave saw the cold smile on Jung Lee's face. His body was wreathed in gray smoke as he combined the six Affinity spirits that were in his body, reaching new heights of power.

Dave's opponent moved with lightning speed, their spear elusive, quick, and powerful at the same time, seemingly like a snake bobbing around as it looked at its prey. He advanced on Dave, who was feeling just a little bit pressured.

Dave let out a shout as the man got closer. His voice was greatly amplified, making the spear wielder grunt. But injuries were nothing new to him; instead, anger surfaced on his face, as if annoyed with himself for being injured by such a lowly being.

Dave disappeared and reappeared. In his hands, a cannon appeared, the barrel next to his opponent's face. The cannon glowed with resplendent light, firing out a grand working shell that tore through the opponent's head like paper.

"Overkill much?" Steve barked.

Dave didn't say anything as weapons and parts started coming out from his items of holding. The items that had been hovering in the air supporting the forces now shot to Dave. The panels came together and the vault soul gems added to one another as a torso built around Dave; then shoulders, a neck, lower legs. The parts came together like some grand puzzle, forming into a massive person.

"Oh, for fuck's sake!" Steve yelled, looking at the goddamn magical mecha Dave had created. "When the shit did you have time to build that?" Steve complained. "Trying to become a damn Transformer?"

Dave's power surged as he rushed forward into a group of the battlefield lords and their retinues. A blade formed in his hands and tore through the sky with a howl. Dozens died in the attack as he teleported into the air. The gravity under his feet increased. Those who weren't allied with them dropped to the ground, their eyes bulging out at the pressure that rained down on them. Dave waved his hand imperiously, throwing out pins into the sky. Behind them, spell formations activated as they shot toward the ground in a deadly shining rain.

Dave conjured another sword, leaving a path of death behind him as the pins ended those who had been below his feet.

The cannon on his shoulder fired. The shell slammed into a defensive structure on the ground. He teleported away. Once again, the battlefield lords barely held any interest to him, the basic fighting forces nothing more than ants to him in his most powerful form as the cannons and orbs around him unleashed spells and enchanted shells upon the Jukal defenses. His display of overpowering might made those on the battlefield tremble in fear.

They had lived fighting one another, but seeing the ease with which Dave destroyed their lines, their morale plummeted.

"Someone jealous?" Suzy yelled.

"Think he's making up for something?" Gurren asked Lox slyly, over the party chat.

"Well, screw this!" Steve yelled. He disappeared from the battlefield as Dave finished forming his new body that was fifteen meters tall, covered in runic lines. It looked like a much larger version of the Devastator armor, except it was covered in orbs at its joints and there were two massive cannons mounted next to his head.

"Excuse me—coming through. What's the right of way with a portal?" Steve asked.

"Go through the other way, dumbass!" Lox yelled back.

"Be back in a mo!" Steve said sweetly. Steve disappeared through the ship portal that was allowing the flying citadels through.

"Wait!" Lox barked.

"What the hell is he doing?" Deia asked.

No one said anything, as if collectively shrugging, and continued on fighting.

Around Dave, gray smoke seemed to cover his massive war machine. The gravity was much higher and it was harder for the battlefield lords and their minions to control their Mana.

Dave brandished two swords in his hands. "I'm getting that damn weapons master class!" He roared and disappeared from where he had been. His body flashed as he appeared next to a fighter. His sword lashed out, aiming to cleave them in two; they dodged, and struck out. A Mana bolt shot out from one of the orbs, vaporizing their shield as needles that had been hidden from them shot out. Their body withered away and fell into dust. Their power rushed toward Dave, being absorbed by his mecha.

"I thought you were a conjuration mage!" Suzy asked.

"Ah, well, I'd say I'm more of a crafter," Dave replied.

"You took a fantasy-class mage and you turned it into a techno mage," Malsour said.

"Guess so," Dave said.

"This is broken, so broken," Gurren said.

"Will you just shut up and fight? Don't worry—the terrible techno mage is all just an illusion," Lox said, as if he were the authority on it.

"I really don't want to do my maths again to learn all this techno stuff," Gurren said.

"Fat chance of that," Jung Lee said.

"Look, even the samurai-possessed ghost dude alchemist is arguing!" Gurren said, sounding depressed.

Even as they talked, they were fighting the battlefield lords and their minions to their limits. The fights weren't easy, but on the party chat, they could talk freely. They weren't the most normal batch of people when it came to being in fights.

"How have we survived this long?" Induca asked in a voice filled with curiosity.

"I have no idea," Deia said.

"Can someone help me with this druid? He looks like the world's most messed-up potted garden rolled into one! I don't know if he's trying to get a pruning or saying hello." Gurren sounded confused.

Deia and Induca turned. Deia's bow created layered spell formations and aimed the arrow at Gurren's opponent that looked like some vine, tree, shrub, and herb garden, making it scream out in pain as it fought against the Fire spell that was contained within the arrow.

"That's not a druid. Druids take on the shape of animals!" Dave said as Induca's fireball landed.

"Fine! It's a holy, burning, plant-changing weirdo-twig!" Gurren said as the creature was now indeed on fire in a spectacular manner.

"More importantly..." Jung Lee paused as he weaved through a defense of a minion bending backward. His right palm reached out to touch the minion; a flash of white light appeared as the minion was hurled to the side by the spell Jung Lee had insta-cast. Jung Lee moved in a flash and his blade pierced through the minion before he continued on. "What is Steve doing?"

"Good point," Anna said.

"Shit," Lox said.

"I'm not getting him this time," Malsour said.

"Who's Steve? I don't know a Steve," Gurren said.

"So, Dave, what inspired you to make your magical mecha of doom?" Anna asked.

"I'm putting the blame of this on anime," Dave said. His body shifted to the side, escaping a swipe as he rushed forward. His twin swords rippled in the air. Air blades hit his opponent; he teleported, unleashing Mana bolts from one side, then needles from another. He teleported from place to place, overwhelming the battlefield minion.

"Incoming!" Induca said.

Flames appeared around Dave as he quickly dodged away. He had been so focused on the battlefield lord he hadn't noticed the three minions trying to hit him from behind. As he disappeared, their attacks landed on the battlefield lord.

Arrows pierced through two of the minions, others following the third.

"No one hits my fiancé!" Deia yelled.

Malsour's claws shot out shadows through the air, hitting the battlefield lord and tearing them apart.

Lu Lu unleashed a lightning attack on them. Dave's cannon fired; the explosion covered where the battlefield lord had been until the bloodied lord came shooting out of the cloud left by the explosion. Bob appeared behind it. Just as it started to turn around, a look of shock and fear on its face, a claw tore through their back and chest before pulling out, leaving a ragged hole in the lord's chest.

Deia's arrow broke the third minion's defenses. They were set aflame as they dropped toward the ground.

"Miss me?" Steve's voice rang through the party chat as they all looked to the portal that he had exited through.

"Oh, come on! You look ridiculous!" Gurren said as Steve, a new eighteen-meter-tall Steve, stepped out from the portal.

"Ah shit!" Steve yelled as he *fell* out of the portal. His runic lines flared to life, not before he crashed into the ground, leaving behind a crater.

He soared up into the sky, bits of rubble and dirt on him. He no longer wore the Devastator armor but instead had armor made from soul gem composites and a new axe.

"I thought you loved Alex the Axe," Lox said.

"Well, this is Alex the Axe the second," Steve huffed, sounding more like a petulant child than an eighteen-meter-tall monstrosity.

"Let's keep advancing. We still have a lot of distance to cover." Deia shook her head. To anyone else, they might seem downright insane.

"Woo-hoo, Weapons Master Three!" Dave yelled, sharing a message with the others as his power took another step upward. Nothing could even attempt to stand in his way. He flashed across the sky, his weapons transforming in his hands. With every appearance, dozens fell from the sky. He was an unstoppable god of war.

Deia glanced at what he had shared.

Quest: Weapons Master Level 4

One handed and shield 1000/1000

Two handed 1000/1000

Dual wielding 1000/1000

Archery 1000/1000

Rewards: Unlock Level 5 Quest

+20 Vitality

+10 Endurance

+15 Strength

+15 Agility

+300,000 EXP

Passive skills from other weapons increase from 25% to 50% when designated weapon is not equipped. (Example: While using Dual-wield blades, one is able to gain 50% of the archery skill's abilities.)

Class: Weapons Master

Status: Level 5

+100 to Vitality

+50 Endurance

+75 Strength

+75 Agility

Effects: Passive skills from other weapons increase from 25% to 50% when designated weapon is not equipped. (Example: While using Dual-wield blades, one is able to gain 50% of the archery skill's abilities.)

Steve let out a sound of complaint as he, too, teleported. Deia's eyes went wide as he appeared in the midst of the enemy. Both he and Dave were now able to show off the power that they had been hiding from the Jukal for so long.

They had made fusion reactors, Mana wells, and grand working missiles and shells. Even if they only spent part of the time thinking about ways to augment their abilities, it greatly increased their combat ability.

A new wave of destruction covered the land as people started using their most powerful abilities. Their enemy now realized they had poked a slumbering dragon.

Chapter 17: Endure

The emperor smashed his hands against his chair. The reinforced armrests were beaten into submission as he watched his battlefield lords being torn apart by the Emerilians.

They'd been taught with the Mirrors of Communication, armed and armored by the Pandora Initiative, and tempered in the fighting of the event on Emerilia and the fights across the Jukal Empire in order to remove the Jukal's influence.

They might not have lived a life filled with bloodshed, but instead of only knowing how to fight, they had a goal, a purpose. They had people to defend because if they lost, Emerilia would fall. With such a purpose and goal, how could they allow themselves to fail! The Jakan beside them were fighting to become allies with the Emerilians, to be shown how to gain star travel in order to expand through their system and to also allow them to fight.

They threw themselves into the fighting right beside the Emerilians, their reasoning odd to the humans. But at that moment, they didn't care, only thankful to have more allies on the battlefield.

"They're making their way into the battlefield!" the emperor bellowed. As the needles had struck the ground, the battlefield underneath had been crushed and a massive pit revealed itself. The Emerilian forces were pushing the slaves back into this uneven territory.

"Nephew, for now we will endure. Then we will send out our true army," the emperor's uncle said, comforting him.

The emperor thumped his hand into his armrest one more time, but didn't say anything to refute him. "Get me a new chair!" he bellowed, his anger reaching new heights.

***

"I don't understand how dwarves can like this so much," Kim muttered.

"I'm a dwarf and I'm digging a hole, diiiiigging a hole, yada yada yah, lumde dum de!" Dwayne said. Even as they were flying, he moved his body as if he were marching.

Yemi, who was leading them, snorted at their actions.

"Seems like Party Zero rubbed off on you idiots," Josh said as they flew through the ground. Several Blood Kin were in front, chugging potions as if it were two-dollar tequilas on a Friday night.

They hadn't been so happy with that comment when Josh had made it.

Their speed was incredible. In front of them, the ground opened up as they flew on. Behind them, the stone, dirt, and ores would close back together, leaving them in a perpetual open sphere.

All of them were using party chat to talk as they had Mana barriers keeping their air in.

"Are we there yet?" Kim said.

"No, not yet." Lucy rode on her magic carpet, wearing her caster's robes and reading a book.

"How much longer?" Kim played with her hair, a bored expression on her face.

"Four more hours," Yemi said.

Kim blew a raspberry and pulled out a crossword. "What is seven letters long and makes people smell better?"

"This really the time for that?" Josh asked.

"A shower?" Dwayne said.

"Not enough—*seven* letters," Kim said, the two of them ignoring Josh.

"Perfume?" Josh sighed.

"Fits!" Kim said as they continued through the heart of the Jukal planet.

***

Frank checked his screens looking at the ground. The Emerilian forces there were pushing back the slave army in vast numbers. They had entered the caved-in area that had been their home and battle-field. It made it hard for the units to stay together, making it so that they had to break into smaller units, getting into fights all over the place as the sky above the area were still covered in aerial forces.

More of the flying citadels were joining in on the fight. Their fire-power joined to demolish more of the floating defensive structures and helped those on the ground. Now all of the flying citadels were on the Jukal home world.

Frank checked over the ship's systems. After coming through the Jukal fleet, they had destroyed five Jukal ships, losing one destroyer along the way. The *BloodHawk* had also been heavily damaged and needed to teleport out of the battle to the rally point. The rest of the fleet followed and immediately worked on repairs.

They'd left behind the portal relays they'd taken into battle. They'd been able to take out another three ships before they were overwhelmed with fire and destroyed.

The main fleet was just seconds away from clashing with the Jukal fleet. Already their battle was heating up. It was impossible to say what the outcome would be as weapons fired and destructive forces rained down on both groups.

"We've got a station coming into range in two minutes!" Sensors called out in a panic.

"Why didn't we see them before?" Xiao hissed. The tension in the room ramped up. "All ships to full readiness. Start flushing mis-siles and get some portal relays out to support!"

"It was hidden among the civilian stations. It only just started opening its weapon ports," Sensors said.

"I hate it when the enemy are trying to be sneaky bastards." Xiao cursed.

Portal relays that had been placed onto the spine of the battle-ship now had a surge of power go through them as they expanded rapidly. This way, their redeployment would be a lot faster than if they were relying on just their own power to get the first portal start-ed.

The portal was flung out into the space above the Jukal home world, quickly transforming. A half-dozen of them populated the outer Jukal atmosphere. Quickly, portals started to grow out from them as the station noticed what they were doing and started to open fire on them.

"We've got orders to defeat that station! If it continues on its path, then it will be right in front of our fleet as they come through the Jukal home world fleet. They're going to get hammered," Xiao said, his face grim.

It had taken the wealth of fire from the entire fleet to down the other stations.

"Frank, what are you going to need?" Xiao asked.

Frank's mind worked as he checked out the information that came from the spells locked on the station that was shedding its out-er skin, leaving panels behind as weapons and missile ports became visible.

There was a grim look on his face as more and more information started to compile.

"Launch all of our missiles this minute. Flush out the portal re-lays, all that we have—get them to pour out more missiles. Have our portals shoot out missiles as well. We're going to need to have Nal-heim avatars prepared and the kinetic energy needles for our broad-sides, as well as many of the shield orbs as possible. Those laser can-nons will tear through what's remaining of our shields with ease," Frank said.

"I'll see it's done and pass word to the rest of the fleet," Xiao said.

Moments later, the portal relays pumped out compact portal relays and missiles. The Pandora fleet ships' missile ports fired constantly as their portals glowed with the light of arcane fire flight drives.

They were wreathed in a corona of missiles.

The light cannons of the station came online and started firing. They cut down the missiles that acted as a screen, creating clouds of debris that made it harder for the light beam to cut through.

With their items of holding, the fleet had missiles to spare as they fired out everything they had, creating a cloud of them in front of the portal relays that were advancing, many of them still forming and growing.

The light cannons made it through the missile screens every so often. The portal relays, even if they had Mana barrier protection, were torn apart.

Some beams went wide, but others struck the vessels of the three Pandora fleets that were gathered together.

"Give the order to the fleet—rotate so that their belly portals are facing the station. Compute the kinetic energy weapons' trajectories," Frank said.

"Aye!" Communication said as Nav shifted the ship. Xiao left it all in their hands, knowing that these seconds counted, separated them from winning and defeat in a space battle.

All of the fleet started to rotate their ships.

The orbs around the *BloodHawk* were burned out as a laser cannon hit them. Three layers of Mana barriers were destroyed in an instant. However, there were still two more layers and the Mana barrier of the battleship that was still recovering from the previous battle.

If it made it through those two barriers, the ship's barrier would fail and there would be penetration.

"Fire the needles!" Frank said.

The ship's portals connected and their needles shot out. They didn't have any guidance as such: the ships had all altered their point of aim to bring them into line with the station. Two fired from every vessel, the rest of their portals all firing out missiles.

The first wave of missiles was taken under fire by the defensive weapons of the station, but there were too many of them.

From around the portal relay stations, Nalheim warriors appeared behind the wall of missiles. Holes appeared in the missiles as the Nalheim's spears shot the station, all of them focused on the same area.

Their bodies faded as the disruption attacks landed. The Jukal Mana barrier shook, changing colors before shattering like glass. Missiles reached into the station, their explosions hammering the station that was now a wealth of fire.

Missiles sprouted from the station; explosions dotted the skies around it as they smashed into the impeding waves of missiles from the Pandora fleets. Even as it seemed like a waste, they were able to clear the Jukal home world's orbit, opening up their cannons to fire on the Pandora fleet.

The portal relays facing the station changed; kinetic energy needles shot out and targeted at the opening. The rest of their portals fired missiles nonstop.

A Pandoran destroyer was struck by a light cannon. Their Mana barrier orbs were destroyed; their main barrier failed and a chunk of their rear section vaporized.

"Put the ship on automatic and evacuate them immediately!" Xiao barked as the ship started to drift.

Its portals and its missile ports continued to fire. The ship rotated. The force of the impact threw it into a spin. The weapons along the broadside started firing, the ship fighting to the last.

The full strength of the missile barrage arrived. The shields all over the station started to fluctuate and dim.

Sections started to collapse as the station tried to rotate to bring more shields into place. Barrier-disrupting grand working spells started to play havoc with the shields, creating massive interference and opening them up to attack. Through the openings, tens of missiles that had survived so far hit the hull of the station. Its hull couldn't be compared to the hulls of the Pandora, Deq'ual, or Jukal ships. It could take the hits, weathering them as the Mana barriers fought to come back online.

The Pandoran destroyer that had been wounded exploded as three more laser cannon blasts tore it apart.

Light spells poured out from the station, seemingly unstoppable as they broke shields, pierced armor, and left the ships of the Pandora fleet battered and torn.

The needles fired by the three fleets landed on the station. The station was forced backward by the impacts. Mana barriers shattered; weapons were scoured off the face of the station as it reeled from the massive damage.

The *BloodHawk* shuddered as it, too, was struck by light cannon spells.

The Mana barrier orbs had created four layers but they were unable to stop the blasts.

"Mana barrier failed. We have strikes on the fourth and fifth floors!" the officer overseeing the Mana barriers said. The others had pale faces but they bent down to keep up their work.

"Teleportation runes are offline. Channeling power into them!" Navigation said.

"Start evacuating the ship!" Xiao barked. His words rang through the ship as people quickly started rushing through onos, leading to the portals inside, and quickly evacuated back to the asteroid base.

Wounded were hauled through the ship, their hull open to space as Frank continued to man his station, watching the station in the distance.

A missile boat was struck, going up in an explosion of spell formations as missiles in their tubes had their grand working warheads activate, tearing the ship apart.

Frank poured power into his console, unlocking the limits on the spell formations around the battleship. The fusion reactors ramped up past their limits as spell formations appeared around the ship. Light spells shot forward; multiple light beams shot off, striking the station and puncturing its hull. Dozens of spell formations appeared and then dissolved around the *BloodHawk* continuously.

"Frank, we need to go!" Xiao yelled. All of the personnel in the command center made for the emergency ono at the rear of the command center to evacuate.

"Go! I've got this!" Frank barked, his eyes red as he looked at the station. Its weapons were failing, being torn from its surface as the weapons started to open up its thick hull, gaining access to the vulnerable areas inside.

Frank continued to control the spell formations, controlling them manually as the ship was hit by another blast, eroding the control of the AI that assisted the *BloodHawk*.

The station was covered in weapons fire, a juggernaut that wouldn't give up.

"Focus on this point!" Frank yelled to the other fire controllers.

Light spell formations flared to life. The other fire controllers listened to their brother, pushing the limits of their magical coding. The second fleet's battleship's Mana barriers failed, a hole appearing in her hull.

A Pandoran destroyer was ruptured and another missile boat sent adrift but their weapons kept firing, their attacks landing on the station. They didn't teleport away; they didn't try to escape. They knew that if they didn't destroy this station, then it would recover its Mana barrier and tear apart the combined fleet.

Those in the main fleet and the Jukal home world fleet looked at the two forces locked in combat, neither giving an inch. The station continued to tear apart ships with ease while the Pandora fleets held on, pouring out all of the potential that they had.

It was savage and brutal as ships were turned to shrapnel, decks opened to space.

A hole opened up in the hull of the station under the onslaught of Frank's attacks. Multiple light beams tore into the hull of the station; portal relays that could bear on it fired out needle rounds.

They smashed into the opening. Armored panels were contorted and destroyed. The needle turned to shrapnel that ripped through the interior of the station.

Another needle round slammed into the point that the ships were focusing on, opening it wider and rushing through it. It hit what must have been a missile bunker on an inner section of the station. The whole quarter of the station exploded outward as a miniature sun exploded inside the station.

Sections of the hull were contorted and shaken. Many of the weapons systems failed. Missiles and needles that had already been fired didn't stop as they mercilessly opened up the hole in the station's hull and tore through everything inside. The station's systems were broken and destroyed as it started to break apart, nothing more than a broken hull.

Frank leaned back in his chair, noticing that things were floating around. A ping on his interface told him that his Mana barrier had automatically activated, as the command center was open to space and without atmosphere.

A pop-up appeared in his face, asking him to join a private chat. He accessed it.

"All right, Navigation. Try to see if we can't level her out. Engineering, let's link some of our portals up to a power source in order to speed up the recovery of the soul gem constructs. I want us sealed up first and the air sorted. Communications and Sensors, direct teams to those wounded or trapped—let's get them sorted out. Once we've got that, we'll render assistance to the other forces. Frank, could you send orders for those portal relays to return? Let's have them on defense, covering us," Captain Xiao said from his command chair.

Frank looked around the room, seeing the core members of the command center all there.

"Sir, why didn't you evacuate?" Frank asked.

Xiao chuckled slightly, holding back from replying as Navigation spoke up.

"Well, you needed someone to keep you level. Don't tell me you didn't notice we were drifting," Navigation said.

"The sensors were a bit wonky—not going to let the targeting be thrown off by that," Sensors offered.

"Needed to make sure you didn't break all of the runic lines. Was a pain managing that power so the spell formations didn't collapse," the officer for Mana barriers said.

Frank choked up as he looked to them all. Even as they joked around, he could sense the care that they showed toward him.

A smile appeared on his face. He rubbed his eyes, clearing away any signs of tears, his emotions a mess from it all. He sat back, realizing how close he had come to death and how they had stood beside him, facing the same struggles as him, without a second glance.

"Thank you," Frank said simply. The atmosphere turned awkward.

"Well, you'd do it for any of us," Xiao said. "Now let's get to work. That second fleet is almost here and the main fleet is tearing the home world fleet to shit," Xiao said.

Frank looked through his sensors, seeing the three Pandora fleets giving everything they had. The combined fleets seemed to have found new strength as they tore through the Jukal home world fleet.

The Jukal were unable to withstand the combined fleets' firepower. Already weakened by the three Pandora fleets from before, they had lost the initiative and were getting worse.

A grim look appeared on Frank's face. He'd escaped death, barely, but even with that, his battle wasn't over.

The Jukal fleet that was returning was taking the time to gather their forces now. It would take them a total of two days to reach the Jukal home world.

The combined fleets and the Jukal home world fleet separated. The Deq'ual ships had taken the most losses. Without the teleportation spells, they couldn't escape after their barriers failed. However, they had been swarmed by Mana barrier orbs in order to make them harder to kill.

Even as the two fleets broke apart, the Jukal were still in the midst of the portal relays that had been left in the combined fleets' wake. The bastion continued to fire backward and the portals around the ships moved to unleash attacks on them.

A battleship trailing behind received their combined attention. Its shields failed as its hull was scraped and opened up. Deep grooves appeared in the hull before a strike rammed right up its engine. The ship's rear exploded and the ship blew apart.

The Jukal fleet tried to get another ship but were unable to do much more than damage their hulls.

It continued for another twenty seconds before they were truly out of range.

The combined fleet altered their course, aiming for Pandora Fleets One, Two, and Three.

The Jukal fleet changed their course as well, heading for the rest of the Jukal fleet that had returned.

There were still dozens of defense stations around the Jukal home world to contest the combined fleet holding the home world's orbitals, leading to a standoff.

Frank turned his attention to the damage. Looking to the reports on his people, he let out a heavy sigh upon seeing the dead and injured. It was not his first time losing people, he knew, but it never got easier.

***

Bob let out a yell as his conjured spear cut through the sky, piercing the battlefield lord that was running away. The slaves were also in a full rout. The Emerilians chased them from behind and above, pressing them harder and harder.

The battlefield lords, after seeing their fellows being slaughtered, started to retreat, only to find the Emerilians were not willing to let them go.

As the last battlefield lord fell, the slaves' morale plummeted. Here and there, they would fight, but most of them just kept running.

"Slow the pace!" Lox barked.

The Emerilian force slowed down, the slaves quickly leaving them behind. Suddenly, those who were running away started exploding.

Dave frowned as he connected to the flying citadels. *Where are you? Come on—what's the frequency?* Dave's mind moved a million times a minute as he looked through reams of information on his interface.

"There you are!" Dave found what he needed before he sent commands to the flying citadel.

A massive spell formation appeared over the slaves. They shot upward, trying to destroy it, but how could they compare to the power of sixty-four flying citadels?

Streamers shot down from the sky and landed on the slaves. Immediately they stopped exploding and the spell formation disappeared.

He'd found out the signal for the kill switches in the slaves, blocking it and sending down a spell to destroy the implanted kill switch in their bodies.

The slaves didn't pay it any heed and kept running.

"Reduce the fire on the slaves," Lox said.

The flying citadels responded. The rate of fire decreased as the slaves ran and flew off into the distance.

"Forces on the front lines, hold position. Fresh forces, move up. Everyone check your gear and look after any issues you have." With Lox's orders, their forces started to move about. The flying citadels' rate of fire came to a halt.

The forces on the front line rotated out, Party Zero included. The floating defensive structures were now holding back after having lost thirteen islands; they had started gathering their forces instead of wasting them away with fighting the flying citadels. It was clear that they were readying another offensive.

The Emerilian forces were quickly moving through the pit that had once been the slaves' home. For them, the distance of ten kilometers wasn't enough to make them feel even out of breath.

Missiles shot out from the flying citadels as spell formations appeared above the floating defenses. Beams battered the floating islands, smashing them down.

The missile grand workings activated, creating teleport points through which attack spells were sent through.

"Looks like the floating islands aren't quite out of range," Steve commented. Dave looked over to him. Their size could almost be compared to a dragon's. Steve's attacks shook the heavens and earth. With one swipe of his axe, he had killed hundreds of the slaves and three of the battlefield lord's minions.

The arks kept any Jukal forces out, with their portals creating sealing shields. The flying citadels suppressed and destroyed the floating defenses; scouts patrolled the sky and the ground as the entire Emerilian and Jakan force advanced, taking the portals with them.

It seemed as if their advance couldn't be stopped. As they sped along the ground, the combined fleet tried to repair their ships as best as they could and prepare for the coming battle. Their original fighting force of a hundred and thirty-three was now down to eighty-nine ships. Eighty-nine against nearly two hundred Jukal fleet ships and defensive stations around the Jukal home world.

The Jakan continued onward. The defenses hidden in the emperor's residence and the ambushes by the slaves were found by the forward scouts and ended before they could begin.

Those who surrendered were sealed by overseers and sent to Emerilia. The ground shook with their advance, none of them daring to slow down. They no longer marched in lines but rather jumped and crossed over the broken battlefield below in a fashion similar to tree tag that the Stone Raiders had played when moving between locations on Opheir.

In front of the emperor's main palace, a new force was showing its face. Massive floating defenses hovered in the air; drones moved around them in groups. Below them, sections of the ground opened up, revealing massive defensive works, missile batteries and artillery.

Mechas were located behind walls, organized in groups of nine.

The ground all around the palace started to change, revealing more defenses and weapons emplacements. Armored Jukal moved to and fro, organizing the defenses and turning the majestic palace into a fortress.

Chapter 18: Victory or Defeat

In the space of a day, the Emerilian and Jakan forces on the ground were closing in on the Jukal emperor's palace. While the combined fleet were repairing their ships, engineers, mages, and people from the asteroid base and the Deq'ual outpost swarmed through their ships to help with the rebuild and repairs that they desperately needed.

Their ships were not in the best condition but they only had one day before the Jukal reached them.

The worst of the Pandora ships stayed behind with the Deq'ual ships supporting them. They were constantly releasing needles. Jeeves worked out the math for the needles' trajectory, using the gravity of the home world and the best firing angles and speeds imparted on the needles to curve around the planet's atmosphere and hit the stations.

Five had fallen under the steady and unending barrage laid down by the combined fleet.

Frank was deep in the weapons decks of the *BloodHawk,* working to get different systems online when he got an alert for Pandoran Fleets Four to Eleven were moving out. Most of the fleets had lost a ship or two at this time. They had beaten the Jukal, but they hadn't had any definitive victories in the Jukal home system yet.

Frank and the others slowed their work as interfaces were activated, all of them watching as the rest of the Pandoran ships were sent out.

They teleported out from where they were stationed, taking portal relays and the bastions with them.

Although they had been able to repair themselves in record time, the Jukal fleet hadn't been able to regrow their armor panels and electronics, putting them at a disadvantage in one aspect.

The bastions portaled into the middle of the Jukal force, flushing out portal relays through their teleport pads and onos.

The teleport pads and onos could increase the size of their event horizon, allowing them to move the fully functional portal arrays out. They were like a shoal of baby fish around a moth compared to the bastions. They unleashed chaos among the Jukal without warning.

Pandoran ships teleported around the Jukal, isolating ships, unleashing everything they had and teleporting away.

Frank watched for a few more minutes before he looked away. The strategy worked by manipulating the teleportation spells to their limit and the precise command and control and communication between the fire control and their weapons techs.

"Let's get back to work!" Frank said.

***

"Well, that is a fucking mess," Lox said.

Party Zero, as well as Fire, Mal, Air, Water, and Bob were all on one of the flying citadels, looking out over the terrain ahead.

The slaves from the battlefield were fighting against the Jukal defenses. However, there had been little chance for them to get close. Many had been cut down, the ground covered in craters and destruction where the slaves had been cut down. Bodies littered the fields and only a few of the slaves remained. As they had advanced, the Emerilian and Jakan force had come across more and more of the slaves looking to surrender.

The Emerilian and Jakan force wasn't far behind the slave force.

They had finally left behind the pit that was the battlefield under the emperor's residence and been greeted by the remains of the slaughter.

They were all looking to the defenses around the palace. There were light cannons as powerful as the ones mounted on the defensive station looking out at them. There were hundreds of Jukal mechas, swarms of drones, and a sea of defensive structures, both in the sky and across the ground.

"Well, looks like we'll just have to take their aggro and keep them off-balance," Dave said. He was now just wearing his normal armor, the parts of his mecha form secured within his bags of holding.

"Let's make camp, get settled. Use long-range attacks—poke them a bit and see what happens. Have the Mana barriers deployed," Deia suggested.

"Nothing like getting a rogue to earn their pay," Dave said.

***

Kim released the Jukal in front of her. They collapsed, the ground eating them up—the Blood Kins' work. They were hiding a few hundred meters under the ground.

Kim opened her eyes, blinking a few times as her eyes shifted from side to side. "All right, takes a bit of time when running that soul search stuff, and people with less nanites are harder to pull memories from." Kim took the time to organize herself. "All right, I have a good idea of where he is. Going to need another person to corroborate, however—got a bunch of possible targets in mind."

Under Kim's guidance, they moved through the ground, bypassing tunnels and structures that were buried under the Jukal palace. Finally they came to the side of an underground structure.

Kim cast a sensing spell, allowing her to find out what was on the other side of the wall. "They're home—grab 'em!"

The wall opened up as Josh stealthed forward and disappeared into the room. He flitted through the shadows, finding an officer poring over an information terminal. Josh stabbed them with a poisoned blade; they stiffened, their eyes wide as they looked up at Josh.

"Hello there, sweetheart." Josh turned back to the hole into the room. "Dwayne!" he hissed.

"Coming." Dwayne made it into the room, helping Josh as they pulled the Jukal out. The Blood Kin sealed up the wall and they disappeared into the depths under the palace once again.

Once they were sorted out, Kim put her hand on the Jukal officer's head. Light appeared around her hand as she closed her eyes. It took some time for the light to fade. Kim killed the Jukal with a bolt of electricity through the brain. She gathered her thoughts once again and started to go through the Jukal officer's memory transfer.

"Okay, I know where the emperor is. I also know where the command console is. It's going to take some time to get past the security to get to either. Might be best if we split up." Kim's fingers moved over her interface as she pulled out a Mirror of Communication. She closed her eyes and accessed the Mirror of Communication.

"All right, Lucy, you go with the Blood Kin and get that command console sorted out. You've got the programming for it and the information from the Pantheon, Dave, and Malsour. We'll deal with the emperor," Josh said, his hands resting on the curved blades in the small of his back.

Kim opened her eyes some time later as she shared something with them all. "Okay, just used the conference room builder in the Mirror of Communication to come up with this map. It's really rough but it's accurate," Kim said. A map appeared of the underground facilities under the emperor's palace. An overlay appeared, with blueprints and information that they had been able to collect on the palace as well as what they had been able to scan from the various sensory enhancing spells that the Emerilian and Jakan ground force had used.

Most of them glanced to the massive array of defenses that covered the area around the palace, facing their allies.

There had been a lot of traps and sensory spells laid over the ground around the palace. However, most of them were made to contain the slaves that had lived in the battlefield. Digging deep enough, they'd bypassed it and entered the sphere of detection spells. Now inside, there was little that would be able to detect them.

Once they had gone over the information that Kim had given them, they said their good-byes and split into two groups, headed in different directions.

***

The emperor had a dark expression on his face as he looked at the screens of the command center. Everyone inside was careful to do nothing to incite his anger.

He had requested again and again to go to the front lines to join in the slaughter of the Emerilians. Imagining it to be the same as when he had flown over the slave-filled battlefield, laughing, killing any who drew his attention with a swipe of his hand—that was what he loved more than anything: feeling as if he were a god looking down upon all creation, waving his hand and leaving nothing more than death and destruction.

His uncle and the man in charge of his personal guard had done everything to keep the emperor in the command center.

He frowned, looking at the screens. "Why haven't they attacked?" the emperor asked, his face grim.

No one replied to him for some time.

"They are probably scared of the might of your forces, nephew," the emperor's uncle said.

The emperor's countenance brightened, pleased by his uncle's praise-filled words. A smile appeared on his face as he sat up straighter, mist falling on him.

"Very wise of you to say, Uncle. I did not realize it myself. Indeed, anyone would be afraid to act upon witnessing my anger," the emperor said, naturally raising himself to a higher position.

"But this will not do. They have come for battle and we must remove this scourge from my residence. Send out our forces to destroy them or get them to act," the emperor said.

The commander of the emperor's personal forces glanced at the emperor's uncle for a split second before he relayed the orders.

It only took a few moments before a group of mechas started to move and some of the defensive floating islands started to advance. Spell formations appeared in front of the flying citadels as Mana beams shot out through the skies.

Light spells ignited in the cannons of the Jukal; beams hit Mana barriers that covered all of the Emerilian forces.

The Mana beams were stopped by the Mana barriers of the palace before they could reach the floating islands.

It wasn't long until the floating islands started to leave the defenses of the Mana barrier.

The flying citadels waited for them to build up some speed and exit the Mana barrier before they all focused on one floating island, overwhelming it with firepower. Missiles shot through the sky; artillery cannons blared and ranged spells beat the floating island back. It was unable to do anything until its Mana barrier shattered and the attacks started to rain down on the ship itself.

The floating citadel lost its power and started to fall toward the ground.

"How dare they!" the emperor yelled, standing to his feet, unable to accept that such lowly creatures would dare to even fight back against his might. His plan and excitement for the battle dimmed. This was being broadcasted all across the Jukal Empire. *Wasn't it just showing how weak he was if his forces were defeated so completely by the Emerilians?*

A shimmering glow appeared around the emperor. On the battlefield, a shadow appeared. It was hit by multiple rounds from both sides, making it harder to establish. It started to solidify as the emperor in his command center unleashed a punch in the direction of the Emerilians.

The emperor let out an angered roar as he poured more and more power into his body. His fist struck the Mana barrier in front of a flying citadel, only to find that there were layered shields covering not only the flying citadel but all of the attacking forces.

His rage reached new heights as the barrier failed to crack under his punch. He roared again. More power ran through his illusionary body. Rounds smashed against him from the Emerilian side; the Jukal held their fire for fear of hitting their emperor.

Seeing as it was just a projection, the flying citadels disregarded it and fired on the floating islands, bringing another crashing down. Its engines tossed it backward as it flew toward the ground, breaking apart and raining down on the Jukal defenses.

The emperor's second punch landed on the Mana barrier, making it shudder and change colors. The emperor kicked out at it in frustration, making it shake again as he let out another punch. His fist became solid as he smashed it down on the Mana barrier. The barrier shattered like glass as the emperor let out a satisfied grunt that seemed to stir the air of the sky. His illusionary body started to disintegrate in that same wind.

"No one stops the emperor of the Jukal Empire!" the emperor barked inside the command center, a look of satisfaction on his face as he turned to the commander of his personal forces. "Send out everything we have. We'll show them my might and wipe them out of existence!"

The commander didn't even look to the emperor's uncle, knowing that there was no way to get the emperor to reduce his orders.

***

"Crap. I was hoping that we could just stay out here, hit them at range and distract them." Deia looked at the entire Jukal defense that was mobilizing. Her words were tinged with worry.

Dave gripped her hand. He, too, was stunned by the power of the projected emperor. With three simple hits, he'd destroyed the combined Mana barrier. It wasn't their only Mana barrier but it was their strongest one.

"Hit them with every damn ranged weapon we've got. We're prepared for the possibility that it will come down on us in order to defeat the emperor's forces," Jung Lee said.

Lox and Deia looked to each other. Lox was still wearing his armor but they nodded to each other, the same idea held in their hearts.

They opened up channels to the Emerilia and Jakan forces. Portal relays, flying citadels, mages, archers, aerial forces—anyone and everyone who could hit the Jukal at range were called to action.

The Jukal, in turn, used all of their weapons: missiles, plasma cannons, light cannons—all of them fired.

"The strength of their weapons is more than I thought it would be." Dave grimaced.

"What does that mean?" Induca asked.

"It means that our Mana barriers are going to break sooner than we thought," Malsour said, his voice emotionless and barren.

"We need to make sure that the portals are ready if we need to retreat," Dave said.

"I'll help you," Malsour said.

Dave shared a look with Deia as he and Malsour disappeared. Dave looked to the portals that were arrayed behind the Emerilia and Jakan forces. They quickly gathered mages and people to help them.

"We'll keep some of them connected to Ice Planet and other places of aid; then, the others, if we angle them up, we can connect them to Gunboat Isle," Dave yelled. The noise of the fighting made it hard to even hear over party chat.

"Got it!" Malsour said.

They distributed the portals behind their forces and then the mages got the ground to grab the portals, creating supports and pointing them up on an angle. As they finished, the portals connected and missiles tore through the air, bringing more damage down upon the Jukal.

Malsour and Dave worked quickly. A thundering explosion made them duck, looking around before they saw one of the flying citadel's shields were deflecting under the massive damage as it was brought under fire.

The citadel started to fall apart, the different sections breaking. A surge of power rushed through the citadel as a spell formation solidified in front of the flying citadel. The entire vessel retreated with a burst of speed. Instead of trying to re-establish their shields, they had pushed themselves away from the forces on the ground. The flying citadel crashed into the ground, leaving a deep groove. It finally came to rest after a few moments. The people on the citadel recovered and started firing back at the Jukal, even wounded and no longer able to fly.

Light spells tore through Mana barriers on the ground; artillery landed among the Emerilians and Jakan. Light cannons cut through them in swathes. However, they didn't charge them but maintained control and continued to hit the Jukal from range.

They had been lucky to not take many losses in this war yet. Now they were being torn apart on the ground while the Jukal emperor's shield was madly fluctuating.

Dave could already sense the shield that was waiting just behind it.

"Come on, Josh. Kill that fucking toad." Dave saw an artillery round coming down toward him. Orbs shot out and created a barrier. The artillery round exploded; the force broke the Mana barrier and damaged Dave's personal barrier, throwing him into the ground.

Dave's head was ringing as Malsour picked him up.

He looked at the battlefield that had turned into chaos and at the approaching mechas that were nearing the dwarven lines.

It was a sight that he would never forget. Shields and Mana barriers were failing all over the place. There was little that they could do. Malsour and Dave disappeared, reappearing back on the flying citadel that was now wreathed in fire as it unleashed all of its firepower at the Jukal.

Everyone had pulled their weapons out and were circulating their Mana, ready to fight. Bob stood at the center of them, flanked by the members of Party Zero as well as Water, Fire, and Air.

Dave held out his arms. Metal plates appeared around him, joining together to form a new body that was only slightly shorter than Steve's body. The two of them didn't stand on the walls but rather hovered between two defensive walls.

In Bob's hand, a spear formed. His cloak fell away, revealing his wolfkin body and resplendent armor with gray smoke falling off it.

In the air around the flying citadels, the aerial forces waited. Up on the walls, Legendary figures had gathered and stood there in defiance and looked down at the Jukal.

"For Emerilia!" Bob yelled, running and leaping over the crenellations, diving toward the mechas.

"EMERILIA!" Their voices reached up into the sky. Fighters jumped from the walls, the ranged attackers covering them as they charged forward. The aerial force's voices joined with theirs, the beasts among them letting out their own war cries as they shot downward.

Dragons led the charge from above, with Denur leading them. She combined the power of their attacks into a blast of force that radiated out toward the Jukal. It came in waves. The first cut open armor and tossed those who weren't ready for it head over heels. The second made the ground rage under the Jukal, turning against them. Moisture in the air turned into raindrops that shot out with enough force to pierce armor while a shimmering shadow made armor rust and those caught outside of armor to wither as if their life force was being drained from them. A golden wave shot through armor, as if ignoring it without cutting through it. People started screaming as it felt as if they were burning from the inside out. A blue wave of concentrated fire caused armor to crackle and pop, melting the faces off the mechas.

Those leading the charge let out their own attacks, the mechas only slightly stunned while those who were on the ground were washed away with the force of the dragons' combined attacks.

The aerial forces behind the dragons came into range and unleashed their own attacks.

The floating defensive islands sprouted defensive fire as drones shot through the sky, raking the forces in the air. Bodies dropped to the ground below as the aerial forces broke into smaller groups, evading the defensive islands' fire and hunting down the drones while trying to support those racing toward the Jukal.

Bob let out a shout. His body stretched to the limit before he straightened in one motion as he tossed his spear. It smashed into a mecha, exploding with Mana as another spear appeared in Bob's hand, shooting into another mecha. Whatever his spear hit, it was destroyed.

"Lo'kal! I thought you had died on that pitiful creation you called Emerilia." The emperor's voice rolled through the sky as a projection of his head appeared above the battlefield looking dominating and well, imperious.

"Still hiding in your bunker like a widdle bitch!" Lo'kal laughed. Spears appeared around him and shot out at the mechas.

Mechas started to drop, their barriers and armor unable to stop Bob, who stood in the air like some war god. With a glance, destruction landed on the mechas.

"You *dare* to lecture me? You, a traitor to your own species? You should cut your own throat!" the emperor bellowed.

"Hah! I tried to keep humanity alive, then my esteemed race turned them into nothing but entertainment. How great is my race," Bob spat vehemently.

"You! You!" the emperor bellowed. His face turned into a body as he lashed out at Bob.

Bob laughed crazily as he charged up to meet the hundred-meter-tall projection of the emperor. It looked impossible for him to win, nothing more than a hair on the emperor's body.

Spell formations rotated around Bob, channeling down his fist as he punched out. Mana poured through the formations, then into his arm, a shining gray light solidifying on his hand.

Their fists met. A powerful shock wave rumbled out as the emperor's body became fainter and Bob was tossed backward.

His arm was destroyed, nothing more than a mangled mess but in front of everyone, it started to reform.

"So, the emperor only equals this?" Bob laughed and charged forward again. The emperor raised his hands, trying to defend as Bob flitted around. His body glowed with power as he lunged at the emperor's projection.

"Come here!" the emperor said, infuriated as he tried to grab and hit Bob. There was no technique to his movements; he had relied on his position and the power of the AI and his energy reserves to dominate the Jukal Empire.

Now he was a hundred-meter-tall projection. Without any fighting training, he was little match to Bob as he conjured weapons, empowered his body and unleashed attacks in every direction. The emperor's projection started to fail, only to have a larger surge of energy run through it.

Dave looked at the sight; he wouldn't be able to do what Bob was doing. The power he showed was unparalleled on Emerilia and capable of contending with the strongest single being in the empire.

Plasma cannon blasts hit the distracted Dave, his body lurching away.

"Time to play a game?" Steve said in a deep voice as they shot through the sky. Streamers appeared around their bodies as they moved at incredible speeds in the air.

Dave gave out wild laughter. The orbs on his body rotated into position; the cannons on his shoulder locked into position as magical formation appeared in front of his hands. Mana blasts poured out from his weaponry. The air distorted under the sea of fire that tore through anything in its path.

Steve let out a roar. His speed increased to new heights. It only took him a few seconds to reach the ground. His axe flashed; light tore out, cutting down those in its way before he smashed into the ground. The ground shook and was hidden in dust from the impact.

A roar filled the air as Steve rushed out, dust breaking over his body as his axe tore out.

Jung Lee let out a crazed laugh as the free Affinity souls poured into this body. He seemed to grow taller; power rolled off him and distorted the very air around him as his hair became longer. Rounds exploded around him as his hand slowly wrapped around his blade. His mouth stretched out into a line, the corners of his mouth lifting slightly, making those who looked upon him shake in fear as they felt their hearts pound. His hair breezed behind him as he shot ahead. He landed on the ground, with his sword flashing out of its scabbard so fast that a gray light shot out with it; as with Steve's axe, the cutting force sliced through all in its path. Those on the ground were cut apart without time to fight back; the mecha tumbled as they lost their feet.

Jung Lee's sword flashed in front of him, blocking the incoming rounds and piercing out. An artillery round in the sky exploded before reaching him as he shot forward. Dust shot up behind him as he left imprints in the ground. He was a vengeful spirit, the calm smile on his face unshaken as he looked at the Jukal as a man who had already seen their death. Blood colored his clothes and fell on his face, his expression not changing in the slightest.

Armor appeared around Fire and Water's bodies from their elements. They turned into red and blue streaks; their staff and trident moved in patterns to summon powerful spells. Their attacks weren't flashy and didn't seem powerful. The entire strength of the spell was wholly contained, only unleashing its might at the moment of impact, tearing those who faced them to nothing.

Mal called upon his demon avatar as he dropped to the ground. A crater formed around him. He clenched his fists and roared into the heavens as lava heeded his call. He truly looked like a demon risen from the bowels of hell as lava shot into the sky.

"Death." His voice rumbled across the battlefield as he pointed at the Jukal. The lava heeded his call and rushed forth, forming into rune-filled hounds and let out howls that made one's blood run cold.

Around Deia, red flames turned to blue. Her eyes turned red as her bow's runes glowed brighter and brighter, turning into actual flames that went from red to blue. The air around her was a series of shock waves as she moved across the sky, her face calm and emotionless as arrow after arrow rained down from the heavens. They seemed to have eyes because they followed their targets as they tried to escape.

Induca and Malsour shot down at the Jukal. Armor swarmed over their bodies, as did runic lines of power as their auras surged; they reached down and cut through those on the ground, their bodies bursting to flames or disintegrating under curses. Their breaths destroyed everything that had the misfortune of being in their path.

Malsour and Induca crashed into several mechas. Their claws tore them apart as their powerful bodies took the impacts of the weapons mounted on the mechas.

A spell appeared around Malsour that made the mechas explode into their components and then rush back together into a ball of junk. The air around Induca surged in temperature, melting the mechas into slag.

The air around Anna was turned into a frenzy, pulling around her and becoming more and more solid as she slowly pulled out her sword. Her short hair fluttered behind her as her eyes turned white. A smile that was not a smile spread across her face. Her aura surged ever higher as the air became thicker and harder, revolving with cutting blades that tore apart all that was coming at her.

The air turned into a paladin superimposed over her. The paladin's eyes were devoid of life as its arms and legs formed; a great sword appeared in its hand. The sword was lowered toward the ground and with a simple gesture, released cutting air that left a half meter cut in the ground.

She let out a cry, the wind whistling around her as Anna'kal's great sword once again played its deadly tune. Anna shot up through the sky with her blade. Drones fell or were thrown aside, unable to keep up with the demoness dominating the sky.

Suzy reached out her staff and stomped it down. Her cores flew out from her bag of holding and created a cloud around her as all of the Affinity energy in the world seemed to turn into streams of color, becoming thicker and more substantial as it revolved around her. Suzy created a sphere of concentrated Fire Affinity Mana of amazing power. Her staff tapped on the ground. The energy flooded toward the cores as the gem in the top of her staff was released and all of that energy reached into the air above the staff. She looked like a monarch of all creation as materials from the air, ground, even mechas were shredded and pulled toward the cores that then surged forward. As they moved, they turned from twenty-sided cores into creations—ranks upon ranks of creations, an army heeding the orders of their monarch.

Air was hard to look upon. Her face was placid and any signs of the joking girl from before had disappeared without a trace.

Her minder Venfik glided through the air, unleashing powerful attacks that sheared through metal and people with ease, his figure elusive and untouched by the mechas and those on the ground, his fighting style more akin to a dance.

Air seemed to glide across the battlefield, appearing behind unsuspecting victims; she flicked out her finger, releasing a fingernail of compact air that shot through her target. She then disappeared from that spot as that fingernail of compacted air would explode with force; the winds of the area stirred up into violence, tearing her targets apart—her attacks calm, unseen, and calculated.

All of these actions happened as one. The tide of destruction spread out through the Jukal lines as they found they had hit a steel plate. Party Zero and all the Legendary figures of the Emerilian forces had been holding back their power; now was the time to let loose.

Across the lines of the Emerilians, destruction was dealt on a massive scale unseen in history. As people clashed, those on the ground fired up at the transcendent beings that seemed to rule the battlefield.

The true fight was between the all-powerful Jukal mechas and these beings. The mechas poured out their power, displaying their full abilities, as magical formations and circuits appeared around them. They stepped into the sky to meet those who shot down from above and wielded massive swords as they engaged in close combat, discarding their gigantic plasma weapons.

Deia darted through the sky as explosions appeared around her. Hits batted her around with massive force, some even sending her reeling.

Dave's eyes turned red as he looked at where the impacts were coming from. He let out a roar and teleported from his position. He appeared under a floating island that was firing on the Emerilian forces. His body turned into a sword covered in runic lines, he himself at the hilt of the blade as arcane fire shot out from under the sword. It smashed through the floating island's shield. The blade shone with golden light as it cut deep into the island.

They had dared to touch what shouldn't be touched. Nothing stood in his way as he reached upward.

He stopped in the heart of the island. In his hand, he pulled out a grand working and tossed it out of the sword, which rearranged itself into a spear wreathed in gray shadows and smoke as arcane fire now blasted it downward.

The grand working ignited behind Dave. The fusion spell ripped through the island. The shock waves caused the island to crack and break apart as Dave rode the shock wave. His spear smashed through the now falling debris as the island was blown apart, losing its ability to float and dropping back to the ground.

He burst out from the debris. Altering his course slightly, he aimed for a group of five mechas. They saw him and started to fire at him. Their attacks were smashed apart by the air around the spear.

"Too late," Dave said as they started backing up, fearing for their lives.

In his spear form, he smashed through one of the mechas. The impact threw three off their feet as the remaining two fought to stay on their feet.

Spell formations appeared around Dave as spears shot out at the mechas. The spear pierced into them and then exploded; Dave didn't even look at them as his avatar body started to reform, tearing parts out from the mecha it had impaled.

Power from the dead and the mechas rushed toward Dave's body, recharging his vault soul gems seeded through his massive avatar.

Dave ripped off a section from the mecha, adding it to his arm that had been damaged. Gray smoke appeared over it, forming runic lines and reaching down his arm to form a massive sword. Dave let out a roar as he pushed up. The ground erupted under his feet as he shot toward another mecha. Before he could get there, an axe came from the side, tearing through it.

A foot followed the axe and smashed the mecha back.

"This is Emerilia!" Steve yelled.

"This is the Jukal home world and you're supposed to say that before you punt them!" Dave yelled, rushing off in another direction. He clashed with another mecha, changing attacks before Dave increased the gravity on them and made their joints smoke under the strain. It wasn't long until Dave's sword pierced their body and power surged into it, destroying everything inside. Its soul energy rushed toward Dave's mecha, making his body hazy as a terrifying aura spread out from it.

Those Jukal watching shuddered as they looked at Dave, their scans showing that he had recovered his peak condition.

Dave teleported. Weapons appeared in the sky and spell formations appeared around him, leaving nothing but broken opponents in his path. He fought in the sky; he fought on the ground, teleporting to his next victim.

Emerilia's hidden strength was now brought to the fore, clashing with the emperor's projection and his forces. In the sky, Bob and the emperor continued to clash. Even the fists of the emperor that missed let out a terrifying pressure that promised death for anyone else in its path. The ground around them was turned into a scene of destruction, the air around them clear of everyone else for fear that they would be destroyed in an attack that missed or by the shock waves when the two clashed directly.

This was battle; this was chaos; this was the Emerilians giving vent to all of the pain and suffering that they had lived with being under the observation of the Jukal who tore their lives apart and hurt their loved ones simply for their entertainment, disdaining them and all of their kind.

The emperor's fist rushed out, but it started to fade away as it collided with Bob's spear. Instead of Bob being forced back, the emperor's fist was pierced through.

The emperor looked at his hand blankly, as if not understanding what was happening.

"Seems that the emperor of the Jukal Empire is only this much." Bob laughed and charged. The air around him raged with power as his spear's light smashed against the emperor's body and tore him apart.

"What is happening?" the emperor yelled, looking at his disintegrating projection. He struck out at Bob, trying to destroy him.

*****

Josh's blades silently slipped out from his sheaths, the wicked curved Xelur blades feeling familiar in his hands. The others around him all prepared their weapons and readied themselves.

"It's done," Lucy said. "You won't have long before they find out."

"No worries." Josh looked to the others. Dwayne and Kim nodded to him before they followed their Blood Kin, the dirt moving around them as they disappeared.

Josh sent out his senses, closing his eyes as he cast spells to enhance himself and see through the walls in front of him.

Dwayne and Kim rotated their power to the limit as they charged through the ground, turning and then coming toward a heavily armored room at speed.

In the face of the Blood Kin, such defenses were useless. The walls peeled away and the armor opened up like a door, revealing the emperor and his command center.

Kim unleashed hexes across the room as Dwayne let out a roar that shook the room. He shot forward, his armor glowing with power as he launched a sword attack, killing dozens of Jukal in the room and clashing with the guards who were protecting the emperor.

Guards appeared around the room and charged Dwayne and Kim. Dwayne stopped any getting to Kim as she unleashed spells that killed dozens in seconds.

The command center was under the Blood Kin's control; the consoles, walls, ceiling, and floor listened to their command, forming into golems or attacking the Jukal in the room.

The emperor, who had been waving his fists madly, fighting in his projected body, was now pushed back behind his guards as they tried to keep him safe.

"You dare touch me!" the emperor yelled, unleashing a fist that turned the guard into nothing but a bloody pile.

The emperor's uncle surged with alarming power. It was clear that the emperor was not the only one with an AI to create spells.

Still, Josh waited patiently as the first group were put on the defensive.

The guards moved so that they were between the emperor and the attackers, while the commanders and leaders ran in a panic with those who had been manning the command center's consoles, trying to escape.

With the Blood Kin in the room, it was their domain; they hammered on the doors that wouldn't open for them.

"You have the power of the Earth Lord, and you the power of the Lady of Light," the emperor's uncle said, a shocked expression on his face.

"Looks like he's got some good senses." Kim's power surged upward.

Malsour and Dave had relinquished their power that they gained by becoming people of the Affinity Pantheon as well as connected Kim to the Lady of Light's divine wells and then charged them up with fusion reactors and soul gems. These divine wells had been spread out to the flying citadels above.

Dwayne's body was covered in a green light as he fought back five opponents at once. A tree appeared on his shield. The tree opened its eyes; branches shot out to impale or capture those in front of it.

Josh rocked on his feet, a predatory look in his eyes. "Now!"

Yemi and the remaining Blood Kin let out a surge of energy. The area in front of Josh opened up as he burst through, nothing more than a shadow as he called upon the power that had been bestowed on him.

The Dark Lord's power surged through him, filling his body with boundless energy. The room darkened with the outpouring of power.

He arrived behind his target in a moment. His blades, covered in writhing shadows, burned through the protective barriers. The power sent out shock waves that rocked people back on their heels as his blades passed through the finest clothing and stabbed into the flesh underneath.

The room was silent as Josh's blades tore upward and then sliced across, the back of his target bleeding severely from the attack.

"Kill him!" the emperor's uncle yelled in a panic.

Josh kicked his target, using the force to jump back and away.

As the blood dripped from the blades, seals appeared around the target before shooting toward Josh as if he had gained their acceptance.

The target turned in mid-air. The emperor's face showed shock at the incredible pain he was feeling. His body turned dark and withered as power shot out from him and into Josh. Dark lines ran through his skin, the poison curses and effects of the Xelur blades tearing the life force from the Jukal emperor. Under everything, he was a weak being, nothing more than a prop held up by the AI he controlled. His body was just incredibly weak when all was said and done. Josh felt new power surge through him as he raised his hand. Those who were chasing him were turned into mist.

"What!" Power drained from the emperor's uncle's body as he looked at Josh with wide eyes as he sensed the aura around Josh. "That's the emperor's power."

With the program Lucy had inserted, she had weakened the emperor's connection with the divine wells under his command. However, it wasn't enough. The blades in Josh's hands had been modified by Dave so that they would forcibly break the connection the emperor had and shift it to Josh. The people of the empire didn't have much familiarity with the divine wells. However, Dave was connected to one, as was Malsour, and he could talk to Bob, Fire, Water, and Air. He had increased his knowledge of them in leaps and bounds before coming up with a way to wrest control away from the Jukal emperor.

"So it is," Josh said as power started to flood his body. The seals sunk into his body as he was now connected to the divine wells.

"Who are you?" the emperor's uncle barked.

"Josh Giles, leader of the Stone Raiders, rogue and also leader of Party One." Josh laughed, throwing out another palm that destroyed the emperor's uncle.

A spell formation wrapped around the Blood Kin and members of Party One. They disappeared from inside the emperor's palace. With Josh now controlling his power, it was possible for them to teleport freely.

They arrived in the air above the battlefield.

"Pull back through the portals!" Josh bellowed to the forces below. Power surged through him as a truly massive spell formation appeared in the sky. Spears started to drop from the sky as curse spell formations filled the ground.

The Emerilian and Jakan forces turned and rushed back toward the portals at their rear. The portals disconnected from Gunboat Isle and were tilted, connecting to the Jakan home world and portals under Emerilian control.

People rushed through and unleashed their most powerful spells on the way out. Spell after spell rained down on the Jukal palace, overwhelming all inside with destruction.

The flying citadels covered the retreat and shot to the larger floating ship portals. Josh gathered the others and flew them onto one of the flying citadels. Party One also did what they could to help cover the ground troops by unleashing attacks at the Jukal who were still trying to attack them under the deluge of attacks.

Josh lowered Party Zero down to the wall. All below them could see them stepping on top of the walls of the flying citadel.

Bob landed on the flying citadel near them, looking resplendent as people gave him looks of respect. In their hearts, Bob was a true Emerilian, the savior of not just Emerilia but the victims of the empire.

The Jukal wanted to give chase and hold them down, but they simply weren't able to as the Emerilians and Jakan retreated quickly and orderly.

Josh looked over the Jukal home world before he turned and walked into the flying citadel.

The forces on the ground departed, the portals melting down into nothing but scrap.

Just as the last citadel, the one that Party One had landed on, was about to pass through the portal, the ground started to shake as powerful Mana fluctuations rippled through the air.

Josh looked over the notifications that blinked at him.

New Class: Jukal Emperor

So, did you just wake up this morning and think "Oh, it would be nice to be a FRICKING EMPEROR!"

Okay, so now that you are one, you get access to divine wells that are just off the charts. Hopefully you don't throw a fit with them, unlike the last idiot.

Status: Level 1

        +100 to all stats

        Access to Jukal Emperor's Divine wells.

        Ability to use magical aid to create any spell possible as

Effects: long as you have sufficient power (see divine wells power levels)

        Individual control over all infrastructure of the Jukal Empire.

"Can I destroy the palace?" Josh asked.

"Yes," a monotone voice replied.

Command: Destruction of Jukal Emperor's Palace and Residence

Are you sure you wish to do this?

You will lose access to administrative rights as well as this class and divine wells.

Confirm

Y/N

"Can I destroy the portals and the infrastructure of the Jukal Empire?" Josh asked.

Command: Destruction of Jukal Empire's infrastructure

Are you sure you wish to do this?

You will lose access to this infrastructure.

Confirm

Y/N

"Will this kill anyone?" Josh asked.

"It will not kill anyone," the monotone voice replied.

"Okay, let's destroy everything in the Jukal home system. Can we disable the charges and kill switches in everything else not in the Jukal system?" Josh rubbed his chest and the Band-Aid that was still there, stopping any kill switch signal from ending him.

Command: Destruction of kill switches and destruction charges outside of Jukal home system

Are you sure you wish to do this?

You will lose access to these programs.

Confirm

Y/N

Josh selected Yes, feeling a heat through his own body moments later as he checked out the next information box.

Command: Destruction of Jukal home system's infrastructure

Are you sure you wish to do this?

You will lose access to infrastructure in the Jukal home system.

Confirm

Y/N

Josh selected Yes for that as well before heading back to the first command screen.

"Have all my orders been transmitted out?" Josh asked.

"They have," the bland voice replied.

"If I destroy the palace and residence, will it stop my orders being carried out?" Josh looked at the nearing portal.

"It will not," the voice said.

"Good." Josh looked at the screen once more and hit Yes. He felt the power under his control but he didn't care. If somehow he lost this new class or it was disrupted for even a moment, then he would lose it all and the Jukal would still be at their peak. With his actions, all of the fighting in the Jukal home system was just a backdrop. This was their true purpose in coming to the Jukal home planet.

Command: Destruction of Jukal Emperor's Palace and Residence

Are you sure you wish to do this?

You will lose access to administrative rights as well as this class and divine wells.

Confirm

Y/N

Class: Jukal Emperor

You have lost this class

Josh closed the notifications, not looking back as the flying citadel exited the Jukal home world, and appeared in the moonbase.

On the Jukal home world, the last portal closed and started to disintegrate.

The rumbling turned into blinding white light as all of the built up and unused power controlled by the Jukal emperor was turned into rampant Mana. The portal that was already falling apart was torn to pieces as the palace, its defenses, the battlefield—all of it—was torn apart in the waves of destruction emanating from where the emperor's palace had been, raging against the shields created by the arks.

As one, the arks teleported away. The destructive forces caused the seas to seethe and strike the land around the emperor's palace.

Water poured into the hole that the palace had been turned into, the forces of nature turning the once proud continent into another part of the sea.

***

Frank looked up from the weapons system that he had been working on as alarms started to blare in the ship.

"Prepare for immediate teleport!" Admiral Adams's voice rang through the ship and the fleet as Frank stood up.

The fleet had already destroyed what was remaining of the ships that were stationed around the Jukal home world.

They'd returned to the fleet, seeing to their damage before advancing on the Jukal. They were on the way to engage with the Jukal fleet when Adams's announcement had come.

Frank dashed off toward the command center. As he started to pull up information on his screen, the first thing he saw was that victory had been secured on Emerilia. The arks had teleported and met up with the forces above the Jukal home world.

The walls glowed and then dimmed.

"Teleport successful." Navigation's voice carried across the ship as Frank made it into the command center, quickly taking his station.

"We're heading back to the Emerilia system," Captain Xiao said to Frank's questioning look.

He looked to his screens, seeing that one of the arks that hadn't used the ship portals was already erecting one to help them exit the system.

"We just had an explosion inside one of the Jukal ships," Sensors said.

"Looks like Lady Light's thoughts were right. Once the emperor is removed, then the empire fights to claim any of the territory it can," Captain Xiao said.

"They're fighting one another?" Navigation said, her voice shocked.

"Their entire society has been built on politicking and taking advantage. Now that there is no emperor, the different forces that had been held down can now act. The Jukal home system is the center of the empire. As such, it's going to become the most chaotic place to be," Xiao said.

"But we're still a threat to them," Communications said.

"It doesn't matter to them. In their minds, they've always seen us as nothing more than entertainment. Do you think that you would worry about a cartoon character? They're so far removed from what they see on their screens and interfaces that they don't even think that the things that have happened to the emperor could possibly happen to them. Even if they saw the destruction, they're out of touch with the realities of the world." Captain Xiao shook his head.

The ark finished off the portal as they started to head back to the asteroid base. They exited into the asteroid field. Shuttles and other ships waited for them to see to their repairs.

Frank and all of those on the main deck looked to one another. There was no one to tell them that the war was over, that they had won.

They cast their thoughts to the future, wondering what they would do while also carrying out their jobs. They still had to see how the fallout in the Jukal home system went. Leave them to deal with one another.

It was surreal as the fleet was moved around, many of them entering the asteroid base or leaving the Nal system for the Emerilia station for repair or to be put on patrol as leave schedules were sorted out.

Is that it? Is it finally, all of it, over? This thought filled the minds of thousands as they watched the information coming from the scout ships.

Chapter 19: Look to the Future

The people of Emerilia were like a spell, readied and waiting to go off. They had defeated the Jukal emperor, something that many had doubted. And although they had hoped for it, they had never thought that they would be able to do it.

The truth of the matter came to light, how the leadership from the Stone Raiders had been imbued with the power of the Affinity Pantheon, moving with the Blood Kin to gain access to the emperor's palace.

Once they were inside, they had removed the emperor's ability to call down spells and act on the battlefield. Dwayne and Kim had distracted the Jukal and Josh had landed the last attack.

With his orders, everything under the control of the emperor was destroyed. The emperor of the Jukal Empire barely trusted those in their own family. Through the ages, they had seeded kill switches into nearly anything of importance.

The portal network that they had tried to seed through the rest of the Jukal Empire was destroyed, as were key Mirror of Communication relay stations and infrastructure. The Jukal home system, the seat of power for the Jukal Empire, had been a seat of plots and treachery. Many of the clans found out that their power crumbled overnight without the backing of the emperor and found that what they did have was destroyed. His "favors" to them had always come with an option for him to tear the power out from underneath them in a moment.

The Jukal home system was in chaos as Jukal were fighting over control, rights, settling old debts and killing one another.

They had been repressed as much as the people who were under their command. Now without the stature of the emperor, someone who had existed for as long as these clans' varied histories, they were able to act out again. The *peaceful* Jukal race showed just how much they could tolerate one another as they devolved into savagery. Clans started to take command of stations, ships, and anything they could get their hands on. The clans started to use them as their own weapons and started their own fights with one another, leading to them destroying even more of the strength they had built up.

Some tried to leave, only to find the Emerilian and Deq'ual fleets following them. The combined forces of Deq'ual and Emerilia easily picked them off. The overseers had their work cut out for them as they processed hundreds of Jukal a day, with many awaiting trial. Shard, Jeeves, and Anna all had long been inserted into the Jukal Empire's information networks, making it possible to put together profiles on all of them, sorting out those who had committed crimes and those who had not.

Those who were innocent were given the option to go to Emerilia and the Nal system. Sending them to a planet that was part of the old Jukal Empire was akin to sending them to their deaths.

Arks and destroyers moved from the still occupied systems, dropping off portals and allowing the Jakan to fight out battles with the Jukal forces that remained.

The people of the empire were grateful to the Emerilians and many were working to establish governments and sorting out trade routes now that they had the ability to support themselves. But still they needed more than they were able to make by themselves.

They started to adapt. Ships that had been captured from the Jukal and merchant vessels that had remained in their ports once again had work. Some people went back to their old jobs; others used the Mirror of Communication school to gain a greater understanding of all things magical.

Nanite injections went through the roof as game AIs mirrored off the ones on Emerilia were added to systems, allowing them to also be able to calculate stats and of course to have interfaces and party chats and cast magic.

The Jukal were on their way to being defeated, while the empire was now blossoming more than ever. The people were searching out new opportunities; people were coming together from multiple systems, pooling their efforts and creating things that would change star systems.

Portals were placed in different systems; a hub was created on the Nalheim's planet Nal. People from across the galaxy were able to walk from one planet to another with ease.

It had the potential to lead to a crazy explosion of ideas and possibilities.

As this all happened, the people of Emerilia helped where they could, with some going to different planets; others created businesses to expand across the entire system. The nations and empires of Emerilia all had a seat within the Alliance of Terra and there was a move to create a new system of government that the AI would pick the candidates for. Most of the leaders were fine with this. With all they had gone through, seeing the stress that came with being a leader and the possibility to regress, they agreed. Those who didn't agree found that their people didn't care much for what they thought. They cared little for the nations and groups they were part of, besides the fact that they were Emerilians. They'd stood as one in the face of their greatest enemy and nothing would wipe away those ties.

***

Dave sighed as he put down the project he was working on. It had been two months since the Jukal emperor had died. The Jukal system had very few remaining ships capable of flight left anymore; the orbitals were nothing more than wreckage and the ground had been turned into a wasteland. The fight for the emperor's seat had caused them to destroy their own planets and people.

"Lunch, you three!" Deia's commanding tone made it clear that they were to hurry up.

"We can get to this afterward," Malsour said.

They were covered in dirt and grime, with smiles on their faces. When they had been working on creations before, they had been tired and worn out, forsaking food, drink, and sleep in order to gain the Emerilians an advantage in the coming war.

Dave looked over what was his first house, the one he had built with his very hands so very long ago. He stepped out of the door with Malsour and Bob.

Bob let out a sigh filled with memories as he stepped on the porch and overlooked the fields that surrounded Cliff-Hill. Among the fields, the glowing soul gem growing apartments could be seen; past them, the gentle stream curved around them with bridges connecting the fields to the wilds of Opheir and the Kufo'tel forest.

"Strange to think that this was where it all started." Bob smiled to his two friends.

They each thought back on past events, both good and bad, sad and happy.

After some time, Bob moved first. "Well, we should get a move on before Deia comes to find us!" Bob chuckled. The other two showed content smiles and pushed their memories away.

Dave stepped off the porch, looking to the Mithsia Mountains and the region where the Kufo'tel elves lived.

Malsour and Dave walked from Dave's first house that had now been turned into a workshop, to his second house, that now housed his family and friends. The rest of Party Zero were there already, enjoying the wild boar sausages and timber wolf burgers.

Deia, Fire, Mal, and Quindar were talking to one another as they nursed drinks and watched the kids as they played. Steve was manning the grill. He wore a massive apron and thankfully, after the battle, he'd returned to his normal size. Lox and Gurren were laughing with Kol, Jung Lee, Induca, Suzy, Josh, Esa, Jules, Dwayne, Kim,

Lucy; Josh and Cassie were retelling adventures and ridiculous moments they'd had.

Dave couldn't help smiling, his heart filled to the brim.

Water, Ela-Dorn, her husband Ela-Gal, and Air appeared in the sky—of course with Venfik trailing after her. Jung Lee waved to Venfik. The two of them had made fast friends, finding out the other was interested in potions.

Air and Water moved to join Deia and her group.

"All right, now everyone's here, tuck in!" A mischievous smile appeared on Deia's face. "Though, it does seem some people weren't able to clean themselves up!"

Dave stopped in his tracks, a feeling of unease filling him.

Water and Air turned to Dave with smiles as Water descended from the heavens.

"Ahh, it's cold!" Dave and Malsour danced under the rain before Air blasted them. Bob had quickly chosen to run out of range, a satisfied smile on his face.

Fire waved her hand; heat fell on the two, their clothes drying in just seconds.

"Grandma!" Malsour yelled indignantly.

Water, Fire, and Air looked to one another, guilty looks on their faces, marred by a look of "well, it was fun, wasn't it?"

The group laughed at the others' misfortune while Bob lowered himself from the sky. Suddenly, rain descended on him.

"You rascals!" Bob yelled, his curse filled with laughter as he was blasted with air and dried.

He had a displeased look on his face as his fur was in a poof. He narrowed his eyes at them, promising to get them back for their prank. His body changed, no longer the wolf, but rather Bob the gnome, his clothes changing as he pulled out a pipe and lit it.

"All right, you lot! We've got dirty dogs and sloppy stacks. Come and get 'em!" Steve said, doing his best impression of an old grill house cook.

Dave and Malsour couldn't stay annoyed for long as they joined the masses in heading for the food.

Dave and Deia sat beside each other.

After a moment, Dave frowned. "Where's Anna?"

"She's gone to see Alkao," Deia said with a heavy expression.

They knew how much it tore at Alkao's heart to see Anna but knowing that she had few true memories of him, all she could rely on was the recordings she had watched.

Dave squeezed Deia's hand. They all cared deeply about them both. It hurt them to see the pain they were both going through.

Deia smiled to Dave as there were no words to say.

"So, have you decided what your dress is going to be yet for the wedding?" Dave asked.

"Dress?" Deia asked, her voice raised in confusion.

Heads at the table seemed to snap onto Deia, who turned around slowly as the table descended into silence.

She looked at them all. "It's just a dress," she said, confused by their reactions.

"Just a dress! You're Oson'Deia, lady! You're going to be getting THE dress!" Fire said.

"Shouldn't you be getting one of those soon too?" Mal seemed to ponder aloud.

Fire's face went red as Bob chuckled.

"Shut it, old man," Fire snapped before she looked to Mal. Her eyes shone as she bit her lip, excitement filling her.

"Seems we've got a lot to organize for the wedding." Dave laughed.

"The wedding—now?" Deia said, her anxiousness showing.

"Well, I did make a promise," Dave said, his eyes soft as he looked to her. In that moment, they stared at each other and the world seemed to fade away.

A red blush appeared on Deia's face as she looked away, looking nothing more than an innocent girl once again. Dave squeezed her hand and laughed, the sight causing his heart to move in joy.

"When's the date?" Jules asked. Her question seemed to set off a chain reaction as they were inundated with questions.

***

Anna had gone to the spiraling towers that rested in the middle of Unity City at the center of Devil's Crater, only to find out that Alkao wasn't there.

She'd been given a waypoint to where he was and she'd set off, flying toward him.

He was helping out with some of his people with establishing a new mine. He and some other members of the Devil's Crater Army were assisting the miners to create an opening for them to place the automated miners in. Once they were placed in, then they would carry out the hard work and start to pull out the resources buried deep in the ground.

Anna glided down from the sky as she watched Alkao swing an axe that caused the ground to shake and left a crater behind. After the strike, he and others worked to pull out the debris, loading them onto the automated carts that populated Terra and the other bases made by the Pandora's Initiative. Now that the war was all but over, the Grahslagg Corporation that controlled the Pandora Initiative was selling off their carts at a reduced cost.

They could have charged twenty times the price they had and people would still buy them. However, Dave and the leaders of the Initiative wanted the people of Emerilia to grow. They were the power behind many projects that were underway across Emerilia and the stars. Already, the dwarves were eyeing their own asteroid and making bids on the resources coming out from the asteroid refinery.

It seemed inevitable that the dwarves would head out into space to become asteroid miners.

Alkao wore a simple shirt and pants; on his wrists, he had the coded bracelets that Dave had created.

Anna's eyes roamed over Alkao's body.

"Like what you see?" Alkao said in an amused tone, looking at her as he drank from a canteen. The corners of his mouth pulled up into a smile.

"Hmph, can't I enjoy the sights?" Anna propped her fists on her hips.

"Pfft!" Alkao sprayed water everywhere as the others laughed at his actions.

"It came out of my nose," Alkao complained. As he wiped his face, a necklace fell out from his shirt, a spiral that sparkled in the light.

Anna's eyes stuck to the spiral as she moved forward.

"Thought you were just admiring? It's more to touch," Alkao joked.

Seeing there was no reaction, he frowned. A hint of pain flashed through his eyes, as if remembering that the woman he loved had been lost.

It quickly disappeared as he smiled to Anna. Even if she didn't have the same feelings, his heart was full seeing her alive once again.

Her hand reached out to the necklace on Alkao's chest.

Alkao and those working froze. All of them knew of the relationship between the two and how Anna had lost her memories. Many people in Devil's Crater could only look to their king with sad smiles, wishing for him to find happiness once again. But none of them pressed him. There were many women who were interested in him but they rightfully left him time to recover.

Now, a bit of hope showed in those around their king. He had become the pillar of their crater and they only hoped for him to find happiness.

Alkao looked at Anna. Her eyes focused on the necklace, a confused look on her face as if hints of memories were peeking through. However, there was a wall blocking them.

Her hand touched the spiral.

It shone with brilliant light. Runes and spell formations appeared around the necklace, appearing in front of Anna.

Anna's face appeared in front of her, projected by the spell matrix within the spiral necklace. It was Anna but it wasn't. There was a difference to them—they looked identical but their experiences had created two different women.

"Remember," the projected Anna said, fading into magical runes that drifted forward.

Anna took a deep breath as the runes passed through her eyes, absorbed through her mouth and lips.

The light on the necklace started to dim, the last of the power transferring to Anna. She slumped forward.

Alkao caught her and looked at her with worry and concern, pushing her hair out of her eyes as he looked to those around him. "Get a healer!" Alkao yelled, using spells to increase his senses, searching through Anna's body to check her condition.

Anna, meanwhile, was lost in her own world. It was as if her mind had been opened up and memories were unlocked. What had been broken was now reformed and absorbed. A rush of memories filled Anna.

She opened her eyes, looking at the frantic Alkao, who paused, his eyes captured by hers.

His heart lurched as she smiled up at him. This smile was completely different from the smiles she had given him since she had awoken to her new body.

"Silly man. Didn't I say that I wanted to stay with you forever?" Anna's hand touched his face.

Tears fell down Alkao's cheeks, as a dam seemed to break. He pulled her into an embrace.

"Anna, *my* Anna." Alkao's voice filled with incredible joy and released the pain of before.

"You dolt." Anna hit him lightly on his shoulder, her smile enough to brighten the heavens. Tears appeared in her eyes as she pressed her face into Alkao's shoulder, smelling his familiar scent. Her tail moved in happiness, wrapping around him, and her ears twitched.

His wings wrapped around her, unwilling to let her go.

Chapter 20: A Promise Realized

Sato stepped through the portal. With him, there were Admiral Adams, Edwards, Councillor Wong, and a heavy security detail.

He exited the asteroid base where he had arrived, touring the facility before he and his party met up and traveled via portal to Terra and then through an ono and teleport pad to Cliff-Hill.

There was a festive feeling in the air. Cliff-Hill had expanded in just a few months. There were soul gem-created inns; the roads to Cliff-Hill were packed and people were swarming in through the onos and teleport pads.

There were two dozen flying citadels arranged around Cliff-Hill. Their weapons were secured, as banners covered them.

All of Emerilia seemed to have come to Cliff-Hill.

It was now six months since they had killed the Jukal emperor. The combined fleets had returned to what was left of the Jukal home system. People were evacuated and relocated from the terrible conditions in the system. Those who had crimes were taken by the overseers, who now had multiple races within their ranks, turning them into a police force of all the various races, backed up by the combined fleets of the Deq'ual and Emerilian people.

The Deq'ual system had built their own portal, connecting to the Nal planet's hub. They were still hesitant but it seemed that they had finally broken through a barrier. People were interacting with the other races, and the Deq'ual system, although not accepting general visitors, were in talks with different ambassadors and creating ties with the people who had been part of the Jukal Empire.

The system was changing as they no longer needed to hide anything. The stations grew at an explosive rate; ships were being created constantly and now they had one of the larger fleets to move goods from system to system. Even with the portal network, there was a need for freighter ships to move between ship portals and systems.

Sato's face broke into a smile as he looked over Cliff-Hill. This was where Dave had first contacted him through the Mirror of Communication.

They quickly joined with the people moving through the city.

They reached a blocked-off area in the middle of the city. It was a decent-sized compound with large soul gem buildings. The signage said that this was the Stone Raiders' first guild headquarters that they had formed after defeating Boran-al's citadel.

"Sato!" Josh said, appearing in a swirl of darkness. He held onto Cassie's hand as he looked to Sato and the others, greeting them with a smile. "Admiral Adams, good to see you again. I'm guessing you must be Edwards and Councillor Wong."

The others nodded back as Sato felt the pressure that seemed to roll off Josh. Unless someone was looking for it, they wouldn't sense it. Sato's eyebrows pinched together slightly. The power coming from Josh surprised him. He'd seen many battles and although they had looked grand, he hadn't been there in the flesh to feel those shock waves, to sense the overwhelming power of spells and explosive power of Mana.

Sato met with a number of others and was introduced to even more. Josh and Cassie were well versed in being hosts and creating ties. The group from Deq'ual were quickly left in the capable hands of others who would be beneficial for them to talk to.

Sato found himself looking up as a half-dozen dragons flew through the sky. The largest of them turned toward the gathering. The dragon's body distorted and changed, turning into their human form. The two people on her back floated down with her, landing on top of one of the soul gem buildings.

"That's Fire, Mal, and Denur," Cassie said, seeing where his gaze landed. A large smile broke out on her face, as if remembering something. "They should have Desmond with them too."

"You just want to spoil the boy, and Koi as well," Josh teased.

"So?" Cassie said, not denying it as she looked at Josh with a mischievous smile that seemed to ask "whatcha gonna do about it, lover boy?"

Josh could only laugh, his body shaking as he smiled and pulled her closer.

Sato's heart was warmed seeing the scene.

A spell formation appeared in the sky, projected through the soul gem buildings of the Stone Raiders' compound.

Soul gem seeds reached into the sky in the center of their own spell formations.

The flying citadels around Cliff-Hill shone with resplendent light, looking like the war palaces of gods as threads of power entered the spell formations around the soul gem seeds, making them expand faster.

The dragons in the sky let out their roars; others shot up into the sky, changing into their dragon forms as they poured power into the construct.

Stone Raiders stepped into the air, power gushing out of them. Dwarven master smiths poured out their power, the council leaders of the Aleph and other Aleph people, Alkao, his brothers and leaders of Devil's Crater, leaders of nations and their aides: all of them added in their power.

Bob, Air, Water, and Fire ascended into the sky, releasing their power as well. The sky shook and power built. Sato poured out his meager power, guiding it upward as threads of power from all those in attendance reached up to the spell formations, creating gentle swirls and a beautiful kaleidoscope of colors that weaved together. The seeds reached out to one another, creating a floor. Once they were connected, the floor became stronger and more real. An island appeared underneath it, formed of soul gem that swirled with power and beauty.

Walls rose up into the sky, covered in murals of the six Affinities. Instead of being in opposition, these artworks weaved together. Six pillars reached up from the floor, three on either side as they depicted one of the Affinities each. Balconies were formed at different levels, floating through the massive temple. The walls and pillars stopped growing upward and instead started to form into a roof that dominated the sky.

Balconies were formed from the ceiling, dropping down to float around the hall, their movements gentle, as if they were truly the clouds above.

The members of Party Zero walked into the clouds, unleashing the full might of their auras that contested with the surviving members of the Pantheon. Power rolled off them. Stairs appeared in the temple, rising up until they formed a platform within the temple.

A multicolored mist appeared, shrouding the temple as people stopped pouring their energy into the floating temple that hovered there. Its sight made people let out sighs of happiness looking upon such beauty.

A man appeared in the sky ahead of the temple. Sato's smile grew wider as he looked to Dave.

"All right, I know most of you came for the open bar but I guess we best get this started!" Dave laughed. "Thank you for coming and witnessing Deia and my wedding. I hope you have a great time."

Dave's words were heartfelt and everyone there smiled at the kindness he shared with them.

"Go, get dressed," Suzy chided and waved him away. Dave teleported away as Suzy and the Dracul family organized everyone as they poured into the temple. The temple expanded to try to fit all, but there were still screens on the outside to share with those who couldn't make it inside.

Sato took his seat in one of the floating balconies that moved through the air in a soft dance. He was at ease as he waited.

***

Dave took a deep breath and checked over his suit one more time. His nerves made it feel as if his body was hot and cold at the same time, while his stomach was churning.

Bob and Kol looked to each other, fatherly love in their eyes as they looked back to Dave.

Bob clapped Dave on one shoulder. Kol did the same to the other shoulder as they both looked in the mirror.

There was no need for words as Dave felt his emotions welling up. He had been raised by an AI within Earth's simulation, formed to play Emerilia. He'd come to escape the world, to escape the fake people who surrounded him. He'd met so many great people—those who cared about him, those who had become a family to him.

He let out a laugh as his eyes teared up.

"What's wrong, lad?" Kol asked.

"I don't think I could ask for two better dads." Dave looked to them both, moving his lips and sniffing to try to keep the tears at bay.

"Oh, you bugger," Bob said, his eyes making it hard to see as he clasped Dave into a hug and pat him on the back.

They separated as Kol took his turn clapping Dave on the back.

"We couldn't be prouder of our boy," Kol said, his voice filled with emotions.

Bob nodded in complete agreement. "Now, let's get you married before that lass wises up, huh!" Bob laughed and clapped Dave on the back.

Dave let out a short laugh before he let out a deep breath. He straightened his tie and nodded to himself.

A spell formation appeared around them as they teleported from the fitting room into the temple.

Standing there on the platform was Party Zero. They were split into two groups on either side of the platform. Induca was on the other side with a giggling Koi.

Bob and Kol moved to join the others on Dave's side.

"Don't mess it up," Dave warned Steve with a mock serious expression, pointing to him.

"Me mess it up?" Steve had a shocked expression on his face. "I'll let you know I am one of the best rated officiants!"

"You haven't married anything in your life," Jung Lee stated.

"I have in spirit!" Steve said.

"Yeah, see, just *nothing* in there," Gurren said.

Dave grinned and moved to Induca, playing with little Koi. She seemed happy to see her dad and hugged him. He laughed and pat her back.

"She's on her way." Fire appeared in a wreath of flames before she took her seat in a nearby balcony, with Desmond in her arms.

"Very well, Mrs. Oson." Dave smiled.

Fire blushed, playing with the ring on her hand. She and Mal had married just a few weeks ago in a quiet ceremony.

Dave made to pass Koi back, only to have her start complaining. They tried a few more times before Dave gave up.

"I'll hold her," Dave said just as music started to flow through the room. Bards raised their voices together as the room became quiet.

Deia floated up, with her arm in the crook of her father's. Blue flames disappeared from under their feet as they stepped into the temple.

Deia and Dave looked to each other, their faces filled with smiles as Mal guided her down the aisle. She wore a dress with a slit that reached up to above her knee. The bottom of her dress looked alive as it was weaved with soul gem threads that depicted scenes of all six Affinities weaved together. They came together at her abdomen, forming together into a gray scene. The depictions from below had now been combined together into a great scene as gray smoke gently framed her dress and her face. Her hair was pulled up into a bun to reveal the curve of her neck and the outline of her jaw.

Dave's suit was a subdued gray with faint runic lines trailing through it, showing off his powerful body underneath.

Mal and Deia approached. Mal smiled to the two of them and his granddaughter Koi. "Keep her happy," Mal said.

"I'll do my best." Dave turned and hugged him, while also looking out for Koi.

The two of them separated. Mal spared a glance for Deia once more as he stepped off the platform. Flames appeared under his feet as he joined Fire. The two of them held hands and looked at Dave and Deia.

Dave held Deia's hand as she opened a private chat with him.

"She's her daddy's girl." Deia looked to Koi, who was playing with her lips and looking around wildly at everything, wearing a dress similar to her mother's.

"You bet." Dave squeezed Deia's hand. They cut the private chat and looked to Steve.

Steve looked at them with a smile plastered over his face. There was no joke hiding in his eyes, only pure happiness. He looked to everyone in the hall, his happiness clear to all.

"Thank you all for coming today. We're here to watch David Grahslagg and Oson'Deia to be joined in marriage. I know we all want to drain the open bar, so we'll get to it." Steve looked back to Deia and Dave.

"Oson'Deia, do you take David Grahslagg to be your husband, to be attached to him through everything? No matter if he's sick as hell, or hasn't taken a shower in a few days, or he's gone out with the boys, adventuring without telling you?"

"Seems a bit specific," Dave muttered.

"I'm looking out for you, bro," Steve said behind his hand, winking at Dave.

Dave couldn't help but laugh, shaking his head.

Deia rolled her eyes, a smile on her lips. "Sure, I might as well."

"Thanks—feel like a nice sack of potatoes," Dave said.

"A handsome sack of potatoes." Deia winked.

Steve let out a giggle before he cleared his throat. The other members of Party Zero on the platform were unable to hide their joy, their eyes shining.

"Do you, David Grahslagg, take Oson'Deia to be your wife? She's way better than you anyway, so I'd say it's a good deal." Steve pursed his lips and nodded, looking like a wise elder giving him some sage advice.

"I'll take her." Dave let go of her hand and pulled her to him.

Deia pressed her lips together, giving Dave a mock glower. Their wedding was about as far from official as it could get.

Steve smiled to them both and pinched Koi's cheek. Koi giggled, trying to capture his fingers. Steve pulled his hand back in time to escape her as he drew himself up to his full height.

"Then today, I present you with a wedding contract." Runes appeared in the air, forming a contract with Deia and Dave's names on it. "Could those who have witnessed the contract please pour forth your power into the contract?"

Party Zero let out threads of power, the contract becoming more solid.

Across Emerilia, from the asteroid base to Terra, people who had been watching the scene let out a thread of power. It gathered together, passing through portals, teleport pads, and onos. It flowed over the lands, fell from the flying citadels, and gushed forth from the teleport pads and onos of Cliff-Hill. The temple was filled with glowing lights of millions as they seeped into the contract.

The contract glowed with great power, turning from a shadow into an object that radiated power. Its strength was enough to shock those in the temple.

"Dave, Deia," Steve said softly. With a movement of his hand, the contract floated in front of them.

Dave and Deia both reached out their hands. Threads of power, gray and red, appeared from their fingers. The contract underwent a change as Deia and Dave's names on the contract solidified.

"The wedding contract is complete! You may kiss the bride!" Steve said.

Dave pulled Deia to him, stealing a kiss.

Their lips parted, Dave's face filled with smiles, as Deia looked like a bashful girl. She blushed, pulling a piece of hair behind her ear.

People clapped and then cheered, filling the temple, then all of Cliff-Hill; celebrations started on Emerilia and even up on the asteroid bases.

They had won against the Jukal Empire; they had freed themselves and stepped into reality. The future was unknown, but they were filled with hope and excitement. This adventure had ended, but another one was bound to appear in the future.

Dave laughed and smiled, holding his two girls as they looked out over the crowds in the temple as Party Zero whistled and did their best to compete against them all.

A pop-up appeared in Dave's vision.

Quest: Friend of the Grey God Level 8
Defeat the Jukal Empire
Rewards: Unlock Level 9 Quest
Increase to stats
+10 to stats (stacks with previous class levels)
+900,000 EXP
Class: Friend of the Grey God

Status:	Level 9
	+90 to all stats
Effects:	Access to hidden quests
	Access to the Imperial Carrier
	Datskun

Quest: Friend of the Grey God Level 10
Live Free
Rewards: Unlock Level 11 Quest
Increase to stats

Quest Completed: Bleeder Level 8
Defeat the Jukal Empire
Rewards: Unlock Level 9 Quest
+10 increase to stats (stacks with previous class levels)
+600,000 EXP

Class: Bleeder

Status:	Level 8
Effects:	+80 to all stats
	Ability to use Jukal Link

Quest: Bleeder Level 9
Live Free
Rewards: Unlock Level 10 Quest
Increase to stats

Level 244

You have reached Level **267**; you have **115** stat points to use.

Character Sheet

Name:	David Grahslagg	Gender:	Male
Level:	244	Class:	Dwarven Master Smith, Friend of the Grey God, Bleeder, Librarian, Aleph Engineer, Weapons Master, Champion Slayer, Skill Creator, Mine Manager, Master of Space and Time, Master of Gravitational Anomalies
Race:	Human/ Dwarf	Alignment:	Chaotic Neutral

Unspent points: 115

Health:	63,100	Regen:	27.02 /s
Mana:	17,530	Regen:	65.45 /s
Stamina:	6,820	Regen:	57.90 /s
Vitality:	631	Endurance:	1,351
Intelligence:	1,753	Willpower:	1,309
Strength:	682	Agility:	1,158

New Class: Husband

Thanks for the good times, Dave. You've kicked ass, taken names and hell, you even pulled a mecha out of your ass. I don't think that you'll be getting many of these class descriptions or new skills in the future, but saying that, there's endless possibilities. Now, this class is one of the hardest to master. There is no right or wrong way to do it. You've done well so far. Stay classy, Dave. Know that there's a whole world cheering for you.

Seize the day and make your own adventure. Nothing is impossible.

-Mike

Thank you for joining Party Zero, the Stone Raiders, myself and the people of Emerilia on this crazy trip!

I would like to say a big thank-you to all of the proofers, editors, and betas who have helped turn Emerilia into what you see today.

And thank you for reading Emerilia and supporting this series! ?

Hope you have a great Day! ☺

Want a bigger map of Emerilia and the continents? Check out

http://theeternalwriter.deviantart.com/

You can check out my other books, what I'm working on and upcoming releases through the following means:

Website: **http://michaelchatfield.com/**

Twitter: **@chatfieldsbooks**[1]

Facebook: **Michael Chatfield**[2]

Goodreads: **Goodreads.com/michaelchatfield**[3]

Thanks again for reading! ☺

Interested in more LitRPG? Check out **https://www.facebook.com/groups/LitRPGsociety/**

Continue on for Character Sheet!

---

1.   https://twitter.com/chatfieldsbooks

2.   https://www.facebook.com/michaelchatfieldsbooks/?ref=hl

3.   https://www.goodreads.com/author/show/14055550.Michael_Chatfield

In Alphabetical Order
Ankol

Dwarf

Dwarven master smith. Smithing Art: Metal Spinner. Lives in Grorart Mountain.

Boran-al

Lich

One of the Dark Lord's Champions. Works directly under the Dark Lord. Creates Creatures of Power and carries out the Dark Lord's orders. His citadel was destroyed.

Alastair Montgoa

Arch Lich, aka former Lord Vailyn. Gave up his fellow Aleph to have everlasting life; used the centuries to build strength and knowledge.

Barry

Dwarf

Dwarven master smith. Smithing Art: Unknown. Wandering smith.

Cassie

Elf/Human Halfling

Holy warrior. Leader of the Golden Sabres. In a relationship with Josh Giles.

Dark Lord

God

    Embodiment of the Dark Affinity. Created demons. Normally an ally with the Earth Lord. Always looking for a way to tip the power balance of Emerilia in his favor.

Dasano

Dwarf

Dwarven master smith. Smithing Art: Metal Press. Lives in Gro-rart Mountain.

Akatol Dracul

Dragon

Water Mage. Was the second dragon, Denur's, husband. Went mad and started a genocide; disappeared.

Denur Dracul

Dragon

Fire mage hailed as "Mother of dragons." First of her race, a Creature of Power created by the Lady of Fire. Seen as her daughter. Sister to Oson' Deia.

Gelimah Dracul

Dragon
  Dark Mage. Brother to Induca, Louna, and Malsour

Fornau Dracul

Dragon

Earth Mage. Quindar's mate. Malsour and Induca's grand-nephew.

Induca Dracul

Dragon

Fire mage. One of the youngest from the first generation of dragons. Sister to Malsour, daughter of Denur, aunt to Quindar, great-aunt to Fornau. Member of the Stone Raiders and Party Zero.

Kinal Dracul

Dragon

Louna Dracul

Dragon
    Induca, Gelimah, and Malsour's sister.

Malsour Dracul

Dragon

Dark mage. One of the oldest dragons in existence, firstborn of Denur. Deia and Induca's guardian; Stone Raider and Party Zero member. Brother to Induca. Great-uncle to Fornau Dracul and uncle to Quindar Dracul.

Quindar Dracul

Dragon
    Wind mage. Wife to Fornau. Niece to Induca and Malsour.

Wokui Dracul

Dragon
    Water mage

Xednai Dracul

Dragon

One of the first dragons; had several offspring, including son Fornau.

Gorpal Dunsk

Dwarf

Dwarven master smith. Lives in Akrimon Mountain. Created three Weapons of Power—Mace of Fury, Tower Shield, Boots of Smash. Smithing Art: Paint Copy

Earth Lord

God
   Embodiment of the Earth Affinity. Created Earth sprites.

Edmur

Dwarf

Dwarven master smith. Had been in the dwarven warbands as a shield bearer. Former pupil of Quino's. Brother to Endur. Smithing Art: Metal's Song

Edwards

Human. Military scientist within the Deq'ual system. Friend of Sato's.

Edwin

Beast Kin. Beast Kin representative on ruling council.

Endur

Dwarf

Dwarven master smith. Had been in the dwarven warbands as a shield bearer. Former pupil of Quino's. Brother to Edmur. Lives in Zolu Mountain. Smithing Art: Hammer Blows.

Esa

Human

Melee fighter. Member of Mikal and Jules's party. Fought at Boran-al's Citadel.

Member of the Stone Raiders. Going out with Jules. Works under Dwayne as a fighter. Being trained for a leadership position under Dwayne.

Lord Esamael

Human
  Lord of Emaren within the Gudalo Kingdom.

Ela-Gal

High Elf

Warrior living in Aleph, married to Ela-Dorn. Persecuted by high elves as heretic.

Ela-Dorn

Orc

Researcher and professor at Aleph College. Aleph Council Member. Married to Ela-Gal

Fend

Dwarf
  Lord Under the Mithsia Mountains.

Geswald

Human
Trader's Guild chapter head in Emaren.

David Grahslagg (aka Austin Zane)

Dwarf/Human halfling, in-game character of Austin Zane. Dwarven master smith. Resident of Cliff-Hill. Member of Party Zero and the Stone Raiders Guild.

Josh Giles

Human

Rogue. Leader of the Stone Raiders. Was an investment broker on Earth; became an E-head. In a relationship with Cassie from the Golden Sabres.

Gimel

Human
    Warrior.
    Fellox Guildmaster.

Gorrund

Dwarf

Dwarven master smith in Benvari Mountain with Jesal, teaching four apprentices. Smithing Art: Blood Bender.

Goula

Demon
    On the ruling council for Devil's Crater.

Gurren

Dwarf

Shield bearer. Member of dwarven warband under Lox's command. Sent to guide people to Cliff-Hill. Friend of David Grahslagg. Kol's grandson. Member of the Stone Raiders.

Helick

Dwarf
    Dwarven master smith.

Kim Isdola

Human
   Cleric/alchemist. Lieutenant in Stone Raiders.

Ishox

Demon
   On the ruling council for Devil's Crater.

Archmage Jekoni

Human/item

Soul bound to Staff of Growing. Over 2,000 years old; missing legs. Held within dwarven vaults with other Weapons of Power.

Jeeves

AI

Made by Bob to assist the dwarven master smiths.

Jeremy

Human
Fellox Guild member.

Jesal

Dwarf

Dwarven master smith. Dave's master smith trainer. Smithing Art: Nature's Guide.

Jules

Human

Healer. Member of Mikal and Esa's party. Fought at Boran-al's Citadel.

Member of the Stone Raiders. Used to be an army medic. E-head without legs IRL. Going out with Esa. Works under Lucy as support. Leads the healers of the Stone Raiders.

Joko

Dwarf

Shield bearer. Member of dwarven warband under Lox's command. Sent to guide people to Cliff-Hill. Friend and trainer of David Grahslagg.

Deceased.

Anna'kal

Wolf Beast Kin/Administrator AI24681

Air mage. Originally a program meant to assist Lo'kal with the running of Emerilia. Anna was uploaded to a player body and inserted into Emerilia. She became emotionally attached with her charges. When the Beast Kin people were wiped out from Emerilia, she went into cold storage, waiting for her father to awake her when a chance came to fight against the prison they had created.

Member of the Stone Raiders and Party Zero. Daughter of Bob.

Lo'kal

Jukal

Scientist. Created Emerilia. Awarded the position of the Grey God. Maintains Emerilia, its people and players. Other names: Bob, Bobby McMahnon, the Balancer, Grey God.

Kino

Demon
   On the ruling council for Devil's Crater.

Kol

Dwarf

    Dwarven master smith. Gurren's grandfather. Resides in Cliff-Hill. Taught Dave how to smith. Runs Dave's smithies. Smithing Art: Blind Man's Touch.

Lady of Air

Goddess

Embodiment of the Affinity Air. Known for causing mischief. Her Champions act as spies and information brokers, tilting the balance of Emerilia.

Lady of Fire (aka Ignil)

Goddess

Created dragons, Mage's Guild and College. Gave gift of "knowledge" to the people of Emerilia. Mother to Deia. Lover of Oson'Mal and best friend with Bob.

Lady of Light

Goddess

Sent players to kill/capture dragons to make her own Creatures of Power. Created the race known as angels. Large rivalry with the Dark Lord.

Lena

Demon
   On the ruling council of Devil's Crater. Wife to Vrexu.

Lovan

Dwarf
  Mithsia Mountain warclan leader.

Lox

Dwarf

Shield bearer. Was the commander of the warband sent to guide people to Cliff-Hill. Friend of David Grahslagg. Member of the Stone Raiders.

Suzy Markell

Human (IRL)

   High Elf (Emerilia)

   Austin Zane's secretary and best friend. David Grahslagg's best friend and assistant with running Cliff-Hill smithy and factory. Summoning mage. Steve's contractor. Member of Party Zero and the Stone Raiders.

Max

Dwarf

Shield bearer. Member of dwarven warband under Lox's command. Sent to guide people to Cliff-Hill. Friend of David Grahslagg. Deceased.

Meda

Dwarf/Elf

Aleph Council member. Deals with the food within Aleph cities and facilities

Melanie

Human
  Archmage Alamos's wife.

Melhoun

Water snake made by the Water Lord.
  Sealed away.

Mikal

Human

Rogue. Jules and Esa's party member. Member of the Stone Raiders. Friends with Party Zero.

Oson'Deia (aka Ouluv'Deia)

Elf/Demi-God Halfling

   Elven ranger and Fire mage. Daughter of Oson'Mal and Lady Fire of the Affinity Pantheon. Resident of Cliff-Hill and member of the Stone Raiders Guild. Leader of Party Zero.

Penelope

Human
    Fellox Guild member.

Pete

Human
Geswald's secretary.

Queen Farun

High Elf
    Queen of Raolor.

Queen Mendari Selhi

Human
Queen of Selhi.

Quino

Dwarf

    Dwarven master smith. Lives in Zolu Mountain. Trained the brothers Endur and Edmur. Smithing Art: Internal Cutting.

Rola

Dwarf

Dwarven master smith. Smithing Art: Puppeteer. Lives in Aldamire Mountain.

Sato/Communications Officer Sato

Human

Lives in Deq'ual system.

Communications Officer. Becomes Vice Commander of Deq'ual military forces. Grandfather original settler.

Emperor Talis

Human.

Ruler of the Xeugrera Empire, located in the Ashal continent.

Deli

Dwarf

Shield bearer. Member of dwarven warband under Lox's command. Sent to guide people to Cliff-Hill. Friend of David Grahslagg. Deceased.

Demon Prince Alkao/Alkao Travezar

Aerial Demon

Melee fighter. Commander of the Third demon Horde and leader of Xerzit lands. Oldest of the five remaining demon princes of Devil's Crater.

Dwayne Trebault

Human

Melee fighter. Lieutenant in Stone Raiders. Leads and trains the melee fighters in the Stone Raiders.

Venfik

Elf
    Lady Air's adviser.

Lucy Vernia

Wood Elf/Human

Lieutenant in Stone Raiders. Spy master. Deals with supporting the Stone Raiders and paperwork.

Vrexu

Demon

One of the seven remaining demon princes. General in the Devil's Crater Army. Married to Lena, the youngest of the five remaining demon princesses.

Water Lord

God

    Embodiment of the Water Affinity. Created the merpeople and Water creatures. Created the Water Serpent Melhoun. Rival to the Lady of Fire.

Austin Zane (aka David Grahslagg)

CEO of Rock Breaker's Corporation. Engineer specializing in space vehicles. Background in Astrophysics.

Wis'Zel

Wood Elf

Bard. Works for David Grahslagg, managing his ceramics factories in Cliff-Hill.

Made in the USA
Coppell, TX
07 September 2020